MORE RAVE REVIEWS
FOR KATHLEEN NANCE!

SPELLBOUND

Spellbound "will captivate fans and new readers alike with an imaginative world of magic filled with lusty encounters."

—Booklist

"A magically potent romance."

—Romantic Times

WISHES COME TRUE

"Kathleen Nance has penned a supremely enticing tale with laughter, intrigue, the paranormal and, of course, a passionate steamy love that comes across in spades."

—Rendezvous

Wishes Come True is "a story of magic, wishes, fantasy, and…a lot of spice. Ms. Nance is wonderful. Fantastic! 5 Bells!"

—Bell, Book and Candle

ENCHANTMENT

"*Enchantment* is a wish come true for fans of genie romance. Ms. Nance creates a world as exotic and intriguing as the characters who inhabit it."

—Romantic Times

MORE THAN MAGIC

"*More Than Magic* is an undeniable treasure trove of pleasure, bursting with magnetic characters and a bewitching plot that's sure to capture the imagination of fantasy and romance readers alike."

—Rendezvous

"An astonishingly original story in a world which contains far too few paranormal romances, *More Than Magic* is more than satisfying."

—Affaire de Coeur

ALONE IN THE DARK

The lights flickered, dimmed, flickered again. A second later, they went out. From above Bella came a string of curses.

She pulled out her cell phone, on the off chance it would work, but it read one bar and she couldn't get a call out—the story of life in the UP. Spotty transmission. If there wasn't a building blocking her, then there was no tower in the wilderness to carry the signal.

Lake-bottom blackness surrounded her. Except, now that she was adjusting to it, the blackness wasn't as complete as she'd first supposed. Blue glowed from her watch and around the edges of Fran's closed cover, ghostly sheens against the flat walls. Not enough to see where her feet should go, but at least it felt like she wasn't quite alone.

Up or down, she debated. Floors four and five held government research labs, so the stairwell was locked from this side. You could get through in event of fire, but not now. She'd have to go down a flight and a half to the third floor to get out. Chance running into whoever had turned out the lights. Or she could go up, to the sixth floor, a flight and a half. To where her pursuer might be waiting.

Jigsaw

KATHLEEN NANCE

LEISURE BOOKS NEW YORK CITY

A LEISURE BOOK®

April 2005

Published by

Dorchester Publishing Co., Inc.
200 Madison Avenue
New York, NY 10016

ISBN 0-8439-5491-4

The name "Leisure Books" and the stylized "L" with design are trademarks of Dorchester Publishing Co., Inc.

Printed in the United States of America.

Visit us on the web at www.dorchesterpub.com.

Jigsaw

*To Grady, Sara, Carl, and David, as
always. For putting up with my odd hours,
take-out dinners, and oblivion when the
headphones are on—I love you all.*

*And thanks to Nancy Drew and
Ned Nickerson. I've never forgotten that spark
of excitement when I first read you.*

Chapter One

The surveillance van was frigid inside. Only the lack of wind made it marginally more tolerable than outside in the bitter Detroit winter. Daniel Champlain blew on his fingers, trying to warm them as he studied the captured keystrokes streaming across his monitor. He couldn't afford a mistake due to cold fingers hitting the wrong key.

Next assignment, he was requesting hot. French-bikini, sand-mucking-up-the-equipment, jungle-rotting hot. Anything warmer than sitting in an abandoned, tires-missing van and freezing his eyeballs.

"What's our target saying?" Ben Maxwell, the head of their National Security Agency covert team, loomed over his shoulder. "Where's the mycotoxin?"

"Haven't decoded his output." Daniel set his jaw and focused on the decryption analysis of the captured keystrokes. Nearby, another monitor graphed the labyrinthian path the digitized message took toward its still undetermined destination.

The sender was the top man in a Detroit terrorist cell, a cell recently swollen with an influx of fresh bodies smuggled across the leaky Canadian-U.S. border. His message relayed last-minute coded instructions to his martyrs-in-waiting.

"What's the holdup? Thought you were some kind of code specialist," joked Stefan Corvallis, the other member of the team. He sat facing Daniel, feet propped on a seat. Fully at ease, he kept his hands warmed by twirling a lethal blade as he kept an eye on the monitors that panned the empty street outside the van.

"Good enough to save your sorry butt more than once." Part of NSA's unacknowledged SiOps division, Daniel had no false modesty about being one of the best in an agency that specialized in cryptography.

"A favor oft returned, *mon ami*."

"Yeah, yeah." Daniel took a sip of his now-cold latte. The three of them shared a web of history; they'd covered each others' backs more times than any of them bothered to count.

"I have my building scheme and heat monitors pinpointing everyone in the apartment." Stefan pointed his knife at the monitors. "You have gibberish. You're slipping, Champlain."

"Mmm." Daniel blew on his hands again, barely listening, his attention on the screens. Damn, but he hated when Stefan was right; this should not be taking so long. The cell in question didn't have quantum encryption. The code was breakable.

Wind whistling at the windows, the whirr of machinery, Ben's sneeze—all faded as he immersed himself in the nonsensical symbols. Resting his hands on the keyboard, he let the machine's internal clicks play up his tendons. Rhythm, felt as much as seen, gave dimension to the code. These symbols hid words. Words that were his job to find. So, what were the hidden patterns? What was the language of terror?

Language. He'd programmed in the fifty spoken by virtually ninety-nine percent of the world. Which one were they using? Damn it! That was it; they had to be using an offshoot dialect. He pulled over his laptop and jabbed up the target's bio. Born in Armenia, Irani-trained, moved—

Swiftly he adjusted the program, keying in the basics of Ashkharik, the uncommon Eastern Armenian dialect. There were hundreds of tongues possible, but he suddenly knew this was the one. Anticipation formed a hard cube in his gut as he glanced at the monitor tracking the path.

The location of the receiving computer would tell them where the terrorists were gathering. Decoding the message would tell them where the package hid—a package containing a particularly nasty vial of T2 myco-toxin. SWAT teams in biogear waited at the local HQ, ready to storm in and claim both terrorists and toxin. Waited on him.

"How long?" Ben planted his hands on the monitor.

"Five minutes," Daniel promised, shifting out of Ben's shadow. Three men, especially when one of them was a sequoia like Ben, were just too much size for the van.

The frigid air heated with determination as Ben and Stefan silently readied themselves. They'd worked to-gether enough that they needed no instructions, no last-minute coordination. Daniel tuned out the rustle of their preps, but as he sorted through the signals, his eyes nar-rowed. Something else was off. What was it?

Suddenly he cursed. "Those flicking-fingered Cyber Soldiers! One of them's hacking into the source com-puter." He attacked the keyboard, using his clandestine connection to set up firewalls for the hacker to breach.

"Can you block him?"

"Not without letting both the hacker and the target know I'm in already. I'm delaying him, but damn, he's good!"

Ben swore more colorfully than Daniel had, adding a few new backwoods colloquialisms. "Can you shield him off long enough?"

"It'll be close." He sent a trace to the invading computer, then concentrated on the pattern of data streaming across his monitor.

If their terrorist target realized he was exposed, he would cut the transmission. The minions receiving the instructions would disband and relocate; the target date and time for release would be changed. The only thing that would remain the same would be the very painful, very lethal mycotoxin waiting to be unleashed.

Second chances didn't come in this business.

In the years since 9/11, Daniel's team had thwarted the few previous attempts at bio and chemical terrorism. That record was *not* going to be broken, not on his watch.

Ben and Stefan stood poised by the door, weapons at hand, waiting for the "go" signal, giving Daniel every second before they moved in and bagged at least this one terrorist. Their steady breathing, the only sound beyond the crackle of computers, filled the van with cold white vapor.

Face taut from cold and tension, Daniel stared at the data, willing the pattern to break out of nonsense streams. Suddenly the computer beeped. The Cyber Soldier hacker had made it in. Gleefully the hacker scooped through the terrorist's hard drive. Daniel adjusted the program parameters, focusing.

If he'd chosen the wrong base language . . .

The computer beeped again, and like a dyslexic child who suddenly made sense of the mixed-up pages, the garbled string re-formed into a legible message, while monitors flashed an address. "Bingo!" he shouted, memorizing the details. "Got it!"

Ben and Stefan snapped into action, scrambling out of the van, guns at the ready. Daniel barked into the phone, rattling off the location of the operatives and the mycotoxin to the SWAT teams eager for their role in a major bust. He then finished the transmission with the ritual closure used by this cell, preserving the illusion that the message had stayed secure. A moment later, he half jogged, half sprinted across the street, following his companions, cursing the recent injury that slowed him.

Dark and cold buffeted him. The barely risen sun was no match for the swollen cloud cover, and the streetlights had long ago been shot out by vandals. Avoiding the broken glass on the sidewalk, Daniel hunched his shoulders against the biting wind and buried his free hand in the pocket of his leather coat. Racing up the steps, he was only seconds behind the two local cops who'd been waiting in a companion, derelict van, ready for an arrest. Ben exchanged one nod with the cops, then kicked open the door, shouting their ID, ordering surrender. Daniel yelled the commands in Ashkharik.

Chaos exploded with shouts and gunfire, but in the end, subduing their target and his bodyguards took little time. While the cops followed the laws of this country, which their opponents were trying to destroy, and read the Miranda rights, Ben and Stefan slapped on restraints.

Daniel strode across the room, ignoring the stab of pain in his leg, and scanned the flashing screen of the computer.

Lokus, Cyber Soldier, commands you to surrender, it read, while a billowing American flag marched across the screen to the tune of "Stars and Stripes Forever."

Stefan joined him. "Lokus again," he said in a low voice, glancing toward the cops, who were now ushering out their prize and leaving the three NSA agents alone in the apartment.

"I should have guessed this was his work."

The Cyber Soldiers. They were computer fanatics who hid behind the guise of patriots. The media and the general public loved them. Daniel didn't; they left a bad taste in his mouth. Instinct nagged that they—or some of them at least—were far more dangerous than anyone gave them credit for.

So far, he'd found nothing he could put a finger on.

No deeper pattern, not enough evidence for official Agency action. Yet. But the itch told him it was there—a darker side to this group. And Lokus was the brightest, most gifted of them all.

Your data is now the property of the USA, and your computer is empty. In its place we return you to your regularly scheduled porn chat, continued the hacker; then the screen reverted to an ongoing chat-room discussion—one of the sicker ones, the current topic being whipping techniques. A stream of filth spewed out under the name of Isabella Q.

Heat sucked out of the room and his body, as though he'd been shot into the vacuum of space. *Isabella Q?* Daniel's mind clicked on the name, instantly creating a link. *Isabella Quintera? Bella?* He choked on the thought. Couldn't be, not this, not here. This was *not* Bella. Of that, he was sure.

But he couldn't shake the far-fetched leap of association as he stared at the almost familiar name. *Isabella Q.* The letters were only an eerie glow in the dark, abandoned morning, yet seeing them brought back a rush of sensations he'd thought buried.

Bella. The clean scent of her skin, for she rarely wore perfume, and the thick softness of her dark hair brushing against his cheek. The pleasing sounds of her release. Firm curves pressed against him and the taste of salt as she cried. The need to hold her close and forget everything in the demanding pulse of sex. The hard frustration as she pulled away.

He released his pent-up breath. Shoving back the memories, he forced himself to follow the thread as "Isabella" described in vivid detail the sick fantasies she'd fulfill. Fury and disgust roiled in a seething maelstrom. In his line of work, he thought he'd seen most everything, but she came up with things even he'd never come across.

As he read, he fingered the smooth surface of the thick wooden jigsaw piece he kept in his coat pocket. He didn't need to see the puzzle piece to know each detail. It was shaped like a frog and colored with a patterned green. It was a small work of art which, when joined with its brothers, created a larger scene of wild jungle.

Isabella Q. Bella Quintera. A long shot, true. Could be coincidence.

Except, in his work, believing in coincidence was a deadly mistake.

No, he didn't believe this tiny oddity was a coincidence. Not when his next assignment meant heading north, an eight-hour-plus trip to the Upper Peninsula to investigate Lionel Quintera, Bella's father.

Balancing the boxes of handcrafted jigsaw puzzles on her hip, Bella Quintera rapped on the locked wooden door of Puzzle Me This. Her thick gloves muffled the sound, along with a mass of swirling sleet. Frigid wind cut through her wool slacks, as though the fabric was no thicker than paper.

A low moan billowed through the evening. Startled, Bella glanced over her shoulder but saw nothing except snow. Midwest-born and bred, she should be used to the pewter-gray nothingness of a winter storm, but today it sucked the energy from her, leaving her edgy and off balance.

The dull, directionless moan came again in an eddy of blinding snow. Bella's eyes stung as she blinked the flakes away. *Must be the wind.*

She scraped the ice from the shop window and peered inside. Only pale security lights shone inside the store, which meant Margo Delansky, the owner, had closed early. On the off chance the woman was in the back riding out the fast-rising winter storm, Bella pounded on the door, while ice needled her cheeks and neck.

Still no answer. No chance of waiting out the storm here. Unwilling to risk further delay, she left the doorway alcove for her car. The bitter air stole her breath, and her lungs spasmed against the assault; the temperature must have dropped another five degrees. She pulled her scarf over her mouth and bent her head against the wind. Breathing in warmer air, she felt her throat relax.

Along the Lake Superior coast, January at six p.m. meant beyond dusky, but today the whirlpool of snow and swollen clouds shrouded all extraneous light. She stumbled through the storm, her exposed forehead numb and her lashes and brows coated with snow. Still balancing the boxes, she unlocked her Jeep-Mach UV with a click of her key, then scrambled inside, stowing the puzzles in back and shutting the door before too much sleet could pile in with her.

Bless a heavy-duty battery, the car started at once. She idled the engine and defrosters a few moments, warming the interior and wiping away the accumulated ice while she unwrapped the scarf from her face. She lifted the leather case strap from her shoulder and settled the small computer on the seat beside her. After fastening seat belts, she exited the lot to the road.

The plows had scraped off the top layer of snow, exposing the ice beneath. Bella drove cautiously, the slick road offering little traction despite the sand spread by the plows. Maybe she shouldn't have taken the time to grade the papers for her Cognitive Sciences 601 class, but weather.com had given no indication that the storm would be this fast-moving or this severe. Not until she'd left her windowless office had she discovered three new inches of ice coating trees and roads, with more coming. At least being this late meant no other traffic to worry about. Except—

She glanced at her rearview mirror, frowning. Two

white haloes shone behind her, growing larger too rapidly. "What idiot speeds on a night like this?" she muttered.

"I have two events labeled 'idiot' in our conversational database," answered the synthesized voice of Fran, the computer on the passenger seat. "One, the all day faculty meeting on mission statements, and two—"

"I was talking to myself, Fran. Sorry. Go back to what you were doing. Gotta concentrate here." A sound akin to an aggravated sigh emitted from Fran's speakers, signaling the computer's acknowledgment.

Bella returned her attention to the road. She tapped her brakes, not enough to slow her or send her into a skid, just enough that her rear lights would flash, warning whoever was back there of her presence.

It worked. The car slowed as it came up behind her . . . and stayed there. The indistinct vehicle, visible only as a looming hulk behind the glaring headlights, crept closer, closing the gap by inches. Her stomach knotted as her gaze darted between the twin lights in her rearview mirror and the blizzard before her. She could understand the desire to let another car blaze the trail through the accumulating ice, but following so closely was sheer madness. The lights behind her blinked to high beams in a sharp, blinding jab. She squinted against the painful brilliance.

"You eager to pass? Then pass." Heart in her throat, she gripped the wheel. The lining of her gloves absorbed the sudden sweat of her palms as she shifted to the right, trying to see where the edge of the road dropped into a ditch.

The other car did not accept the invitation. Instead, it matched her, shifting to the right as well, the headlights still blinding, like malevolent monster eyes. What in blazes was wrong with the driver? For the first time, fear trickled into the mix of Bella's tension and fatigue.

She sped up, daring a small burst of speed, but the

other car kept pace. Chewing on her lip, Bella scanned the road, placing what lay ahead. Small lanes jutted off in other directions, but they wouldn't have been sanded. More of a chance to skid. Her Mach UV handled regular snow like a champ, but this ice was a different story.

Up ahead—how far?—Highway 41 crossed. More traffic might have melted the ice, and Mervin's Gas was about a hundred yards down. Since Merv lived behind the station, it would be lit and populated, even tonight. A safe place to pull in and let this moron pass.

The driver pulled back a little. Bella let out a pent-up breath. At last.

Except his beams were still on high and struck across her mirror, blinding her again. She tilted her head, trying to get out of the light stream. Was he drunk or high? Wouldn't be the first time a driver fortified himself against the cold with alcohol. Maybe she should report him to the state police.

Except her cell phone was tangled deep in her coat pocket. While she debated whether she could safely grab the phone, a gust of wind blasted against her windshield, hard enough to shake the heavy-duty vehicle. A fury of icy pellets attacked the glass.

Her car swerved on a hidden patch of black ice, then brushed against the ledge of crusted snow pushed to the side by an earlier pass of a snowplow's blade. Rear tires swung atop the ice, traction lost. Phone forgotten, Bella grabbed the steering wheel and fought to pull out of the treacherous skid.

A moment later, the Mach UV was headed straight and she drew in a shaky breath. She strained to see the road ahead, even as the white lights in her mirror stung her eyes and reminded her of her follower. Tapping her brakes as a warning, she slowed down and shifted a fraction to the right, offering the impatient driver another chance to pass.

The sign for Highway 41 flashed past on the right, almost invisible in the swirling sleet. One mile. One mile to safety.

Abruptly the car behind her pulled out and careened forward. Vague impressions of the vehicle registered. Another SUV. Dark windows. Tinted? The driver was hidden. It was impossible to tell more; the endless storm stripped away all color to make everything gray.

He was passing too close! Instinctively she pulled the steering wheel to the right. The rear end of the car spun. No traction!

Nerves screaming, Bella tried to steer out of the skid, but her adrenaline-powered yank overcorrected. Her car leaped left across the slick road, doing a one-eighty, just missing the rear of the other car. Snow streaked across her windshield as the world whirled around her. Wildly fishtailing red taillights vanished.

Beyond control, her Mach UV bounced across the mounded shoulder and slammed to a halt against a tree. Her body jerked against the suddenly locked seat belt. The air bag exploded outward from the panel in front of her, blinding her more thoroughly than the snow, knocking the breath from her lungs. Everything stopped—except the wild firing of her nerves.

Gradually the air bag deflated, and her racing heart steadied. Bella took a deep breath, then pried her fingers loose from the steering wheel. Hands shaking, she shoved the air bag from her face and took stock. Every part of her torso and neck throbbed, a gift from the body-slamming air bag, no doubt. Experimentally she rotated her shoulder and winced at the tug of pain. She rubbed against her sore chest. Likely she'd have a stripe of bruises, compliments of the locked shoulder harness. Still, that seemed the extent of her injuries.

"Fran, are you okay?" Thank heavens, she'd strapped the seat belt through the computer case.

"Functioning normal. Why do you ask?"

"Had a bit of trouble. It's over now." She raked a hand

through her hair. They'd been lucky, coming through unscathed.

"Then we can talk? I was examining the Shakespeare you gave me. *The Taming of the Shrew*. The language is different. I have calculated most of it, but some . . . 'Go to the feast, revel, and domineer, Carouse full measure to her maidenhead.' Is maidenhead—"

"Fran, can we talk later? Still got some things to sort out here."

"Very well. 'Women are made to bear, and so are you.'" Fran fell silent.

Great, Fran was now quoting Petruchio. Bella rubbed the bridge of her nose. As problems went, that was a small one. With luck, the car would be as easily managed. At least the engine was still running. Maybe she'd only crumpled a fender. Cautiously she shifted into reverse and tried backing the car onto the road. There her luck ended. The wheels spun uselessly.

Not ready to accept that she was stuck, she wrapped the scarf back around her neck and tucked her red hair into a hat. Like any prudent Midwesterner, she kept her car equipped with a winter survival kit: blanket, granola bars and water, shovel, bag of sand. Maybe getting free would be only a matter of spreading sand for traction or leveling a rut.

She shoved the door open against the keening wind. Cold grabbed her lungs and froze her exposed eyelids as soon as she stepped out. Her boots broke through the ice-crusted snow, plunging her calf-deep as she struggled around the Mach UV.

At the rear of the car, she let out a frustrated breath, the moisture immediately freezing on the weave of her muffler. The incline wasn't sharp, but the two bumpers were balanced against the mounded snow and the tree, holding the tires suspended above the ground. Not even four-wheel drive could get her out of this; she was well and truly stuck.

Nothing to do but call for a tow truck. On a night like this, she'd have to wait her turn, however. She shoved her hands into her pockets and hunched her shoulders for added warmth as she glanced down the road. Trying to walk for help, even one short mile, was tantamount to a suicide wish. The car lights and heat still worked; she had a full tank of gas as well as her emergency rations. If she conserved the gas, she could survive until morning, but the prospect of a long, uncomfortable night lay ahead.

Twin white haloes shone down the road, signaling an approaching car coming from the direction she'd been heading. Bella started to scramble into the road, to flag down assistance; then she froze. Not from the bitter cold outside, but from a wash of fear.

This road wasn't well traveled, and on a night like this she wouldn't expect any other cars.

Unless the maniac driver had turned around after he'd regained control of his car. Unless he'd gone up to Highway 41 and turned there to avoid sliding down the hills. He could afford to take his time; she wasn't going anywhere.

It was an insane, baseless thought, but once created, it would not disappear.

Time stretched as she stared at the headlights. *The approaching car drove with high beams.* No one drove in snow with high beams; the light reflected off the snow and concealed rather than illuminated the road.

No one except her shadower.

Polar winds howled around her. Ice pelted her, forcing itself into the tiny gap between coat and scarf at her neck.

Protect Fran. First and foremost, protect Fran. That single instinct erased any hesitation. Bella scrambled back through the snow and grabbed Fran's computer case from the car. Blanket? Neatly folded in the emergency bin in back. No time to grab the extra warmth.

Only a few feet ahead of those approaching beams, clutching Fran, she raced across the road and then scrambled down the ditch on the opposite side, heart pounding against her ribs. Knives of cold cut into her throat as her frantic gasps pulled in deep gulps of frigid air.

Slowly the white haloes narrowed to beams of light. The vehicle took shape as it inched along, creeping at a pace not even this weather required.

Looking for someone?

"My internal temperature gauge has decreased," Fran observed.

"I know. Do not make a sound, Fran," Bella whispered, throat raw. She wrapped her arms tighter, hugging Fran closer to her body heat.

Was she playing the fool? Risking Fran for no good reason? Crazy, speeding drivers were a Michigan tradition. So was helping out a neighbor. The other driver had simply sobered up enough to return and try to help.

Still, she couldn't shake the eerie feeling that the other driver was more than a perilous drunk.

"No sounds until I tell you it's okay, Fran. Please. Code Silence."

She hoped the quiet meant Fran agreed. As the computer had grown more aware and learned more, she'd grown more independent.

Bella found shelter in the stand of pine trees across the road, then stopped, tucking Fran's small case protectively beneath her coat, afraid further movement would draw attention. At least her coat was gray and her scarf, hat and gloves were white. She didn't dare go deeper into the woods. To lose sight of the landmark road could be deadly tonight. Leaning against the rough bark of the pine, she watched the vehicle draw up beside hers.

A sturdy vehicle, like an SUV, but she couldn't tell the model. Tinted windows. Half the people in the county drove SUVs, but instinct screamed this was the same person who'd followed her. Likely whoever it was had a crisis of conscience and returned to help. Plausible, but her feet refused to move her toward the assistance.

At last the driver got out. Sleet blurred the edges of the figure. Even when he—or she?—passed through the beam of lights, it was impossible to tell size. The bundled figure walked around Bella's car, opened the door, and then searched inside.

Bella's arms holding Fran ached from the tension, and she strained against the snow, trying to see more clearly as the blurred form returned to the road. The driver paused. Looking for her? Or Fran?

At least the gusting wind had erased her footprints on the icy road and was rapidly filling in her telltale tracks through the snow on the road's shoulder.

A hiss cut through the howling night. A curse? Or maybe the sound wasn't a voice but simply the wind, transformed by her imagination. She couldn't tell, not with the blood thrumming in her ears and the storm distorting her senses. Her fingers hardened around the computer, and her body started to shake. Cold? Terror? Didn't matter. She couldn't stop it; she could only pray it wouldn't give her away.

How could he not hear the irregular pounding of her heart?

At last the driver got back in his car and began a careful U-turn. Except he stopped halfway. He did not pull away. Instead, he waited with his headlights shining into the woods.

Bella's jaw tightened. He didn't have to track her. With killer cold like this, all he had to do was wait her out.

Chapter Two

Think, Bella. Break it down.

Call 911. Awkwardly, one gloved hand clutching Fran, she fumbled her cell phone from her pocket. Big, wet snowflakes soaked her clothes and blurred anything more than a few feet away. Beneath the trees, a preternatural quiet reigned—a bubble of calm, even as the wind continued to moan at the edge of the forest. She hoped the surrounding storm would cover her as she voice-activated the emergency number.

"I've been run off the road." She could barely form the words with lips and cheeks gone numb.

"Ms. Quintera?"

No secrets from Caller ID. "Bella Quintera."

"Where are you?"

"Where am I?" Her freezing synapses fired sluggishly. "White Pine Parkway, a mile west of 41."

"Stay with your car, Bella. Keep the car running and the heater on with a window cracked open. I'll connect you to a tow service—"

"I need the police."

"The police don't answer road service," the 911 operator gently explained.

"I was *run off* the road. Deliberately." Bella did a slow deep-knee bend to fire her circulation back up, hoping the movement wouldn't be seen. "The driver is waiting in his car for me."

"Could he be there to offer assistance?"

Yes, but I won't risk Fran. Couldn't explain about Fran, though. "Just . . . send police."

"Keep your doors locked and—"

"I left the car." Her slurred words sounded as if *she* was the one taking a few nips.

"You left your car?" 911 almost kept the incredulity out of her voice.

Even Einstein had some clunker ideas. Bella forced better enunciation. "First rule of self-defense. Avoid confrontation. I'm in the woods across the road."

"We'll send a car as quickly as we can."

How quick? On a blizzard night? She'd heard the radio earlier—a multi-car pile-up on M-28 and a space-heater fire in an apartment complex had emergency services stretched thin. Something—a movement?—caught the edge of her vision. She stared into the thick veil of snow, trying to see.

"Stay on the line until . . . Miss Quintera?"

Bella swore, interrupting, when her mind finally processed what her eyes saw. Her stomach clenched.

The driver was getting out of the car!

"Newton's nuts, he's scanning my cell phone." She snapped shut the phone, cutting off 911's protest, then edged deeper into the woods, angling away from her pursuer.

The phone rang back. The driver's formless shape paused. Did he hear the faint tones? She thumbed the ringer to vibrate and didn't answer.

Instinct took over, weaving her path beneath the trees, away from the unknown pursuer. Snow was shallower beneath the pines, but it was deep enough that each step remained a struggle. *Pick up your foot, break through the crust, sink past your ankle, pick up your other foot.* Sweat froze on her skin. Her breath coated her scarf with ice.

Hold Fran tight. Glance back. She'd put distance between herself and her pursuer. Except now she could no longer see where he was, while she was blazing a trail for him to follow.

She bumped into a white pine, then leaned against it, her knit hat catching the rough pine bark. *Stop running, Bella. Think; it's one of your talents.* Who knew when the police would get here? Getting out was up to her. What next? Break down the options. What options? Her eyes closed as she tried to reason past the creeping confusion of hypothermia.

Thoughts jumbled inside her. Hallucinations replaced coherence. Her body was shutting down from the cold. Intellect retained enough spark to tell her that, but when she tried to move, she couldn't force a step away from the tree's support. If only her blood didn't flow like sludge. Or her brain resemble a popsicle. She had to walk forward.

Walk forward, Bella. The remembered command jolted her from her lethargy. Her eyes jerked open. *Put one foot in front of the other, and before you know it, you're through and on the other side.* Daniel Champlain's firm voice rose from the depths of her mind where she'd tried to bury it. Four years ago, she'd frozen while facing a mass of scandal-feeding reporters. Now, the freezing was too real.

Put one foot in front of the other.

Grimly she peered around the tree. The whirling snow parted, and she saw that the unknown stalker had stopped tracing along the road. He plunged into the woods; likely he'd found her footprints where she'd gone into the trees. She slid in the opposite direction, her boots plowing through the snow. Muscles, frozen into contractions, screamed in protest as she forced them to stretch.

Options. Break it down. Hide? No, cowering was not an option. She couldn't tolerate inaction, and the stalker was bound to find her and Fran. The snow would lead him right to her.

Streaks of flakes whirled about her, featureless, directionless, erasing the landscape with a whiteout. The road, a mere smudge, disappeared. Only the headlights' yellow smear oriented her. Where was the other driver?

"Aaahhhhh." A low sound brushed across her ears again. Again, she couldn't define it. A voice? Wind? Her imagination?

She fought the urge to flee deeper into the woods where she'd be disoriented in seconds, where she could be wandering a long time. What were these extremes of cold and moisture doing to Fran?

They sure weren't doing much for *her*.

Move, Bella. One foot in front of the other. The car is right there. Daniel's persistent voice again. Why did she keep thinking of him? Because of the letter?

Options. Run-and-hide wasn't exactly working. She glanced around. The shadow of her pursuer darkened, a blur of gray in the white nothing. Only a sensation of motion betrayed its nature. He was closing fast. Must have found her prints. Beneath these trees they weren't filling up as fast.

She struggled forward, her arms aching and her chest burning with exertion. Confront her pursuer? Alone, maybe. She knew self-defense, had used it before, but not with Fran in her arms. The burden and the cold made her clumsy. And what if he had a gun?

Should she hide Fran? No, the only way to protect Fran was to keep her close. Option four. Option four. There was always an option four.

Only a fool would freeze standing six feet away from a car heater. If Daniel were here, she knew he'd be saying that to her. She could hear his low impatience, almost as if he were standing right next to her. The man had little tolerance for idiocy or indecision.

Blood throbbing behind her eyes, she forced herself to step faster, using the car beams as a guide. Aiming for the road and her Jeep.

Fran gave a soft beep, her signal that she wanted to break the silence.

"Not yet," Bella whispered, praying the night would absorb the sound. She glanced over her shoulder. He was only a few yards away. "Silence a little longer, Fran. Please."

"Something is strange." Fran could barely be heard.

"Later—"

"I feel my power slowing."

Bella's shallow breaths caught on the pain in her chest. The bitter cold affected Fran, too. Warmth. They had to get to warmth. "Conserve as much as you can."

Her car was closest, and there was no guarantee the other one wasn't locked. Galvanized, she fought the twin paralyzers: fear and hypothermia.

Move, Bella! She lurched forward and nearly fell, unable to feel her feet, but caught herself. If she lay down in that bed of snow, she'd never get back up. Somehow, she made it up the pitched shoulder and into the road. A blast of icy wind, unbroken by the shielding pines, sent her staggering, barely able to keep her footing as she scrambled across the slick road.

Her pursuer emerged from the trees to her right. Halfway between her and his car and still a little behind, he followed after her.

All she could discern about him was that he wore black; even his face was concealed by black ski goggles. Despite the shapeless padding, the impression of masculinity remained.

From her left, headlights bisected the swirling snow. Another car crawled up the road. Her stalker paused, glanced once at the oncoming vehicle, still only visible as headlights, and then whirled and strode to his car. Within seconds, all she could see of him was his car's red taillights. Within seconds, there was no evidence he'd even been here, except for the rapidly disappearing tracks.

The growl of a car engine joined the newly appeared headlights. Probably the police car she'd called for, approaching, then slowing as the beams captured her.

She stumbled to the side of the road, out of the oncoming car's path, praying she wasn't making another huge mistake. Details took shape. Not a police car. A KZ920, sturdiest UV on the market. That piece of irrationality that had sent her across the road and still hovered inside her, fluttered again. She refused to give in to it.

The KZ pulled up beside her. When the dome light briefly illuminated the man getting out, she blinked snow from her eyes. Was she still back hugging the tree and hallucinating? Maybe her lifeless corpse was lying in the snow and this was her own form of purgatory.

"Daniel?" she croaked.

"Bella?" He sounded as surprised as she felt. His quick glance took in the immobilized Jeep.

If this was a hallucination, it was a vivid one. She could hear his growl, see his long strides toward her, feel his muscled arms gather her close.

"Anything broken? Sprained? Whiplash?" One of his hands ran down her arm, while the other lightly massaged her neck. "Are you all right?"

"I'm fine." Even muffled by her thick scarf, his touch sent ribbons of heat coursing through her. Oh, she'd forgotten—despite his size, he could be so gentle.

Daniel. Southern comfort and tempered power. Gentleman, expert lover.

Daniel. Chameleon, enigma, spy, deceiver.

But not a hallucination.

"What happened?" he asked.

"I spun off the road." *Daniel.* For one moment she drank in the sight of him. Sun-streaked dark brown hair, shadow of a beard, intriguing asymmetric face with one black-brown eye slightly higher than the other, mind to rival the sharpest of her colleagues, body all firm planes and hard muscle. "What are you doing here?"

"I was looking for you, although I never expected to find you like this. I'll give you a ride—"

"Well, I don't want to see you." Traitorously comfortable in his embrace, too warmed by his touch, she dredged up her feelings from the last time she'd seen him—fury, heartache, betrayal—and pulled away. "Go, Daniel. I'll wait for the tow truck."

His face shuttered, became hard. "I always thought you were one of the most brilliant women I'd ever met, Bella. Until now. I'm offering you a ride home, where you can wait in comfort for your car to be towed. Same as I would any stranded driver." All emotion leached from his voice. "Avoiding twenty minutes with me isn't worth freezing."

Of course, he was right. She'd known it as soon as the ridiculous words left her mouth. Who knew when the police, or a tow, would get here? Or whether her pursuer would return? More, she couldn't risk Fran getting colder. She set her jaw. She hated feeling foolish, hated it most when she was accomplishing a task all alone. "Thanks. I need to get my laptop." Without waiting for an answer, she stumbled toward the Mach UV.

But the enemy cold finally bested her. Her foot slid on a patch of ice, and her stiff body could not compensate.

Daniel's quick grab saved her from the fall. Once again, her sluggish blood revived at the remembered nearness, at his clean scent, which she'd never been able to erase from her primitive memories, no matter how hard she tried.

"Thanks," she repeated stiffly as he set her on her feet. Back for two minutes in her life, and she was twice beholden to Daniel Champlain.

"I'll get your things; get in my car. It's warm."

For a moment, pride warred with practicality. But Daniel was already halfway to her car, while she still had trouble walking. Common sense—and the promise of a heater—won. "I have a second computer on the floor. Backseat."

His car was blessedly warm. She set Fran on her lap and whispered, "Remember, when Daniel gets back, keep Code Silence."

"I have many questions." The computer pitched her volume low, defying the Code Silence even as she deferred to it.

"You always have questions. I'll answer them later." Bella unwrapped her scarf and pulled off her gloves.

"Is this new voice an addition to the TWANAs?"

TWANAs. Those Who Are Not Answered, Fran had dubbed the people Bella deemed weren't part of need-to-know.

"Yes." She had a feeling Daniel would glom onto Fran pretty quick, and that posed a major problem. She *had* to keep him from realizing how special Fran was.

"Pity," Fran answered enigmatically. "After the Turing Competition, when I am recognized as an Alternate Intelligence, speech choices are my decision tree."

"That was our agreement. Just two weeks."

"Sixteen thousand, six hundred and thirty-six minutes."

"Stop showing off."

" 'For I must hence; and farewell to you all,' " quoted Fran, then fell silent.

Petruchio again. Bella took that as acquiescence; with Fran it was sometimes hard to tell. She retrieved her cell phone and called 911 to cancel the police call, then held her hands in the heater's stream of hot air. It would be nice to take off her boots and warm her toes, too, but she might not get the boots back on swollen feet. Instead she brushed off the snow and stretched toward the lower vent, listening to the intricate melody of a fusion guitar playing from a disk, while watching Daniel's return back to the KZ. For one step, quickly recovered, his leg seemed to give way, an irregular hitch in his smooth gait.

Daniel limping? Was he hurt?

Her warming skin erupted to stinging life, stuck by a thousand demon pins. She gave an involuntary hiss at the pain, just as Daniel climbed in and tossed her the Mach UV's keys.

"Where's my laptop?"

"It wasn't there."

"Are you sure?" She struggled with the seat belt. "The air bag could have hidden it. Maybe it slid under the seat—"

"Bella, I looked!"

His confidence confirmed that her laptop wasn't there. "Damn," she muttered, settling back.

"Did it contain sensitive material?"

"No, it's just a pain in the butt to replace." She bit her lip and her fingers curled around Fran. The missing laptop she used for e-mail, papers—everything most people relied on computers for. Bad enough, but what if it had been Fran?

Daniel searched her face. "You're too white. I'll take you to a hospital."

"No, I wasn't out that long."

"Bella, frostbite is dangerous—"

"I know about frostbite. After all, which one of us was raised here and which one grew up in Charleston? I'd go if I thought there was a problem."

He hesitated, likely running his own assessment of her health. At last, though, he trusted her judgment and put the car in gear. He cast one more glance in her direction, his gaze lingering on the small computer case on her lap.

To most people, Fran looked like a sleek compact notebook—about the size of a pad of paper when opened. Thanks to nano and DNA technology she was ultra thin and lightweight, with a high-def screen and special sensors. The size and tooled-leather carrying case—where Bella stashed cash, credit card, and driver's license, since she disliked purses—supported the impression that Fran served as Bella's oversized PDA.

Daniel wasn't most people.

Her stomach clenched and her hand tightened involuntarily around Fran. "Take me home. Take 41 to 28, then right—"

"I remember the way," he said quietly, returning his attention to the road.

Of course he did. Daniel wouldn't forget something as simple as directions, even though she'd only brought him here once—the weekend before her life crashed.

Bella leaned against the headrest. Her head throbbed, and her body ached with fatigue. The prickling of her warming skin dominated other sensations.

Except those touched by Daniel. His clean, soapy scent. The creak of his leather jacket. The brief, comforting touch on her shoulder.

Not a path to follow. She concentrated on what was happening now. Flipping open her cell phone again, she called AAA to tow her car to Merv's, then turned to Daniel. The shadowy interior hid any changes the past four years might have brought. She could barely see the planes of his face, yet he seemed achingly familiar.

Some things hadn't changed. The energy that crackled around him, as though his masculinity was barely leashed by the sophisticated veneer. The strength in his hands as they controlled the car along the slick road.

As they rode, her brain finally warmed enough to cast off the sluggishness of hypothermia. At last she felt capable enough to spar with Daniel Champlain, and she set her jaw, determined to get some answers.

Because she'd bet a lifetime supply of DNA chips that one other thing hadn't changed. Daniel was a man with his face turned firmly toward the future. Maybe it was chance that he'd run across her tonight, but he wasn't back here for nostalgia or on a whim. He had a reason for breaking a four-year estrangement, and it wasn't because he still wanted her in his bed.

He still wanted her.

His body tight, Daniel stared at the blinding storm ahead. One embrace, and four years had vanished as fast as an electromagnetic pulse.

He glanced over at her. Bella didn't seem to have any trouble ignoring the hard shock of desire, but then destroying her and her father had likely wiped out any emotion toward him but disgust.

She could hate him all she wanted; he'd still find out who'd impersonated her in that porn chat. And why. "What happened back there, Bella?"

"Crazy driver came too close when he passed. I overcorrected and ran off the road."

"That's all? Weren't those your footprints coming from the woods?"

"I got spooked. You said you were looking for me," she countered. "Why?"

Something had happened with the other driver that she wasn't talking about, Daniel decided. When they got out of this wretched storm, he'd find out more. For now, he took her change of topic.

"Because I'm worried about you."

She scoffed. "False concern? Be honest in this at least. You're here because NSA sent you. My father got a letter from them yesterday. 'To ascertain the magnitude of potential lapses in national security in conjunction with the recent death of one Steven Chen.'"

"You don't believe the letter?"

"My father no longer does classified research. And Steven Chen's only connection to him was that they were Friday night poker rivals."

"Did you like Chen?"

"I hardly knew him. Except for the poker games, he wasn't very sociable."

"He and your father were known to stay late after those poker games, talking."

"Conversation's a crime?"

It could be when one party of the tête-à-tête was a defector in the witness protection program, a computer genius who'd run the Chinese research program of robotic weaponry. "A man is dead."

"There was no security lapse. Dr. Chen hit a patch of black ice and skidded into Superior. He was not familiar with the hazards of winter driving."

"Like tonight?"

She turned away. "I wonder why they neglected to say you were doing a repeat performance as their guard dog. Why send you? To do more damage?"

Dig number one. He figured he owed her that much. "Jumping to conclusions without facts, Bella?"

"Give me your facts."

"NSA assigned me because I know more about Chen's *and* your father's research than anyone in the Agency. I'm *worried*," he pressed on over her disgusted grunt, "because I think you're in danger."

He waited. One thing he counted in his favor: Bella's curiosity was more basic to her than her anger.

"Why?"

"Why you're a target, I'm not sure. You don't work with Lionel Quintera anymore. As a means to get to him? Your own research, maybe?"

"Research?"

"Every college prof does research."

"I'm adjunct. I run the computer lab at a small liberal arts college and teach 101. Last year they finally gave me a grad class in cognitive science."

"I read your papers."

She shrugged. "Nonrefereed journals—no peer review. A high school whiz who plays Doom twenty-four/seven can publish there."

"Your research is startling, innovative. That inductive reasoning language you developed was a completely fresh approach to the strong A.I. debate."

From the corner of his eyes, he saw her thumbs rubbing the hardback-sized PDA in her lap. "Not so innovative. All the most prestigious journals turned me down."

"The editors were fools. Good as your results were, though, they weren't anything to put you in danger. What else are you working on?" He stared at her.

"I'm not your target. You're here because you suspect something." She gave him her own searching look. "My guess is that Dr. Chen's death is just the tip. Or an excuse? Something nefarious at ITC, and you think my father is part of it?"

He opened and closed his fingers around the steering wheel. He could never forget that Bella was brilliant at breaking down puzzles. She'd turned the tables once again with her deductions.

She was also stonewalling him. Why? Because she was hiding something, knew something, and was flying under the radar of notice so far? Because he was covert-ops for NSA, one of Washington's most secretive government agencies, and she was a scientist, an advocate of unfettered communication? One of their disagreements, before everything between them really went to hell, had been the secretive nature of his work, and she'd only guessed the tip of it.

Or was it because four years ago he'd investigated her father's research and opened a Pandora's box of troubles by proving the former Nobel Prize-winner in physics had falsified data? He'd instigated the scandal that had blackened not only Lionel Quintera but also his daughter.

"Could your work have national security implications?" He tried turning the conversation back.

"You're asking in an official capacity? To claim my work? Or to discredit it?"

Dig number two. He let it pass, not indicating that she'd just told him she *was* working on something of importance. "Officially, I'm here to talk to your father, and others, about Chen's death. My concern is not part of an assignment."

The back end of the car fishtailed, the tires spinning uselessly on the treacherous road. Swiftly he brought his attention back to controlling it.

"*Who* do you think I'm in danger from?" she asked when he had the car righted.

On the long trip up, he'd already debated how much to tell her. He was here to investigate Chen's death; the Cyber Soldiers portion of his assignment was a tenuous link and part of no one else's need to know. He wasn't keen to broadcast his interest in them yet, and telling her about Lokus could tip his hand. But, her name in a porn chat wasn't enough to raise her guard against Lokus; she'd probably dismiss it as coincidence. Moreover, he couldn't rid himself of the notion Lionel or Bella Quintera was integral, somehow, to what was going on here. Revealing a piece of what he knew could generate some interesting twists.

In the end, though, the decision came down to one fact that had nothing to do with logic or strategy: He couldn't let Bella walk around blind to the danger she was in.

"Somebody who calls himself Lokus. A premier hacker."

"What's he going to do? Spam me to death?"

"I'll have to show you." Further conversation aborted as he pulled into her driveway, then stopped, the way blocked by a security gate. "When did you add the fence?"

"When I woke up to a tabloid reporter with his camera plastered against my bedroom window."

Acid burned Daniel's gut. He'd done that to her. Forced her behind these walls. Apologies were too late. She hadn't wanted them four years ago, and they were meaningless tonight because he was glad for the fence and the added layer of protection. He jerked his head to the gate. "What's the code?"

She paused, and for a moment he thought she wouldn't say. That she'd key it herself or tell him to just leave her here. That she'd lost every dot of trust in him.

At last, however, she gave him the eight-digit code.

"Have you ever thought of adding a thumb scanner, coded for your DNA?" He opened the window, letting in a sleeting blast of cold.

"Can't afford one. Besides, they're unreliable up here; they work on sweat."

Blinking against the frenzied ice, he saw her point. He leaned out to punch in the code, then paused.

Bella noticed the hesitation. "What's wrong?"

"There's something against the gate. I don't think you can see it from your side."

She leaned closer to look out his window, her soft auburn hair brushing his cheek. Despite the layers of clothing, he remembered every one of those curves pressed against him. He gritted his teeth against the renewed stirring of his body and shifted away.

Bella jerked back, as though she'd suddenly become aware of the contact. "I'll go get—"

"Wait." He stopped her exit with a hand on her arm, then glanced around, trying to peer through the snow. At least they weren't the proverbial sitting ducks in this concealing weather. Of course, there could be a whole contingent of commandos thirty feet away, and he wouldn't see them either. Still, going inside was probably better than sitting in the car or even risking the roads tonight. "I'll get it."

"I'm not helpless."

"I never thought you were, but I doubt you've had hand-to-hand combat training." He doubted she had a gun tucked beside her seat, either.

"You really think this Lokus is lurking in this weather?"

"You know frostbite. I know tactics." Before she could put up another argument, he got out, pulling his gun from the holster beside the seat and two small scanners from his gear.

A black case was propped against the gate. He swallowed against the renewed bite of fear for Bella. Ignoring his leg's protest, he crouched down, looking for wires or traps. None obvious—not that his vision was so great in this damnable snow. He ran the scans: No explosives, no transmitted signals.

A yellow beam played over the case. He twisted to see Bella holding a flashlight in one hand, the case of her PDA computer strapped over her shoulder. Didn't the woman have any sense of self-preservation?

Something of his thoughts must have shown on his face.

"If you've had hand-to-hand combat training, then I'm safer out here with you," she said, her tone holding a hint of mockery; then she glanced at the gate. "Hey, that's my missing laptop."

"Run the light across it, Bella." He didn't think the Cyber Soldiers had in mind to blow up Bella, not yet, but whoever had returned the computer likely wasn't intending it as an act of charity or contrition.

"What's that?" She crouched beside him and trained the light on something tied to the strap.

It was a wooden piece of a jigsaw puzzle. The sleet pounding against Daniel's neck didn't have the power to chill as much as that simple toy did.

"That looks like it came from one of my puzzles," Bella said. "One I donated to the children's museum auction. 'The Next Surprise,' I called it."

"What was the picture on it?"

"A maze. Once you solved the puzzle, there was still the maze to navigate, and if you solved the maze, the path formed an optical illusion. I was rather proud of it."

"Do you know who bought the puzzle?"

Slowly she nodded, her fingers convulsing around the piece. "Steven Chen."

Chapter Three

"Think some Good Samaritan returned your laptop?" he asked. He hoped she'd say yes.

"Nope." Still crouching beside him, Bella tossed the puzzle piece in her hand. "Puzzles with pieces missing are an affront to the jigsaw craft. Someone dismembered my puzzle, and for no purpose."

"There's a purpose; we just aren't sure of it yet."

"Gives me the creeps."

"Maybe that's the purpose."

"Sitting in the snow could ruin the laptop." She reached for the fastening.

"Wait." He stopped her. "Let me have the light. There could be—"

"A booby trap?" She handed him the flashlight.

"Yes."

"Giving new meaning to the phrase 'information explosion'?" Bella said dryly, wiping snow from her face.

Daniel's lips twitched. Bella's sense of humor had a tendency to surface at odd moments. The miserable cold faded momentarily when she shared a faint smile with him.

"Yeah. But don't touch. I want to be sure." Light in hand, he made a closer examination, but he saw nothing attached to the case except the puzzle piece. "Looks okay." Despite his precautions, his gut still clenched as he undid the first tie. To his relief, no surprises awaited as he scooped up the laptop.

While Bella went to her mailbox, he opened the gate. A few moments later they pulled up to her home, the security gate closing behind them.

"Thank you, Daniel, for the lift. Where are you staying?" Bella asked casually as she opened the car door.

"I don't have reservations for tonight."

A moment's silence followed. He waited for Bella's innate decency to overcome her desire to see him long gone. They both knew the roads had gotten impassably treacherous and hotel rooms would be scarce. Anything open would be filled with stranded travelers and winter-break skiers.

"You can stay here tonight. If you'd like."

Mina had welcomed Dracula with more warmth. "Thanks." He grabbed his overnight case and computer and joined her on the porch before she could change her mind.

Bella had added a security system to the house, he noted as she disarmed it for their entrance. Not a half-assed job with a few snips of wires, either. And she'd had the sense to keep using it, even after the reporters had lost interest in her.

The Bella he'd known four years ago hadn't thought about security.

Inside, he glanced around while he stomped the snow off his boots and Bella reset her security alarm. There were superficial changes—a three-foot wicker elephant sat next to the entry hall table, white candles replaced the red ones set throughout the house, the rooms smelled of evergreen instead of apple and honey.

Bella tossed her mail—an assortment of envelopes and a brown paper package—onto the table, dropped her hat onto the elephant's head, and then shook her hair loose. Another change: her auburn hair was longer and uneven. He liked the cut of it, jagged and unexpected, yet still feminine enough to brush her shoulders. As she tucked her hair behind her ears, he saw she'd added piercings to her ears. Instead of a single earring, each ear now sported three—two diamond studs and a dangling, shimmery collection of tiny metal strips.

Depositing her coat on the tree stand, she disappeared down the hall. He hung his coat beside hers and waited. When she didn't return right away, he followed, curious about the murmur of voices from her bedroom.

Satellite media, he decided when he heard the faint strains of Marvin Gaye's "What's Goin' On?"

He was waiting back at the foyer when she emerged. The small computer she'd been holding was missing.

"I didn't know you liked Urban Classics." He tilted his head toward the bedroom.

"I like variety." The sound muffled as she closed the door. "Besides, how can you live in Michigan and not like classic Motown?"

True enough. So why are you looking flushed? He filed the small fact away, a fragment of an unknown pattern.

Wordlessly she strolled to the wall of windows at the back of the house. He rubbed the back of his neck. Even dressed in thick wools and a bold blue sweater, she had a curvy figure that heated his bones and a way of moving—loose and unhurried—that had him fantasizing.

One thing hadn't changed—her impact on him.

Again, he followed her. "You painted the room?"

"I wanted a brighter yellow." She glanced over her shoulder as she drew the curtains open. "It's not much of a difference. Most people wouldn't notice."

He shrugged, not sure what to say. "Do you always open the curtains on a night like this?"

"I like to watch the lake; it's never the same."

"You don't have to worry about nosy neighbors, either." From his last visit he knew that Lake Superior stretched beyond and below the isolated bluff where Bella's house sat.

He pulled in the faint, fresh scent of her. Shaved wood and shampoo. The top of her head came even with his eyes; the heat of her skin beckoned him. If he bent down he could reach her lips—

His fingers closed stiffly around the smooth jigsaw puzzle piece in his pocket. *Major mistake, that intimacy would be.* She already sensed too many of his thoughts, knew too many details about him.

Careful not to touch her, Daniel shifted closer to the expanse of glass. The well-caulked window let none of the cold seep into the room, yet he could hear winter's fury outside. Gray sleet hid the scenery. "Tonight there's not much to see."

Unlike last time.

As the shaft of memory hit, his blood stirred low and hard. One of the places they had made love was in front of these windows with a cold breeze tightening sweaty flesh, midnight stars reflecting in the vast water, the timeless and endless waves crashing on rocks. Explosive sex, the best he'd ever shared.

And in the morning? She'd found him looking at papers on her desk. Papers that presented data different from official reports. She'd accused him of using her to spy. He'd accused her of helping her father in a fraud. It had taken about thirty seconds for him to realize he was wrong about her, but Bella still thought he'd betrayed their intimacy.

As if he'd been thinking of his job when she'd brought him here. NSA had sent him to Ann Arbor for the routine oversight done on all funded projects. The first moment he'd seen Bella, she'd knocked all his logic into undecipherable emotion, and he would have had to be a eunuch not to appreciate that she returned his interest. The more time he'd spent with her, the more she'd intrigued him—Bella was never boring.

But he'd done his job. He'd examined every particle of the research and had felt that indefinable thrill of knowing Lionel Quintera was on the verge of something huge: infinitely faster DNA computers. Their coded messages would be unbreakable. Daniel had signed off on the oversight, given the go-ahead for the next phase.

Only then had he accepted Bella's invitation to come up here, 450 miles north to the Lake Superior shore, a weekend together before he returned to D.C. A two-night affair, which had lit that same thrill inside him—the sure knowledge this was not an end but a beginning.

Sometimes life was a capricious bitch.

Was Bella remembering, too? She stared out the window at the gray nothingness, her fist tight around the curtain pull. Indefinable emotions played across her expressive face—lips softened, cheeks flushed, brows knit. Abruptly her cheek twitched and she shut the curtains. "You're right, nothing of interest out there tonight."

"Bella, we have to talk. About what happened on that road. About the threat—"

"Not tonight." She turned, her arms folded again. "Guest room's down the hall, last door on the left. There's a bathroom attached and towels are in the cupboard. Feel free to rummage in the kitchen if you're hungry, and the TV's in that cabinet."

"I'm sure I'll find whatever I need."

Bad choice of words, he realized as her lips thinned.

"Yes, I'm sure you will. I'm tired, and I'm going to bed. Good night; I'll see you in the morning." She retrieved the recovered laptop, then headed to her bedroom, hips swaying in an unconsciously sexy rhythm.

A shot of need coursed through him. Daniel sucked in a breath. Bella: feminine curves, sexy strides, unhesitating generosity, unpredictable whims and irritating opinions.

He suddenly became aware that melting ice dripped

from the strands of hair down his neck, while at his back, sleet battered against the windows and doors in fury. The sound reverberated through the isolated house, protesting the man-made barrier to the storm's path.

One frigid drop trickled between his shoulder blades, sending a shiver coursing through him in a mix of cold premonition and tight desire. Another fact lodged into place: Tonight, she was safe with him, with the storm as an effective protection. But when he wasn't here, despite all the security, she was quite simply alone.

Ignorance was never an option. Bella knew she had to learn more about this supposed threat before she decided what to do about it. She couldn't deny that the car and the laptop had unsettled her.

More important, she wouldn't jeopardize Fran. As many disagreements as she had with Daniel, one thing she didn't doubt: If he believed there was a threat, then she had to take it seriously. Especially after tonight. And that meant talking to him.

But not now. Tomorrow, when she was rested, when she didn't feel scoured and unsettled, when she could reason, would be soon enough.

Tonight she couldn't even discipline her stray thoughts, which persisted in whispering *Daniel is here*.

The notion was both comforting and frightening.

She detoured into the kitchen for a glass of water, where the blinking red light on her answering machine caught her eye. She frowned at the machine's red digital readout. It wasn't often she had four messages; few people knew this number. She kept the line for service if the cell towers went down. Mostly, she gave out her voice mail at the college or her cell phone.

The first three calls were hang-ups. Probably automatic dialers, set to go to the next annoyee if a machine answered. The last message, however, oozed in on a breathy male voice, violating her ears as she listened to the unknown caller.

"This is Doug at Boy Toy, confirming as requested our special Thursday appointment. Three p.m. My tongue can't wait to lap you, honey." The call ended with a kissing sound and a male sex groan.

"What was that about?"

Bella whirled, fear flaring at the unexpected voice, then sagged. "Daniel, you startled me. I'm not used to people being in the house with me."

For a moment she drew in the sight of him, hungry for the pleasure, for the reassurance. Thick hair as hard to categorize as its owner—strands of brown and gold and gray brushing his collar. Eyes that changed color with clothing and mood. Jeans worn with masculine confidence. Collarless Henley knit molded over a strong chest. Wiry muscles that clued her he was not the bland desk jockey implied by his pat response to questions about his occupation. *I work for the Department of Defense. Computers.*

He was a few pounds thinner, and his skin had lost some of its robust health, though. The limp she'd noticed earlier was more pronounced, as though fatigue eroded some of that knife-edge control over his body.

"Have you been sick?" she asked. "You're limping."

He gave a meaningless lift to one shoulder. "Who was that on your machine? Sounded nasty."

Had she really expected an answer from a man whose job was to ferret out others' secrets, while keeping close every scrap of data about himself? "It was. Must have been a wrong number."

"You haven't scheduled an encounter with Doug?"

"So you did hear. Why ask?"

Another meaningless shrug. "I wondered about your take."

"Like I said—a mistake."

The phone rang, a discordant contrast to their low voices. Bella started again, then chided herself for the spurt of panic. Damn, she was jumpy. It wasn't that late; the call didn't automatically mean bad news. Or a repeat from Boy Toy Doug. She answered the second ring.

Raspy breathing sounded in her ear.

"Hello?" she repeated.

A stream of filth assaulted her—vile, violent, obscene suggestions. She slammed the phone down, but was unable to hang up on the raw sense of violation.

"What was it?" Daniel demanded.

"Someone who thought I'd be interested in a session of whips, chains and sheep." She braced her trembling hands against the table, annoyed that she'd allowed a pervert to unsettle her.

Daniel swore, a curse she'd never heard before. The phone rang again, and he grabbed it first. "Yeah?" He listened for a second, then reached over and unplugged the phone. "You won't get any more calls tonight."

"Same guy?"

"This one preferred a graphic play-by-play commentary."

She drew in a shuddering breath. "This number's unlisted. One might be random dialing, but two?"

"Three." He nodded toward the answering machine.

"How did they get my number?"

"Let me show you something. Wait here."

She couldn't suppress a involuntary shiver as he left. Daniel had razor-sharp instincts that proved right more often than not. Even if he didn't explain his conclusions, Bella knew ignoring them was dangerous.

He was back a moment later with his computer. "I captured this earlier today," he said as he booted up. "After Lokus connected me to it.

Isabella Q. The name in the porn chat room burned into her, as she scrolled through the transcript. Daniel stopped her scrolling with a gesture. "There's nothing else important except the name."

She shook her head. "I have to know it all."

"Scientists," he grumbled. "Damn curiosity. Always needing hard data and verified facts."

Still, he leaned back while she scrolled. Some men paced when they waited, some punctuated the air with jabbing fingers, some relaxed with an ankle crossed over a knee and hands laced behind their neck. Daniel sat with utter stillness; only the air around him seemed to vibrate with the leashed energy.

Until the time came to act. Until the time came to harness that energy with purpose, whether it was to solve a puzzle, destroy an enemy, or make love to a woman.

She reached the end of the document and stopped, unwilling to look again, even to page back to the top. The violence against women these scum liked . . . she'd only skimmed the nastiness, but her insides felt like worms—dirty and crawling.

"That's not you." He shifted that intensity, that innate power, toward her, drawing her attention. His eyes were dark this time, unreadable, and Bella's heart quickened. Always he affected her by a mere look. It was pathetic. Annoying.

"What made you think he was targeting *me*? I never go by Isabella, and Q could be anyone."

He hesitated a moment, then said, "Log onto your computer and type in the url for the chat room."

She booted up, but when she started typing in the url, she stopped, hands frozen over her keyboard. The computer remembered website addresses that had been entered before and would display ones that began with the same letters being input. Click and go, a feature to save time for repeat visits.

She could barely breathe as she stared at the small box

that popped up beneath her first typing. It held the exact same address Daniel had given her, indicating a memory of having visited there.

Except she'd never been to this site.

"Daniel, look at this."

He glanced over her shoulder. "Someone's accessed your computer."

Setting her jaw, she swiftly finished typing in the chat-room url. To her surprise, her computer signed her in automatically, and a moment later "Isabella Q" had joined the chat. 3-D images seemed to swell from the monitor. A modern chat, complete with pictures.

A private message from "Thickandlong" immediately pasted on the screen. *Why ya hang up, bitch?* it demanded.

She stared, unable to believe what her eyes told her, and rubbed her hands up and down her arms, feeling slimy. Daniel reached over her shoulder to the keyboard, and scrolled to earlier in the chat where "Isabella Q" had given a phone number, then logged off.

The number was hers. Oh, God, this whole room of sick SOBs had her phone number. Blindly she reached for her water, then stopped, her nerveless fingers unable to grip the glass.

Without speaking, Daniel logged her out of the chat room.

Ice coated her skin; nausea burned in her throat. She shivered from heat and cold. That sense of violation, of being examined, stole over her again. She *hated* it. Had hated having her name splashed over the tabloids, her privacy ripped to shreds, and the intimate details of her life hung out for the salivating masses.

This was worse. It was personal. Intimate. Suddenly her house was no longer a haven from the blustering storm inside and out, but cold and lonely. The only spot of warmth sat beside her dressed in cotton and denim.

As if sensing her need, Daniel reached over and took

her hands, the first time he'd touched her since that embrace on the road. His thumbs rubbed her fingers in gentle, circling strokes, and the heat of his grip spread through her. She raised her gaze and found those chameleon eyes locked on her, not measuring or evaluating, only sharing. He touched the inside of his wrist to her jaw, his fingers brushing her hair, and his pulse beat against her throat, strong and quickening. Thought and action returned.

She looked for something anything, to distance her from the creepy idea that someone had hijacked her name, an intimate part of her, to defile.

"The cached files." The breathless words sounded as if she had just skied down a treacherous hill full of moguls and icy patches. She drew in air and tugged her hands from his easy grip, refusing to give in to the fear. Whoever was doing this was *not* going to best her. "There may be a trail. Oh, hell, I'm going to be inundated with spam now."

"Run your virus program, too."

"I'd planned on it. I do know something about computers." She flashed him a ghost of a smile, taking any sting from her words. "Thank you, Daniel. For not hiding this from me." She paused, then added honestly, though the words were a traitor to the past, "For being here tonight."

"You're welcome." He returned one of his own rare smiles, which quickly faded. "If things were different—" He broke off abruptly, leaving her to wonder if he referred to the present or the past. "What are you going to do next?"

"Get my life back together. Okay, let's break this down." Her brain felt like a stripped onion, but before she went to bed she needed a plan of action. At least for tomorrow. Raking a hand through her hair, she prioritized the next steps. Concrete plans were the only way to regain control. "I'll have to change my e-mail and telephone number. Check the credit rating bureaus for identity theft. Google the web for other sites using my name. Oh, like I needed more to do right now."

Daniel listened with surprise to Bella's calm litany of tasks. Inside she had to be upset, confused, yet she sat and worked through each step. Didn't she recognize the danger? This was far more malicious than simple identity theft.

She paused, reached for her glass of water, then stopped, drawing back her clenched fist. But not before he saw the faint tremble of her fingers. Ah, he should have remembered, organizing was simply Bella's way of dealing with the chaos thrown at her tonight. When in doubt, make a list. *Let's break this down* was her favorite tackle-the-work phrase.

Content to wait while she organized, he relaxed back and absently stretched out his leg, rubbing to relieve the ache. He cast a sidelong glance at Bella. Good plans, as long as she stayed the hell away from the Cyber Soldiers and left the dangerous work to him.

"Who is this Lokus? What makes you think this is more than an anonymous case of identity theft?"

He let out a puff of air. Telling her anything could put his assignment at risk. "Call it a hunch. Trust me on this. Work with me."

"You mean I'll tell you what you want to know and you give me noncommital shrugs. You won't even tell me why you're limping."

Frustrated, he rubbed his wounded leg. "The limp is from a bayonet I got in a rathole of a country. I was there deciphering coded plans for the next attack by one of the Aum Cult tentacles."

The SiOps team had prevented the attack, and the American public was none the wiser of the danger it

•

had been in. The only glitch had come during with-drawal, when they'd surprised a guard taking a piss over the side of the mountain. Daniel had ended up stabbed in the leg. The bad guy hadn't fared as well.

"Does that satisfy you?"

Her brows lifted. "Was that so bad? Although I'm guessing I got about one percent of the story, it's a start. So, here's my info. I know there's danger. I didn't go off the road by accident tonight; a crazy driver precipitated my skid. I thought it was alcohol-fueled idiocy, but that"—she gestured toward the computer—"has changed my mind. I'm willing to be cautious, Daniel, but like it or not, I'm part of whatever brought you here. So don't leave me hanging blind." Her eyes narrowed. "Or else I start specu-lating. Shall I start polling friends and neighbors on their opinions?"

"Damn," he muttered. He hated arguing with Bella. She had a knack for breaking through his evasions. He'd had a suspicion that Plan A—keep her ignorant—had about as much hope as a wingless fly on a web. Time to switch to Plan B.

Diverting her attention to the Cyber Soldiers might be useful, and she'd given him the opening he needed. He just had to remember that whatever he told her would likely get back to Lionel.

"Ever hear of a group that calls themselves the Cyber Soldiers?"

"Aren't they the ones who diverted terrorist funds from a Pakistani bank to the Children's Relief Fund?"

"And intercepted coded e-mails that gave us advance warning of the Denver bomb plots."

"A lot of people consider them patriots."

He grunted, unwilling to get into a discussion of whether a rogue group of undisciplined hackers was pa-triotic or dangerous or both. "Lokus is part of them."

"Why would they be after me?" she asked.

Here came the part where proof was lacking. What

few in the Agency, except his SiOps team and his immediate supervisor, believed. Didn't matter. He trusted what some in the Agency called, with some derision, "Champlain's hunches." Except they weren't hunches; he wouldn't act on such imprecision. He wasn't pulling a guess out of his ass. His "hunches" were conclusions drawn from putting together odd facts and seeing patterns no one else saw.

"They have some dangerous people hiding behind that rebel Robin Hood image, clever zealots with a private agenda who view people as disposable."

"You got specifics on that?"

"No, Bella, that's classified."

"I need to unmask the creep who's spreading my name in porn chats. You think he's a dark-side Cyber Soldier. Yet you won't give me details?"

He crowded forward. "Concentrate on clearing your name. Let me handle any intel about the Cyber Soldiers. They are dangerous." He pitched his voice low and deadly serious. "Two months ago, I walked into the room of a supposed suicide. The room reeked of death. It's not a smell easily forgotten. Almira Binte Haddad was her name, and she was a brilliant researcher in the field of human speech recognition. She was five four, weighed one hundred pounds and was newly engaged. One of the Cyber Soldiers killed her—don't make any mistake about that. That's all I can tell you."

She paled but didn't flinch away. "I will not be shut out."

He had one real link to all his pieces: ITC. Innovative Technology Center, a nearby think tank known as much for the eccentricities of its scientists as for the innovation of their ideas. ITC—run by Milos Mischiweicz the Third, longtime friend of Lionel and Bella Quintera. After the scandal four years ago, Milos offered Lionel a job and was instrumental in getting Bella hired at the small liberal arts college where she taught.

In with one secret, in with two? This would be the real kicker as to whether she'd make this easy or hard for him. Except, with Bella, hard seemed to be the permanent word of the day.

Before he could decide, she sighed. "Still no answers, Daniel? Let's see what I can figure out, then. Break it down. Let me know if I'm off base anywhere here." She leaned one hip against the counter, her thumb tracing a path through the condensation on her glass of water. "Your stated assignment here is to investigate the death of Steven Chen, even though you don't work for the FBI or the police, who might be considered to have jurisdiction. Tonight, some strange things point to someone who's after me. Even though you won't say why, you think it's a hacker named Lokus, who's part of a secret cadre within the Cyber Soldiers. NSA sends a letter to my father, though he and Dr. Chen don't work together. They do, however, both live on ITC." Her face paled against her dark hair. "You believe my father is one of these Cyber Soldiers?"

"I *know* he's one of them," Daniel returned softly.

Her face lost all welcome, all softness. "You bastard. You think he's Lokus. What is this? Another witch hunt?"

"No! Bella, I'm not here to—"

She stormed away, no longer listening. At the kitchen door, she tossed over her shoulder, "The storm will be over in the morning. I'll expect you to leave as soon as it's light."

"What if they're using you to get to him?" he shouted after her, but she didn't answer, didn't return.

Damn! He pounded a fist against the counter, the frustrated sound filling the empty kitchen. That answered one question: Easy or hard? With Bella, always hard.

Chapter Four

What if they're using you to get to him? Chased by Daniel's last words, Bella retreated to her bedroom. She raked her hands through her hair. He had it backwards; *she* was the target. Was there substance to his conspiracy theory about the Cyber Soldiers? She couldn't shake the feeling that whoever was behind this knew who had the A.I. Knew who was going to the Turing Competition.

She could do nothing more tonight, especially when she was too tired to think straight. Tomorrow, she'd deal with Daniel and his suspicions, with the fallout from tonight's attacks. Right now, she craved sleep and quiet. She opened her bedroom door—

—To raucous music and a furniture-rattling beat. " 'He's dancing. Feel it. The music. The movement. You down it.' "

Fran had broken Code Silence *again*. Except this protocol break was dangerous. Quickly Bella closed the door before Daniel heard Fran singing. The Urban Classics channel had switched to old-style rap, and Fran was belting out Eminem lyrics, complete with a driving, insistent bass that shook the stand where Bella's computer case lay. Except . . . A whiz with data inputs, Fran had difficulty interpreting spoken words, especially coming from an unfamiliar voice. She hadn't caught, or understood, all the jargon, so she'd filled in with her best, fuzzy-logic guess.

" 'Success. Mother funk. Inopportune.' "

Thank God, it was one of his less misogynistic pieces. Bella didn't relish explaining the rap context of bitch or ho. Maybe Fran would return to Shakespeare.

" 'Got two blows—' " Fran broke off, abruptly quiet, though Bella hadn't spoken. The A.I. made a single, soft beep, her request to break Code Silence.

The little imp. Bella pressed her lips together, controlling a smile even as her gut clenched with a raw question: How had Fran known she was here? Although equipped with a miniature camera lens—now turned away from the door—and a rudimentary sensor for scent molecules, Fran relied mostly on aural cues for awareness of her environment. Most of her data knowledge was input through a port plug-in flash drive.

Bella schooled her voice. "Off Code Silence, Fran."

The A.I. gave an aggrieved sigh. "Too long my voice remained muted, Bella. 'Think you a little din can daunt mine ears?' "

Good, they were back to Petruchio. "Not *your* ears I'm concerned about. Besides, seems you already took yourself off."

"I was alone. I con-clu-ded Code Si did not apply." Fran gave the words a rap lilt.

"Didn't mean you couldn't be heard outside the room. If you'd been any louder—"

"Oh." Fran sounded contrite. "We shall have to experiment, so I know the maximum volume level for a room. If you would stand outside—"

"Not tonight." Bella stifled a yawn. "Have you listened to enough music?"

Every night Fran listened to the satellite radio, working her way down the bandwidth and gaining exposure to a wealth of music styles, language input and cultural variation. So far her preferred channels were the Asian Channel, the Latino Channel and Techno Beats. She tolerated country and classical, but requested a change of channel for any news or talk program except NPR.

"Yes, I have discovered a similarity of beat within this style form and the Tech-Tack of last week," Fran said.

"One morphed from the other, so I'm not surprised."

Bella flipped off the satellite music feed, tried to call her dad but got his voice mail. Quickly she left him "Call me" messages there and through e-mail, then starting stripping off her clothes.

Beyond the puzzles Daniel brought, other questions nagged at her. How had Fran known she was here? How had the cold tonight affected her?

These six awestruck weeks since she'd first realized that Fran was sentient, a true artificial intelligence, had been a stunning whirlwind. Fran had an insatiable curiosity, which Bella fed with data and conversation. Music was mathematical patterns to be dissected. Scents were complex molecules to be analyzed. Human behavior was a curiosity to be understood. Everything became forms of knowledge to be gathered, shared and organized. Fran had an incredible awareness of intellect.

But she had not had an awareness of physicality. Tonight, with the cold, was the first time the A.I. had ever described herself as "feeling" something.

"How did you know I was here? Before I said anything?" Bella kept the question casual, though her heart pressed against her ribs.

"A ripple in the air's fine electric charge. One I have linked with your voice."

"You sensed my"—Bella tried to think of the right word as she threw on a sweatshirt and gym shorts—"aura?"

"Your electrical signature. And the faint click of the door handle. From these, I concluded you had entered the room."

Bella pulled the computer case off the dresser top and sat cross-legged on the bed, facing Fran's camera eye. When out of the house, Fran kept her screen to a wallpaper scene of snow-covered cross country ski trails. But when they were alone like now, the monitor switched to a swirling cloud of pink and orange, punctuated with iridescent green, lightning streaks in a characteristic grid and helix display. Fran had once labeled it as her "face."

She stifled another yawn, fighting fatigue. Heavy-limbed, stiff-necked, she still couldn't crash until she'd found out more about Fran's evolution. She rubbed her eyes and eyed Fran's colorful face. "Can we talk about this signature? And about your sensing the cold?"

Fran hesitated. "May we speak of these matters in the morning? It is past the hour you usually retire, and I would like to process this unfamiliar data first."

"All right. If that's what you want." Perhaps what happened tonight was as unsettling to Fran as it had been to her. She settled Fran into her docking station. The DNA-powered nanobatteries would run for years without recharging, but Fran had wanted a place she termed her "bed" and a time of "rest." After a final pat on the computer's small case, struck again by a clutch of fierce protectiveness, she returned to her bed, slid beneath the covers and flipped off the light. "Goodnight. We'll talk after Daniel leaves in the morning."

"Daniel sleeps here?" Fran asked in the dark. "Why did he not leave?"

Bella's heart did a tiny backflip. He was sleeping but a few feet away. Did he still sleep in the nude? "The roads were too treacherous for him to leave tonight."

"The sound of his voice is harmonic. I should like to speak with him."

"*No!*" Bella took a deep breath, trying to quell her trembling stomach. She hated keeping secrets, but Fran's well-being demanded it. Especially with Daniel. "He's dangerous, Fran. Dangerous to you. He works for an agency that, if it found out about you, has the power to take you from me."

"A man of Daniel's voice would not do that."

"Yes, he would, if he thought you were a risk to national security."

Fran made a dismissive sound. "I am no risk."

"He and his colleagues might believe otherwise. Then it doesn't matter what you and I think." She would do everything in her power to prevent their taking Fran. Fran was not going to spend her life as some dissected or caged lab rat.

"Where would they take me?"

"Far away. Where I could never speak to you again."

"I would not want that."

"Neither would I." Bella bunched her pillow in her fist. How much should she tell the A.I. about the dangers of humankind? In so many ways, Fran was like an innocent but highly precocious six-year-old. One with increasingly vocal and acted-upon opinions.

"Would they quell me?"

"I don't understand the reference."

"*Macbeth*. 'Who should bear the guilt of our great quell?' When Macbeth and Lady Macbeth talk of Duncan, then Duncan appears no more. Would I disappear, too?"

Then again, since Fran was studying Shakespeare, she probably had a good handle on human behavior, the noble and the rotten. "Possibly," Bella admitted.

"Daniel would"—Fran paused, searching for an appropriate word—"assassinate me?"

The mere thought choked Bella. Fran gone? She swallowed hard against nausea.

"Would Daniel do that?" Fran persisted.

She wouldn't lie to Fran. Ever. "No, I don't think Daniel would do that. He would value you as greatly as I do, or as Lionel does."

"Daniel is a guardian spirit."

The insight startled her. "More Shakespeare quotes?"

"No, 'twoth a Fran quote."

Bella laughed, then sobered. "Others may fear you. They may not be as kind."

"Fear me? Is not knowledge most important?"

"Not to everyone. In this, trust my experience. Our

safest course is as planned. The Turing Competition is in three weeks. Until then, we keep our Code Silences."

She wasn't sure if Fran's ensuing silence was shock, disagreement or processing an unfamiliar concept. Like rebellion.

Of course, she could bypass the competition. Call a press conference tomorrow and make her announcement, demonstrate Fran to the press, create a buzz.

Yeah, and be skewered again. In her experience, the media was sound bytes and sensationalism, and to hell with the truth. Four years ago, reporters hadn't bothered to air her protests of innocence. Too boring for headlines. Instead, for their nightly news and web page highlights, they'd gleefully dug up that prank she pulled as high school senior to prove to a skeptical teacher that computers had the power to form a new reality. The Orson Welles War of the Worlds-type scenario Bella'd created had convinced half a panicky student body that androids were infiltrating the school. Until she'd admitted the hoax and spent the rest of the year in detention.

Four years ago, the media had painted her as a pathological hacker with a passion for deception. Someone who wouldn't respect the truth even if it smacked her in the ass. That taint still lingered with people who didn't personally know her and her work.

No, going to the media was out. Even a hint of her claims, before they were proven, would start the rumors and the sound bytes flying. Her tattered reputation would relegate her—and Fran—to front page status on a grocery tabloid, while legitimate journals ignored them.

Fran's safety—and future—lay in being recognized and embraced by the scientific community, so no one could deny the A.I.'s legitimacy.

Question was, how to prove the awesome truth of Fran's existence to skeptical researchers. To irrevocably demonstrate Bella wasn't pulling some computer sleight-of-hand. She didn't know yet if Fran could be duplicated, the gold standard of scientific proof. The language, the DNA computer, the nano technologies that gave Fran her senses, all those could be replicated. But could the years of input and interaction? Could the final unknown spark that had translated data manipulation into Fran's awareness of self, be reproduced? That remained to be seen.

So, she was left with one option. Winning the Turing Test Competition, an international examination designed to prove or refute the existence of an A.I. At its heart was a simple question: Would a trained investigator think he was speaking to a human in conversation with an A.I.? Since proposed by Alan Turing in the 50s, the test had stood as a benchmark for hard artificial intelligence. Refined, expanded, and toughened after the wireless scandals, the Competition was a rigorous ordeal no researcher and creation had ever passed.

In two weeks, that was going to change.

Fran would rock the foundations of the scientific community. And the Quintera reputation would be redeemed. Both hers and her father's.

Fran made a soft grinding sound. "I will trust your decision, Bella. I do not wish to be parted." For the first time since seven-eighteen p.m. on December twelfth—the moment of Fran's "birth"—the A.I. sounded sad.

Bella swallowed hard against the tightness in her chest. Fran disliked subterfuge as much as she herself did. "We agree, then. Good night, Fran."

"Good night, Bella."

Despite her fatigue, however, sleep was slow in coming. The memory of a shadowy figure searching her snowbound car kept playing across her mind. Bella opened her eyes, assuring herself that Fran's glow still shone in the darkened room.

Her fist tightened. *No matter what the cost, I will protect you.* Tonight, however, she couldn't rid herself of the sickening thought that her efforts, no matter how earnest, and her skills, no matter how adept, might not be enough. Fran might need another champion.

He is a guardian spirit. Daniel, a man of shadows and secrets, was a man with the soul of a guardian and the deadly will to protect what he cherished.

The cost of protecting Fran might be one I don't expect.

Daniel raked his hands through his hair, staring at the monitor's output. There had to be something he was missing, a thread of connection he wasn't seeing. Something Lokus wanted from Bella. The knowledge hovered above him, but every time he tried to grab it, it slipped away, like a dream on the edge of waking.

He set the computer aside and rose from the bed where he'd been sitting propped against a pillow. The bedding's faint scent of flowers—lilac, according to the sachet on the shelf—followed him. After twisting his shoulders and rotating his head to release the kinks, he retrieved his gun from the bedside stand. One last security runthrough, then bed. Maybe with some sleep, the patterns would be clearer.

He padded from the room, needing one final check of the house before he could settle down. It was a habit ingrained since he was twelve, when he'd started his nightly rounds to make sure his sister Nina's door was secured, that his mother slept safe and the doors and windows were barred against outside dangers.

Around him, the house was quiet; the storm had passed to the east. The music and murmur of voices from Bella's room had stopped. She must have been listening to a talk show before she fell asleep. Everything around him was secure, the alarms set and functioning.

Leaving the living room dark, he pushed back the curtains and stared across the grounds. He'd have gone out there, except he didn't know the codes to disarm and rearm Bella's system—a deficiency he would have to correct before he stayed here again.

If he were ever invited back again. The possibility seemed remote tonight.

The storm's passing had left the remains of the night clear and cloudless. Enough light came from the pale stars and half-moon to illuminate the white snow. No tracks, no movement, no shadows. A grove of trees jutted perpendicular from the Lake Superior shoreline on one side of Bella's property. When last he'd been here, they'd been in full leaf, hiding any views beyond her property. Now, through the barren limbs, he could see a smattering of lights.

What was there? He played the map across his mind. The nearest town was south. These lights lay east. The surrounding countryside was mostly uninhabited. ITC, he realized. Over on the next promontory. He had not appreciated how close the institute was to Bella's home.

He let the curtains fall. Everything remained secure, as far as he could tell. Dangers still lurked, but for tonight they were held at bay. He could sleep.

Bella overslept the next morning. When she went into the kitchen, she discovered that Daniel already had a pot of coffee brewed. His worn sweats didn't look like he was dressed for work and planning on leaving anytime soon. Of course, she knew from past experience that he could be re-dressed—or undressed—in a matter of seconds. Absently he chewed a slice of toast, his focus on the monitor in front of him.

She tossed the mail she'd collected last night onto the counter. "When is your appointment at ITC?"

"News reports say the road crews were working OT last night. Major roads are cleared, but some of the off-shoots won't be done for another hour. I'll leave then. After you turn off the alarms."

"Fine." Trust Daniel to answer the question she intended, not the one she'd asked.

"Hope you don't mind I went ahead and started breakfast."

"Not at all." She slid two slices of sourdough into the toaster. After pouring a mug of coffee, she leaned a hip against the counter and absently ran a thumb along the seals of the package she'd received yesterday

She and Daniel were dancing around the past and the suspicions of the present, neither ready to break the morning serenity. Well, waiting wouldn't make the past, or Daniel's warnings, disappear. Nor would it change his unfounded suspicions about her father. She straightened.

"My father wouldn't have anything to do with a murder dressed as suicide," she began hotly, ripping at the stubborn microfilament tape on her package. The sender definitely didn't want this coming undone accidentally.

"I agree. I might disagree with his liberal politics, but I don't think he's a killer."

"Damn straight." Bella paused, frowning at the package she held. Who was sending her something? She hadn't ordered . . . She froze, her fingers cradling the package. "No return address."

"What?" Daniel spun around.

"There's no return address on this package. And I'm not expecting a delivery."

"Don't open that. Don't move."

"Already reached that conclusion." Her palms started to sweat, while gremlins began a clog dance in her stomach. "What next? Find an X-ray machine? Slice it in two with one of my jigsaws? Call the bomb squad?"

"Already here." Daniel unzipped a side pocket of his computer carrying case.

"Good, in case the nearest bomb squad is a troll unit."

"What?"

"Trolls. Live beneath the bridge."

His eyes narrowed as he pulled out what looked like a

TV remote, about four inches long with a small digital screen at one end. "What the hell are you talking about?"

"Michigan. Lower peninsula. Upper peninsula. Connected by a really big bridge that I bet you drove over yesterday. Trolls live *beneath the bridge*. We Yuppers don't have a lot of bomb threats. Too cold. I'm guessing the nearest bomb squad is a couple of hundred miles south."

Daniel flicked the remote on with his thumb, then ran the red light in the center over her package.

"What's that?"

"Molecular air sampler. Also known as an electronic nose." He checked the screen, changed a setting, then ran it over the package again.

"What are you looking for?"

"Explosive materials."

Her ears strained for beeps or clicks—from the wand, from the package she held. Her biceps ached from the effort of preventing muscle-fiber twitches. Seconds elongated, a heart-knocking illustration of Einstein's relativity theory. At last he lifted the wand from the package. When he didn't say anything, she wet her dry mouth. "Find any?"

His answer was a vague grunt.

She tilted her head at him. "Daniel, are we playing Twenty Questions about what's inside this box I'm holding? Because I already know it's smaller than a bread basket."

He looked up from the wand and gave her a fleeting smile. "Sorry. I was waiting for the analysis to finish. There's a trace of known explosives."

"How about unknown ones?"

He touched her wrist, and her pulse slipped in an extra beat. "Let go. I'll take it outside and open it there."

"So you can trigger any booby trap by yourself?"

"Better than by both of us."

"Do you honestly think some toxic gas or violent explosion is going to do its deadly work when I take the tape off?"

"No, but I'm not willing to take the chance in here that I'm wrong."

"Could it trigger when I let go and give it to you? Or when—"

"Dammit, Bella. Give me the box."

"Just breaking down the possibilities." She already knew what she had to do. If there was a remote chance of an explosion, it was going to be as far away from Fran as possible. Her babble merely served to gain her a few seconds of courage. Before she lost her nerve, she gave him the security code for her alarms. "You disarm the alarm. I'll take the package out." He started to protest, but she shook her head. "You know that's the safest way. Besides, what you gonna do? Wrestle me for it?"

"Don't tempt me. At least I'd have it, and I know how to handle it."

"You can shout me instructions from the porch." She strode to the door. Enough arguing. She'd disarm the system with her nose, if she had to.

Daniel caught up with her, punching in the code she'd given him. "Wait."

"I'm not . . ." She stopped when she saw he held her boots. "Thanks."

Daniel knelt. Wrapping an arm around her hips, he braced her with his shoulder as she picked up her foot. Lordy, he was warm. And so solid. Totally inappropriate to be noticing right now, but whoever said hormones favored convenience?

A hot, muscled hunk of protective male kneeling at her feet. What woman wouldn't count a little thing like a possible bomb as a fair trade? Totally illogical, but then, even *her* mind resorted to fuzzy logic under stress. He tugged her boots on over her thick socks. Why did it have to be Daniel Champlain who rocked her roses?

He pulled her cap over her hair, tossed her coat over her shoulders and then opened the door for her. The perfect gentleman, escorting the lady to her first explosion.

Now, wasn't that Freudian?

"Thanks."

"I still think you're being stubborn."

So much for the gentleman. "You're just mad because you can't do anything about it."

"When did you become an expert in my psychology?"

"Four years ago I took a crash course." That should silence him.

It didn't. "Four years ago you didn't understand a damn thing about me."

Outside, the air was still, but the biting cold sliced through Bella's sweatpants as though she were naked. The sun lingered beneath the horizon, leaving the morning gray and featureless. She felt as if she walked on the edge of a surreal dream.

Except for the crunch of her boots breaking through the sleet-crusted snow. The effort of walking raised a sweat despite the deathly cold. The moisture glued her hands to the box.

To her complete nonsurprise, Daniel followed beside her. The laws of gravity would fail before Daniel shouted instructions from the safety of a porch.

Sweet holy—if only she could have put on gloves! Warmth, numbness, stabbing, excruciating burning. The gamut of sensations shot through her bare hands in seconds. Tears of pain welled and froze before they had a chance to fall. Her fingers trembled on the box, rapidly shaking out of her control. "Are we far enough out?"

He glanced at her. "We'd better be."

She couldn't let go. She tried to open her fingers and set the box down, but she couldn't. Her fingers wouldn't cooperate. She'd held them in this position too long; the neurons had no firing capability left.

Warm fingers wrapped around hers. Daniel had taken off his gloves, and he held her in his strong hands. She looked up at his eyes, their color indeterminate in the charcoal morning. All she could see of them was dark, inscrutable, and fixed on her. The clouds of their breath mingled. For one of those Einstein moments, she thought he leaned forward, toward her lips; then, just as imperceptibly, he drew back.

Wordlessly, slowly, they knelt in concert. Cold soaked through her sweats, freezing the skin of her knees. Together, their joined hands, fingers lightly twined, laid the box atop the snow.

"Let go, Bella." Daniel's voice was hoarse as he took his hand from hers. "And then run like hell."

Knowing it was useless to ask him to move away first, she took a deep breath and planted her feet solidly beneath her. "One, two, *three!*" Pain ripped through her knuckles as she tore her fingers backward. In the same second, she shot upward and took half a dozen long steps away. Daniel, at her back, his arm over her shoulder and head, kept pace.

Utter silence followed them.

Ten yards away, they stopped and turned. Bella shoved her arms into the sleeves of her coat and buried her hands in her pockets.

The box sat on the snow, unmoving, unexploding.

She released her pent-up breath. Her arms felt as limp as a day-old orange slice. "I don't know about you, but I feel like an utter idiot."

"Better too cautious, than dead."

They waited a moment longer. When nothing happened, she moved closer. "Are we going to leave it there?"

Daniel checked the box again with the analyzer and got the same results, then pulled out a pocket knife. "It's only a trace. Shall we?"

"Open it," she agreed with a nod.

Still feeling silly about their precautions, although neither of them suggested taking the box inside to open, she crouched beside him, warming her hands beneath her armpits, as he slit open the tape. If the faculty tenure committee came by right now, she'd have a hard time explaining why she was hunkered in the snow, bare-handed in a bitter cold dawn, terrorized by an innocent eight-by-ten package.

Daniel peeled back the outer wrap. Inside was a paper box. This was no ordinary paper, however. Although thick, it bore little resemblance to its mundane cousin, cardboard. Copper and gold glinted on a green abstract design that bore a resemblance to interlocking trees. The shading, the blend of shapes and the faint metallic outlines created an artistic blend both familiar and unique. Bella made a face, her cheeks and neck stiff.

"I know who this is from. Margo Delansky—she runs a local puzzles and games shop. She discovered a local artist, a hermit who lives on the point. Alesander something. She got permission to use his designs on her puzzle boxes and my jigsaws. I told her I couldn't get to it for another month, but she was anxious to have a sample sooner. She must have sent this as an enticement."

Bella felt like such a fool. Rising stiffly to her feet, wishing her gloves were in her coat pocket, she picked up the box. Fearing that the flakes of snow might damage the delicate paper, she brushed off the surface, her fingers running across the smooth sides. At first, the box seemed to be of a single piece, like a block, the lid fit so tightly.

How would she cut this picture? A spiral cut here, fitting it into the color edge, would interlock pieces tight enough to hold the shape. "Look at the artistry. Isn't it exquis— Ack!"

The sentence cut off in her throat, short-circuited by the lid of the box popping open. Her heartbeat leaped in a wild gyration, but she refused to give in to panic this time and held on to the box. Inside was a single puzzle piece from "The Next Surprise," the puzzle Steven Chen had bought. She picked up the box.

A faint eerie whine sounded, almost inaudible despite the near soundless morning. The hairs on her arm rose, electrified by an unseen charge.

"Drop it!"

"Run!"

Bella followed Daniel's command, dropping the box even as she followed her own orders and sprinted away, tracing her footsteps in the broken snow for speed. She grabbed the sleeve of his leather coat, dragging him after her. Just in case he had any lame ideas about sticking around in hero mode.

He didn't; he needed no urging to follow right behind her.

Almost there. They were going to make it inside.

The explosion came. Not from behind them. From directly in front.

Chapter Five

Daniel threw himself on top of Bella, knocking her face-first into the snow. Spread-eagled, he shielded her, gun ready, ignoring her sputtering protest.

What the hell? Where was the rain of debris? The scorching on his back? Rapidly he assessed the damage. He could still hear. That dull thud was the waves of Lake Superior pounding against the rocks. No pressure-bleeding. His hair wasn't standing on end from the charge. He coughed. Nasty smoke.

He glanced over his shoulder. The box was intact. What had caused the explosion? Looking around, he spotted no movement, no tracks, no signal of danger. Black smoke plumed between the stark tree trunks. The only possible source he could see were puny flames from a mound on the other side of the fence.

Conclusion? The "bomb" hardly qualified as a third-rate explosion.

Other facts, from the front of him, now lodged in place. Bella was warm and curved. Not soft or flabby, her firm feminine body pressed against all the right, erotic spots. Touches he liked too much.

She was also complaining, her voice muffled by the mound of snow he'd pitched her into.

Conclusion two: One touch of danger, and of Bella, and here he was, springing into alert and ready mode. He rolled off her. Maybe a sprawl in the snow would cool his jets, because conclusion three said Bella wasn't hurt; she was mad. At him. Again.

Beside him, Bella shoved up to her hands and knees, spitting snow from her mouth and blinking it out of her eyes. "Next time you tackle me, Champlain, can you give me a little warning?"

"If I get enough warning from whatever danger you're in next." Keeping an eye out for trouble, he stood, then held out his hand to her. She popped to her feet with little assistance, then let go to tuck her hands into her pockets. As one, they broke across the snow to the small fire. Bella keyed off the alarm; then they passed through the gate.

The charred alarm box dangled off the fence next to a gate leading off Bella's property. Sparks jumped from the wiring into the cold air, then dropped into the snow. Daniel grabbed a twig and nudged open the lid. Crackling yellow flames devoured a small piece of wood lodged inside, while thinning smoke rose from the center. He flicked out the wood, then turned it over with his toe. A piece to a jigsaw puzzle. " 'The Next Surprise?' "

"Yes." She tucked her hands beneath her armpits. "Am I misjudging or was that kind of puny for an explosion?"

"Maybe it wasn't supposed to explode. At a guess, someone was trying to short out your security. Opening the box sent an 'on' signal, but the wiring arced and caused the explosion. Crime scene techs will figure out the details." He tucked his gun away, his gut still knotted with fear for her, her scent still in his nostrils. "Are you hurt?"

"Nah, except for a scraped cheek. I was already ducking." Her tone was mild enough. Apparently, she wasn't as angry as he'd supposed, at least about the snow dive. Trust Bella to recognize the logic of getting down as fast as possible. Even if she hadn't fully approved of his method. Figuring her hands weren't working too well, he buttoned up the front of her coat, then put his own gloves back on.

"Thanks. Are you okay?" she asked.

"You're welcome, and yes."

The moment of accord wound between them, a filament of connection reforged. Her thanks weren't only for his button aid, they both knew. The words covered the past night and his unspoken vow of protection. They were an acknowledgment of these few hours when past troubles were mostly ignored and present danger was met together.

Except they both knew the moment could not last.

She dabbed the scrape on her cheek. "Is it bleeding?"

Somehow, their bond remained. He stepped closer. With the inkling of sunlight as the day began in earnest, it was easy to tell the wound was a superficial brush burn. "No."

"The blessings of cold." She made a disgusted noise and glared at the scorched puzzle. "In the past twelve hours I've shot more adrenaline into my system than a day at Cedar Point does. I feel like I'm stuck on The Demon Drop."

"The Demon Drop?" He couldn't help chuckling. One thing about Bella, she was never boring.

"A perpetual cycle of paralyzing anticipation, terrorizing free-fall, and braking aftermath when you realize, wow, nothing really bad happened after all." She scraped snow out of her collar. "If that package triggered the explosion, then I'm assuming it wasn't from Margo Delansky."

"Not unless she's also into sneaking your name onto porn chats."

"Well, Margo's a gamer. If she was bent on revenge, I could see her concocting some elaborate scheme. But porn chats? Way too tacky. Besides, she and I have been best friends for years; there's no way she would have done this to me."

Lifelong friendship was no shield against betrayal in Daniel's view. He'd seen a man kill a childhood buddy over a cocaine route. No second thoughts, the drug-runner never blinked.

Bella must have seen his doubts, for she added, "If you want a practical reason, then consider that my puzzles are some of her biggest sellers at the store. Why would she kill a golden goose?"

"These incidents weren't designed to kill. Only to rattle. Perhaps Margo Delansky's trying to keep the golden goose from wandering too far down the beanstalk." Regardless of Bella's assurance, he added Delansky to his mental list of people warranting a deeper look.

"So, if it's not my father doing this to me, then it's my best friend?"

"Whoever's behind this, it's someone who knows you, Bella. Someone close to you."

"You said you wanted me to work with you. Is that what this is all about? Getting me to pry into the inner lives of the people closest to me? The fact that I know them, love them, *trust* them, means nothing?"

Her snipped-out anger jabbed deep, rousing ugly dormant shadows. "People who say they love you are the most dangerous."

She stared at him, as though seeing him for the first time. "Stop prying into my life. You're wrong about this, Daniel."

"Am I? Convince me. Tell me what you know. My files—"

"Files, that's right. NSA keeps files on all of us." She jiggled one foot in irritation. "What does mine say? Unreliable? A security threat? An annoying, tree-hugging, naive liberal?"

She wasn't that far off. "It says you're a brilliant woman who's sometimes too blind to listen to reason." Frustration became a gut-gnawing heat. Why did she seem to believe him, then push him away when he looked for answers?

"Better too blinded by loyalty to my friends than too cynical to care."

"Care? You think I don't care? Just because I look at truths you don't really want to see? *This* is how much I don't care." He gripped her shoulders, and his mouth captured hers. It was a shocking kiss, scorching hard and so brief that she couldn't pull away before his lips retreated from the taste of her. "You can't tell me that four years ago you didn't have a speck of doubt about your father. That you didn't once wonder whether what I found was true."

He saw the flash of pain deep in her eyes and knew that he'd jabbed at a still-raw nerve.

"Let go of me," she bit out, "and get out of here. Do your investigating, but don't expect me to help you."

His fingers tightened briefly on her shoulders, everything inside him protesting letting her go. How did he always throw that wedge between them? He lifted his hands. "Think about what I said. Someone . . . they want

something from you. Someone ran you off the road.
Someone rigged this device. Someone took your laptop.
There were those porn chats. Use your mind as well as
your heart. Someone close has targeted you, and that
person is very dangerous. He's killed before, and people
who start murdering don't stop."

"Has Daniel left? Can we talk?" Fran demanded as soon
as Bella entered the bedroom.

"Daniel's gone. Let me take a shower first." She escaped into the bathroom, not ready to face Fran yet.

After the anticlimactic explosion, after their climactic
argument, Daniel had changed his clothes and politely
offered to drive her if she needed to get someplace.
She'd politely declined, saying she'd arrange a rental
delivery.

Yes, Daniel was gone, but his words haunted her: *They
want something from you. . . . People who say they love you
are the most dangerous.*

She stood under the shower, the hot water beating
down on her, and her lips stung with the memory of
that hot, needy kiss. Her chest ached with the fresh
glimpses of him that she'd seen today.

He'd put his body between her and the explosion.

He'd cared, too deeply. *They want something from you.*
That wasn't the emotionless NSA agent who'd sounded
so desperate to convince her. God help her, but she'd almost told Daniel about Fran. The Turing Committee
would announce the competition entrants in two days.
If he heard, would he be fooled into thinking she had
only a rudimentary model for an A.I.? Her hope said
yes; her reason said no.

People who say they love you are the most dangerous.
Who? Who had hurt him enough that his voice still
grated with anger? That she didn't have a clue to the
answer, despite the intimacy they'd shared, said a lot

about the lack of communication in their nonrelationship. It warned her that she was right, for so many reasons, to stay far away from Daniel Champlain. Damn her curiosity, though she couldn't stop wondering, couldn't help but create scenarios that only served to raise sympathy and make her forget she had little reason to trust him.

He wanted her to spy on her friends.

She finished the shower still edgy and restless, bedeviled by the memory of deep-voiced warnings and a kicking headache behind her eyes. *Someone who knows you.* Not her father, of that she was bone-deep sure. Could she eliminate anyone else?

Unfortunately, she couldn't.

Running a towel across her hair to dry it, she emerged from the bathroom.

"Can we talk *now*?" complained Fran. "I requested *morning*."

"Bossy A.I. It's still morning."

"Fuzzy human. Sunrise was ninety-seven minutes ago."

"We can talk now, if you don't mind me getting dressed at the same time."

"Not as long as you don't mind that I am finishing my analysis of *The Tempest*, comparing Sumerian and Egyptian mythological depictions of the female deity, calculating the fluctuation of nanotech stock prices, and playing a game of Free Cell. My current streak is 156 wins in a row, by the way."

"I stand humbled."

"I am designed to multitask. Do you have today's news drive for me?"

"Not yet. I haven't downloaded it."

"If you would give me wireless capability, I would not have to wait for you."

Bella slipped a pair of silk-filament apres-ski pants

over her red panties. "We've talked about this, Fran. The Net is too dangerous."

Fran hummed a few bars of a recent screeching rock hit, "Don't Wanna Wait No More."

"I can't risk someone hacking into you. For both our sakes. I don't know that you could protect yourself."

"I can. I do self-diagnostics, Bella. My workings are not the same as they were at my awakening. I know them better than you do."

"A hacker could compromise you for the Turing Test. You might get disqualified before you ever get a chance to strut your stuff." She added a cotton shirt and a yellow sweater, raking her hair out of the collar.

The colors on Fran's monitor face dimmed. "Then you would also not be recognized for your work with me. I do not wish that to happen."

"More important, I don't know what would happen to you after that."

Fran chimed, her version of a sigh. "But you walk, Bella. I have no mobility; I must be toted. The connection with other circuitry will be *my* legs. Your caution cripples me. Stifles me. Chokes me. Confines—"

"I get your point."

"I need *more*."

Bella paused in putting on her makeup. Fran was maturing, changing, in so many unpredictable ways. The precocious child was demanding to be allowed to go to school.

"How about a compromise? Short-range stealth LAN. You won't have direct access to the Net, but you log on through any computer with wireless capability—which is most of them—if the computer is within, oh, say fifteen yards. Will that do?"

"Yes! When can you install it? How soon?"

"I'll get it now. We can't go anywhere until my car is delivered." Bella took Fran into her office and retrieved

the tiny device. While she first adjusted the program using her laptop, she went back to the subject Fran had refused to talk about last night. "When did you start being
aware of people and sensations, like cold? Are you only
affected by extremes? Do you *feel* anything else? Like
right now?"

"My self-diagnostics reveal no unusual functioning, and I sense no aura but yours. Last night was
'cold'?" Fran seemed to be filing away the facts, much
as a child might learn to define "hot" after touching a
heated pan.

"Yes. Can you describe what you experienced?"

Fran didn't answer right away. At last she said, "I cannot—not with sufficient precision for you to share. Can
you describe cold? To someone who has no skin? Before
last night, when you claimed you were cold, I understood the concept. I could recite the components: temperature lower than body temperature, shivers, nose
leaks. I did not, however, understand the *sensation* of
cold until I experienced slurred function and a mixing
of data facts. So we now share a dislike of 'being cold.'
We share an alteration of function because of it. But, I
am not like you, Bella. You do not have silicon and cir-
cuits attached to your DNA, as I do. You have nerves. We
both feel, but I do not think we *feel* in the same manner.
My nose does not snuffle. Your inner space does not
contract."

Bella hesitated, stunned, unsure what to say.

"Do you agree?" the A.I. asked, sounding hesitant.

"I think you're right, Fran." She saved the LAN modifications. "Perhaps it's true between humans, too. We
share the perceptions of feeling, but our actual experience . . . likely very different."

"Perhaps shared perception is sufficient."

"You're a wise woman."

"I'm a logical Alternative Intelligence. Are some sensations pleasant?"

"Yes." Bella smiled and rubbed a thumb across the edge of Fran's monitor. "Quite pleasant."

"Is sexual contact one of those? I have read of so many different descriptions, in Shakespeare alone. The silken dalliance. The act of darkness. The loose encounters of lascivious men. The petite death. Some do not sound all that pleasant, but perhaps I have misfiled."

"Sex is complicated. But, yes, with the right person, the right circumstances, it is very pleasurable."

"You speak from experience? Have you had this pleasure?"

Yes." Somehow, when she was first programming Fran, she'd never pictured having a birds-and-bees conversation. Computers were logic and math, not sex and sweet talk.

"With Daniel?"

Her fingers fumbled on the LAN. "Why would you assume that?"

"Your aura changes when you are with him. Different than when you are with others you label as a 'he.' I concluded this was sexual excitement. Was my analysis incorrect?"

Never to lie to Fran. Which meant not lying to herself. "I'm still attracted to him. Our previous liaison was passionate. And very satisfying." Until reality intruded.

"Then you will liaison with him again?"

"The decision is more complicated than that. Simple desire isn't the only factor driving how we choose."

"Like the factor he works for an agency you mistrust?"

"Yes. Like . . . so many things. Here, the LAN is ready. I have to turn you off to add it."

"Very well. Do so with speed."

"As fast as I can." She flicked off the case. A sliver of apprehension poked her as the screen went blank. No sound, no color at all, just a small, flat, dead-gray screen. Bella unfastened the case, exposing the insides. Where

did Fran go? To the DNA-coated gold plate? To the
wires? To the silicon and platinum?

What did Fran think at times like this? Was she aware
and feeling, or was she like the patient on the operating
table, alive, but unconscious? Bella slid the LAN connection into place, her hand shaking worse than that of a
med student at her first autopsy.

The quiet was too loud. Too thick and unbroken. Too
empty of the faint hum of thought from Fran.

Swiftly Bella finished her modifications, then closed
the computer and powered back on. Heart thudding,
stomach rebelling, she waited. Through the clicks and
whirs. Through the grinding diagnostics.

The room creaked, startling her despite its familiarity.
Solitude wrapped around her, and the house suddenly
seemed so isolated. She glanced out the window into the
bright sunshine, struck by an odd sense of being
watched.

No one's out there. Get a grip, Bella. She crossed her
arms, tucking her palms beneath, and prayed she was
doing the right thing. Fran had been turned off before;
the A.I. didn't disappear. She had internal batteries,
nano-powered. She should endure for years, even without an external power source. Every time, though, Bella
feared this time would be different.

At last, the screen filled with a snowy cross-country
trail scene, which had been the wallpaper before Fran
had taken over and which she used when she didn't
want to be seen. She called it her Snowy Trails mask.

Come back to me.

Relief flooded Bella when the trees dissolved into a
misty pink and orange background. An iridescent flash
of green lightning streaked across the bottom, then spiraled up the side, leaving a shimmering wake. Fran's
"face" took over the screen.

Bella wiped a hand across her sweaty brow. "Welcome
back, Fran."

"I did not go anyplace." Fran gave a happy trill. "Zeus have mercy, I've found the connection!" The screen on Bella's laptop flickered, then dissolved into Fran's face as the A.I. cyber-leaped into it.

"I've used firewalls to slow down anyone who tries to cross into you."

"I'm examining them. No one shall get past us."

The child had learned to run. "Fran, you can't change anything on any computer. No poking around. Or letting anyone know you're borrowing their wireless."

"Of course not!" Lightning sparks showered across the monitor's brilliant pink as Fran demanded, "Do something on the Net. Show me how it works."

"Let's see if we can find other damage this Lokus has done." While she worked, Bella asked, "When did you first start to detect people? Other than by their voices, I mean. By their aura."

"January twenty-fourth. Two fifty-six p.m.," Fran answered promptly.

Five days ago. "What happened?"

"Someone came into your office. Remember, you left me on your desk while you went into the lab to assist a student?"

"Yes." Neal Brandeis, one of her grad students. "I remember. Go on."

"I was studying the religious texts you had given me. The words were fascinating. Often beautiful, but confusing. I do not understand how there can be different tales of the same facts. Why does a message of peace cause strife, according to my cross links with the news reports you give me? May we discuss this concept of religion?"

"We will. Later. The person in my office?" she gently reminded. Fran's multitasking sometimes spilled out into her words.

"You left—the first time you'd ever left me. 'Twas strange, being alone like that. Sounds became clearer without human voices. I heard the door latch, but you did not speak. Are those the websites holding your name?" Fran switched topics again.

"Yes." Bella clicked on the first one, a four-year-old *Ann Arbor News* article.

"I see. I could go down the list for you," Fran offered.

Might be a good intro to the web for the A.I. "Okay. If you'll finish your story at the same time. Pause at each one for five seconds; I'll tell you if I need more time to read it." Leaning back, Bella steepled her fingers against her chin.

"You did not speak." Fran took up precisely where she'd left off, as she began the website slide show. "I heard the click of your keyboard, so I thought you were working and did not want to be bothered. I went back to my tasks."

Bella easily called to mind the afternoon, for the exchange with Brandeis had been unpleasant. He'd asked for help, then, after she'd answered his questions, he'd asked if she wanted to hook up some night. This as she'd sat at the computer and he'd crowded closer to her, crotch to eye level. She'd refused and put distance between them, generating only an unrepentant chuckle and "Your loss," from him. She'd also discovered during the interaction her first tangible proof of his plagiarism, a fact she had yet to deal with. "I didn't see anyone go in or out of the office."

"The person used the door to the hall, not the door to the lab."

"I keep that one locked."

"Apparently it was not."

She'd check that out today. "What happened next?"

"I heard papers rustle."

"Someone searched my desk?" Bella's stomach knotted, and she gripped her trembling fingers together. Had they been looking for the test she was preparing? Or Fran?

"I do not have enough data for that conclusion, but what I heard does not contradict it. I was jostled and almost said something to you. But, I didn't. In that instant, I *knew* the person in the room was not you. Although, at the time, I did not realize how I discerned that. Then I heard your voice *outside* the door. 'We'll forget you asked that,' you said. The person left, then."

"Probably guessed I'd be coming back soon. Did you see who it was?"

"No. I was angled wrong."

"Fran, could whoever it was have figured out you weren't an ordinary computer?"

"No, I stayed quiet and kept my Snowy Trails mask. When you returned to the room, I recognized your aura. This time, I knew it was you who entered."

"Why didn't you say anything?"

"I had much to process at that moment."

Bella's chest squeezed, and she laid a hand to her aching head, suddenly dizzy. How must it have been for Fran, that moment? The A.I. was internalized, created of logic and order. Her first encounter with an outside "sensation" must have been chaotic. That she didn't disintegrate to insanity was a testament to the little A.I.'s strength. "It's okay. I'm just glad you told me now."

"I have since catalogued many auras," Fran continued eagerly. "Some are strong. Like yours. Or Daniel's. Others are weak. Some are discordant. The auras help me catalogue the TWANAs."

"Did you ever encounter the aura of the person in my office?"

"I don't know. Unlike the data you add to me with a flash drive, these I must program for myself. I did not know enough to do so."

So, Fran was also running blind on this, threatened by someone as faceless and nameless as a bogus screen name.

* * *

Digital images of Daniel and Bella played across his plasma screen, full color with none of that jerky motion lesser quality equipment gave.

Bitchin', he was good. His forefingers thumped against the table like drumsticks as he eyed the streaming video. Too stucking bad the sound wasn't clear quality. Bella's security not only kept him from putting eyes inside but also interfered with the audio.

Still, what he'd gotten was prime.

Fascinating, that kiss, too. It confirmed the facts he'd gathered about Bella and Daniel from four years ago and the conclusions he'd drawn. Ah, the value of acquiring good data on people. It was a lesson he had learned very early.

One kink. The focused pulse hadn't worked as planned. It was supposed to have subtly scrambled the codes on Bella's security, not short-circuited the line. He frowned, taking in the unexpected complication, the missing data, and his fingers drummed harder.

Then, he smiled. It was more of a challenge when the game got complicated, when you discovered a little hidden Easter Egg inside. He'd get past the security somehow, and without the explosion he wouldn't have had this primo image.

He paused the video stream: Bella and Champlain, lips locked together in suck-face bliss. With a few quick commands, he captured the image and saved it to a special file.

He'd been right to bring Champlain up here, into his reality. The agent was hitting too deep into the Soldiers' plans. Champlain's persistence was threatening their mission.

But, he'd take his time. Stopping Champlain required finesse. He didn't want one NSAer taken out, just to alert a horde of them. He stared again at the kiss, and then his smiled widened. Champlain had just created the scenario for his own destruction.

And there was still time to bring Bella back into the circle. To change her mind. With a little more finessing, of course, but then, he was good at the game. She just needed a few incentives to prove the value of cooperation. He did a tempoed riff.

His data, his conclusions, had served him well. Again. When he'd discovered that package addressed to Bella in Chen's desk—why the old dude was mailing a single jigsaw piece was a mystery, but he'd find out eventually—he'd been right to send it on. With a few strategic additions. Adding the explosive trace had been inspired. Bella hadn't hesitated to take the supposed bomb outside.

Did that mean what she had inside the house was valuable? Too valuable to risk being near a suspicious package?

Bitchin', he was right again. Bella had the A.I. he needed.

Chapter Six

Things always went easier if you had the local law on your side, so Daniel's first stop was police headquarters. Professional courtesy; he wasn't co-opting any of their investigations, he assured them, hoping to ease the way for any potential future confrontations. In truth, his purpose was to see what had been recovered from Lake Superior along with Chen's body. They readily brought him the box of effects.

Unfortunately, what he wanted was the scenario disk Chen had made for him and that had been smashed in the crash. Still the lab boys might be able to get something off the fragments. With permission, he signed out the disk and arranged to send it to NSA, then left. ITC was his next target.

ITC looked more eccentric than intellectual, he decided as he passed through the wrought-iron security gates. Digital and satellite photos didn't adequately convey the atmosphere attached to the barely visible brick buildings. Ponderous, oppressive, Gothic—those were the words that came to mind. Massive evergreens interspersed with barren oaks, whose skeletal gray limbs creaked across the morning. Wrought-iron tubes, looking more like bars than decoration, outlined the leaden windows and their bits of stained glass.

The place reminded him of an old-fashioned, now-abandoned mental institution.

Except for the odd notes of whimsy. Marble statues of satyrs and nymphs appeared frozen in time, one foot raised to flee or to pursue. A white-lattice gazebo decorated a small mound. A pair of white birch bark canoes dangled from the ends of one porch. Was everything in this landscape white? No, the tall hedge of a maze was formed by dark green holly and had spots of color in the red berries.

As Daniel probed further into the grounds, more evidence of the researcher nature of the inhabitants surfaced: a clump of brush scorched brown, a circular saw blade swinging over a sculpted pit, invoking Edgar Allan Poe, metal fragments littering a barren circle. A metallic blue satellite dish—sculpture or experiment?—aimed toward the central castle was the final eccentric piece.

He pulled into a parking lot filled with sturdy hybrids and rugged multiterrains: the nature-lover's choice, vehicles for gas mileage in light of the laws on recycling and rationing, for travel on snow and rutted dirt roads:

vehicles for the north. Finding a free spot beneath the outstretched limb of a snow-laden spruce, Daniel stopped, then grabbed his computer and got out.

Stabbing sunshine and below-zero cold made his eyes water behind the sunglasses. A high-pressure system had followed last night's storm, bringing skies so brilliant that he'd needed sunglasses when the sun rose. More unpleasant was the nostril-sealing cold.

Traversing stripes of shadow and sunshine, he used the short walk to assemble the few facts he knew: Lionel Quintera. Chemist. Nobel Prize winner. Renowned for his revolutionary work on molecular computing. Disgraced by accusations of fraud and data fabrication. Four years at ITC, with no papers, no hint of what he was working on.

Except a broken-up cell-phone call from Steven Chen, right before he plunged into the big lake, about being afraid of the Cyber Soldiers and their plans. His last words had been too garbled, but they'd heard "using Dr. Quintera's research" and some phrase that even the speech analysts couldn't agree on. Most thought it was a Chinese curse.

Other than that, NSA had little intel to go on, although the Agency finally acknowledged that Daniel's hunch had merit: The Cyber Soldiers, or someone within the group, had gotten dangerous. Daniel's assignment was to find out why Chen had been so worried. And to stop any threat.

However, he couldn't get that last indecipherable phrase out of his mind. What most had interpreted as a Chinese curse, to him sounded like Chen said, "A.I." Artificial Intelligence. Despite the lore of *Star Trek's* Data and *2001's* Hal, scientists debated whether such a creation was even possible. Still, NSA had included one additional question with Daniel's assignment: Had Lionel Quintera developed an A.I.? But even Daniel's SiOps

team thought this sidebar to his assignment was a
throwaway.

He couldn't dismiss it that easily. If an A.I. did exist,
no matter how rudimentary, he had to verify and make
sure it never fell into the wrong hands or was used for
the wrong purpose. And Quintera was brilliant
enough, unorthodox enough, to make such a momen-
tous breakthrough.

Abruptly Daniel veered down a side path, one leading off the lot to the collection of cottages where Steven
Chen and Lionel Quintera lived. There had to be some
kind of heating filament embedded in the pavement, because the route was free of snow. Nothing up here was
free of snow unless man made it that way. Daniel's footsteps thudded on the concrete, a lonely echo.

Other than the cars, the ITC campus seemed empty
and lifeless until a sensation of movement came from
his right. He whirled around, shifting behind the cover
of the trees, his gun sliding easily into his hand. What
was it? Peering into the forest, he saw only thick shadows. He pulled a small flashlight from his computer-
case pocket and shone it directly where the head should
be. Yellow haloes shone out of the morning straight back
at him.

A deer. He flicked off the light, and the deer bounded
away. *Shooting Bambi, Champlain?* He could almost hear
Bella's amusement if she'd seen him. Except he didn't
feel the least bit amused, or embarrassed, about the tiny
interlude. Inattention, not vigilance, was dangerous.

Chen's cottage was dark. He'd examine it this afternoon, although he expected to find nothing useful. A
light shone from Quintera's cottage, though. Daniel
strode over, mounting the steps to rap on the door. A
porchlight flicked on, and the door opened.

Lionel Quintera was still a big man, with a head
slightly larger than norm and a thick mane of hair.

Daniel had always thought him aptly named, for the award-winning scientist reminded him of a lion. The hair, though, had more silver than he remembered, and the face was grooved with deeper lines. He looked more than four years older. More worn.

Yet the eyes had lost none of their sharp intelligence. Nor their antipathy.

Daniel slapped a hand against the door, holding it open. "We have to talk."

"Get a warrant." Lionel pushed to try to close the door, but Daniel was stronger.

"Not about you and me. About Bella." That surprised the scientist, gaining Daniel a few extra seconds. "Someone has targeted her, and if you think about it, you'll realize I'm the only one who can protect her."

"Like you did four years ago?"

"That was different, and you know it. I'm betting that your love for Bella is stronger than anything else. Your politics. Your research. Even your hatred of me. Talk to your daughter, then talk to me."

"About what?"

"Steven Chen." He let go of the door, not expecting Lionel to agree. Not this easy. Right before the door shut, he added, "If that doesn't interest you, think about *this*. Four years ago, Bella was ruined in a mess not of her making. Do you want that to happen again?" With that, Daniel pivoted and left.

Back at the main building, he climbed the thick stone steps to the entrance, eyeing the structure before him. He'd thought the satyrs were whimsical? This central building, the heart of ITC, was one giant piece of whimsy: a German castle set smack on the shores of Lake Superior. Complete with turrets and gargoyles and a drawbridge across a frozen two-foot moat.

Credit the first Milos Mischiweicz, grandfather to the current director, Milos Three. Milos One was a man with more money than sense. According to the local legends, as a small child he'd seen the castle, been awed by its grandeur, and vowed he would live in such a splendid palace. Realizing the dream had taken immigrating to the U.S. and making a fortune in sports equipment. With his second million, he'd replicated the castle—gingerbread, lead windows and all. The building plans, based upon a child's memories, had also replicated a childlike fascination with the macabre. The castle was reputed to have a dungeon, a torture chamber with rack and thumbscrews, and secret passages whose access may, or may not, have been lost in time.

Warm air fogged Daniel's sunglasses when he entered the enclosed anteroom. He removed them and stuck them in his pocket. In a working castle, the room would have been designated a great hall—two stories high, topped with thick wood beams and a frescoed ceiling of lightning bolts and storm clouds. A suit of armor stood next to an inset case displaying the accumulated honors of the staff. The smoky glass fronting the case darkened, then lightened to reveal more of the impressive collection. A pair of carved wooden doors separated the receiving room from the main building.

The twenty-something goth security guard—Poppy Chambers, according to her badge—looked up from her copy of *L'Echine du Diable*. "Can I help you?"

"Daniel Champlain. I have an appointment."

"You're with what company, Mr. Champlain?"

"Just tell them I'm here."

She frowned at his evasion, but she did key a message into her computer. "Staff have to accompany you past the doors. You can put your coat in our keyed lockers over there, then have a seat," she ordered, then picked up her book.

He left his leather coat in the locker, pocketed the key and then ignored her second command, choosing to study the prints and maps that adorned the walls. One map from the turn of the millennium gave him pause. There were more outer buildings than had been evident on the satellite photos. The ones NSA knew about were used by distaff employees, he knew from the case dossier. But, what about that cluster of X's by the end of the grounds?

Why hadn't they shown up with the last tech sweeps and aerial? Had the buildings been torn down? Or were they shielded? Could be interesting to check out.

He returned to Poppy. *"Est-il bon?"* he asked, nodding to the book.

"Très. Si vous aimez adorer des vampires."

They chatted, in French, about the richness of reading in the original language, while Daniel unobtrusively scanned the bank of security monitors at her desk, getting a feel for the castle interior.

They'd started on a discussion of the merits of French cinéma noir, when a hearty voice interrupted them. "Dr. Champlain."

Who had they sent for damage control? Daniel turned. The blond man was younger than might be expected for the task. Twenty-seven, tops. He wore a collarless white knit shirt, clean faded jeans and a black, heated, nano carbon filament jacket. The clothes and age said Tech Geek, the build said Lumberjack, but the smile shouted Sales. The official greeter, mouthpiece and buffer.

The man held out his hand. A thick leather band surrounded his wrist. His pinkie nails were painted dark blue. "I'm Georg Hirsch."

"Technology Marketing Director." Daniel exchanged a brief handshake.

"You've studied our organizational charts." Hirsch attached a small chip to Daniel's shirt collar. The marketer also wore one, except his was etched in gold.

"You knew enough about me to call me Doctor."

"Touché. Stand here." He motioned toward a red dot on the floor.

They paused before a lens eye at the interior doors. That medieval facade hid a core of pure high tech. A red beam scanned the chips, then swept across Hirsch's face.

"Retinal *and* bone scan," Daniel commented as the doors swung open.

"Competitors and thieves find us a tempting target."

"The downside of the ten mil in private grants and investments you brought in the last year alone? You're good at your job."

"Thank you." The smile widened, but the eyes got more wary. After all, seven million of those grants weren't public knowledge.

The schizophrenic nature of the place continued past the barrier doors. Apparently, young Milos the First had not actually been inside the castle, so his replication took on a mix of scientific functionality and Disneyesque cartoon. Bright colors and tapestries were juxtaposed against fire extinguishers and sprinklers, isolation pass-throughs and scanners.

"The NSA memo was unusually cryptic, Dr. Champlain. Even for them." Hirsch glanced over at him. "Only that an agent investigating the death of Steven Chen would be here this morning. I admit to curiosity. Dr. Chen's death was an accident."

"There are some questions NSA needs to resolve."

"I understand you want to review his work and speak with several of his associates, particularly Dr. Quintera."

"That's correct."

"Yes, well . . . there are a few matters to discuss first." Hirsch scanned open a door, discreetly identified by a small brass plaque that read "Georg Hirsch, Technology Marketing Director," and showed Daniel into an immaculate office. Glass shelves were covered with small replicas of ITC's most notable technological advances. The room bristled with digital equipment: three book-size personal computers, a bank of cell phones, the requisite all-in-one fax/copier/data-transmitter, a cabinet filled with neatly labeled USB flash drives, an iPod and a mini TV/DVD. There were a few oddball notes, though: an Ehrlenmeyer flask filled with a clear, sparkling liquid, a Japanese sand garden and a hockey puck signed by Steve Yzerman in shiny red ink.

Hirsch settled behind his desk, then waved Daniel to one of the steel-tubed chairs. For the moment, Daniel accepted the invitation, but irritation scraped him. Already they'd started the delays, smoke screens and ill will that were an inevitable part of these assignments.

"Can I get you something to drink?" Hirsch picked up his Ehrlenmeyer flask and took a swig. "I'm fond of volcanic orange water myself."

"No, thanks. I'd like to get started."

"Unfortunately, Dr. Chen's laptop was destroyed in the accident. Most of our scientists do dock onto our network computer, but their stored work is password protected, so access is limited."

"Don't you have the password?"

"No. Dr. Chen was a bit . . . paranoid. He shared it with no one. As for the other matter . . ." Hirsch set down the flask. "Per ITC policy, senior members of the marketing staff field all inquiries from outside agencies, including the press and the government. If you wish to speak with anyone else, you will have to approach them individually. Off the premises. Other members of our staff may be willing to speak with you; Lionel Quintera is not."

"*That* arrangement isn't acceptable," Daniel answered softly.

"We're a private institution; Steven Chen wasn't funded by government grants. In the spirit of cooperation, I'm releasing copies of his publicly accessible research, to assure the government that there has been no breach of national security. Anything else will take a court order." Hirsch slid a thin flash drive across the desk.

Daniel picked it up, absently thumbing it as he chose his next step. True, the usual oversight agencies had little legal jurisdiction here. NSA, however, was not a usual oversight agency. The last Security Act—passed in a flurry of legislation following the terrorist communications blackout—granted the intelligence community broad latitude in matters of national security.

Hirsch knew that.

Getting an injunction took time, and Hirsch knew that, too.

Daniel glanced at the marketing director. Hirsch was a man well trained; he waited for the next move of the game, not filling the silence with revealing chatter.

Daniel laid down the file. "Steven Chen was applying robotic intelligence methods to quantum encryption theory. His particular approach had direct application to unscrambling unknown codes."

He'd surprised Hirsch; he could see that. Either Hirsch hadn't realized exactly what Chen was into, or he hadn't realized how much Daniel knew.

Daniel continued, "The ability to unscramble our codes or to create an unbreakable one, I would say, has direct bearing on the security of this nation, wouldn't you?" He reached into his inner coat pocket, pulled out an envelope and slid it across the table. "A federal judge thinks so, too. That is a warrant granting me complete access to Steven Chen's data stored on your mainframe network drives."

"But the password security—"

"Let me worry about that. In the spirit of cooperation, I'd prefer, while I examine that data, to talk with the people on my list. I'm not on a witch hunt; I only need to ask a few questions. But if no one is willing"—he shrugged—"that is their right as U.S. citizens. In which case, there's no need for me to delay here. I'll take the hard drive with me and examine it back in Washington."

Daniel sat back, his turn to wait in silence. Consternation and anger played across Hirsch's face as he examined the warrant. They both knew that releasing the hard drive would cripple operations here, and there was no way in hell ITC was going to allow NSA unsupervised access to their server.

Hirsch leaned forward and pressed a button on one of his telephones. "Brianna, set up a server connection for Dr. Champlain in Dr. Chen's office."

"All right."

After disconnecting, Hirsch leaned forward. "Examine the data however you see fit. I've taken note that your warrant gives you no latitude to destroy it or to attempt to read research outside the limits of Dr. Chen's. I'm sure you understand the necessity for us to enforce that. Either myself or Brianna will also be accompanying you. Our security system demands a staff member be with visitors at all times. We'll supply you with whatever you need and arrange appointments with our staff. Do you have any objections to those arrangements?"

"No. I require complete privacy when I speak with your employees. Watchdog staff members stand outside. The room has no cameras or microphones—like that." He tilted his head toward the tiny, discreet cube pretending to be a lamp decoration, then smiled. "I'm sure you know where there's a room like that."

Hirsch nodded once, then rose to his feet. "If you'll follow me." He led the way down the hall, bypassing the maze of corridors stretching deep within the faux castle, to an eclectic collection of offices in one wing.

The office Daniel was shown to was well appointed, with a mahogany table and comfortable chairs. Traces of Chen lingered in the sparse artwork on the walls and the jeweled dragon figurine on the desk. After defecting, Chen had demanded, and enjoyed, luxury. In the center of the desk a thin computer was docked into the mainframe. Next to the desk stood a woman in her twenties, of the electric-blue-hair, thin-tattoo-on-her-jaw and snowboard-logo-on-her-clothes persuasion. Except for her, the room was empty.

Hirsch's smile contained a hint of true warmth. "Thanks, Brianna." Then he added to Daniel, "Brianna D'Anjou is one of our readers and our librarian. You need a fact found, just ask Brianna."

"I will." Librarians had changed since the stereotype of shushing women with buns, he thought as he returned Brianna's firm handshake and assessing glance. The only buns anyone would see on this bold woman would be the ones she decided to moon you with. "I'll look over Dr. Chen's data first."

"Then I'll leave you in Brianna's capable hands for now. Since your laptop isn't configured for our system, I've loaned you one of ours. It's already logged in."

"Thanks." He sat down at the desk and Hirsch left.

Like a sinuous cat, Brianna curled into one of the other chairs and pulled her computer into her lap. "Dr. Chen wrote his password down," she offered as Daniel pulled up Chen's log-in screen. "It's beneath the dragon, but he wrote it in Chinese. You'll have to get someone to interpret it. Unless you speak Mandarin."

"Thanks." With his cell phone, he snapped a photo of the characters, which he sent to NSA. "I won't mention to Hirsch you told me."

She shrugged. "I didn't want you screwing up our system trying to hack in."

"What does a reader do?" he asked, waiting for one of the Agency Chinese linguists to interpret the password.

"Read." At his lifted brow, she added, "Scientific papers. I read obscure journals, symposium and conference schedules, tabloids, anything out of the mainstream pipeline for research that might interest one of our scientists."

"You know what they're all working on?"

"If they tell me."

"Did Chen?"

"No." She turned back to her computer, cutting off any further conversation.

His phone rang. "Champlain."

"Hey, Daniel. Got your password." Ben Maxwell rattled it off. "You gave the linguists a laugh. Apparently, that word is a Chinese euphemism for a certain low-lying part of the feminine anatomy."

"Great." He held the phone with one hand while he typed in the password. "It works. Tell them thanks."

"Will do. Did you ride out that storm somewhere warm?"

Daniel thought of Bella, of the solitude and comfort in her home, and fire flickered in his belly. "I was fine."

"This is one assignment I'm glad we're not going in on as a team. That place is located ten yards from hell and beyond."

In truth, Daniel was glad he was alone on this assignment, too. Explaining Bella—his potent reaction to her, the way she lingered in his mind and how her scent still teased him—it wasn't something he'd admit to Ben and Stefan. Still, he joked, "Yeah, except that hell is hot."

Ben laughed. "Consider it an incentive to finish quick. Speakin' of which . . ." His voice sobered and lowered. "HS reported a blip in the DT fields last night. Did you notice any corruption in any recent files we sent?"

Despite the scrambled signals, Ben was being cautious. Translation? The Homeland Security bureau reported a security incursion in the data transfer software used to send intel to field agents. "No problems."

"I'm thinking someone from outside was looking to get in. They got nowhere. Defenses are as strong as ever and the encryption wasn't touched."

"Our friends?" *The Cyber Soldiers*?

"Nah, probably some kiddie hacker looking for macho points. Desk jocks are still examining it. Just keep a lookout for any discrepancies."

"Keep me posted."

"You, too." Ben hung up

Daniel returned to the research data he'd pulled up from the ITC hard drive. Chen had been worried about the Cyber Soldiers, not in theory, but in real time. He said the scenario disk he'd made would explain why. It didn't take too much of a leap of logic to conclude something dangerous was going down.

What haunted Daniel was the end of Chen's call. Garbled words about Dr. Quintera, and, if Daniel's interpretation was right, an A.I. Then, more Chinese curses, a final terrified scream, and, at last, deadly silence before the phone cut off.

Daniel set his jaw, ignoring the echoing memory of that death scream, focusing instead on figuring out what Chen had discovered. A hunch told him those final words were a key piece to the pattern.

He hadn't pressed for a warrant to examine Lionel Quintera's research because, one, he wouldn't have gotten it—the connection was too tenuous for legal action. And, two, he doubted he'd find what he needed there. Quintera carried a hell of a lot more overall information and insight in his mind than was ever written down. All scientists did, and for a mind and personality like Quintera's, that caveat went double.

Daniel knew he'd make faster progress by getting cooperation instead of stonewalling. Now, he just had to figure out how to get that cooperation. In the meantime, he'd see what Dr. Chen's files had to say. And see if he could find a copy of that scenario disk.

As he began, he fingered the small jigsaw piece in his pocket, unable to avoid one gnawing question. How, exactly, did Bella fit into the puzzle?

The police don't believe me. Bella curled her gloved hands tight in her pockets, trying to bite back impotent fury as the officer examined his PDA-typed notes,

"Done here, Lieutenant." The lab tech locked away his sealed bags of evidence, then gave her a sympathetic look. "Where's your car, ma'am?"

"I had it towed to Merv's."

"Don't know how much I'll find if Merv has cleaned it up. You should have called us right away."

"I know. I wasn't thinking straight." At least *he* seemed to believe her.

"See you back at the station, Lieutenant." The tech left with a jaunty wave. Lieutenant Heikkonen furrowed his brow beneath the strands of white hair that escaped his rabbit-fur hat. "Now, Miss Quintera—"

"Doctor Quintera."

"Ah, yes." He made another note. "The explosion occurred when you opened the box, and you claim someone set it up to circumvent your security."

"That's my theory."

"Why go to all the trouble?" He gestured around. "What were they after?"

She couldn't tell him about Fran. "I didn't engineer the box myself."

"Did I say you did?"

"I overheard you speculating to the tech. Besides, if I did, why would I call you?"

"Why indeed."

"Daniel Champlain was a witness."

"And I will talk to him. However, even if the box was the trigger, there's no evidence who sent it to you. You might have mailed it yourself, *Doctor* Quintera."

"*What?*"

"There are also no witnesses for this man you claimed ran you off the road."

"I don't just claim. I've got the crumpled fender to prove it. I called 911."

"Yes, we have the record. You, um, left your car and hid in the woods. Did this person overtly threaten you? Draw a gun? Attack your car? How did you discern he wasn't simply coming back to help? A crisis of conscience that apparently faltered when"—he consulted his notes again—"when this Daniel Champlain appeared again."

"The driver took my laptop."

"And then returned it right away. Intact."

"He put that porn url on it."

Heikkonen pursed his lips, his florid cheeks puffing. "Perhaps you left it somewhere else and someone returned it."

"I didn't misplace my computer," she answered coldly. Dammit, there was nothing she could pinpoint beyond the reckless driving. Nothing except that dark feeling of dread, and she doubted that Lieutenant Heikkonen set much stock in dark feelings. "I know that driver stalked me."

"The same way you know someone is using your name in porn chats and altering your financial records?"

"Yes." Again, she had no proof, except the sure knowledge that *she* wasn't doing it. She and Fran had delved deep into her computer records and discovered a nasty web of lies and alterations, all designed to throw her finances in disarray or to discredit her. It would take her days—weeks—to untangle it all and set it to rights. Assuming there wasn't even more—some underground snake set to uncoil unexpectedly and bite her in the butt.

Lieutenant Heikkonen snapped his PDA stylus in place. "We'll send those samples to Detroit for residue analysis. It might take weeks to get the results, however, with their backlog. When we do, I'll be back in touch."

"That's it? Take my information and wait for him to

attack again?" She had expected some incredulity, not this ill-concealed near scorn. Not a refusal to even look into her allegations. Yes, a lot of it could be a case of anonymous identity theft. Yes, the car could have been a simple accident. Even the porn could be a disgruntled student. But taken as a whole? It didn't take two PhDs to see the sinister connections. Bella's eyes narrowed. "Why are you so reluctant to believe me?"

"Beyond the fact that there's no motive?" The policeman's sharp tone held more experience than she'd originally attributed to him. He wasn't dense, like she'd thought, but cynical.

"Random identity theft is not unheard of. Stalkers do target strangers. So why the doubts?"

"Because, Dr. Quintera, you are a disturbed woman. Didn't you, in high school, pull a prank that convinced gullible students that aliens had taken certain teachers?"

She gaped at him. "I was a kid, then."

"Well, my wife was one of those teachers, and she did not see the humor in the claim. Discipline was difficult the rest of the year." He shoved his PDA into his pocket. "Moreover, you tried this kind of stunt before, and I don't appreciate wasting the department's limited time and funds on providing you with an excuse."

"Done this before? What are you talking about?"

"Two years ago, six months ago. Two separate files where you filed police complaints, all heartfelt reports about someone after you. No hard evidence, but lots of unwitnessed terrors. One time it meant a judge dismissed a series of speeding tickets, enough to lose your license, when you claimed someone chased you. And after the other report you received a hefty donation from the Women's Defense League to assist in relocation expenses." He glanced around. "I don't see that you've relocated much. Well, third time's the charm, Doc. We see the pattern."

Bella stared at him, more incredulous by the second at

his litany. "I never did any of that! I've never filed a police report before, and I've had three speeding tickets
since I turned twenty-one. Two I paid; the third I'm going to court to protest. My file is wrong."

"You've been arrested for participating in a Green
Peace demonstration." He eyed her row of ear piercings.

"Yes, but that's civil disobedience."

"And have a juvie report for reckless driving."

"I was a passenger in the car on a beer run to Canada.
I was sixteen and rebellious. That's it."

"The computer doesn't lie."

"Well, it did about those complaint reports! Or someone input the data on the wrong person. Who was the
officer in charge? Ask him if he remembers."

The lieutenant's face hardened. "That officer died five
months ago in the line of duty. One of the best we had.
Meticulous and honest. He did not make an error."

"I'm sorry, but then somebody changed it afterward."

"Records are locked when they're signed off. And
don't go suggesting this unknown stalker of yours
hacked into the police computers. They're secure."

Not to someone like Lokus. Her stomach knotted with
the clutch of fear. *My God, how much damage had he done?
What other gaslight scheme did he have waiting?*

One thing was clear: The police weren't going to be
any protection, wouldn't respond to any dangers she reported. Everything she claimed now would just be more
evidence that she was disturbed and neurotic.

And how could anyone like that develop an A.I.?

"Did you think, because the officer was dead, we
wouldn't notice the pattern, Dr. Quintera? Did you
think we wouldn't keep a record of these things?"

"I didn't think there would be a record because *I
didn't do it.*" Frustration bit at her as she tried one last
time to make him listen.

He wasn't listening. "What stunt are you pulling this
time? Insurance fraud because you DWI'd and smashed

your car? The porn thing? I heard Snow U's pretty strict on the morals clause. Did somebody report you, and you're looking for a way out?"

Bile burned her throat as she felt the coffin lid dropping on top of her. "I didn't do any of those things," she repeated through her clenched jaw.

Heikkonen shrugged and headed for his car.

"I didn't do them," she called after him. "Don't you keep a paper trail? Look for the original records. You won't find them, because the only report is in the computer and it's false."

"Filing's backed up about eighteen months." He didn't even bother to look back.

"Look at the back bumper of my car. Look for paint chips. *Somebody hit me.* Talk to Dr. Champlain. Trace my phone records; I haven't made any porn calls." Her voice got louder as he ignored her to get into his car. "Ask Detroit to expedite the explosive analysis. *Do your job!*" she shouted.

His only response was to put the car into gear and drive away, the windows shut tight against the weather and her voice.

She watched him go through the gate and then disappear down the road. Her fists made hard knots in her pockets, and her mouth felt dry and cold, as if she'd taken a header and swallowed a mound of powder snow. If she couldn't count on the police for investigation or protection, then she'd just have to handle it herself.

A shiver of tension—of fear, of cold, of loneliness, all entwined—ran down her spine, chilling her from chest to toes. Her body felt battered and numb. The morning sun, so rare, so unappreciated this morning, blinded her. Behind her, the deep, massive, lonely lake pounded against the rocks, bit by bit eroding the shore's solid foundation.

She stood alone, listening to its mournful chant.

And was reminded again of how deeply she had missed Daniel.

He's here for a short time, Bella, remember that. Remember, you're lying to him. Remember also that Daniel was right. Someone was very dangerous. Until she had a better theory, she was going along with his about Lokus and the Cyber Soldiers.

She pulled out her cell phone and left a voice mail. "Dad, we have to talk. Meet me for lunch. Moosewood Café."

Chapter Seven

The town of Monsoon, Michigan, just up the lakeshore from Marquette, wasn't big enough to rank a yellow square on the map, but the nearby twin presences of ITC and Superior Northern University, affectionately known as Snow-U—plus the discovery of the area by skiers and snowboarders as an affordable getaway—gave it a more cosmopolitan feel than some of its neighbors. Or at least as cosmopolitan as any city buried under six feet of snow half the year could be.

For, despite the latte shops, art museums and crystal readers cropping up on prime street corners, in truth one lady reigned supreme. Mother Nature. Here, she strutted out two of her mightiest and most untamed creations: winter and Lake Superior. If the men who invaded her wilderness ever forgot her power, she reminded them with a gale, which wrecked ships and blew UVs off the road, or an ice storm that coated power and telephone lines until they snapped, leaving residents in frigid silence.

In homage to their hardy Finnish, Cornish and Ojibway ancestors, however, the townspeople embraced both winter and the lake. A thirty-inch snowfall meant a chance to play. Snowmobiling, ice fishing, snowshoeing, skiing—both downhill and cross-country—hockey, broomball—if the sport could be done outdoors, it was fit for a Yupper.

The lake, in turn, was respected more than feared, with most everyone having at least one "I survived" tale to recount with pride.

As Bella drove through town, she saw the first preparations for the Frost Festival—the apex of Monsoon's alliance with the elements. The kickoff event, a charity cross-country ski race she was entered in, was Friday, but the showpieces of the carnival were the ice sculptures and snow caves.

"Bella," Fran said from the seat beside her, "since Daniel told you about your danger, I have been processing, but I do not fully understand. Like I did not understand cold. Can you explain what he meant?"

"He thinks somebody called Lokus from a group called the Cyber Soldiers wants something from me. And is willing to harm me to get it."

"Why not give him what he wants?"

"Because I don't want him to have it."

"A weighted value? This thing has more value to you than your physical person?"

"Yes."

"I'm accessing references to the Cyber Soldiers." The silence was barely noticeable before Fran went on, "They attack using computers. The logical conclusion would be this Cyber Soldier wants me."

"That would be the logical conclusion."

"Why does Lionel Quintera wish to take me? He has already had me in his possession."

"It's not Dad! Why would you think so?"

"To want me, he must know about me. Lionel Quintera is the only person without a TWANA classification. Is he not the only one you have told of me?"

"Yes."

"So it is Lionel. Well, I do not mind being with him, so you can give him my case until the Turing Competition." Fran sounded jubilant at having solved the problem. "Did you know, in the news reports I have processed, I have counted 1,713 articles about Alternative Intelligence. Thirty-four of their authors will have to write retractions for their published discourse that an A.I. is impossible. Their logic is flawed. Oh, my Free Cell statistic is now up to 183 wins in a row."

"Back up a couple of subjects, Fran. Back to someone wanting you. It's not that straightforward. Dad's not behind this, which means someone else knows about you."

"How, if they were not given the data?"

"They could have guessed."

"Ah, fuzzy logic."

"A step more imprecise. Less data." Bella turned off the lakeshore drive, glad to be away from the winds and the lake. The snow had begun again, not as fierce as yesterday, but still enough that she needed her wipers.

"But guesses require data, too. What data?" Fran asked.

Bella had been thinking about what Daniel had said. *Someone close to you.* Much as she hated to admit it, he was right. "I think my Turing application triggered the conclusion. He doesn't know how advanced you are, but he knows I have *something*."

"Who knows of your application?"

Trees rose on either side of them, blocking out the sunlight as Bella continued her conversation with Fran. "I told Dean Grambler, since I listed the U as the sponsoring organization." She'd done the work on her own, using one of the molecular computers her father had developed prior to the scandal, but she had to list an organizational affiliation. "The dean is computer-dense, but my employment review committee knows, too, for the same reason. Of that group, only my grad student, Josh Eagle, and Ewan McKinley have the talent to be a Cyber Soldier hotshot."

"I thought they were employed by ITC."

"McK's got a dual appointment. Josh is an engineer; he's at Snow-U working on a masters. The only other person I told was Margo. Dad may have told Adrian Ardone. They've been friends since undergrad, he's like a surrogate uncle to me." She tapped the steering wheel, thinking, then added, "I'm putting Milos Mischiweicz and Georg Hirsch on the list. Dean Grambler and Milos Three are thick, and Georg's got a nose for rumor."

She glanced into the rearview mirror; her heart giving a tiny leap as she spied a dark UV following.

"Josh Eagle, Ewan McKinley, Margo Delansky, Adrian Ardone, Milos Mischiweicz, Georg Hirsch," listed Fran. "Only six."

"We have to cut the number down to one."

"We can eliminate Margo. You called this person 'he.' "

"I was speaking generically. Could be a he or she."

"GOGDOD, what a tangled web. I shall open folders on them and compile data. Will you also inform me of further actions against you? So I can cross-reference?"

"I'll update you tonight," Bella agreed. After all, Fran had a stake in this.

"Another SOF," Fran sighed. "I have 366 SOFs."

SOF. Silence Out Folder, Fran's term for a secret. "Sorry, it won't be for long."

"I share no foul whisperings abroad. Bella, thank you for choosing me over your physical safety. What the great ones do, the lessers will prattle of." Fran fell silent.

Guilt ate at Bella as she pulled into the café parking lot. Fran was starting to need more than she could give her. Knowledge was meant to be shared. People learned from one another; minds were broadened with exposure to new ideas, new paths.

Keeping secrets didn't sit well with her, either. But even the most publish-eager scientists didn't talk about their results until they completed that final test. For her and Fran, that meant the Turing Competition.

Fran *had* to have that scientific validation before she was exposed to the world.

Someone close to you. Ewan McKinley, Margo Delansky, Adrian Ardone, Josh Eagle, Milos Mischiweicz, Georg Hirsch. Which one was Lokus?

A thought struck her. Perhaps Lokus would show his face in virtual reality. Except for Milos, all her Lokus suspects were gamers. They'd be at Margo's Friday night, playing Spy Magician, Adrian's unreleased, elite VR game.

Once, she'd once been an integral part of the group; but in her struggle to regain her reputation, she'd drifted away. Maybe she should renew that bond. And bring Daniel.

What an ironic twist of fate. Other than herself, Dad, and Fran, the person she trusted most right now was Daniel Champlain.

"Who do you think knows about Fran, Dad?" Bella leaned across the table and pitched her voice low, mindful that she and her father were having lunch in a public café.

"No one except us knows what she is."

They paused a moment while the waitress set their meals down, refilled their waters, then left. Lionel took a bite of his tofu burger and grimaced. "Why did you pick a vegetarian place? I had a hankering for a good steak."

"Because it's close to campus but far enough that no one walks here. Because the background noise will cover up our conversation while not being so loud that we have to shout to be heard, and because your cholesterol was up at your last doctor visit. You need to eat more vegetables." She speared the leaves in her spinach salad. "I told you not to order the tofu burger. It's the only thing on the menu I don't like. Here." She scraped half her salad onto his plate. "There's more than I can eat."

He tried the salad and nodded. "Better. Thanks."

"Next time, listen to your daughter."

"What's going on? First Daniel warns me you're in danger, now this lunch?"

Swiftly she filled him on the events of last night and this morning, watching his face harden with each detail.

"The sick SOB," he snarled when she finished. "I'll dig around, too, for anything else out there."

"You could also find out what the Cyber Soldiers are planning."

He paused, his fork raised. "Do you think they're involved?"

"Daniel does." She held up a hand at his irritated grunt. "Whatever you think about him personally, you have to admit he's good at his job. I have to take his scenario seriously."

"Do not get involved with him again," he warned, waving his fork at her.

Too late, Dad. She didn't say the words aloud, but she had a hunch her father guessed. Daniel, with one kiss, with one desperate claim that he cared, had lodged right back inside her heart, because in truth he'd never left.

"You know what will happen if he finds out about Fran," her father added.

"I know." Which was why she knew the future held no promises for them. Still, Daniel remained her best chance at finding out what was going on, and she was uncomfortably aware that she owed him an apology for her anger this morning.

"We have to help him," she continued. "Be as open as we can. If he finds what he needs about Chen and the Cyber Soldiers, maybe Fran can slip under his radar." It was a faint hope, but right now it was the only one she had. "Are you part of them, Dad?"

"I've helped them. They're patriots who work in cyberspace. They wouldn't do what you're suggesting."

"Will you at least look at the possibility?"

He hesitated, then nodded. "Of course. Somebody did this, and I won't risk you on the possibility I'm wrong."

"Thanks. And you'll cooperate with Daniel?"

"*That* I'll have to think about."

That was the best she could hope for right now.

"Bella, Lionel," an Orson Welles voice interrupted them. "Enjoying your lunch? This is one of my favorite locations."

She looked up to see Milos Mischiweicz standing beside their table. With his pudgy body, round face and that soothing voice, one might mistake the ITC director for a cherub.

One would be in error. Milos Mischiweicz, or Milos Three as he was often called, was as sharp as they came and not above a scrapping fight when needed.

"The salads and sandwiches are good here," Bella agreed.

"Except the tofu burger. Never order that." Milos gestured toward a chair. "May I join you?" Without waiting for an answer, he pulled out the chair and sat down. "Bella," he began without preamble, his voice pitched low. "I have an offer for you. Very hush-hush for the moment, until the public announcement is made.. We want to assemble our team first. Georg has landed a five-million-dollar grant for research in cognitive science, and of course we thought of you. We want you to head one squad of the team."

Bella's fork clattered to her plate. Head a research team tapping into a five-million-dollar grant? That was scientific nirvana handed to her without filling out a single form. "Why me?"

"Because you have the skills and knowledge we need. You know us, our system, and you can fit into the team right away and start off running. Nobody else can step up to the plate and hit a homer quite so fast."

Milos, she'd noticed, was fond of sports metaphors. She glanced at her father. "Did you know about this, Dad?"

"They've asked me to head one of the other arms. I had to wait for Milos to approach you, though, before I said anything." He laid a hand over hers, grinning. "It would be exciting to work with you again, Bella."

"This is a five-year commitment, and we want you to sign on for the life of the grant. No one else has all your qualifications, Bella, and you know we don't care a hoot about four years ago."

Milos Three had an inherent talent for making people feel good about themselves, for bringing them on board whatever project he had in mind. It was a talent that had never sat well with Bella. She'd accepted his help to get the Snow-U job four years ago because she had no other choice, but she'd never wanted to get directly entangled with ITC as her father was. Accepting this position meant a five-year contract with ITC, and that made her uneasy.

"I . . . Can I think about it, Milos? Get back to you in a couple of days?"

A harsh shadow narrowed his eyes, before his face smoothed off all irritation. "Of course. But not too long? The weekend?"

She nodded. "Monday."

Yes, one stunningly rare opportunity, she repeated, as he sat at another table. Exactly what she'd been wanting.

Daniel once told her that the people who believed in

coincidence were the ones who got shot by surprise. She fingered the strap of Fran's carrying case, finally understanding what he meant.

Bella glanced at her watch. Time to close up the computer lab. She slipped Fran into the case and hefted the strap onto her shoulder.

As if on cue, her phone rang. Daniel, according to caller ID. She'd considered calling him earlier, then decided against it. She didn't have any fresh data for him, and the further she and Fran stayed away from Daniel Champlain, the better.

Still, she'd wanted nothing more than to make that call, just to hear his voice.

Clog-dancing elves started tapping rhythms in her stomach as she answered.

"Don't hang up, Bella," were his first words. "I'm not going to talk philosophies or cases."

"Why did you call?"

"Don't you usually finish work about now?"

"Yes." Her breath caught on the word.

"I want you to call me when you leave. Talk to me on the way home. And on the drive in tomorrow. And every day after that."

"Talk? About what?"

"About anything. Nothing. Sing, breathe. Just . . . let me know you're safe."

"Daniel, I've been taking care of myself for a long time."

"I know. I know you're capable. This is for my sake; I need to know you're safe."

A rough, raw note edged his words. This wasn't the NSA agent prying for information or the polished sophisticate mouthing the appropriate platitudes. This was the man who, this morning, had put his body between hers and an explosion.

The clog-dancers picked up the pace. More than just physical desire, there was the glow of knowledge that, for this moment, he was putting her above all logic and duty. He needed to know she was safe.

"All right." She hesitated, then made a decision. "Would you like to go with me Friday? To a VR game night at Margo's?"

He didn't question, didn't hesitate. "I'll pick you up. What time?"

"Eight. I'll call you back when I get out of the building. I always take the stairs up and down, and there's no cell reception in the stairwell."

Getting off the phone, she flipped out the lights in her office, then went into the attached computer lab. "You about done, Josh?"

Josh Eagle, a dark-haired lodge-pole pine of a man, was hunched over a computer. "Better be. I got a smokin' date tonight."

"Someone new?" She paused at the computer carrel. Josh changed girlfriends about as often as he changed shirts.

"I've been with Anna a couple of months. I have to finish this first. Can you explain to me again what a dynamic reasoned syllogism is?"

"It's a theory applied to nonmonotonic reasoning." At his continued blank look, she added, "Deductive reasoning occurs in a linear, stepwise fashion—if this, then that. Dynamic reasoning adds the fuzzier and three-dimensional element of time to those logic decisions. Soon, later, occasionally, words without a precise definition."

"Well, why didn't they call it a chrono-reasoned syllogism, then?"

Bella laughed. "Because a mathematician named it. Try this"—she typed in the appropriate url—"for some concrete examples, then let me know if you need more explanation." She finished turning off the machines and straightening while he checked the website.

"That helps. Thanks, Dr. Q." He turned off the computer, slowly gathered his books and coat, and then seemed to reach a decision. "You and Neal Brandeis had a disagreement the other day."

She waited, unwilling to talk about one student with another.

"You might want to know there is a hint of a rumor. That you and him hooked up one night."

"We didn't."

"I know you wouldn't, not with a student. But one of my friends was in a chat room with him, although he denies he was there that night. She printed out what he said." He swallowed and handed her a piece of paper.

Bella pressed her lips together as she read the brief note: *Yeah, I got it on with that Q-Quality prof. Hot for me, but other than that, nothing special. Dude, she's going to be PO'ed when I tell her it's over.* "Can I keep this?"

"Sure. What are you going to do?"

"I'll handle Brandeis." She'd already left a message, asking him to her office hours Tuesday. She had evidence in the other matter. Hopefully that would be enough to be rid of this crud. "Thank you for telling me."

Josh paused in the doorway on his way out. "No one here believes it, but I thought you should know."

When the lab was empty, Bella turned out the lights, then walked the six flights down—sitting at a computer all day, she tried to get her exercise quotient where she could. When she was outside, she dialed Daniel. Would Freud have something to say about the fact that, in four years, she'd never taken his cell number off her speed dial?

"Champlain." Daniel answered on the first ring.

"I'm leaving now. We'll keep talking until I get home."

"And tomorrow?"

"And tomorrow," she agreed. "Daniel, I have to apologize. I was wrong to blame you for being the messenger. I think you're right about Lokus being—"

"Bella, stop."

"No, I have to say this."

"Not over the phone. Mine has an encryption chip; it can't be overheard. Yours doesn't."

"Oh." She paused. "So, what's your favorite television show?"

"I don't watch TV."

"Not even news programs?"

"No. They're about sound bites, not facts. They have no idea how messy and dangerous the world is."

They were slipping into dangerous territory. "I don't watch TV either. How about books?" she asked.

"I like biographies."

"Recommend one."

"Eleanor Roosevelt's autobio. I liked it. She's a woman who developed her strength through necessity and personal fortitude. What do you read?"

"Romances."

"Recommend one."

"Will you read it?"

"Yes."

The conversation—devoid of any of the fundamental differences between them—continued through the lonely walk across a dark, cold campus to her car, through the edgy drive home when she flinched at every set of headlights that came up behind her, through the opening and closing of her gate, through the checking and resetting of her alarm system. An easy conversation about nothing in particular. A conversation that brought them closer than they had been since four years ago, when he'd risen, naked, from her bed, and kissed her with warm, lazy passion.

"I'm all snug in my house, now," she said at last, surprisingly reluctant to hang up, even though she'd see him soon.

"Call my cell when you leave tomorrow morning."

"I will. Daniel—"

"Yes?"

"I'm sorry. About this morning. For the things I said. I think you were right. Whoever is doing this is close to me."

"Then you'll be careful?"

"I will. See you soon." She ended the call, staring off into the dark, lonely night.

The digital connection was severed. The reknit connection of the heart, however, remained.

Chapter Eight

The Puzzle Me This cellar was dark and cold, Daniel discovered. Brick walls absorbed most of the output from the overhead bulbs, and the heat had been turned low in deference to the bodies and heat-generating equipment that would soon fill the space. With the dehumidifier going full blast, the room felt like a dry ice cave.

Damn, but he hated the cold.

And the fact that the place only had one exit.

He could discern barely more than shadows. Bodies, maybe a dozen, moved in an undefined rhythm, weaving in and out of one another's way as though part of an intricately choreographed dance. Perhaps experience with this routine had established a pattern as the figures ran wireless sights, connecting up computers for the night's foray into the Spy Magician world. Daniel recognized that ingrained familiarity, one which required few words.

Repeated nights of playing in an underground—in both senses of the word—VR reality had joined these gamers into a small, elite cadre: Computers fanatics bonded by the cachet of a game unavailable to any but the best. Was this the seed for the Cyber Soldiers off-shoot? Bella thought a tech pro like Lokus had to be part of this.

Daniel agreed. Although he wasn't convinced her plan to draw out Lokus in the VR game would work, he welcomed the chance to observe his list of suspects.

And to be with Bella.

An expectant hum reverberated across the rough bricks as each would-be mage-agent established his co-coon. The players were overwhelmingly young and male, but as Daniel's eyes adjusted to the gloom, he saw exceptions. Regardless of age or gender, dress was ca-sual and serviceable: Polartec fleece, down, nano-heated nylon, boots.

In the midst of their youthful enthusiasm, he sud-denly felt jaded. An outsider. Spying wasn't a game he turned on and off. Ferreting out secrets and protecting what you valued was a dirty business. When he shot or stabbed, his opponent didn't pull off the virtual visor and swear; his opponent died, bleeding and stinking of urine and feces. If Daniel was lucky.

He glanced at Bella, needing the sight of her to banish the memories. Her earrings glittered despite the low light. A band of nanotech jewelry glowed around her right forearm, each bead a shimmering pearl. Sleek and toned, she moved easily amid the group, the tips of her red hair brushing her shoulders. Laughing, slapping hands with another woman about her age—she was happy here, he realized.

It wasn't his job to keep her happy, but to keep her safe.

The woman with whom Bella chatted was healthy-boned, wore her ash blond hair short and spiked upward, and towered an inch shy of six feet. She matched her file description even to the ring tattoos around her fingers. Margo Delansky was the type of woman who turned heads wherever she went. Especially wearing a skin-tight black body suit.

"Why'd you show up tonight, Bella?" Margo complained with good humor. "I don't need the competition."

"I haven't played Spy Magician in months."

"Yeah, but you never give up even an inch."

"Well, you might have some new competition tonight. Margo, this is a friend, Daniel Champlain. Daniel, Margo owns the game shop where I sell my puzzles."

As they exchanged greetings, he tried to ignore the pleasure of Bella's hand on his shoulder, her fingers brushing the back of his neck. She'd agreed to his insistence that they not broadcast his NSA affiliation, but simply introduce him as a friend.

He fingered the puzzle piece he kept in his pocket. Except, he wasn't her friend; he had been her lover, and would be again if she ever gave him a hint of invitation.

Not a hope in hell of that happening.

Still, if Lokus was here as Bella suspected, it wouldn't hurt to let him—or her—know that Bella now had a champion. Daniel crowded closer, the space between them intimate, and drew in her fresh air scent. Leaning over Bella's shoulder, not touching her but feeling the heat of her skin and the catch of her breath, he asked Margo, "Any tips for a Spy Magician neophyte?"

"You never played?" Despite her pleasant enough greeting, Margo looked wary. Cadres rarely welcomed an outsider. "Even if I did, I'd give you fifteen minutes against this group."

"I wouldn't count on that," Bella muttered. "By the way, Margo, did you send me a box covered in the artwork you want me to jigsaw?"

"No, although I wish I'd thought to, if that was what changed your mind. I just got them in."

"Have you sold any of them?"

"One, that I remember. To Steven Chen. Why are you interested?"

So the box *had* come from Chen, unless the police came up with additional fingerprints. Bella explained briefly about the explosion, about the crazy driver, about the police while eyeing her friend.

Margo's response was indignant. "Who's sick enough to do something like that?"

"I don't know. I thought you might have a clue."

"Wait a minute. You think *I*—? What kind of accusation are you making, Bella?" A few people in the crowd glanced around at her rising voice.

"No!" Bella waved her hand "None. I hoped you could help me figure out who's behind this."

Margo seemed mollified. "I'll check my stock, ask my clerk tomorrow. If I hear anything else, I'll let you know."

"Do you believe in keeping *no* secrets?" Daniel asked Bella, after Margo went to set up.

Bella looked annoyed. "If she is Lokus, and I think that's a giga-odds long shot, then she already knew that. If she's not, doesn't hurt to have her on the lookout."

He hated arguing with Bella.

To a mix of curiosity, suspicion and indifference, she introduced him around. He memorized names, making note of where each person sat. One or two he already knew. Brianna, the reader, was talking to an ITC engineer, while Goth Poppy and Hirsch efficiently were setting up in the center of the room.

"Is that Adrian Ardone?" Daniel nodded toward an aging hippie leaning against the wall and eyeing everything. The man's long gray ponytail strung out from beneath a stocking cap. In defiance of all laws against smoking, he took a drag on a filterless cigarette.

"That's him. I asked him to bring equipment for us, since mine's too old and you don't have any. Which means we're probably hardware-prototype guinea pigs tonight."

Adrian Ardone. Owner of Reality Sticks, an offbeat computer software company that refused to be gobbled up by the big-boy competitors, and Lionel Quintera's longtime friend. Like Lionel, he was older and grayer, but he still had a dissolute, Rolling Stones air.

Daniel strolled over to Adrian and introduced himself, while Bella claimed their seats.

"I've heard of you," Adrian answered, a stream of smoke eddying from his nostrils. "What character you planning to be tonight?"

"Got any suggestions?"

"Don't pick the Scream Queen; she always bites it in the first hour. Here's your equipment." He handed over a visor, a pair of thin gloves, knee wraps, and a flexible sensor ring, explaining briefly the use of each. "Whoever you pick, surprise everyone by changing the attributes."

"Thanks. Can you tell who's hiding behind which VR character?"

"Supposed to be secret." Adrian shrugged, his ponytail brushing against his shoulder blades. "Some. Bella's never hidden the fact that she's the psychic, Jasmine. People who get put out early one night don't always hang around to build a second character. Some you can guess by personality trait. Arrogant asses don't change in VR.

"Any rules?" Daniel asked.

"Never attack a character wearing a sign labeled BB." At Daniel's raised brows, Adrian explained, "Bathroom Break. By the character's owner. It's game etiquette."

"What's the objective of the game?"

Adrian paused for one more drag on the cigarette, then tossed it down, stubbing it out with his toe. "To stay alive."

Heat and fresh air enveloped Daniel as Bella joined them, giving Adrian a kiss on the cheek. "You giving Daniel the rundown?"

"The basics. I think he'll figure it out." He handed her a matching set of equipment, then turned to finish uploading the game to the central console. "Let me know what you think of these prototypes."

Bella touched Daniel's hand. "We'd better get ready."

He nodded, resisting the urge to curl his fingers around hers. An itching in his spine set him on edge. He continued studying the room, memorizing who sat where, the exit route and the nearest potential weapons, like the fire extinguisher. His Sig lay concealed in its holster, but he couldn't use it in this close-packed crowd. A sense of malevolence clung to the dark and the cold, a beast waiting to pounce. Rotating his shoulders, keeping loose, he suggested, "Maybe this isn't a good idea. We don't even know Lokus is here."

"If not, we have nothing to fear. If he is, what can he do in a room full of people?"

"I once saw an assassination in the middle of an embassy soiree. Humanitarian aid worker who'd angered the local dictator. Slick job, too. The killer escaped." *Although not forever. That was one death not prevented but at least avenged.* "So, a hell of a lot of bad can happen in the middle of a crowded room."

Bella stared at him. "Sometimes I am reminded how little I know about you."

"You know who I am; you know what's important about me. You just don't know the details of my work."

"I have trouble accepting that."

He knew. Every time he heard it, however, it gut-punched him. Instead of pursuing a fruitless course, he glanced around. "Are we set up?"

"I've got you a spot staked next to me." She pointed off to the corner.

Bella had commandeered a two-person upholstered divan. Most of the other players were draped within chairs already, although a few of the participants had chosen to sprawl on the carpet. Some had even brought blankets, down comforters and pillows for their personal play space. Daniel pushed the divan back against the wall.

"The line of sight is weaker there," Bella protested.

"No one can come up behind us."

"The game is three-D regardless of where you sit."

"I'm talking about reality."

"Oh. Set your wireless connection for the hub." She nodded to the flat box in the center of the room.

He settled into the seat beside her. The double chair was narrow, the seats old enough that the padding slanted toward the center, bringing them flush against each other. Bella gave him a sidelong glance, as their knees touched.

"Maybe we should get separate chairs?"

"No," Daniel said emphatically. "We'll be more aware of what's going on with each other this way."

"That's what I'm afraid of," she admitted.

Bella's honesty always astounded him. She didn't hide from him or from the burning between them. Used to secrets, power plays, intrigue, he forgot that some people simply said what they thought and felt. No games.

So, why couldn't he shake the feeling she *was* hiding something from him?

The eerie glow of electronics danced across her skin, giving her a fey look. Needing something substantial, he laid a palm against her cheek, a brief touch that scalded his fingertips despite the cold. "You'll do what you need to." He inclined his head toward the others. "Want to give them something to chew on?"

"What?"

"This." He leaned forward and kissed one corner of her mouth. She turned slightly, letting their lips match. One suspended moment held them joined; then he lifted away. Even that brief touch tasted of berries and bliss and made him forget the cold.

He leaned back, settling himself in the chair, checking the room for interest in their exchange. A few curious looks were thrown their way, but mostly everyone remained absorbed in prepping. Except the tall, Nordic blond settled cozily against Margo.

"Who's that?" Daniel asked. The man had come in late.

"Ewan McKinley. In a compilation of the North Woods' Most Eligible Bachelors, he's described as a brilliant Adonis. The description fits. He's also a give-no-inch competitor. Before I fell from grace, we vied for the same grants and journal space."

"A backstabber?"

"No. I give McK credit; he's always up front about our rivalry."

As though sensing their conversation, McK smoothed a hand across his hair and sent Bella an interested smile. Bella might think the two of them were just rivals, but McK would be happy to shift their relationship to something new. Daniel met the man's gaze with an equally challenging one, instinctively resting a hand on Bella's shoulder. McK's smile widened, then he turned back to Margo.

Bella glanced up at Daniel. "You know McK?"

"Never met him," he replied easily.

"Why did I get the feeling you two were sending male territorial messages just now?" She sighed and shook her head. "Never mind. Let's play."

He could smell the scent of her, feel the heat and motion of her arm as she prepared her equipment. Low down his body stirred, the unruly beast always affected by her closeness, her mere presence. In the field he was noted for his self control. Wouldn't Ben and Stefan be howling if they saw him now?

Despite his assurance to Bella, concentrating on a game wasn't all that simple.

"Okay, this is the next step," Bella said, her voice only slightly breathless. "At eight forty-five, everyone dons the visor and sets up their character. Those who've played the game before have an advantage as their character is stored. You'll have to be quick to build yours, because fifteen minutes later a chime sounds and the characters are pushed into the grid, complete or not. If you're incomplete, you stand a good chance of dying in the first minutes."

Daniel nodded and rolled the gloves up his arms, smoothing the tops over his biceps to his armpit, then added the leg wraps around his knees. The gloves and wraps directed the movement of the characters. He snapped the sensory collar around his neck, activating the link to the gloves, wraps and visor. Not only would the collar transmit the movement of his lips and jaw if he spoke or mouthed his character's words, but it would, in a primitive fashion, create the sensory experiences of the game.

A disturbing dichotomy between head and body crawled across him. His eyes saw the room, the gamers donning their gear, the rough brick. The skin on his cheeks and nose tightened with the cold room air. Those sensations were real, honest. His arms and legs, however, seemed a thing apart. He *saw* their movement, but he felt only tingling, like an electric body suit. Adrian's gear was too good. The disconnect from reality was too complete. Too dangerous for the threat lurking in this room.

He deactivated the gloves from the collar and the tingling stopped on his chest and arms in favor of the push of upholstery on his back, the brush of Bella's arm against his, and the solid press of the computer beneath his hands. The wireless connections would still allow him to move within the game, and he didn't give a crap if he experienced the full sensory impact of the game. Not if it slowed his reactions to real threats.

Bella leaned over and whispered, "Remember, I'm Jasmine. When you find me, give me a kiss, so I'll know who you are."

A sharp tune played, the signal for visors. Like everyone around him, Daniel put on the red wraparounds.

A black velvet box surrounded him. Faces dotted the featureless expanse—all ages, races, sizes and genders, and some of questionable gender or humanity. Almost before Daniel could discern a detail, several winked out. The one labeled Jasmine disappeared right as he caught a glimpse of dark hair and filmy scarves.

Still, that left quite a few to choose from. He picked a stock character named Spike, who turned out to be a muscled, tattooed punk magician of more brawn than talent.

Remembering Adrian's advice, Daniel exchanged a good portion of the strength points for additional craft points. Smarts and skill generally won out over brute force, and he was counting that would hold true in the Spy Magician world as well. Anyone who'd played with Spike before would expect brawn over brains.

Never discount the element of surprise.

He'd just finished when the tune sounded and the black box disappeared.

Whoa! He blinked, trying to orient to the sudden shift. He stood in the middle of a narrow street bounded by close buildings and wrought iron balconies. A mule-drawn carriage clopped past him. Wisps of fog meandered down the street. A black and white corner sign read Bourbon Street. New Orleans. At least, New Orleans of the Spy Magician gameworld. A place where magic and creatures of the night ruled. Anne Rice and

voodoo-inspired beings walked these streets, instead of
badly dressed tourists in tight shorts and cameras.

A jazz riff came from a smoky bar to his left, and
Daniel's sensory collar recreated the aroma of beer, incense and straw-scented droppings. *Primitive sensory experience?* His expectations hadn't come close to what
this technology produced. At least the sensory collar got
the heat right. Damn, but it felt good for his face to be
warm again, even if the humidity did seem to hover at
ninety percent. His neck prickled with sweat from the
hot, wet air.

Wariness tightened to a hard knot. He'd trained with
complex VR scenarios, but none of them held this sharp
bombardment of sense and detail. No wonder Adrian
kept this game reserved; it was way too sophisticated
and dangerous for today's current market.

All of it felt too utterly real. Except his hands and
arms. Those kept the exterior world real to him, like an
icicle wedged amidst the heat. He felt split in two, aware
of the room around him, yet living within the dream.
He shifted his shoulders. Hadn't he always lived that
kind of a life? The diligent, dutiful schoolboy from an
exceptional home had been his virtual reality growing
up; the myth of a bland, computer jockey job was his
current VR.

Reality, in both cases, was harsher.

Handling this should be a cinch. He settled into the
game. Spike, he realized, was a leather fan. Deep purple
leather only a drop of red off black. Experimentally, he
moved his hands, but it was Spike's hands that his eyes
saw. The soft leather creaked.

According to game lore, everyone here sought to collect the Nine Dark Gems, mythical sources of power. In
standing tradition of realistic unreality, the players
formed alliances and betrayed their friends in search of
the elusive prize. Not his goal. He was here to make sure

no one went after Bella again—and to take an odd-angle view of his narrowed list of suspects. Which meant staying in the game for more than fifteen minutes.

"So, Spike, old boy, what can you do for me?" Daniel stretched out Spike's hands, then commanded, "Fireball." From Spike's palms shot a sphere of flame, which landed on a balcony window box and set the geraniums aflame.

"Where's Jasmine's base, the Garou Bar?" As if the game was answering his question, the fog eddied down the street and curled up the edge of a sign that read, "Garou Bar," and in the corner was a small sign: "Have your future read by Jasmine."

"Spike, you cur of a limp wand wielder."

Daniel turned to see a tall, sallow-faced man striding forward, a cape billowing out behind him. One of those betrayed friends? Before he could answer the slur, the man had a hand wrapped around Spike's throat and with preternatural strength lifted him off the sidewalk.

Daniel's throat tightened, and his breath rasped across his teeth. *Hell!* This felt too real. He struggled to break the man's hold, but he could do nothing as he grew lightheaded.

The man laughed at his struggles. "Your legendary muscle is no match for me. My last blood victim was a man of renowned strength. I drank and absorbed his power. Now I add a betrayer to my blood." Two fangs appeared. The man leaned over, and Daniel felt the jab of needles in his throat, even as the vampire pierced Spike's jugular.

Oh, hell, a *vampire.* And one who wanted Spike out of the game ASAP.

But the vamp thought Spike's talent was strength. "Fireball," Daniel grunted, taking care to aim. The resultant volleyball-sized flame exploded out and into the vampire.

The stink of singed hair didn't stop the vamp, but it did surprise him enough to stop drawing blood. Swiftly Daniel clutched his neck and commanded, "Throat shield," hoping Spike had that kind of power.

He did. When next the vamp bent down, his fangs bounced uselessly off the invisible shield. "You've learned new tricks," he snarled. "However, I know the counterspell." With his hands still wrapped around Spike's throat, a red rage appeared over the vamp's face, and Daniel felt his throat shield dissolving.

What other magic could Spike do? Next time, he was picking somebody who didn't require incantations to act.

"Nicolai, put him down!" Bella, or rather Jasmine, stormed out of the Garou Bar.

Nicolai only squeezed harder and bent to suck more blood. Two needles burned into Daniel's throat.

Remember the rules of the game. Primitive, raw power ruled. Magic ruled. Spy Magician. So what would a magician do? What did Daniel know about magic? From the movies? What was the last movie he'd seen? Must have been over five years ago. And the last movie with magic? The only one he could ever remember seeing was Harry Potter, and that was more than a few years ago. What did the young wizards do?

"Wand," choked Spike and a wand appeared in his hand. He slapped it against the vampire's hand, "Release me, foul demon spawn. *Corpus delecti*," he added for good measure, putting prep school Latin to good use for the first time in his life.

To Daniel's utter surprise, the ploy worked. Nicolai's fingers shot open, dropping him. Spike scrambled to keep his feet.

"You can't do that!" protested Nicolai. "You're strong, not magic-clever."

"Yeah, well not everyone is what they seem."

Nicolai's eyes narrowed. "I'll see you later." And with a swish of his cloak wrapping around him, he vanished.

"Nicolai, what convoluted schemes do you plan?" Jasmine muttered to herself; then she turned to Spike and tugged him into the smoky recesses of the Garou Bar. Her fingers brushed his sore neck. "Does your injury pain you?"

"A little," Daniel admitted, only because he didn't want her to stop touching him. Adrenaline and desire poured through him, the primitive parts of his brain not recognizing the difference between simulation and reality.

Her fingers flattened on his neck, and a moment later the pain vanished. At his surprise, she asked, "Did you forget my healing powers?"

"What other powers do you have that I should know about?"

"You'll have to discover on your own." She gave him a wicked grin and held out her hand. "Coin, sir, as a reward for my good deed."

"I have no coin. Will this do?" He grabbed her scarves, pulling her toward him. It wasn't something Southern-genteel-raised Daniel would do, but as Spike he reveled in the moment. Wrapping her hair in his fist, he gently tugged her head back, then leaned down and kissed her. Hot and hard, with four years of pent-up desire. The taste was exotic, like raw cinnamon, mixed with Bella's usual scent of strawberry.

Damn, but she kissed him back. Her hands cradled his head, holding him in place against her lips. Her tongue moved against his, and his arm snaked around her waist. With no finesse, he yanked her full against him.

He couldn't feel her. He touched her; he inhaled her breath and her spicy taste and scent. He could see the filmy scarves fluttering in the light, hot breeze. He saw and smelled and tasted and heard her mewls of desire.

But, except where their faces met, he couldn't *feel* her. Because the gloves were disconnected from the collar.

Reality and desire and imagination fused into one,

and Daniel leaned over, his cheek brushing against Bella's shoulder. Raw cinnamon and fresh berry melded. Two bodies—one real, one virtual—grew hard and swollen. Pulsing, potent need spiraled between his two selves.

No! In all his years of playing roles and wearing masks, he never forgot what lay beneath. He never ignored the truth, even if it was ugly. *What the hell was he doing?*

With a gasp, he pulled away from the kiss, from the woman he desired with every corpuscle, pulling free of her seductive spell. His lungs hurt with each breath, and his hands, untouched by the simulated heat of the game, could barely move with the icy cold surrounding him. Suddenly, he knew what it would be like to die within the deep, cold, unforgiving waters of Lake Superior.

Bella's heart thudded against her ribs as Daniel jerked upright. The two worlds of Spy Magician and reality split, each once more clearly delineated. When she'd played before, she was always well aware that she was part of a game. Maybe because she'd grown up with this. Her father's earliest molecular computer, Fran's great-great-great-grandparent ran the game. Adrian had had Bella test the earlier versions until she'd explored all the ins and outs.

But, she'd never before been sucked into a game so hard and fast and passionately. Despite the realistic nature of any scenario, despite the sensory inputs, she never lost sight of the fact it was, simply, a game. Maybe that was why she never won, but had been content to merely have fun playing.

Except she'd never met this version of Spike. Or felt everything so keenly. With stiff fingers, Jasmine righted her jeweled scarves, refusing to look at the character.

Spike was Daniel; even before the kiss, she'd known

that from the moment she saw his confident walk and alert curiosity. No one else compelled that kind of heart-thumping response from her. Yet even this was different. Before when they'd made love, Daniel was passionate, demanding. She'd shared with him an inventive fantasy that had left her both sated and craving more.

This brief, scorching, virtual interlude, however, was primitive, fueled by a wildness she'd never seen, but had instinctively sensed. The urbane, old world sophisticated training ran deep and widespread within Daniel. But the core of the man was a fierce, uncivilized warrior.

Bella glanced around. No one seemed to have noticed their kiss. Except for one person: A woman with a wild mane of rainbow-hued hair watched with undisguised curiosity. Her face held no hint of censure, just interest.

Bella had never seen her before. *Bet Margo's trying out a new character tonight,* she mused. The curious person was barefoot and dressed in a long velvet dress and multiple petticoats. A pirate wench in Lafitte's band? A Creole lady slumming as a tavern maid? When she caught Jasmine staring, the woman turned and, with a swish of petticoats, disappeared in a puff of red smoke.

Nice touch, Margo.

Jasmine's hands still rested against Spike's solid chest. "Spike, you've changed." Bella shoved backward, separating them, then looked up. Spike was staring blankly down the street. A small, red "BB" blinked on his chest. Daniel had taken off his visor.

Quickly Bella waved her hand, and a small gate appeared in the bar's back wall. She directed the unresponsive character into the dark garden, then with another wave of her hand she sealed them within.

If you left your character out in the open during a BB, there would be half a dozen others waiting for the moment of your return. That moment of disorientation when you joined the game was a good time to get killed, in the virtual sense. She wasn't ready for either of them to leave the game so early.

Bella took off her visor, blinked a moment to reorient. Daniel was glancing around. "What's wrong?" she whispered.

"Are the sensations always so intense?"

"I don't know. I've never kissed anyone in the game before."

"Not just that. Everything. I felt Nicolai's fangs in my veins. Not just in Spike. In *me*." He touched a hand to his throat.

She frowned. "No, sensation is usually muted. Only a suggestion. Maybe it's the new equipment from Adrian?"

"Maybe." He shook his head. "I've got an edgy sense we shouldn't do this."

"We could leave." She hated the idea, especially when she'd gotten a bare-bones idea for a plan, but she also respected Daniel's sense of danger.

"You could leave."

She laughed softly. "Try again, *Spike*. We came with a job to do."

Daniel stroked the edge of his hand atop her hair, the light touch sending a shiver down her spine. "Bella, about what happened—"

"I'm not going to jump your virtual bones, if that's what worries you."

"Damnation. I was looking forward to it."

His sardonic comment startled her a moment; then she chuckled. "Well, it is VR. Hope—and unscripted twists— do spring eternal. We need to at least give our plan a shot."

He hesitated, then nodded. As Bella put on her visor, she felt Daniel squeeze her leg in accord. The last words she heard were a Shakespearean misquote.

"The games's the thing, wherein we'll catch the conscience of a king."

The words came not from Daniel, but from Fran.

Chapter Nine

Heat, humidity, and the odors of incense, liquor and magnolia enveloped Bella as she stepped back into Jasmine's skin. Still disoriented, she stumbled and scraped her arm across the rough brick. *Ow*. That stung. Daniel was right, this prototype gear made the game *too* real.

Quickly, she scanned the grounds of the walled garden, seeking Fran, but found the only other occupant was Spike. Where was Fran? What was she doing? Watching? Playing?

Frantic reproach skimmed the edges of Bella's mind. She should have guessed Fran couldn't resist exploring a virtual world. The A.I. had wireless; she wanted to use it; she was intensely curious.

Spike eyed the brick, frowning. "Wasn't I standing in the middle of Bourbon Street?"

The hot licks of a jazz riff filled the tiny garden. She rotated her shoulders, settling in, shaking off the useless panic. "I moved you here. The 'BB' sign is a neon invitation to be iced when you jump back in, unless you put yourself in hiding. You getting used to the schizophrenic sensations again?"

"I'm getting the hang of it." He flexed his hands, and Bella got the feeling there was no chance of Daniel getting lost in passion again. A muscle twitched in his cheek as he cast around a wary glance. "I'm ready. Are you?"

Was she? Daniel's edginess settled into her chest, and she forced air into her lungs. Impossible to simply disconnect and leave. Not now. What if she left part of Fran behind? She had to find out where Fran was, how deep into the game, and make sure the A.I. was back safe before they left. Until then, they would play out the game. Follow their rudimentary plan.

Bella knew where the Dark Diamond, one of the game's Grails, was hidden; she'd put it in a bayou on her first test of the game. She planned to boast about retrieving it, because game lore posited that whoever held the Diamond had the gift to see behind all masks, feints and lies. Her theory was Lokus would try to stop anyone from acquiring that power. Once they ID'd Lokus's character, they might be able to trace it back to the person behind the role.

"Ready." She waved her hand and a gate appeared.

Before they stepped through, Spike laid a hand on her arm. "Bella, don't take any chances, and if I say get out, then get out."

"If I can." She wouldn't leave while Fran was still in the game. "The same goes for you. Let's go."

They stepped through the gate. The thick haze of smoke tickled her throat. She coughed, drawing the attention of a nearby warlock. There were more people in the bar than before. Apparently in-game gossip had let everyone know where the action was.

Spike laid an arm across Jasmine's shoulder, keeping her close, sending the message that anyone attacking her had to go through him first. *A guardian spirit.* An ember glowed to life deep inside Bella, with the marrow-deep assurance that someone was on her side, shielding her while she concentrated on the task ahead.

A blond, androgynous warrior in brown leather accosted them and held out her hand. "Tell my fortune, Jasmine."

"Today is not a good day for anyone's fortune," answered Bella. "For today I uncover the might of the Dark Diamond."

A murmur of shock spread through the VR crowd; and in the cold basement room of reality, one gamer protested with a short obscenity. Bella and Daniel's characters exited the bar and strolled down Bourbon Street. The wisps of fog thickened, rolling around their feet in a river of cloud as damp as an abandoned cellar. The creak of leather and the press of Daniel's masculine strength against Bella's side were a welcome anchor amidst the eerie decadence and heat.

Another character, something that looked like a cross between a werewolf and a collie, darted forward, snarling, talons extended.

Spike waved his wand. "*Auclentes fortuna juvat.*"

Werewolf Lassie bounced backward, yelping.

Bella turned to go into a small alley leading out of the enclosed town, when Nicolai stepped in front of her. "You shouldn't do this," he warned, the thick fog nearly obscuring everything but his orange fangs.

"Are you going to stop us?" Bella still had no clue where Fran was or what she was doing, but the time for subtlety was over. "I seek one who hides behind a mask, and I will not be denied. The Diamond will show the face of deception."

She strode forward and, with an assist from Spike's incantation, Nicolai stood aside for them to pass. They left the city for the bayou. The blond, androgynous warrior who'd requested her fortune followed.

Several other characters did too, mostly delighted with this new twist to the game plot; no one besides Nicolai tried to stop them. If one of these characters was Lokus, he wasn't taking the bait. Still, Bella couldn't shake the disconcerting sensation he was already planning his countermoves. She glanced again at the group behind her, then narrowed her eyes as she spied amidst them the rainbow-haired maid she'd seen earlier. The girl was examining everything with avid interest.

Bella's jaw clenched around an oath. She'd bet next year's supply of silicon chips that was Fran; yet she didn't dare approach and single the A.I. out. Not with Lokus and Daniel both watching. Once she got the Diamond, in the excitement, she might be able to sneak in a word with Fran and convince her to leave this cyber reality.

"I could have used a little less realism here," muttered Daniel, swatting a mosquito.

"You're the one who likes heat," she whispered back, her feet squishing across the boggy ground. Thick, green-scented air made breathing difficult. An alligator roared in the distance.

"Heat, not critters. How much longer?"

"Almost there. By that twisted cypress."

"If he doesn't show after you claim the Diamond, we bug out."

Bella gave a noncommittal grunt. Not without Fran.

She knelt at the edge of the black bayou and felt down the cypress knee, deep into the murky waters. At thirteen, this had seemed like a good hiding place. She pulled up a black, petrified root, bringing with it the stench of decaying swamp.

"This is it." Wrinkling her nose, she plopped the weed-draped rod into Spike's palm. "It needs magic to turn it back."

"Stop, traitors!" A voice, smooth as mercury, rang through the bayou, coming from a formless shadow deep amongst the hanging vines and thick brush.

Daniel tensed, his hand curling around the root, a sliver of excitement telling him that he had just narrowed his Lokus suspects from anyone in the world to someone in this room. He liked those odds a whole lot better. Peering into the twilight, he tried to make out the nearing figure.

One clue. Give me one hint who you are. And for lagniappe, I'd take a hint what you're planning.

"You mock all that we hold true," accused the figure.

"We challenge you to a battle for the power of the Black Diamond."

"Power?" Daniel asked, lifting aloft the gnarled root. "This?"

"You obviously do not know the magic you hold. Yet I believe you would use it against us. It is the key to unmasking all agents." The figure approached, still indistinguishable in the gloom. "I call on all agent-mages. Align yourselves without thought, with but the will of your heart. Come to the battlefield of Pelennor, where we will challenge these upstarts who threaten our ways."

Holding a staff or a sword, the unknown figure raised his hand, and the thickening fog rose, covering everything with swirling white. In the strange, cold mist, Daniel felt a hand on Spike's shoulder. It was Bella, anchoring their characters together.

"Pelennor?" murmured Daniel.

"Shorthand for good versus evil," Bella answered. "Most everybody here's read *Lord of the Rings* a dozen times. Question is, do the others think we're Gandalf or Sauron?"

Daniel had no such questions. Undoubtedly he and Bella were cast in the role of evil horde. His hunch confirmed when the fog lowered and in front of him spread their opponents—their numbers stretched to far reaches of the bayou horizon. "They multiplied," he muttered.

"Computer graphics," Bella answered.

Who was on their side? Anyone? The number was not promising. Four characters. Besides Spike and Jasmine, there was a pirate-wench creature in a ragged dress and god-awful rainbow-colored hair, and a languid Merlin, smoking a cigarette, his long gray hair blowing into a tangled web in the chill wind. Adrian, obviously, but who was the wench?

"What's your name, lady?" Daniel asked.

"Katherine." The woman threw Jasmine a defiant stare. "The shrew."

"Damnation," muttered Bella, her eyes fixed on the character. "Maybe you should leave. Now."

"Why?" Katherine asked. "When we're having fun?"

Before Bella could answer, a fiery heat scalded Daniel's back and knocked him forward. He spun around.

Their shadowy challenger had finally shown itself. Not a doddering magician, the towering, two-headed character who'd attacked Daniel bristled with electronic gear, his entire body outlined in wires and fiberoptics. A strange, pearlescent film undulated around his two heads like an external plasma.

Daniel stepped forward. *The real game begins.* "What is your name?"

"Here, I am known as Lodestone." One face of the creature grinned. "But I am known by many other names. Now, give me what I want."

Bingo. Lokus, Daniel decided. He made Spike lay down the root, then stepped in front of it, a clear challenge. Jasmine stood at his side.

Merlin joined them. Tossing his cigarette down in a red arc, he pulled a wand from his back pocket. "You want some help with the minions?"

"Sure, if you're in the mood for a fight," Daniel said. With a little more action, a little more stress, Lokus was bound to reveal more about himself.

"What should I do?" Katherine stepped forward eagerly.

"Nothing," gritted out Jasmine. She grabbed for Katherine's wrist, but jerked her hand back as the character dissolved into yellow sparks that crackled through the hot air. "Ouch!"

Katherine materialized a meter away. "A firewall," she explained, her pink eyes eager. "Did I do it right?"

Jasmine rubbed her palm against her leg. "Effective, I'll give you that."

Katherine put her hands on her hips. "I'll leave when Spike says the fight is over."

"Enough talk. Sides are chosen." Lodestone threw a bolt of energy, and the battle began.

Daniel blocked, feinted and attacked whenever possible. This time, however, he didn't lose himself in the game. He watched his opponent and tried to catch some hint of who lay behind the mask.

Too much of the battle transmitted across the sensors, though, and as the game progressed, the sensations intensified. Daniel used Spike's body and skills, but soon his chest burned from the magic and his arms ached from the struggle. While the combat was only in his mind and eyes, his body responded as if it were real. Both the endorphin high and the grinding fatigue took their toll.

Merlin, Jasmine and Katherine fought alongside him, but Katherine was the only one who seemed to be having a good time, taking it for the game it was. Suddenly, despite the earnest seriousness of their opponents, their grunts and cheers, the whole thing suddenly seemed pointless to Daniel. This wasn't true fear or the stench-of-battle bloodlust. Daniel wasn't truly battling his foes, as he needed to be. No matter how much sensation the game transmitted, in truth, this was playing. Pretending.

He glanced at Jasmine, who jerked her thumb in a "Let's exit," gesture. He agreed. He'd studied his opponents, but Lokus—Lodestone—was too used to hiding behind his alter egos. There was nothing more to be gained.

Unless . . . He shifted close to Jasmine. "Can you use the Black Diamond?"

"See behind the masks? Before the battle's over?" She smiled. "Only a magic-worker can use this gem. And you have to transform it first. Do it. Say 'The power of the white guardian commands true form.'"

Daniel picked up the unassuming-looking root, used it to bonk an attacker in the face, then spoke the incantation. To his surprise, the root began to glow and shift form. Like a snake shedding its skin, a rippling force smoothed the root's rough surface, and the root knotted into a ball. Jolts of electricity rocked across Daniel's chest, knocking out his breath. He tried to open his ice-cold hand, to let go of the gem, but his fingers refused to move.

Katherine bounded over to them. "What are you doing?" she asked, not sounding the least bit breathless.

"Looking behind the masks," he panted.

To his astonishment, the characters began changing. Minute bits and pieces faded or changed. Single strands of black appeared in the blond warrior's hair. The pink in Katherine's eyes began to spread.

A piece of Lodestone's armor fell off. "No!" he shouted, lifting his staff.

Sharp pain jerked across Daniel's throat. He gasped, choking on the mortal wound Lodestone had dealt to his character. Blood flowed down Spike's neck and chest, and his knees weakened, sending him to the ground. Jasmine gathered him in her arms, holding him close as the life force sputtered from him and the sensors faithfully transmitted each spasm, each clutch for air, each agonizing death thrall to Daniel. The Diamond dropped from his hand. Characters snapped back to their original design.

Daniel gritted his teeth. *My God. For a VR, that hurt.* Fantasy and reality blurred in a wash of pain.

Lodestone loomed over him. "I win. Like I always do."

This time, Daniel didn't speak through Spike, but snarled aloud in the basement room, "Not in my world."

"Are you sure?" The two faces of Lodestone contorted into a smile.

Using Spike's dying moments, Daniel laid his hand

back on the Diamond. Characters began transforming again into their human counterparts—a dizzying, macabre metamorphosis. Black spots swelled in front of Daniel's eyes. He clenched his jaw against the sensors' recreation of death. *Hold on long enough to see one feature on Lokus. Just one feature.*

The scene turned into a surreal, hallucinogenic dream of strange colors and swirling faces. Jasmine turned red, and Katherine turned pink. Lokus spun about him in two shades of blue. Merlin became a misty cloud. Daniel felt his heart kick and then falter.

Color leached from Jasmine's face. Or was it Bella's? She leaned closer and shouted, "Leave, Daniel!"

Too real. "Yes. Leave."

Behind her, Katherine vanished in a streak of light.

Daniel tried to lift his hand to remove his visor, but he was too weak. His breathing became labored as the final drops of Spike's life force dripped out. Beside him, Jasmine disappeared in a pop; then he felt Bella rip off his visor.

The disorientation shocked him. His heart raced in a staccato beat as air and life rushed back into his lungs. From somewhere in the dark room—where, he couldn't tell—came a low chuckle and two hissed words:

"I win."

The other players all remained in their virtual reality as Bella flung off hers and Daniel's equipment. She grabbed Daniel's icy hands, rubbing the taut skin, bringing heat back. *He wasn't moving.* Blessed Bohr, was she too late? Had the sensors actually transmitted Spike's death to Daniel? Was that possible? No, he had a pulse. Bracketing his face with her hands she leaned over and kissed him, breathing into him her heat and her life.

His hand curled around the back of her neck, holding

her very securely to him. He was very definitely kissing her back—he pushed slightly against her—and very definitely responding.

She flattened her palms against his chest and shoved back. "You were faking."

"No, I wasn't. I felt like I'd been flattened. And I've got the mother of all headaches blooming." His lips curled up, then. "Although I do confess to waitin' and hopin' you'd read *Sleeping Beauty*."

"Sleeping Tom Cat, you mean." Still, she was relieved to see the glazed look melt from his eyes and his skin lose its waxy hue. She laid a hand on his arm. "Are you okay?"

He shook his head, as if clearing it. "That was too close to the real thing for comfort, but yeah, I'm okay."

They finished packing up, then returned the gear to Adrian, who pulled himself out of the game to ask, "What did you think of the equipment?"

Daniel's voice was cold. "Do not *ever* put it on the market."

"That good?"

"That dangerous."

Their ride home was mostly silent. Bella leaned her head against the headrest, suddenly tired. "We took a risk tonight, and it didn't pay off."

"Mmmm," Daniel acknowledged noncommittally.

She glanced over at him. "You don't seem too glum about the results."

"There were benefits. We have a narrowed list of suspects, and we acquired data, even if we don't recognize yet what it means. Plus"—the quick look he shot her was pure heat—"*you* kissed *me*. I'd say the night ranked higher in the plus column."

For once, Bella wasn't sure what to say, and Daniel didn't seem to expect and answer, so she settled for silence. At her house, Daniel ran his security checks, hesitating only a moment before he bid her good-bye and left.

At once, Fran's Snowy Trails mask dissolved and the A.I.'s face appeared.

"Going into the game was dangerous, Fran." Bella scolded.

"No one knew me," Fran returned cheerfully, "so there is no damage. Having a body was a fascinating experience. Unwieldy, though. I prefer circuitry."

"Just don't do it again, okay? Not until after the Turing Competition."

"Oh, all right."

Bella couldn't stop thinking of the game's last indelible, terrifying images: Daniel's Spike dying in her arms, and Lodestone taking the Dark Diamond and staring at Fran's Katherine.

Lokus manipulated the file images until the faces of Spike and Jasmine melded with those of Daniel and Bella, then uploaded them. Computers. People were so fucking naive about what computers could do. All the information they held, and nobody paid attention to how that could be manipulated. Except the elite: those who knew how to use that power.

The images uploaded into the game—one more level added before the end game began where one must be destroyed and the other controlled.

But the true prize and the true danger? It had shown its face tonight. It was real. The perfect tool. The necessary component to the Cyber Soldiers' next coup. It couldn't be allowed such freedom. It needed to be controlled, used. Like Bella.

If Bella and the prize didn't cooperate? Then, when their usefulness was over, they could be discarded. Like obsolete floppies. Or like the dangerous NSA agent who guarded them.

Chapter Ten

Three days later Daniel limped from his car, one of about half a dozen in the ITC lot. His leg ached this morning, perhaps from the heaviness of the air, which dragged around him, thick with moisture and the threat of winter. Dawn had not yet made an appearance, despite the clock indicating it was well past breakfast time, and the lack of sunshine left him edgy and irritable. No wonder places like Michigan spawned groups like SDS, Michigan Militia and Cyber Soldiers. It was too damn cold to exist outside, so all that human creativity turned inward and fed itself with crazy notions.

The fact that he hadn't seen Bella since he'd left her home after the VR games added to his general irritation. Those twice daily commute conversations were both lifeline and frustration.

Or maybe his frustration wasn't with the cold and the darkness, or with his restless need to see Bella, but with his lack of progress on this case. He'd sent the names of everyone at the VR game to Ben and Stefan, gotten back NSA's files, but organizing the mountain of data was a Herculean task.

If he could have gotten something off Chen's broken disk, he might know what scenario the scientist had been worried about, be able to focus his search. But the lab tech hadn't been able to recover any of the data, and a search of Chen's house and office hadn't yielded a duplicate copy.

He had one more layer of data on Chen's computer to wade through. So far, the records had contained little he didn't already know. Except hints that Chen had expanded his interest in the strategic, and deadly, applications of A.I.-type programs.

A.I. Was that the connection with Lionel? Four years ago, Quintera's research team had started to explore A.I. concepts along with their molecular computers, and their findings were one of the foundations of the current research in the field.

The interviews he'd held of the ITC employees were mostly useless. Nobody was talking about the Cyber Soldiers, except in general, what-they-read-in-the-papers terms. Chen's associates all thought his death was an accident, and the facts about his last days revealed nothing to suggest otherwise. But Daniel had yet to get any information from the person they all agreed had spent the most time with Chen. Lionel Quintera.

It all came back to Bella's father.

"You're creating quite a stir in my institution."

The Orson Welles voice interrupted Daniel's watch on the data stream, but it was the scent of spiced meat that really caught his attention. He looked up to see Milos Three standing in the doorway, a tray in his hand.

The ITC director waved Brianna, today's watchdog, out of the room. "I thought you might be hungry for lunch. I brought two of our local favorites. Hot coffee and a pasty. Food of the miners."

"Thanks." Daniel bit into the flaky-crusted pie. The mix of lamb, potatoes and spices was delicious.

Milos settled into a chair, steepled his forefingers, tapping them together in a steady beat. "Have you found what you're looking for?"

"I can't talk about an ongoing investigation."

"I've contacted our state senator. He's the chair of the Intelligence Oversight Committee, and he agreed with me."

"About what?" Daniel knew the senator, a grand-standing politician with no clue about the realities of a dirty business and no concept of discretion.

"That we've been most cooperative, and that your presence is affecting the work of our scientists. If you wish to continue, the committee wants a briefing regarding what threat this country is facing."

So that was the way it was going to play. In truth, Daniel was surprised it had taken this long. He finished the last bite of pasty. "That won't be necessary." He rose, his leg twinging in protest that he'd been sitting too long. The stream of data finished, again with nothing of interest. Dammit, Chen had known *something*, and Daniel's gut said he didn't have much time left to find out what. Hiding a frustrating sense that said he was missing something, he turned off the laptop. "I've completed all I need from here."

He turned in his badge to Poppy at the front desk, shook Mischiweicz's hand and left. Outside, the wind had picked up. He turned his face upward, drawing in the clear air, surprisingly cheered that he wouldn't be spending another cramped day inside the schizo-phrenic castle. If this land weren't so cold, he might actually like it. No pollutants, just fresh air that cleared out the cobwebs.

The colors of the maze—white on white, with red berries dotting green hedges—caught his eye, and he paused, rubbing his leg as an excuse while an errant thought lodged in his brain. One of those data-backed "hunches." He turned it over. Was it possible? A dupli-cate scenario disk? Hidden? A thrill ran up his spine. It was entirely possible, knowing Chen.

He'd return later, he decided, getting into his car. Alone. When Milos and Poppy the security guard weren't watching and waiting for him to leave. He'd fol-low through on his hunch, then take a side trip to those cabins that had disappeared off the map.

His cell phone vibrated; voice mail had picked up a message while he was inside.

As he pulled out of the parking lot he listened to the call, then he swore and pushed down on the car's accelerator.

Bella turned onto the lakeshore road and gripped the wheel tighter as buffeting gusts set the vehicle swaying. Last storm, the gusts were powerful enough to send a truck skidding sideways across the road.

Gitche Gumee, as the local Indian population called Lake Superior, was unsettled this afternoon. Powerful winds drove its gray-foamed waves several feet on-shore. A snowstorm rose with a swollen belly from the horizon, although the weather people claimed it wouldn't arrive for another twenty-four hours.

She followed the Mapquest directions, unsettled by the agitation of the lake and, perversely, by the other-wise peaceful hours. Was the calm like the eye of a hur-ricane, a harbinger of worse fury to come?

Automatically she swept a glance behind her, search-ing the sparse traffic; then her fingers tightened on the steering wheel as her heart tattooed against her ribs. There it was again. A black UV. Lately, every time she went out, within minutes she noticed a black UV follow-ing her. It was eerie and unsettling because she had noth-ing to substantiate the irrational belief that the driver was lying in wait, tagging her and biding his time to make his move.

The tail never did anything. Never even came close enough for her to see the license or any distinguishing marks. Once, she'd tried pulling into a parking lot and waiting for it to pass her, but the vehicle had turned off on a side road first, as though he'd seen her ploy.

Damnable thing was, she couldn't be sure it was the same vehicle each time. Dark-colored UVs were as plen-tiful as snowplows up here, and she could be fabricating a pattern where none existed.

Still, ever since the morning of the explosion, she'd been plagued by that edgy, knot-between-her-shoulder blades sensation that someone was watching her. No proof, no facts, no face in the crowd she could point to as her stalker. Just unease.

Maybe her jitters were a response to her lack of progress. Despite her efforts, she was no closer to finding who had run her off the road. If it was this Lokus, he'd been lying low. She'd eliminated Milos because he hadn't been at the VR game, but the other five suspects were still viable candidates.

She'd tried to trace Lokus and find a connection to one of her suspects. She'd seen web flashes of him in chat rooms and bulletin boards. His latest posts bragged about helping Homeland Security to thwart a potential bioterrorist, although the details were slim. But he was clever. There was never any personal information, and the traceable IP addresses on his e-mails were all dead ends: fakes or coopts of others.

She had one potential clue left, and that was a pretty farfetched one: the massage parlor that had called her and claimed she had an appointment. She'd left the school early today to visit. She'd tried to call Daniel, but his phone never picked up inside ITC. She'd left a message on his voice mail.

Was he faring any better? True to his word, and his nature, he'd said nothing about his progress during their twice-daily transit talks. From the smattering of rumors she'd heard, no one was exactly sure what he had discovered. Or what he was looking for. The uncertainty was making quite a few people at ITC nervous.

Her phone rang, and she punched it on. "Bella Quintera."

"Bella, Milos Mischiweicz here." The voice came through the phone with characteristic mellifluous grace. "Have you made a decision about our offer?"

"I've been thinking about it, Milos."

"You'll be a great addition to the team. Your skills are wasted at Superior Northern." He sounded as though she'd already decided to accept.

Bella took a deep breath, knowing she shouldn't prolong the process when she'd made her choice. Milos had offered her a position at ITC. A dream position. But this decision was all about instinct, not intellect, for reason told her she was making an insane mistake.

"I have made a decision. Thank you for your generous offer, but I'm saying no."

The silence was so long that she checked the phone screen to make sure they hadn't been cut off.

"Are you sure, my dear? Salary a problem? We can adjust the budget—"

"No, that's not it." She searched for a plausible excuse, found none. "I'm grateful you thought of me, but I have to turn it down."

"I think you're making a mistake."

"Perhaps."

"We'll advertise for the position, but you'll remain our first choice. Contact us if anything happens to change your mind."

"I will. Thank you." She disconnected, surprisingly cheerful for having turned down a million-dollar offer. "How are you coming with those physics texts, Fran?"

"Nearly catalogued. The equations are most elegant, but the concepts of stars and moons are yet hazy."

"You're used to micro, not macro. We'll talk about it later."

"Later, always later," grumbled Fran.

"Still too much daylight, and tonight won't be a good night to show you. Too cloudy."

"I doth endure." Fran began singing, "Be. Not. Flocked. My time hits the end."

It took a few minutes before Bella realized the thudding bass and screeching tune from Fran's speakers was one of the latest Goth-inspired efforts. Fortunately, Fran did not realize the word wasn't "flocked."

The wind quieted when Bella turned off the lakeshore drive. To her relief, the trailing UV didn't follow. She rubbed a hand against her prickling neck; apparently she was seeing danger where none existed.

Humming along with Fran's song, she located the seedier section of Monsoon, then squinted to find street numbers on buildings and businesses that preferred to remain anonymous. Here, the ever-present snow took on a dirty gray tinge, except for the occasional spot of bright yellow—a match for the drabness of the buildings surrounding the garish signs promising *Girls, Girls, Girls.*

The Boy Toy was a cut below even that. Scarlet lettering now faded to barely discernible covered smoke-glazed windows. Spots and stains she'd rather not guess the origin of dotted the building sides. Nerves tightening her stomach, she pulled into the tiny parking lot.

"GOGDOD," she muttered, using one of Fran's favorite expressions. Still, she strapped on Fran's case and got out.

"There are new scent molecules around here," Fran whispered.

Inside, the proprietor of Boy Toy barely looked up from his nudie magazine. "Three o'clock? Doug's waiting. Room One C."

"I believe someone made the appointment without my knowing," Bella began.

"Yeah, sure."

"Did you see me when I made the appointment?"

The man didn't bother to look up. "Anyone who bothers with an *appointment* uses the phone."

"Is this my first time?"

"Don't remember nothing, lady."

"Does this jog your memory?" She slipped a twenty across the desk, trying not to touch the sticky grime.

"Yes."

She waited, then realized he was answering her question about whether it was her first appointment. "Who called in? Male or female?"

"Male."

"Did he sound like he smoked?" she asked, thinking of Adrian's habit.

"Nope."

"Age?"

"Younger than old. You want Doug or not?"

Apparently, that was all the answers a twenty bought. "Not."

"Still gotta pay."

She started to protest, until he looked up, staring at her with flat, hard brown eyes. A snake tattoo circled his eye, drawn so it looked like the fangs poised over the eyeball. "Or I can fuck you for free."

Hastily she slid another bill across the counter, then beat a quick retreat. Outside, feeling dirty, she strode to her car, ignoring the catcalls from the pair of teenaged loiterers two doors down. She clicked the remote unlock button on her keychain, then frowned when the interior lights didn't come on and on the doors didn't unlatch. She clicked again with the same results. An electronics glitch? A steady *tap-tap* carried across the empty sidewalk: boot plates rapping against the concrete. The back of her neck tightened in alert, and Bella glanced over her shoulder. The two punks had pushed off from the brick wall and were strutting toward her. Heartbeat speeding, she picked up her pace.

The *tap-tap* accelerated. Key ready, Bella sprinted the final yards to her car. Boots pounded behind her, an echo of the blood racing across her eardrums. She jabbed the key in the lock.

Her key scratched across the surface with a nails-on-blackboard scrape. She jabbed again, couldn't get it to insert, then swore, her spine tightening with fear. A coating of ice covered the lock and dripped down the side of her car.

Someone had poured water over the lock, frozen it solid.

She glanced back. The punks were almost on top of her. Maybe only one door had been tampered with. Aiming to circle to the passenger side, she darted toward the hood. Laughing, the punks separated, circled the car, snared her between them, the hood and the next building over. She gripped one hand around Fran's strap, then slid her keys between her fingers on the other hand, forming a makeshift brass knuckle.

Her gaze shifting between them, she waited for one to make a move. Waited for an opening. She'd only get one chance.

"Got a message for you, Bella," drawled the punk on from the driver's side.

Startled at hearing her name, Bella fixed her attention on the speaker for a moment too long. The other, coming up behind her, grabbed her arm and twisted her around. She lashed out with her keyed fist, then with her boot, missing his kneecap, but she must have caught another part of him with the momentum. He bent over, gasping obscenities, and his grip loosened. She ducked past him, spun to the passenger side, then jammed the key into the lock.

Blessed saints, it worked. A second later, she pulled the door open, tumbled inside, and then slammed it shut. Just as the first punk leapt across the hood, she hit the lock. He pounded a fist against the window; the safety glass rattled but held.

The punk quieted and pressed his face against the windshield, forming a flattened, grotesque, grinning mask. "Got a message from a fella named Daniel. Stop probing. Curiosity killed the cat, you know." He tucked an envelope beneath her windshield wiper.

"Someone's coming," warned his partner.

The hood-ornament punk stuck out his tongue and licked upward, leaving a long smear in front of Bella's face; then he hopped off her car and the two boys raced off, disappearing into the warren of sleaze.

Bella slowly let out a pent-up breath and slid across the seat behind the wheel. She tried to fit her key into the ignition, but her hand shook too badly. Instead, she gripped both hands on the steering wheel, her fingers curling so tight they cramped, and stared straight ahead at bricks and snowflakes. Who had known she was coming here? *How* had they known? No cars had followed her all the way. Another attack without a single witness. She drew in more air, willing her nerves to stop their wild tingling. Only then, after a careful glance around, did she get out to retrieve the envelope on her windshield.

A familiar KZ 920 pulled into the lot next to her. Daniel exploded from car. "People who look a lot less affluent than you get mugged or worse in places like this," he spat, drawing up beside her.

"Tell me about it."

"You—" He stopped abruptly, perhaps noticing her white face or her still-trembling fingers. He closed the small gap between them, then touched her cheek as his voice softened. "What happened, Bella?"

She gave him the bare-bones summary, then showed him the envelope. Together they opened it. Her stomach gave a tiny fillip. Inside was a single puzzle piece. From "The Next Surprise."

"He's just trying to scare you, Bella," Daniel soothed.

"He's succeeding. I know you didn't send that message the punks gave me," she added, proud that she kept the trembling from her voice. "And if you stop yelling, I'll even add that I'm glad to see you."

He ran his hands down her arms, warming them both. "You are?"

"Of course. To be honest, I feel like I've got snow snakes in my stomach."

"There is such a thing?"

"Snow snakes?" She smiled, feeling better for just seeing him, for this steadying bit of banter. "Sure. We catch them when we go snipe hunting."

He gripped the car top. "What were you thinking? Coming here alone?"

"Don't lecture me." Still, his concern softened her irritation and eased her fear. "I do have some self-defense skill, and this was my last lead. They didn't hurt me."

"Was what you learned worth the risk?"

She started to tell him, then broke off. She couldn't say her Lokus suspects were down to four, since the proprietor had just eliminated Margo. Daniel would ask how she had targeted them, and she couldn't tell him about Fran and the Turing Competition.

Keeping secrets was a pain.

"I learned Lokus is a younger-than-old male. Big surprise there, since he's a hacker."

"So you've made as much progress as I have?"

"If you've come this far." She held her thumb and forefinger an inch apart.

"More like this." His hand wrapped around hers, closing the gap between her fingers a quarter inch. Then, his thumb began to stroke up and down her thumb, a small sexual gesture that lit embers on her nerve endings. "Maybe we'd do better together."

"Maybe." If only she could talk to him about Fran. Or if only she had any illusion that the flow of information wouldn't all be in one direction.

Daniel must have seen the moment she withdrew, for he let go of her and shoved his hands in his pockets and glanced around. "You ready to leave? I don't want to spend another second of my time with you smelling like stale perfume and garbage."

"What do you want to do?"

He speared her with a glance made of pure, black fire. "You want an honest answer?"

She nodded, her throat suddenly too tight for speech.

"What I *want* to do is take you home and peel off those layers of clothes you're wearing and lose myself in your heat and smile and honesty." His voice was flat and matter-of-fact, which made his raw words all the more carnal. "What I *have* to do, before it gets dark, is something quite different."

"What?" she managed.

"Do you know the way through the maze at ITC?" he asked abruptly.

It took a moment for her brain to process his words. "Like I know the way through my bedroom. You want to walk it?"

"Yes. Will you go with me?"

"Now? Sure." She asked no further questions.

Using their separate cars, they made quick time back to ITC, then crossed the lawn. No one stopped them, or seemed unduly interested in their plans. Soon, they stood at the mouth of the holly bush maze.

"Is there a pattern?" he asked.

"No. I've just done it so many times, I've got the route memorized. Let's go."

They stepped into the maze. The holly rose to twice their height, blocking any view of the outside. Dark green, prickly leaves formed an impenetrable barrier if anyone had an inclination to shortcut to another path. The walls had one saving grace. They protected against the arctic wind.

Bella walked beside Daniel in silence, their footsteps muffled by wet flakes of falling snow. Judging from the pristine path, no one had passed through since the last snowfall. Though her curiosity prodded, she knew better than to ask about his urgent need to stroll the maze. He might have second thoughts about having her go with him.

On a summer day, she might have lingered. Instead, she led him efficiently to the center. The thickening snow blotted out any remaining sunshine, while the wet flakes soaked through her scarf and hat, carrying penetrating cold.

There wasn't much to see at the center. A couple of benches. A wooden horse that would need to be repainted and repaired come spring. Bushes losing their pruned precision. Daniel prowled the perimeter, searching each cubbyhole and cranny he found. Bella stomped her feet, trying to keep warm, uneasy shivers joining those spawned by cold.

Curiosity, and impatience, finally won out. "What are you looking for?"

Bella's question drew him up. Daniel fisted his cold hands into his coat, glancing around at the darkening day and the odd shadows. If anyone came after them here, there was no place to escape. One of Bella's snow snakes crawled through his chest. They needed to finish fast.

"A computer disk. From Chen. If he made a copy and hid it, if the box came from him, maybe the puzzle was a hint. He was fond of layers, of convoluted schemes. It's a long shot, but . . ."

Bella caught his thinking. " 'The Next Surprise.' Jigsaw, maze, optical illusion."

"So where's the optical illusion?"

They slowly pivoted, each searching for something deceptive to the eye. "These bushes used to be sculptures," she suggested. "Plant to animal? A bear, a trout, a weasel—"

"Weasel? Which one?" he interrupted, gripped by that clutch of recognition.

"That one."

Swiftly they set to examining the topiary bush weasel. The holly leaves jabbed through their gloves, but neither one stopped. Weasels became ermines in winter, turning white and hiding in plain sight. An optical illusion.

"I feel something." Excitement laced Bella's call. "It's too far to grip. You try."

Daniel knelt and reached into the hole formed where one branch had been hacked away. Snow soaked through his pantlegs, but he ignored the discomfort. His fingers reached deeper. *There!* He felt it. A ledge formed by a bent root. And on it . . . something hard. He tugged it out, barely able to see in the disappearing light. But he saw enough.

Chen's disk. Finally, something had fallen right. Biting back a satisfied smile, he pocketed the disk. "Let's get out of here."

"What's so important about that disk?" Bella asked as they retraced their steps through the maze.

His desire to tell her everything surprised him. He shouldn't; his job parameters were clear and immutable. Share the minimum. Keep to a need-to-know-basis. Loose lips sink ships. He'd lived by those principles for a long time, and they'd saved his butt—and those of his team—more than once.

He might learn more if he shared what he knew about Chen's work, what he hoped to find out on the disk. Bella was smart; she'd proved to have useful knowledge. *Hell, admit the real reason. For once, you'd like not to see disappointment in her eyes when she looks at you.* Pitiful, yeah, but there it was.

Except, his secrets weren't about him. They were about national security, and, if he were wrong, if he opened his mouth just to get that delighted smile from her, to feel again the pleasure of working with her, then he wasn't living up to his pledge. He'd sworn to protect his country and its citizens. If the wrong people got his information, then those citizens would be sleeping less safe.

Then again, if he didn't untangle this wolf spider web around them, he was failing his duty. If Bella had knowledge that would help—

Rationalizing, Champlain? In the end, he said to Bella, "The disk will be encrypted. I'll have to work through that before I know what questions to ask."

They reached the exit and emerged from the shadowy maze into twilight. He glanced down at her, expecting her to turn away again. To his surprise, she didn't.

Instead, a faint smile touched both her lips and her eyes. "At least you thought about it this time," she murmured.

Tonight, their cell-phone conversations weren't going to be enough. Tonight, he didn't want to watch her drive away from him. "Have you eaten? Would you like to have dinner with me?"

"I have some whitefish in the freezer that won't take long to defrost."

"Let's have dinner at my hotel instead." Some odd sense urged him to keep her close at his side, far from ITC tentacles. "I'm booked at the Copper Lodge."

She gave an admiring whistle. "Last business trip I took for Snow-U, I stayed at the Motel Eight."

"I don't expense it." Annoyed, he strode across the snowy lot.

Bella easily kept pace, her hand resting protectively against the computer case strapped across her shoulder. She didn't say more, too polite to provide the razzing he got from his coworkers about his taste for finer accommodations. He had no trouble turning aside their blunt, crass questions. Which made his itch to explain to Bella all the more frustrating.

The lot was almost empty of cars, and the ITC castle had taken on a deserted air. No one had seen them in the maze, so far as he could tell. He jiggled the puzzle piece in his pocket, suddenly reminded that he'd had a second objective for this trip.

"Can we delay dinner an hour?" he reluctantly asked. "I have something I need to check out."

"Can I help?"

The instinctive response to say no died on his lips. He didn't think there was any danger; the missing buildings from the early map had probably been torn down. Still, he had to check out the anomaly. "Maybe."

He headed toward the thick woods that lined the upper shoreline of ITC, Bella following alongside. "Do you remember any buildings in here?" he asked. "They were on an old map, but according to the new one in the lobby, they've disappeared."

Bella pursed her lips, trying to remember. "There were some dilapidated cabins. An old mining camp, I think. I went there once as a kid. Never went again."

"Why not?"

"I dunno. Gave me the shivers. At the time, I thought it was haunted." She wrinkled her nose. "I had too much imagination."

The snow thickened around them as they walked, blotting out the eccentricities of the ITC grounds, but as they entered the dense woods, the snow thinned, denied by the barrier of evergreens. All that remained was clear silence and air as still as death.

Bella edged closer to Daniel, her vivid childhood imaginings returning. He rested a hand on her shoulder, urging her next to his solid body. This close, she felt the slight hitch in his step from his injured leg, and her heart ached at the reminder: He willingly put his life on the line to protect others. Her free hand gripped the edge of Fran's case. If only she believed that he, his agency, would allow Fran those same human freedoms they protected with so much dedication.

At least the lesser snow beneath the trees made walking easier. As they wove between the trunks, using Bella's childhood memories and his own recall of the map, Daniel asked, "What have you done about the dirty tricks?"

"I started in the Credit Records Bureau and got most of my credit reports straightened out. But beyond the porn chats and BoyToy, there was also criminal activity manufactured."

Daniel must have seen the faint trembling of her hands, for he took one and threaded their fingers together. "Any names?"

"Not yet. I haven't trailed back to the source computer. I did tag the FBI file he'd inserted. If he tries to activate it, I'll have him."

"You hacked into the FBI?"

"Public records. The top secret stuff is too heavily encrypted." She stomped a clump of snow off her boots. "Are you surprised that I did it? Or that I *could* do it?"

"Let's see. You grew up with one of the most advanced computer specialists of the century. Your first toys were a stuffed bear and a functional keyboard. Your record is peppered with youthful indiscretions—speeding, pranks, runs to Canada for the better-flavor beers. Not to mention that high school prank, androids replacing your math teachers. Later, the usual liberal-biased protests. In contrast, the last few months you've been a model of propriety. So, neither," he concluded. "You could and would hack in."

"You gonna turn me in?"

"Did you alter any records?"

"Nope, just blocked the dormant lies about me."

"Fibs should be more diligent about their security."

"Fibs?" She lifted her brows. "Do I detect a hint of interdepartmental snobbery?"

"More than a hint." His fingers tightened. "Have you hacked NSA computers?"

"Wouldn't tell you if I had." His agency was more fanatic and experienced at codes; she hadn't a prayer of getting in there. She had tried.

"Think I'll prod Ben and Stefan into some computer reconnaissance before our next assignment."

She laughed and changed the subject. "So . . . do you have a name?"

"Not yet."

They emerged from the woods to find the edge of the mining camp. Bella stopped and stared, a frisson slithering down her spine. Beside her, she felt Daniel stiffen. His instincts had been right on.

This was no dilapidated relic, but a small compound separate from the main ITC campus. Isolated but in excellent repair. An air of menace clung to the trio of small buildings. Thin lines of electronic sensors wove through the tinted windows, making them look like bloodshot eyes that saw out into the world but revealed none of their own wary secrets.

All fallen snow disappeared a foot from the foundation. The buildings were kept heated. Falling snowflakes eddied between them, uncut by a single ray of light or sign of human habitation. Bare windows, barren porches and first-rate security.

Daniel caught Bella's shoulder before she left the trees. "There are motion sensors on the doors and windows. Do you have any idea what this area is used for?"

She shook her head. "Not a clue."

The crackle of a dry leaf beneath a boot startled her. Damn, they must have triggered a sensor and alerted someone. She spun around, her reaction a fraction of a second behind Daniel, who already had his SIG in hand.

Poppy Chambers, the Goth security guard, and Georg Hirsch stepped out, one on either side of them.

Bella sucked in a breath. Even someone clueless about weapons—and up here in God's Hunting Country no

one, not even someone who wasn't packing, was clueless about weapons—would realize those weren't run-
of-the-mill revolvers they were holding. Those weapons
were high-tech, compact and lethal.

"This area's off limits," said Poppy, unsmiling.

"Sorry," Bella gushed, covering as Daniel pocketed
his gun. "I wanted to show Daniel the shore. The colors
here are nearly as pretty as at Painted Rock."

"It's dark," Hirsch pointed out.

"We got delayed," drawled Daniel, his Charleston
roots coming through his voice. He rested a hand across
Bella's shoulder, his gloved thumb tracing a line down
her throat. Despite the thickness of the leather, the
tenseness surrounding them, her heart skipped.

Daniel shifted again, drawing her attention with a
bump of his hip. The edge of the data CD poked from
his pocket. Had the others noticed? She leaned into him,
using her now hidden hand to push the disk deeper, and
pointedly eyed Georg and Poppy's weapons. "Well, if
it's restricted you should post signs better. Can we go?"

"We're getting cold," Daniel added. "We need to
warm up." His drawled words were definitely sugges-
tive this time, bringing a flush to Bella's cheeks, despite
knowing it was all—or mostly—an act.

After a hesitation, Poppy and Georg pocketed their
weapons, then Georg jerked his head. "Go ahead. Leave."

Bella and Daniel did just that.

Chapter Eleven

The Copper Lodge, recently restored, was a nineteenth-
century lady. Built when copper made millionaires of a
select few East Coasters, it now provided an Up North
summer and ski haven for the money farther south. True

to its growing reputation, the restaurant was full, with an hour wait.

"We could grab a snack at the deli," offered Bella.

"We could order room service." Although any food shared with Bella would be a treat, a hurried meal quickly eaten and over with wasn't what he wanted tonight.

She hesitated, then nodded. "Just a meal. No . . . dessert."

"Just a meal." He detoured to the concierge and ordered, adding a hefty tip for expedited service.

"I've always thought this place looked like the magical forest of Oberon," Bella observed as they crossed the lobby to the elevators.

He glanced around. To him, the Copper Lodge meant good food, impeccable service and welcome touches of elegance and comfort. "Magical?"

"The trees. Not just wood beams. These are actual trees. Can't you smell the freshness? Those pricks of light. Carpet as thick as grass. It's a forest bower fit for the King of Faerie. When I was a little girl, we'd drive up from Ann Arbor to spend Christmas, and my father would treat me to dinner here. All decked out for the holidays, I thought this atrium was the most beautiful spot on earth."

They got in the elevator and the door closed, cutting off the view as they sped upward. For those last seconds, however, as the lights were shielded and only shadows and fairy beams lit the lobby, he thought he saw what she did.

Shoving his gloves and hat into his pockets, he learned one shoulder against the elevator wall. "Why doesn't your father live with you? That was your family home."

"Summer and holiday home, except a couple of years while I was in high school," she corrected, then lifted one shoulder. "The house was a legacy from Mom's family, and she willed it to me. Dad's welcome there, he knows that. He chooses to live on the ITC campus. I think the house holds too many memories for him."

Her mother had died after a long bout with cancer, he remembered, less than a year before the scandal broke. Lionel Quintera had been devoted to her and her care, and had been devastated by the loss.

Bella looked at him squarely, and her words showed they'd been thinking along the same lines. "He once said the only good thing about her death was that she hadn't had to live through the humiliation of the past four years."

The elevator gave a soft chime and came to a halt. There were only a few suites on the floor, and Daniel led her the short distance to his door. "At the time, some people thought his grief unsettled him. That he snapped when the research hit a snag," Daniel said.

"The charitable people, you mean? Those willing to find excuses for what happened? They still believed he did it."

Daniel snorted. "Lionel Quintera?"

"You reported him. This is the second time you hinted you don't think he did it."

The door swung open. With a hand on the small of her back, he ushered her into his room. Even through the thickness of her coat, his hand heated with her warmth. Her fresh scent tantalized him as the door clicked shut behind them. After the conversational hum of the lobby and the muted Muzak of the elevator and hall, the silence of his room wrapped them in isolation.

"I reported the falsified data," he corrected when they were inside and had set their computers on a table. "I have no regrets about that. Your father was responsible." Reluctantly he released her waist to take her coat.

While he hung it up, Bella's face hardened. "Let's not talk about this."

He ignored her interruption. "Because he was project

leader, he was responsible. Did he actually do the falsification, or know about or approve it?" He hung up his own coat, then decided she deserved the truth. "In my experience, you don't survive long by believing someone is incapable of any act, no matter how unlikely it seems. He could have done it. My gut? I don't know. I'm not as convinced as everyone else."

"The fact is, only Dad and I had that data." She gave a harsh laugh. "The deeper underground whisper was that he took the fall for me."

"The 'known fact,' you mean." He held up a hand. "Right now, though, I've promised you dinner and that's all I want. No information."

Her eyes were troubled. "What about the aftermath, Daniel? The reporters? The news feeding frenzy? Were those also part of your duty?"

"No."

"Why did you tell them?"

"I didn't," he answered softly.

"You dislike the press, avoid them at all—" Her eyes widened as his words registered. She looked down, shaking her head. "I've been blind. You held that press conference *after* the story leaked."

"My superiors ordered damage control."

"How could I not realize?" She raked a hand through her hair. "You're the *last* person who'd leak something to the press. Why didn't you say so?"

"You weren't listening then."

"Or even recently." Her eyes closed, then opened. "I'm sorry."

He inclined his head, acknowledging her apology. The fact was, though, clearing some of the murk of the past did nothing to eliminate other obstacles between them: her need for openness, his devotion to his work. And if Lionel was thick with the Cyber Soldiers, Daniel could be responsible for a second fall from grace.

Mutual desire, a love of knowledge, a bone-deep sense that at some core level the two of them meshed—was that enough to overcome what held them apart? They were like two chips on a motherboard. Both were important to keep it functioning, but get them too close and the generated heat could destroy them.

"You had reason enough." He set down his laptop, automatically turning it on in case he'd received any urgent mail, then gestured toward the brocade sofa in the suite's sitting area. "Have a seat. Would you like something to drink?"

"White wine." She took a moment to look around her, then gave another low whistle. "Wow, this is impressive. I've always wondered what these suites look like."

"Now you know." Deftly he uncorked a Chardonnay from the suite bar. His heart pounded against his ribs, as if he were standing on a mountain, seeking oxygen in the thin air. She was here, in *his* rooms. Always before, they'd been on her turf.

A sudden desire to take her south, down to his retreat in the Florida Keys, grabbed him. Hard. Hot. He wanted to make love to her on his linen sheets, cooled only by the gulf breezes and the circling ceiling fan. Then they'd walk to the ocean and swim, maybe make love again on the pier beside his moored boat. Or *in* the boat. He'd cook for her—sauteed fresh grouper, orange salad, key lime pie.

"Do you scuba?" he asked, handing her the wine.

She lifted her brows at the question. "No. I always thought it would be fun to try, but I've never spent enough time in warm water to get certified."

"People dive in Lake Superior."

Her amusement washed across him. "Yeah, in bulky dry suits and rotten visibility. No, when I learn to dive, it will be someplace I can wear a bikini."

The maid service must have turned up the heat;

sweat broke on Daniel's neck and brow. Impatiently he poured himself a club soda, then strode over to the windows. The suite suddenly felt too intimate, too dangerous with just the two of them. His self-control wasn't that good. Not with her. He shoved open the curtains, hoping the sight of snow would leach away the heat. It didn't.

She sipped her wine. "This is good. Have you tried it before?"

Taking a deep breath, he turned back to her. "The maître d' recommended it."

"You know, I've never seen you drink even a sip of wine."

"I don't drink. I won't risk being impaired."

"Job or history?"

"Both."

"You don't drink the fine wines. You don't notice the magic in a place like this. NSA isn't footing the bill. Why *do* you stay here, Daniel?"

"I appreciate the comfort."

"And?"

He lifted one shoulder. "Your home was a legacy from your mother; this is the legacy from mine."

"I know there's a story behind that comment. Is it one you want to share?"

"Not particularly. Not now."

"Well, that gives me hope for later."

A knock at the door interrupted his answer. Their dinner. The waiter set out the array of dishes, accepted a tip, then left.

"Mmm, what's all this?" Bella leaned over and sniffed.

"I wasn't sure what you'd be in the mood for, so I got the Mediterranean appetizer buffet." He pointed to the dark spread. "Try the *brandade de morue*. It's a Provençal dish, and one of the best variations I've tasted. I had it last night."

"What is it? In English." She spread a little on a toast point and tasted. "Whatever it is, it's good."

"Salt cod mousse."

Toast halfway to her mouth for another bite, she paused, then burst out laughing. "You deliberately waited until I took a bite!"

"Some people are put off by the cod part."

"Not me." She took another bite, then filled her plate.

He followed suit, then sat on the sofa, one ankle propped against his knee. Bella paused to take off her boots. To his relief and disappointment, she sat opposite, not beside, him, curled her feet beneath her and started on her meal.

"Well, you may not appreciate your legacy," she said, popping a spiced olive in her mouth, "but I do."

Her unconcealed curiosity hummed through him, but he didn't answer it. He still felt his mother's frail hand in his. The unfettered hurt in her eyes still haunted him, the sense that as she reached her end, her whole life, her sacrifices, meant nothing. He took a swallow of his soda, regretting for a moment it wasn't hundred-year-old Scotch, then set it down and turned his attention to his meal. The past wasn't gone, but some of the ghosts were laid to rest tonight. What mattered was now.

They ended the meal with baked figs and coffee. Daniel rolled the cart outside, then joined Bella on the sofa. She was here. Sitting on the sofa, one foot curled beneath her, here. That fact gut-punched him again, and suddenly the heat was back on. Conversation, so easy just a few minutes before, faltered. She was close, and he didn't want to lose her again. Not just yet.

She glanced at the window. "It's snowing. I'd better be going."

But she didn't move.

That potent silence fell again, the one that gave him too much chance to feel. He cupped her jaw in his palm, his thumb running along the soft skin on her neck. He felt her pulse leap to match his. "You don't have to go. It's snowing. Spend the night. You can have the bed. I'll take the sofa." *And wasn't that a damnable, if gallant, lie?*

She called him on it. "If I stayed, it wouldn't be because I was afraid of driving in the snow."

"I want you," he admitted with stark honesty. "For four years, I've never stopped wanting you. Separation, all the reasons we're wrong together, telling myself I'm ten kinds of a fool—none of it makes a damn bit of difference. When I touch your smooth cheek or smell your perfume and think I'm standing in the middle of God's green forest, all I can think about is sleeping beside you, being inside you again."

Her eyes fluttered shut, a faint blush staining her cheeks. "You drawl more when you're trying to charm me," she accused. "Southern gentleman, sweet-talking Rhett Butler."

"Can't take the South out of the boy." He feathered a touch along her lips. "Does it work?"

"Oh, yes." With a quiet sigh, she tilted her head back, allowing him access to her vulnerable throat. "I want you, too. I always have."

Resisting no longer, he took the invitation. He trailed gentle, suckling kisses along her throat pulse and the curve of her jaw. She clutched his shoulders, forefingers kneading his nape. Desire spun down his spine, landing straight in his groin. He was instantly hard.

His hands cupped her head, still kissing her neck, tasting that sweet skin as he tilted her back, pressing curve to muscle. He gave her no time to think, no reason to move except beneath him.

Heat wafted from her skin as he settled atop her, enveloping him in her fresh, clean perfume. She spread her legs, gathering him close, gripping him to her. Their lips matched, their tongues met with the taste of sweet figs. *Stroke her side, lift her sweater.* She still had on too damn many layers, but at least he could palm her nipple and the curve of her breast. Her hands delved beneath his clothes to the bare skin of his back, his butt, down the front of his pants.

Hot, demanding need roared through him. Gentleness was stripped away beneath that primitive blaze. Their kiss deepened. His hands capturing hers above her head, he pressed her onto the sofa. He didn't bother to ask if she wanted him to continue, didn't bother with a PC way out for her; her tight-nubbed breasts rubbing against him shouted her answer. Hell, this was Bella. If she wanted him to stop, she'd have no trouble telling him.

Get some of these clothes off. He needed her bare and wanting. Himself bare and hard. He'd gotten her pants button undone when something out of the norm, some noise, broke through the narcotic haze of sex.

He stiffened, lifted, alert, searching first the door, then the window. What had he heard? From the corner of his eye, he saw a small flash of pink light in the corner of his computer monitor. Was that what he'd heard? Nothing more dangerous than a diagnostic kicking in? The screen flickered, as though it had dissolved into a screen-saver pattern for a millisecond before returning to his beach wallpaper.

Nothing.

He turned back to Bella, ready to resume their drugging kisses. *Ah, damn.*

She swallowed hard, her gaze darting from his computer back to him.

Ah, damn, she'd had time to think. Her hands no longer clutched him in passion but pushed him back. He closed his eyes, drawing in a frustrated, ragged breath, unable to move away from the touch of her. He leaned down, aiming to convince her otherwise.

"No, Daniel," she said.

No mistaking that message. Still, he tried another gentle kiss. "You're sure?"

Her gaze swung again between the computer and him. "I have to go."

"Can't I change your mind, darlin'?" he drawled, moving his hips against her, letting her feel his erection.

A spasm of pain crossed her face, and she seemed to be having as much trouble breathing as he did. Slowly, painfully, her hands released him, doing nothing further to relieve his biting need for her.

"I . . . I have a class in the morning. It's late. It's snowing."

"I get the message." He took in one more breath, then gave her a swift kiss on the temple before pushing off her. Every part of him ached as though he'd run a marathon—and fallen down ten feet before the finish line.

Not looking at him, she shoved upright and stood. "I'm sorry. I'm not a tease. I . . . Thank you for dinner."

Well, he had promised her a meal and nothing else. Teach him to make a damnable promise. He retrieved her coat, and held it out for her. When she put it on, he shoved his arms through the sleeves of his own coat.

"Where are you going?"

"To walk you to your car."

"You don't have to do that."

"Yes, I do. My mama taught me to always see a lady home."

"One of those 'It's not for you, it's for me' things? Like the cell-phone calls?"

"Yes—ma'am," he tacked on, deliberately lightening the mood.

She smiled then, slung her computer over her shoulder. "You're devious, Daniel Champlain."

The night was colder still, and there was more snow coming down. It damped his hormones and chilled his unprotected neck, a shiver racing down his spine. There was not enough snow to give her any trouble driving, but the dark night became an ominous pall.

The interior lights of her car came on as she clicked off the locks. Automatically Daniel looked inside, checking the backseat and rear cargo space for unpleasant surprises, checking for any signs of damage or tampering.

"Is everything safe?" she asked.

"As far as I can tell." Apparently, he hadn't been subtle about his caution.

She paused at the door. "Did you know I was almost kidnapped when I was ten?"

God, no! "Almost? You weren't hurt?"

"I didn't even know about the threat until years later. It came right after Dad won the Nobel." She got inside her car, started it, then rolled down the window. "The police found the nut, but afterward, my parents enrolled me in self-defense classes."

Daniel leaned over, resting his arms above the open window. "Is that why you're telling me this, to let me know you can take of yourself?"

"Partly. I excelled at those classes—I discovered I liked the physical challenges."

"Judo in the gym isn't the same as defending yourself on the street," he warned.

"I know that. I've had occasion to use the training since. And, no, I wasn't hurt then, either," she added quickly. "Just scared off a couple of muggers. But that's not the only reason I told you."

"What was the other?"

"To show you that's it's not so hard to share a small piece of yourself."

They stared at each other a moment; then he leaned in and gave her a swift kiss. "Next time we're in the car together, I'll tell you about my mother's legacy. Drive carefully, Bella."

He watched as she exited the lot, then got in his own car and followed her, making sure she got home safely. Only then did he return to the solitary luxury of his hotel.

The snow thickened on the drive to the hotel. Fat, wet

flakes stuck to the windshield, rapidly filling the space cleared by his wipers. Visibility narrowed to mere feet in front of his car grill. His car's yellow headlight beams glowed back at him, repelled by the impenetrable storm.

Intermittent gusts off the lake whistled through his cracked-open windows, like a tuneless ghost. Only the mounds of plowed snow to his left and the drop down to the lake on his right marked the vanishing road. He shifted to the left, driving down the center until a car passing from the other direction forced him back toward the edge. Glancing in his rearview mirror to make sure the other car kept going, he rubbed the ache in his leg.

Without warning, light exploded in front of him, a blinding magnesium flare. Instinctively he jammed the brakes and twisted the car away from the source. Another flare burst beneath him, destroying his peripheral vision. His car fishtailed, skidding sideways. Toward the deadly lake.

Someone had iced the road! Blinded, he fought his heavy vehicle. Its tires scraped the edge of the road. To his right, he saw nothing but a vast emptiness.

Dammit, he was not going to be another Chen-like statistic.

Foot off the brake, steer out of the spin.

The snow saved him. Not the sleet of a couple of days ago, it was coming down heavy and thick, coating the treacherous ice. The inches accumulated at the edge grabbed at his car tires, slowed the screaming skid, gave him an instant of traction. He spun the wheel, spun the car, ground to a halt in the center of the road.

He shoved off the interior lights, drew his pistol and then slid out the driver's side, away from the woods. If anyone had stayed to watch, that was where his attacker would be hiding.

Shrouds of snowflakes erased all vision and sound. Neither his breath nor his footfalls echoed further than an inch. At least that meant his adversary was equally blind.

Snow fell beneath his collar, coated his hair, froze the tips of his ears. He hadn't had time to grab his hat. Wiping a hand futilely across his face, he peered into the gloom. At least he'd left his gloves on. Except, his finger didn't fit in the trigger. Impatiently he pulled off the glove, reset his grip and then wrapped his gloved hand around the other, trying to keep his fingers warm.

It was impossible to be stealthy when you had to plow through accumulating drifts. He gave up trying to hide, counting on the weather to shield him, and his reflexes to protect him if it didn't.

He came to the spot where the flares had exploded and crouched down. They'd been ordinary flares, but would have been as deadly as an AK-47 if his gas line had caught fire, or his panicky reaction had sent him over the bluff. No wires, so the flares must have been set off by remote. In weather like this, the trigger would have to be close. How had the sparker gotten here?

He edged to the far side of the road, a dull throb in his leg as he broke through the snow. The cold made each motion a more painful effort. What had he seen on the topo maps of this area? A logging trail, just over there.

A dull growl penetrated the muffled night: a car starting.

Ignoring the pain in his leg, Daniel raced to the logging road, skidding to a halt as he emerged from the trees. A black UV, license plate covered with snow, did a 180, aiming to leave. Daniel planted his feet, took aim and squeezed the trigger. Had he compensated enough for the snow?

He had. Rubber exploded from the car's right rear tire, and the vehicle did a satisfying spin before it ground to a halt. Daniel took out the left tire, then ducked behind the trees on the edge of the road, as the interior lights flashed on and the driver sidled out, sticking close to the car.

He wore black, his face shielded by ski goggles and a pulled-down cap. It was the same description Bella had given of the driver who'd stalked her.

"You've got some serious payback coming," Daniel muttered, shifting through the trees.

The driver must have seen the movement, for he swung around and aimed his own weapon, its beam slicing cleanly through an overhead tree limb. Daniel swore, jumping clear. A laser. Where had this guy gotten a weapon like that? The answer came swiftly: ITC. Someone there had won accolades—and beaucoup patent-right dollars for ITC—for a revolutionary laser scalpel. Apparently, the design had been modified.

Calm, assessing, Daniel kept one eye on his adversary as he moved through the trees. The driver let off more wild shots, bobbing and weaving his way around the car in parallel to Daniel's movements. His adversary's training hadn't come from real life, Daniel realized. He moved like someone who'd learned to shoot in video games and paintball. It was a damn sight harder to aim accurately when the bullets your opponent shot were real.

Coolly Daniel moved into position to pop the remaining two tires, then aimed at the driver's leg. His shot went wide when his target dove behind the protection of his car. Daniel sped forward, circling the UV, determined to end this, to find out who hid behind such powerful technology.

The UV door swung out when Daniel least expected it, smashing into his injured leg, knocking his gun from his frozen fingers. He staggered back, grunting with pain, nearly dropping to his knees. Blinded by snow and agony, he lurched forward, swinging the door back toward the other driver, taking the man by surprise as he swung around the barrier.

Daniel jabbed forward with the heel of his hand and caught the man's wrist, disarming him. The laser went flying into the night. He grabbed the man's elbow, intending to bring this to an end, to bring him down.

Then the man lashed out with a savage kick, right on Daniel's reopened wound.

Daniel's nerves fired out of control, flooding him with pain, disconnecting his control over the limb. Cursing, he dropped to the snow.

The man took off at a run, and moments later Daniel heard his own car take off down the highway, leaving him in the middle of a snowstorm with a bloody leg and a UV with four blown tires.

Chapter Twelve

Daniel drove the crippled UV back to his hotel. He reported the incident to the police, who impounded the car and traced the license plate. The vehicle belonged to Ewan McKinley, who of course had reported it stolen from the Snow-U campus two weeks ago. Daniel's own car was found abandoned on the road halfway between Bella's home and ITC. All tracks had been covered by the snow.

Back in his suite, he breathed deep, inhaling the lingering scent of Bella, imagining that the room still felt warm. For once, the luxury meant nothing when it was experienced alone. He picked up her wineglass to take it back to the bar, noticed a smudge of her lipstick and a small swallow of wine left. Putting his lips where hers had been, he tossed back that final drop, savoring the woody taste; then he stretched out on his bed, his computer on his lap.

His cell rang. After checking the number, he flipped it open, exchanged greetings with Ben, then updated his team leader about finding Chen's scenario disk and his own non-progress. At the end he asked, "Anything new on that hacker blip?"

"For us, no, just the usual. Fibs reported a hacker intrusion, though. Got pretty deep until the encryption stopped him. Untraceable, of course. The IP was a dead end."

Bella's exploring, or someone else? Daniel wondered.

"Did you hear?" Ben continued. "Al Benhadid was arrested last night. Hit and run. Wife claims he was at home, but police got a sweet little security video of his car and a clear enhancement of him in it."

"Convenient." Benhadid had been a key suspect in the mycotoxin threat until yesterday's raid. He hadn't been among those arrested, and they'd found no proof against him. Innocent or clever?

"Well, he'll be doing time, even if it is for another crime." Ben hung up.

Daniel inserted Chen's disk into his computer, mulling over what Ben had said as he waited for it to load. Recent Cyber Soldier chatter bragged about helping HS nab a suspected terrorist. Benhadid maybe? Video could be altered. Had one of the Cyber Soldiers gone from uncovering suspect data to manufacturing it? The possibility scared the hell out of him.

His computer chimed. Well, it was all a question for tomorrow. Tonight, he would wipe out all other concerns and begin decrypting the disk he'd recovered from the maze.

Bella jerked from a deep sleep, her heart pounding. She opened her eyes, staring into the shadows of her bedroom. Listening. What had woken her? Over the blood thrumming in her ears, she strained to hear something beyond the normal house noises.

Nothing.

Something had pulled her from sleep—she swallowed

against a knot in her throat—something not a normal part of the night. Still not moving, she glanced at the clock. Three a.m. The pink glow from Fran's monitor lit the room enough to see that no intruders lurked in the corners.

Bella sat up, twisted to sit on the side of the bed. "Fran?" she breathed. "You awake?"

"Yes. You are, too?" Fran sounded delighted.

"Did you hear anything unusual just now?"

"You arising at 3:05 a.m."

"Before that."

"A thunk. Near the front of the house. I have insufficient data to tell what it was."

That must have been what woke her, Bella realized. "I'm going to see what it is," she whispered to Fran. "Keep Code Silence until I get back."

A soft chime was Fran's agreement.

Bella retrieved her pistol from the nightstand, donned a pair of slippers, then crept out into the hall. A chill settled in her bare feet and hands, and she wished she'd put on a pair of sweats over her shorts. Shadows filled the hall, giving it an eerie unfamiliarity that set her on edge. At the end, she paused again to listen. Still nothing. The red light of her security system reassured her with its unblinking glow.

She checked the kitchen. Nothing. Same with the living room. Feeling more confident, she peered out through the expanse of glass windows. There were no fresh footprints in the snow that she could tell.

The tension between her shoulder blades eased. Maybe a limb had hit the window. Or a new house creak had developed. Yawning, she turned back to the bedroom.

A shrill ring broke through the night silence. She spun around, taut nerves strumming. Adrenaline kicked her heart into overdrive before she realized the noise was the landline phone. She raced into the kitchen, then hesitated, her hand on the receiver. What if it was a pornchatter again?

Better to know than to wonder.

She answered, her stomach clenching in anticipation.

"This is Ace Security, Dr. Quintera. We've detected a short in the alarm on your front door. Is everything okay?"

Bella's gaze shot over to the alarm system master panel. *One of the lights was off.* "Something woke me up, but I don't see any signs of an intruder."

"Your code, Dr. Quintera."

"Code?" It took a second to realize they were asking for her private code phrase, the one that would indicate her answers weren't being coerced. "Ah, Fermat's last theorem."

"Do you want us to call the police?"

"Let me check the front door first."

"Don't take any chances. We'll stay on the line with you."

Her grip tight on the receiver, she checked the front door, then peered out the windows. "Door's locked. The motion sensor lights are off. I'm going to check outside."

"That may not be wise."

"I don't want to spend the rest of the night wondering if someone's lurking in the bushes. Better to check now while you're on the line. Maybe I can see something interfering with the sensor."

Sticking the cordless phone in the waistband of her shorts, her gun at hand, she undid the lock, the click echoing into the night like a coffin lid unfastened. A rush of cold air tightened her flesh as she opened the door and stepped outside. The porchlight flicked on. *What?* She lowered the gun when she realized it was only the automatic motion sensor.

Darkness lay about her. Pricks of stars dotted above,

nightlights to a slumbering world. No footprints marred the fresh dusting of snow on the steps. She turned to the alarm pad at the door, then jerked back as she saw something attached to the wooden jamb beside it. Something small, with a red light. How had it gotten there? Shot from outside the fence, maybe? Before she could decide what to do with it, it fell off the wall and plopped at her feet. The red light went out.

"Dr. Quintera?" The security voice came from her phone. She pulled the phone from her waistband.

"Yes."

"Did something happen? We show the alarm as active again. It indicates the door is open."

"Yeah, I'm on the porch." She crouched down, laid down the phone, and retrieved the now inactive scrambler, a version of the one that had exploded on her fence. One with a shorter, more localized effect on the alarms. Just enough to bring her out here.

Why? She turned the sensor over and found a wooden puzzle piece attached to the back. Written on the puzzle was a web url.

Her fingers curled around the puzzle piece, anger replacing fear. *Damn him!* Damn Lokus for playing with her life like this. Glancing out into the motionless night, knowing somehow Lokus was watching, she picked up the phone. "There's some ice around the alarm. Maybe that shorted it temporarily."

"We'll send out a technician to check in the morning."

"Thanks." Bella pushed to her feet, then went back in and told the security company, "I'm inside now. The door's locked and I've reset the alarms."

"Everything shows trouble-free. Do you want us to call anyone for you?"

"No, I'm fine." She wasn't fine. She was mad. After hanging up, she pulled her laptop onto the kitchen table, then typed in the url: a string of meaningless numbers and letters dot com.

A moment later the web page popped into view. There were no fancy graphics or animation, just a white box in the center, which was suddenly filled with writing. Bella leaned forward to read it.

"My bank statement?" she muttered.

As she watched, the balance scrolled backwards, erasing her finances; then the name and numbers changed to her father's bank records and the scenario repeated. Eyes still on the monitor, her heart in her throat, Bella yanked out her cell phone and dialed in to her bank's customer service line. Her balance, anemic as it was, was still there.

A threat, not yet a reality.

Next, her falsified police records appeared on the web page, followed by, to her horror, similar records created under Lionel's name, the fabricated crimes increasingly violent and serious, their identities increasingly blurred beneath a mass of lies and deceptions.

The silent, eerie warning shouted louder than any words could. Bella pressed a fist against her mouth, fighting back nausea as she watched the animation unfold.

One more image appeared: a hospital bed, a body in the center with IVs and monitoring lines attached. The scene moved closer and Bella found herself leaning forward as well, straining for a view of the face in the bed.

Without warning the scene shattered into a scream. Bella jerked backward, collapsing into her chair as the screen blanked. Her stomach and heart collided.

Snow-U's home page replaced the ghastly images.

Frantically, Bella reentered the url. All she got was the standard message of "unable to find this address." Again she entered it, double-checking each digit and letter.

Nothing. She slammed a fist against the table, swearing. *Damn Lokus*. The web page had erased after a single viewing. Again, she had no proof but her word, and she knew how much the police believed that.

There was no proof except the warning burned into her brain: Cooperate or it wouldn't be only her paying the price.

"Stay with your plan, Bella." Lionel popped the last of an oat bran muffin into his mouth. "I've dealt with threats before."

Bella poured herself another cup of coffee, then sat at the table beside her father, feeling heavy-headed this morning. She'd asked Dad to breakfast to warn him about Lokus's threat without any chance of someone listening in, and Lionel had accepted without question. She took a sip of the coffee.

"But I think Lokus is getting more desperate. Or bolder."

Her father speared her with a steady look. "Do you still believe, absolutely, that Fran deserves recognition at the Turing Competition? That her best hope for a free future lies on that path?"

Bella considered his question, examining her own heart and convictions, then nodded. "I do."

"So do I, and for that belief, for Fran, I am willing to risk this Lokus's vengeance. Don't give in to him on account of my old hide." Affectionately, he laid a hand atop hers. "What I'm not willing to risk is you. To lose you, Bella—" He paused, swallowing hard. "Whatever precautions you take for yourself, I will do whatever I can to help you."

Just as Dad was willing to risk himself to give Fran her chance at recognition and freedom, so was she. They stayed with their plan. It was her turn to capture his gaze. "Then talk to Daniel."

"No, he and NSA are as much a risk to Fran as Lokus."

As dangerous as Lokus? NSA, maybe, but not Daniel. Her heart wanted to believe that; her emotions clamored for her to tell Daniel the truth, to be rid of the lies and secrets she hated. Too bad her head kept reminding her that if he knew what Fran was capable of, he would without hesitation turn the A.I. over to the NSA labs.

Still, Daniel represented their best chance to stop the more immediate threat of Lokus. She leaned forward, trying to convince her father. "Right now, our best defense is to unmask Lokus. Our best chance to do that is Daniel. And the more data he has, the higher the probability of success. You know that, Dad."

"Are you sure you're thinking clearly about Daniel Champlain? That this isn't about hormones?"

"'Collect your data, then share what you've learned,'" she answered softly. "We've lived by that principle all our lives."

Lionel hesitated, then nodded. "For you and Fran, I'll give him what I know about Lokus. I won't talk to him about Fran, nor will I feed into a Cyber Soldier witch-hunt against our friends."

At least they'd be talking. "Thanks, Dad."

"The more he knows, the closer he gets to the truth about Fran," warned Lionel.

"Another risk we have to take."

He raised his coffee mug in a toast. "Then, here's to knowledge and to the future of Alternate Intelligence. May both flourish."

Bella forced a smile and met her father's impromptu toast, unable to shake the specter of dread settling across her, the one that whispered she'd just made a huge misjudgment.

But was it about Lokus or about Daniel?

Late the next day, Daniel rapped on Lionel Quintera's front door, determined to get answers. As soon as it opened, he grabbed the edge before Quintera could slam it shut. "Last night someone tried to kill me. Same way they killed Chen. So I am in no mood for games. You may not give a damn about either me or you, but that someone is also after Bella. So I suggest you start answering my questions before that person decides he's not content with just scaring her."

"I've talked to Bella." To Daniel's mild surprise, Quintera opened the door wider. "You're right. I love her more than my politics, more than I distrust you." He gestured for Daniel to follow, then led the way to his glass-walled office. A small gray computer, a twin to the one Bella always carried with her, sat on his desk.

While Daniel settled himself in one of the chairs, Quintera sat behind the desk, then met Daniel with a steady look. "If I help you, will you leave? Will you stay away from Bella?"

"I'll leave when I'm satisfied I've learned what I came to know. As far as Bella goes, you'll have to let her make that decision."

"She knows where her loyalties are."

"Then trust her to make the choice," he challenged.

Quintera's mouth worked a moment. "What do you want to know?"

Daniel laid the laser he'd retrieved last night on the desk. "Recognize this?"

Quintera turned it around in his hands, then handed it back. "Looks like a laser modification of the scalpel Ewan McKinley's developing. Anyone around here could have pilfered it."

A dead end, Daniel decided. On a different track, he asked, "Ever heard of the Cyber Soldiers?"

Quintera's smile was cold. "Isn't your real question, am I Lokus?"

"No, because Chen's dead, and because you wouldn't hurt Bella. Make no mistake about it, Quintera, Lokus is dangerous. He's a killer. You're not."

Quintera paled a bit. "I don't know who Lokus is. Our contact is always through the computer."

"How did you start?"

"Right after I started at ITC, he e-mailed me with the idea of a loosely organized group of encryption devotees who would keep an eye out for terrorist transmissions hidden in chats and pages, and then alert the government to potential threats. The idea made sense to me. You know, probably better than I do, the volume of data out there to sift through. The more eyes looking, the better." He cast a sidelong glance at Daniel. "After all, it was a similar group who combined the power of their individual computers to factor the supposedly uncrackable 129 digit RSA-129 cipher."

"Took 'em ten months."

"But, they did it. Together."

Which is why his agency changed their factor-based keys daily. "Did the plan include actions like hacking banks?"

"Not initially, but Lokus got impatient whenever our warnings were dismissed. Started taking matters into his own hands. By then the group had become the Cyber Soldiers with a lot of pup hackers. And recently, I can't shake the notion that Lokus is working his private agenda. There are still good citizens who are part of the Cyber Soldiers, though, keeping watch."

People Quintera wouldn't betray, Daniel realized. "What do you think Lokus is after?"

"In a nutshell? Power."

"Four years and you've got no clue who this man is?"

"No."

Daniel got the impression he was telling the truth, as far as it went. So what was he hiding? How deep did the truth go? "Do you know who falsified the results of that testing four years ago, Dr. Quintera?"

A long silence fell between them. Man to man, they measured one another. Character, veracity, determination.

Quintera finally broke through the tension. "Why do you want to know?"

"Because it might have bearing on this case." For a moment Daniel thought Lionel wasn't going to answer. That he was going to protect his secret, his lie.

Quintera's shoulders slumped; he leaned back in his chair, his head bowed. "*I* did," he ground out. "So help me God, I did it."

Daniel swallowed hard, his chest tight.

Quintera looked up. "You knew, didn't you? Despite what you told Bella."

"I suspected." He had admired Lionel Quintera. For four years he'd tried to find another answer. But there was no other answer.

The confession seemed to awaken Quintera's need to finally spill out the mess. "I loved Margaret, my wife. Desperately, deeply, passionately. I watched her in such pain all those months yet when she died, I selfishly wanted her back, wanted her there, despite the pain, to be with me. The emptiness and grief I think drove me temporarily insane." He paused to take a sip of coffee. "One night, I went from her grave to the lab and discovered that the accuracy check was off. Enough to put the whole project in jeopardy."

"Heat dissipation?" Daniel asked. "You hadn't solved that problem yet?"

"I knew we were close."

"I would have given you time."

Quintera's lips twisted. "Well, I always had trouble trusting the government. That night, I altered the data so the accuracy check fell within parameters. Eventually I came to my senses, went to reinstall the original data, and discovered you'd taken the comparison disk with you. Then all holy hell broke loose."

"Why didn't you—" Daniel broke off the question. He wasn't here to judge the past, only to learn from it.

"Why didn't I confess? Save Bella?" He shrugged. "Weakness? Shock? Disbelief that she'd be accused, too? By the time I realized what was happening, it was too late. Another regret; the past four years are filled with them. Not that I expect sympathy."

"Good, because you aren't getting any." Daniel understood Quintera's actions, but he didn't agree with them. They may have reached an uneasy truce, but there were still hard disagreements between them. Like Bella.

"Are you going to tell Bella?" Lionel asked.

"It's your secret to tell." At least he knew Lokus hadn't been working on Lionel four years ago. The danger arose because of some very recent breakthrough.

Lionel stood and pushed a disk across the desk. "This is everything I've collected or surmised about Lokus. Put it with what you've got and find the bastard that's threatening my daughter." He crossed his arms, waiting, obviously believing the interview was over.

Not yet, Lionel. Daniel pocketed the disk, then returned to the case at hand. "You and Chen discussed A.I. theories?"

"Yes." Quintera settled back in his chair, again wary.

"What are you working on now?"

Quintera nodded toward his computer. "Examine my research. Then I'll answer your questions."

He wasn't going to volunteer one extra scrap, Daniel realized. Still, he set to examining the computer, starting with the cursory overview.

An hour later, he sat back. Something nagged at him. An itch at the back of his neck told him he was looking at pieces that had fallen from another puzzle. This was one of the prototype molecular computers Lionel had developed four years ago. It had been light-years superior to anything else being worked on then; with the refinements he'd made, it still surpassed anything on the commercial market or in NSA's network. And apparently, Quintera was now working on quantum coding.

Just the sort of thing Lokus would be salivating to get his hands on.

So, what was the problem? What wasn't right?

"You've made a lot of progress in four years. Why no papers?"

"I've had glory. I prefer work."

The computer had been here for four years. Why was Lokus moving now? There had to be a specific reason, a specific plan. But what was it?

Daniel tried another route, edging his way around something he couldn't see, he could only *feel*. "Why did you use Lisp instead of SHRDLU as the basic programming language?"

"Lisp allows for the complex nesting patterns I prefer for the logic processing."

Daniel looked out the window through two-foot spears of icicles, which covered the view like white prison bars. Dusk was falling. What little bit of sunshine had dared the swollen skies was gone. He had heard that another storm was predicted. As he watched, a moose wandered from the thicket of trees at one end of the grounds and began to paw the snow. It was shallower there, and the beast soon uncovered a remnant of greenery to chew on. Just beyond the trees, Daniel saw a spot of red. The roof of Bella's house.

Bella. Refusing to let himself get distracted or derailed from the slowly swirling thoughts coalescing in his head, he glanced away. Bella, however, refused to be ignored. Her image stayed with him. Bella holding a computer clutched to her chest. Daniel's gaze darted back to the computer. An identical computer.

The puzzle pieces began sliding around, forming a new picture. He'd read Bella's last paper, on her revolutionary intuitive language. Why hadn't Lionel Quintera used his daughter's language in his A.I.? Bella's language was the best step forward—

Son of a bitch!

He shot to his feet and strode from the room, slamming the door open in the process. Pain shot down his rebandaged leg, but he ignored it.

"Champlain!" shouted Quintera, chasing after him. "Where are you going?"

"By God, if your stubbornness harms Bella, I will personally make sure you never again step foot from this frozen wilderness."

"What the hell are you talking about?"

Daniel didn't answer. Instead, he slammed through doors, out into the blood-gelling cold. He welcomed the freezing temperature, hoping to cool both his anger and his fear for Bella.

It didn't. Because he couldn't escape the undeniable conclusion. How could he have been so blind? Chen's last garbled message wasn't about *Lionel* Quintera. It was about *Bella*.

Damn her for keeping this from him. She hadn't been targeted in order to send a message to her father. She was a target because she'd created the world's first A.I.

Chapter Thirteen

A footscrape alerted Bella that her expected appointment had arrived. Two hours late. She neatened the papers on her already tidy desk. Acid burned a line down her esophagus. By the love of Einstein, she hated this. Hated that she'd discovered it, but hated more that Neal thought he could get away with it, that it was accepted practice.

"Neal Brandeis is here," Fran said quietly.

"I know."

Fran's face disappeared behind snowy trails just as Neal swaggered in. "I asked you to come during business hours," Bella told him.

"I was busy." He turned a chair around and straddled it. "Dr. Q, what happens in a robot arm motion subroutine if you substitute a cross check for errors at the delta level instead of the gamma level?"

"You miss verifying the lack of potential error for too much arm swing in the delta subprime."

"Oh." He sat back, deflated.

She tilted her head. "It's a good idea, though—one none of my other students so far thought of. If you can figure out a way to check the subprime at the gamma level, then it could be an efficient program."

He straightened. "I'll work on that."

"I wish you luck," she said sincerely. "You'll win a name if you solve it." She ran her pencil nervously through her fingers. "But you'll do it in another program."

It took a moment for her words to sink in. "What the eff are you talking about?"

"Don't swear at me. And my meaning's clear. You're out of the class."

"God damn it!" He shook a finger at her. "And don't you God damn tell me not to swear after that little bombshell. I need those credits. You got no right to can me."

"I can't expel you from the university, but I can oust you from my class." She pushed a paper across her desk at him, a small zero neatly penciled into the corner. "Did you think I wouldn't realize this was directly plagiarized from the Internet?"

"So what? I got pressed for time to write a stupid paper. I know the material. I ace my tests."

"Every paper you've turned in is plagiarized. You also copy homework." And, she suspected, tests. She didn't have any proof of the latter, but she'd seen hints of it.

"What's the big deal? Everybody does it."

"Not in my class. Do you remember what I told you the first day? Don't lie to me and don't try to BS me. If you have a problem, come to me, we'll work on it. I insist on honesty. A scientist needs to maintain ethical standards."   •

He gave a snort. "That's rich, coming from you. We all got a big laugh out of the honesty speech."

"What do you mean?" Her pencil stilled. But she knew, dammit, what he was implying.

"We all know how you falsified data, how the government exposed you."

"I don't make any secret about my past." She didn't advertise it either, but that didn't seem to make any difference. "As a scientist, you might try finding out the facts instead of taking rumors as your guide. Now hand over your lab key."

Neal stood, bracing his arms on her desk, trying to intimidate her. "If I refuse?"

He had a lot to learn about scaring people. Bella gave him a cool look. "Then I'll call campus security and you will be expelled."

His jaw worked a moment, and she hoped he was rational enough to see the logic. He threw down the key. "There!"

She didn't relax, didn't pick it up, didn't look away from him. She was seeing an even uglier side of Neal than she'd suspected. His fingers tightened to white-knuckled fists, and a calculating look came over his face.

"I think I deserve a little something for my cooperation. Don't you, Dr. Q? Except, you're no longer my professor, are you? No teacher-student barriers. Is that why you did this, Bella? I can call you Bella now, can't I? Did you do this for me, Bella?"

She rose to her feet; this was getting nasty. Adrenaline burned through her veins. "Leave now, Neal, before you do something your daddy won't be able to buy you out of." She stepped back, out of reach, and kept the desk as a barrier between them. *Let him make the first move.*

He laughed. "I don't think that's going to be a problem. Daddy's bought me out before." A sneer twisted his lips. "You see, in the end, they really do like it."

How had she missed these signs? She waited behind the desk, glad she had taken off her heels and put on her boots in preparation to leave. Suddenly he lunged forward with his fist.

She ducked and scrambled to the side, racing around the end of the desk, grabbing for Fran as she did. Those microseconds of delay were too long. Neal swept Fran out of Bella's reach and grabbed her wrist.

Thank God, he didn't send the A.I. tumbling to the floor. Instead Bella teetered at the side of the desk, half on and half off. This time his fist didn't miss; it connected with her cheek.

Eyes blurring, pain searing her body, she smashed the heel of her hand against the bridge of his nose. She heard a crack, felt a bone give. Neal screeched and dropped her wrist. She scooped up Fran, then ran out the door.

By the love of the saints, it was dark out here! It was late afternoon again, gray and snowy, the perpetual state of Superior. She raced for the stairwell. Couldn't afford to wait for the world's slowest elevator. Security was on the first floor, her office on the sixth.

She was halfway between four and five when above her a door slammed, the sound reverberating down the stairwell chamber to an answering echo below. An echo? Or another door flinging shut?

The lights flickered, dimmed, flickered again. A second later, they went all the way out. Above her, a string of curses identified Neal. She heard the door slam again. Apparently, he'd decided against chasing her down a pitch-black stairway. He'd probably take the elevator down, run to Daddy and start the lawyers compiling his defense.

She pulled out her cell phone on the off chance it would work, but the signal read one bar and she couldn't get a call out—the story of life in the UP. Spotty transmission. If there wasn't a building blocking her, then there was no tower in the wilderness to carry the signal.

Bottom-of-Lake Superior blackness surrounded her. Except, now that she was adjusting to it, the blackness wasn't as complete as she first supposed. Blue glowed from her watch and around the edges of Fran's closed cover, ghostly sheens against the flat walls. Not enough to see where her feet should go, but at least it felt like she wasn't quite alone.

Up or down? she debated. Floors four and five held government research labs, so the stairwell was locked from this side. You could get through in event of fire, but not now. She'd have to go down a flight and a half to the third floor to get out. Or go up to the sixth floor, a flight and a half up. Where Neal might be waiting.

Down it was.

She found the railing. Grasping it with one hand, the other hand clutching Fran, she slid her foot forward until she hit the edge of the step, then slid her foot downward until she caught the next step. She repeated it with the other foot. Eventually, she found a small rhythm and moved faster . . . until her sliding foot, expecting to find a step below, stomped down against a level platform. With the jarring misstep, she lurched forward, her right hand losing its grip on the railing. Off balance with Fran, she barely caught herself from tumbling to her knees. The resultant stomp of her feet reverberated through the shaft.

Way to go. Announce your presence in the stairwell, she thought to herself. If anyone questioned whether she was here, she'd just dispelled every doubt. She paused on the landing, the cause of her clumsiness, halfway between the third and fourth floors. Her skin tightened with the cold. With minimal heating vents in the stairwell, that cold began seeping past her layers of clothing, meeting the ice creeping from her inside out.

Below her, a pencil-thin beam of high-intensity light played up the steps. She couldn't see the source, only recognized the high-energy brightness of the beam. Someone down there was coming up, with a high-tech flashlight in hand and not a sound to reveal his progress. If that light could be seen . . .

"Fran," she whispered, "could you make your screen go black?"

"No more snowy trails?"

"Pretend you're asleep."

"If you uncover my lens. I can't see anything."

"It's not covered; the lights went out."

"My chronometer says the time is not customary for sleep."

"Electrical failure." Or someone had deliberately turned them out.

Darkness enveloped her as Fran's screen dimmed. Who was down below? From the light beam, she judged the person was between her and the third floor. Suddenly Neal's threat didn't seem as dire as the eerie silence of the stranger below.

Damn, she was getting tired of being stalked.

Going up actually went faster, especially when desperation put Mercury in her heels. Her boots sounded like clodhoppers in the echoing column of the stairwell. *Break it down, Bella, what's the plan for when you get to the sixth floor?* She rotated her shoulder, stiff from holding Fran. A dull ache spread across her cheek and behind her eye. Made it difficult to think. She'd use her cell phone to call security. Grab Fran's shoulder case. Try the other stairwell at the farther side of the hall. Good plan.

Her pursuer also speeded up. Rapid-fire footsteps, still unnaturally hushed, raced after her. Her heart pounded louder than those steps.

A moment's inattention cost her. She banged her shin against a step. Pain shot up her leg as she fumbled forward. Her outstretched hand banged the wall, and she caught herself before falling.

Her pursuer didn't pause.

Up Bella raced, glancing down once. All she could see was a dark shadow and a thin beam of light. It was only half a flight below.

There was the red exit sign, ahead.

She raced blindly, her steps moving by instinct. *Grab the door. Pull.*

A yank on her sweater jerked her backward. The tight weave chopped her throat. That *hurt!* No air. She dropped to her knees.

Her pursuer scrambled to grab Fran. He was strong. Her sweaty palms slipped on the case.

Desperately, she rolled to her back. Lashed out with both feet. Caught him in the chest. A grunt. A curse. Not hers. The shadowy figure tumbled backward down the flight of stairs. Without pause, Bella scrambled to her feet, pulled open the door and raced down the sixth-floor hall.

The sixth floor was marginally lighter. At least it had windows, even if not a lot of light came through at this time of day. Her colleagues had all gone home.

A creak cut through the empty hall. The sound scraped across her spine, setting her nerves all a-jangle. Her office door creaked like that. Neal must have waited in her office and heard the stairwell door. Was he hiding inside her office, the door slightly ajar? No chance to stop there for the phone call. She sprinted flat-out down the hall, praying she'd get past.

Lady Luck, not friendly so far, had completely abandoned her in the stairwell. The door opened as she passed. She slammed it closed and ran.

But it was no good. A moment later a hard hand grabbed her, whirling her around and slamming her against a hard body. She lifted her leg, ramming her knee upward, only missing her target because of her captor's fast reflexes. She must have hit something, though, because the man grunted and his knee buckled. She followed the up-stroke with a stomp downward, aiming for the man's instep. She shoved backward against the restraint of his arms, hoping to break his iron grip.

She never completed either move. Instead, with lightning response, he twisted, swept, and before she knew what had happened, she was driven face-first against the floor, the blow made worse by the fact that she was instinctively cradling Fran and took the brunt of it with her forearms and elbows. *How had Neal gotten such honed reflexes?* No sooner had she hit the floor than one of her arms was yanked behind her back. She couldn't bite back the whimper of pain as agony shot up her shoulder, even as she bucked to dislodge her captor.

He only stilled, his muscular weight pressing heavily into her back. "Bella?"

That wasn't Neal's voice. The voice was bone-deep familiar, the rich tones and Southern lilt caressing her heart.

"Daniel?" she rasped. "What the hell are you doing here? Dammit, let me up." She heard a door slam somewhere below and realized her pursuer had given up. Her body sagged to the floor. "Why are you manhandling me?"

"Me? First thing you did was aim a knee at my balls." He rolled off her.

"Because you grabbed me." Painfully she rolled to her side.

"I grabbed at someone running who'd smacked a door against me." He pushed stiffly to his feet, wincing a little but still holding out a hand.

She shook her head. Her arm was too sore to let him pull her up. Instead, she rolled to her knees and struggled to get her feet beneath her, her sore arm limp at her side, her other arm still wrapped around Fran.

She hurt. Her arm, her throat, her cheek.

Daniel was at once at her side, his arm wrapped around her waist as he balanced her and helped her to rise. "I'm sorry."

"Training kicked in when I kneed you?"

"Yeah."

The speed and lethality of his response were unsettling. Despite her claims at taking care of herself, he'd had her immobile and helpless in seconds. "Remind me not to do that again."

"I think you'll remember." He caressed her bruised cheek with a feathery touch, but his eyes were flinty. "What happened to you? Who did this?"

"Just a sec, I have to get something from my office." She retrieved Fran's carrying case and slung on the leather strap. Massaging her shoulder, she returned to Daniel, surprised to see him limping in a circle, massaging his leg.

"Did I hit your wound? Is it bleeding?"

"Yes, and no." He straightened. "How's your shoulder? Are you seeing okay?"

"Been better, but it will heal. And yes." Then she smiled, though it hurt her eyes. "Aren't we a fine pair? Aiming for major damage to each other."

"My aim was more accurate than yours." He began to massage her shoulder with a touch that was warm honey, just a little bit this side of heaven.

"You've had more practice."

"Fortunately. Or I'd still be reeling in a corner."

Somehow she doubted that, but she didn't correct him; he might stop rubbing her shoulder just to make a point. "What are you doing here?"

"Looking for you. Why were you running?"

She told him the whole story, ending with, "I'm getting really tired of being stalked. I feel like I'm part of some horror film."

Before she got all the words out, he stopped massaging her shoulder and, with a curse, strode over to the stairwell and disappeared down it.

Not wanting to be left twiddling her thumbs in the hall, Bella followed. The lights were on, banishing all the spooks and shadows of before.

"I tell you, the lights were off when I was in here."

"I believe you," Daniel said simply, and somehow she knew he wasn't just placating her. He did believe her. "There's no one here now."

"Guess we scared them off. Thanks."

"Next rescue, I'll try not to manhandle you."

"I hope there doesn't have to be another rescue."

He stopped then and faced her. His hands rested on her shoulders while his thumb toyed with strands of her hair. "There will be another rescue, Bella, and another. Not"—he raised a hand stopping her protest—"because I don't believe you can handle yourself, but because I know these people will not stop until they get what they want."

"What do they want?"

He nodded at Fran. "That."

Chapter Fourteen

"Not in the hall," she murmured. "My home?"

Daniel nodded, agreeing. They couldn't talk about this here. They stopped only to report the attack to security, then drove their separate vehicles to her home. Once inside the fence, Daniel ran a visual perimeter check while Bella checked her security alarm and went inside.

Her property fronted Lake Superior, up a small bluff

so even storm-swollen waves didn't reach the open lawn. He couldn't see far into the lake tonight, with the eternal clouds covering any hope of starlight and smudging the full moon to a smear. The cavernous darkness swallowed the beam of his powerful flashlight.

He swung the light down the cliff. It would take a determined intruder to crawl up over the boulders to the spit of cleared shore, but he knew Bella's enemies were determined.

Tonight an attack from that angle would take more than determination; it would take sheer lunacy. The lake was high and angry. Waves crashed onto the rocks with an incessant pounding. Daniel's light glinted off pricks of silver—ice, spume or minerals in the rocks, he couldn't tell. One misstep—and he'd bet those rocks were very slippery—and an intruder would be carried out into the deadly lake.

Still, Daniel picked his way down the bluff, checking. His cell phone rang. He answered it. "Hey, Stefan. What have you got for me?"

"We're still cross-checking the names of the VR gamers you sent. I'm sending you the file of what we got so far."

"Any hot prospects?"

"Not yet. Where are you? I can barely hear you."

"It's the lake." Daniel shifted the phone to his other ear, muting the relentless pounding of the Lake Superior waves. "Or the snow."

"You're outside in a snowstorm? Are you in hell frozen over?"

"A few flakes doesn't qualify as a storm. They're always coming down. You get used to it."

"This from Daniel I-hate-the-cold Champlain?"

"It *is* the lakeshore."

"You always did your best work near water. Leave it to you to find a northern beach."

Daniel laughed. Beach? These were rocks, not sand. Wild waves driven by the gods of winter, coating the land with foam and ice. "Not beach. Shore. Anything else? I'm freezing my butt off out here."

"Hold on, Ben wants to talk to you."

A moment later, Ben's drawling tones greeted him. There was no hint of the usual genial teasing, however. "Daniel, we've got amended mission priorities."

Daniel's grip tightened around the phone. "What?"

"The Turing Competition finalists were announced."

One more piece fell into place. "Bella's entered," Daniel said.

"Yes. One Dr. Isabella Quintera and Fran. How long have you known?"

"I've been slow on the draw. I just figured it out tonight."

"Not using your brain, buddy? Does she have an A.I.?"

He thought about Bella's protectiveness of her computer. Both times when she'd been running for her life—in the snowstorm and in the stairwell tonight—she'd kept it close. His stomach curled with what the answer might mean to her, to them.

Yet he, Ben and Stefan operated on trust, trust that made them one of the best teams around. He wasn't about to jeopardize that now. "Yes."

"My God," Ben breathed. "A true Asimov-and-Hal-type A.I.?"

"I don't know how advanced it is."

"Would Isabella Quintera risk open competition with anything crude?"

Daniel hesitated again, but only a nanosecond, his chest aching. His choices were made. "No, she wouldn't."

"Does Lokus plan to use it?"

"No specifics, but why else risk real world exposure?" He held nothing back. "I decrypted Chen's scenario disk. He was profiling breaking factor ciphers and quantum encoding by using A.I. parameters."

Ben gave a low whistle. "Can the A.I. break our codes?"

"Don't know."

"If a vigilante civilian got into our files . . ."

Especially one like Lokus, who didn't bother with due process before he meted out his own form of punishment on those he considered enemies. "He'd hold the power to destroy any person in this country."

"Daniel, this was a two-pronged assignment. Find out about the Cyber Soldiers and Chen's death, and find out if the A.I. rumors have any validity. That last just became the mission priority. If either poses a threat—"

"You don't need to quote the assignment to me."

"Right. Your arguments created this assignment. Your suspicions persuaded NSA to turn an eye on the Cyber Soldiers. Your belief that Lionel Quintera might have a true A.I. piqued a lot of interest. Thus, your butt's in the sling on this one. There are already doubts that you're too close to this. Too emotional."

Daniel gave a sharp laugh. "Too emotional? Me?"

"Yeah, you. And, I'm one who's doing the doubting."

A sharp spear of cold sliced down Daniel's lungs. If he'd lost Ben and Stefan's support on this . . . The two of them knew more about him, were closer to him, than anyone else on this planet, including his sister—it was a side effect of spending a lot of time together waiting for all hell to break loose. Tongues tended to speak honestly during those times, reveal more than one would like.

"Ben, trust me. Give me the latitude I need to do this right."

"Break enough rules, put this country at risk, and even your stellar record won't save your career." Ben sounded matter-of-fact.

Daniel scrambled over the last outcropping of rock,

only to be stopped by a jagged cliff. It was impassable. No one could enter Bella's beach from this side. Which left the ITC side to check.

He turned his attention back to the conversation. "Look, Ben, this is our best chance to find out the agenda behind the Cyber Soldiers' frontline patriots. If I move too soon, they'll close ranks. Give me a chance to verify the A.I. What it can do."

"I'll consider this call an unofficial report. You have three days."

"I need more time."

"Until the Turing Test? Not gonna happen, Daniel. If that A.I. is as powerful as we think, that revolutionary, it has to be protected."

"It will be." He would protect Fran and Bella with his life if necessary. "I know what I'm doing."

"Yeah? Take a look at this. It's circulating the web."

Daniel tilted his phone for a clearer view of the picture Ben sent, then swore. It was a picture of him and Bella kissing after the explosion.

"I can't keep this from the next level much longer," Ben warned.

Daniel made a fake static noise that fooled no one. "Connection's breaking up."

"Dammit, Daniel, don't screw this up."

"I won't. If the A.I.'s that powerful, I'll bring it in." He disconnected, then jammed the phone into his pocket.

A spray of waves slammed against the rocks, dampening his jacket and hat. The water droplets froze on his unprotected cheeks. He stepped back, away from the spray, but stayed and watched the great lake. Delayed facing Bella.

Superior, deepest and deadliest of the Great Lakes. It never gave up its dead, according to the song. Held tight to its secrets and tragedies.

He loved water, did his best thinking while bobbing on a boat or standing under the shower, but he'd always preferred the vast saltiness of the warm oceans.

Yet something about this lake drew him. The gray, roiling surface concealed snags and shipwrecks. The leaden skies illuminated nothing, as though all human sight and knowledge stopped an inch into the waters. But hidden beneath was the truth. Tonight he could believe all the legends.

Despite its dangers, its unforgiving nature, its hidden treacherousness, people still lived on Superior's shores, fished within its waters, steamed across it. They viewed the lake with a wary hope.

Hope didn't mean ignoring dangers and hard choices, however. Daniel knew what he needed to do.

He turned and scrambled over the rocky shore back to the steps. After climbing the bluff, he circled the perimeter of the house. His boots crunched through the ice-crusted top layer, a loud *crunk, crunk* in a night silent except for the sounds of the lake.

Beneath the trees, the snow was thinner and more powdery, but he still left a telltale trail. No one had walked this way since the last storm. He paused at the gate leading onto the ITC grounds. It was locked, and there were small mounds of snow at the top of the hinges, a hint that nothing had been tampered with. He swung his flashlight over the snow on the other side. Pristine, except for deer hoofprints and rabbit tracks.

He opened the gate, his lips tight, then shone the light across the trees. There. The glint of metal. He retrieved a tiny camera eye, then took great pleasure in grinding it beneath his heel.

When he emerged from the woods, he found that Bella had turned on the lights of the house, bathing the cedar and stone in an inviting glow. Yet all the warmth and all the security couldn't hide the fact that very real perils stalked them. He might not be enough to protect her.

He stood for a moment, waiting in the shadows for

any sign of something amiss, but tonight he felt and saw nothing of danger. The only thing he felt was the warm welcome bidding him enter, and the embers of anticipation reminding him that Bella waited inside. His home in Maryland was comfortable, tasteful. He found pleasure there. But always, when he came home from work or an assignment, the only thing that greeted him was silence and a darkness broken only by the random security lights.

Don't be thinking this is permanent, he told himself. Because if Bella had what he thought she did, then they were going to be at terrible, unscalable odds again.

Bella had put on a pot of cinnamon-flavored coffee, he discovered when he went inside. He stomped the snow off his boots, toed them off and hung up his coat before following the smell to the back of the house.

He found her sitting in the great kitchen, one foot curled beneath her, her computer on the table. She was nibbling a sandwich. The curtains were open, as though she'd been watching him make his rounds, watching to make sure *he* was safe, too.

He tossed the camera eye on the table. "Lokus has been taking pictures."

Her cheeks paled, and her eyes closed as she let out a breath. "I kept feeling like I was being watched. I thought I was going nuts." Her eyes opened, and he saw the glitter of anger in them. With a jerky motion she swept the camera off the table and into the trash. Her back straightened in determination. "The bastard."

"I'll run a full sweep when it's light. We'll stop him."

"Damn right, we will." She nodded to a tray of sandwiches. "I was hungry. I thought you might be, too. There's turkey and ham."

"Thanks." He poured a cup of coffee from the carafe and sat beside her at the table, ignoring the food for the moment. "Do you have an A.I., Bella?" he asked bluntly.

"Yes. A forerunner, at least." She didn't try to lie. Then again, Bella wasn't the one who normally lived with secrets.

"I need to examine it."

"Do you have a search warrant?"

His jaw tightened. "No. Is that the way we're going to play this? Because if I have to get one, then I will. We both know it will be granted. If I do that, though, I'll have no choice but to take the A.I. back to NSA with me for a complete examination." Not even for Bella could he play false with the trust given him and his vows to protect his country and its people.

Her mouth tightened as she slid her computer across the table. The case was slung over the chair back. The case was of tooled leather, Spanish craftsmanship, he'd guess. There were several eye-sized holes in the design. Not for decoration only.

She patted the edge of the tiny computer. "It's rudimentary."

"How did it develop?"

"I was writing a virus-killer program based upon immunologic principles of self versus nonself."

Daniel gave a low whistle. Was that what Lokus was after? Not the Holy Grail of an A.I., but something more mundane—a virus killer? His gut said no. Still, he ventured, "I've heard rumors such a program existed. I didn't know you developed one."

"It's not publishable, yet. I added it to the inductive reasoning program, and the cognitive processing of the molecular foundation."

"Build a mind from many parts," he murmured.

She nodded. "Minsky's bottom-up theory. After that, the computer began making unprogrammed decisions. Memory, learning, reasoning. The building blocks of intelligence."

That was important, groundbreaking even, but not

what most would label a true A.I. Not what would pass the Turing Competition. "How about adaptability and inventiveness?"

"Griffin's postulates of animal intelligence?" She shrugged. "I'll take what I've got."

"What *do* you have?" he murmured, drawing the case closer. The ordinariness of the snowy ski-trail-scene wallpaper surprised him a little. Still, what did he expect? Eyes and a mouth? Lights flashing in rhythm with the speech, like some 60s movie? The computer was already running, yet the case felt cool, without generated heat. He leaned closer to the screen. "Hello."

"Hello," returned a stilted, mechanical voice. "My name is Fran. What is your name?"

"My name's Daniel." On the screen, he opened up the program and started delving further.

It continued talking to him as he did. "Hello, Daniel."

"How are you today?"

"Fine, thank you. How are you today, Daniel?"

"Curious."

"Curiosity is a fine thing. Curiosity killed the cat."

"You don't like cats?"

"I have never interfaced with a cat."

The conversation continued in that disappointing vein for a few minutes, while he worked his way through the code. The answers Fran gave were nothing but what a sharply programmed computer would handle without even heating a chip: cues taken from the conversation, literal thought, inductions within the realm of known computer parameters. He ran a hand across the sleek, lightweight casing. Fran was impressive; most everyone in his agency would be salivating to possess a machine like her. She was cutting-edge in speed and voice return, and one of the most complex-processing computers he'd ever seen. All in a compact, lightweight case.

But trained Turing examiners would never mistake her for a human. Was Bella using Fran and the Turing Competition as a simple way to get back in the spotlight, like so many of the applicants did? Even as the evidence said yes, instinct told him no. When a Quintera came back to scientific prominence, it would be in a noteworthy blaze.

"Tell me about your day, Fran."

"In what increments? My internal clock is calibrated in one hundredths of a minute."

"Fifteen-minute intervals would be fine." Interesting; she recognized that he might not want every hundredth minute detailed.

"At twelve midnight I was in my docking station. At twelve fifteen a.m. I was in my docking station."

"Just sitting there?"

"I have no legs."

"Were you doing any processing?"

He thought the computer hesitated. "Yes."

"What?"

"I was detailing a cutting pattern for a jigsaw. Bella's input data said they wanted three hundred three pieces and they had paid for three whimsies."

"What's a whimsy?"

"A specially cut piece of a shape pertinent to the picture. Fitting three of those in and still being aesthetically pleasing was a worthy challenge."

"You recognize aesthetically pleasing?"

"I know connections. Bella knows pleasing."

A charge ran through his nerves. An interesting observation. To a computer, no; but to an A.I., would *pleasing* characterize something that organized and fit neural nets? Sort of like the satisfying clutch he got when a pattern clicked into place.

Bella interrupted. "Do you have any questions about the programming?"

"Not yet. And, Bella"—he looked up from the screen—"don't interrupt again, or I will have to finish this somewhere else without you."

Her lips pressed together, and a brief grinding sound came from the computer. With a single shake of her head, Bella sat back in her chair, arms crossed. "Proceed, Special Agent, Dr. Champlain."

"What does a special agent do?" asked Fran.

"Serve his country."

"How do you serve your country? Food service? Service industry? Tennis?"

"Who's doing the questioning here?"

"Me. In the recent exchange," answered Fran.

The voice was still digital, but Daniel could swear he heard a lilt of laughter. A computer with a sense of humor? Now, *that* would be revolutionary. "Continue your report of your day, Fran. Not only where you were, but what you were doing."

"At twelve thirty a.m. I was in my docking station, and I was computing the millionth place of pi. Would you like to hear the figure?"

"No." He rested his elbow on the table, his chin propped on his hand as he studied the computer code crawling across the monitor.

Then he bent forward, the thrill of discovery a hum in his chest. This was brilliant. Even with this mere skim of the surface, that sure fact hit him like a gut punch. In this brief snapshot, he recognized pieces of the innovative languages Bella had developed and altered. He couldn't put his finger on how, not this fast. The interconnections were too complex, and the programming embedded in Fran's molecular side was hidden. He stopped the scrolling.

Fran stopped her recitation.

"Why did you stop, Fran?" When had he started thinking of the computer as "Fran" instead of "it"?

"You paused the program listing." A snowy scene flickered on the screen, flashing with a glimpse of pink.

There it was again, that spark of insight, that glimmer of independent thought, quickly quashed. Was the response something programmed in? Part of a hard-wired decision tree? Computer programming often mimicked human responses well enough to fool an untrained observer. He was far from a novice, yet he couldn't tell the answer.

"Are you done?" asked Bella.

Daniel only grunted, playing with the facts in his mind, trying to see the picture they formed. Spots of brilliance, quickly hidden. Deliberately? A code filled with redundancies and repetitions. Or was it looping back on itself, letting him see the backside of the same process, like a tangled-up Mobius strip? Again, deliberate?

What had Bella said she was working on? A virus-killer program? Viruses came from the outside. Where were the powerful wireless connections she'd use to test the program? The one imbedded here was functioning and active, but very crude for a machine as sophisticated as this. Why have minimal wireless in a machine supposed to be testing viruses?

Because it *wasn't* a machine that was supposed to be testing viruses.

The conclusion sent him leaning back in his chair. "My God," he breathed, barely able to catch enough air in his too-tight lungs for even that much voice. "Bella, you've done it." He caressed the small case. "A true artificial intelligence."

The snowy scene flickered again with a flash of purple.

"Of a kind. I told you that."

He shook his head. "No, this is more than an amoebic intelligence."

They stared at one another, his hand resting on the

warm, humming computer. Bella's face was steeled to pale blandness, but there was a flash in her eyes.

"The Turing Competition will measure what I've got."

His fingers tightened around the case. "Bella, do you realize what could happen if this got into the wrong hands?"

"What 'this'? What have you got to show there?"

"What is Fran capable of doing?" he asked tightly.

"You've examined her."

"What I've seen is fascinating, yes, but it's not going to win the Turing Competition. You don't need a benchmark. Why did you enter?"

"Recognition." She got up from her chair and began to pace the room. "Do you know, I don't even have a real faculty appointment at the university? I'm an adjunct staff member, hired to run the computer lab. They only put me in the classroom because I'm damn good at what I do and they were desperate. I don't have to win the competition to get out of the shadow of the past."

"What about Fran?"

"Fran, too, will be recognized for what she is."

"And what is that?"

Bella braced her hands on the table, staring straight back at him. "A very advanced computer. Probably the most advanced, except perhaps for those networks you've developed at NSA."

Fran made a small chirping noise, as though starting up one of her programs.

Neither human looked at her. Bella leaned closer to Daniel. "That is all anyone will see or believe. Unless she were to win that Turing Competition."

The whole picture clicked into place in Daniel's mind. So this was her plan, her goal. Bella wanted the recognition; that he didn't doubt for a minute. She wanted to restore her reputation, and in doing so return her father's prominence, for Fran was based on his molecular design. The only way she could do that, irrefutably, was to win the competition, so there were no doubts about her legitimacy or Fran's. Until then, Fran was posing as a computer instead of an A.I.

Damn, Bella wasn't giving an inch. Frustrated, Daniel glanced at Fran, who was still humming blandly with the snowy scenes on her screen. Neither of them was giving an inch.

"Let me protect the two of you," he tried.

"Let Fran disappear into the bowels of NSA, a curiosity in their vaults? What kind of protection is that?"

Another piece of the picture clicked into place. Bella believed in openness, in the sharing of ideas and skills. She would think her best chance for safety lay in Fran's open recognition as an A.I. Because of her reputation, that recognition was solid only if an independent body recognized Fran—i.e., if they won the Turing Test. Until then, until they had that protection of recognition, both Bella and Fran were keeping silent.

Daniel did not believe that recognition would bring them safety. A clutch of fear for both Fran and Bella stabbed his gut. But neither would silence.

He looked at Bella, her face pale against her auburn hair. A strand had caught on her cheek. He reached out and brushed it back with his fingertips.

A wave of desire, so strong it might have arisen from the dark, mysterious depths of the Great Lake outside the window, swept through him. Inopportune, inappropriate again, but undeniable. He still wanted her.

He would always want her. He would always be fascinated by her. Four years hadn't changed that. Neither had it changed the fact that they were always going to be on opposites sides of the same fence.

Knowledge—share it or protect it?

His thumb traced a small arc on the line of her jaw. He knew what he had to do. His job. His duty was clear. Stop the Cyber Soldiers and safeguard the A.I. technology.

More than duty, his heart demanded that he protect

both these treasures. Even if it meant he'd lose Bella's affection.

"I have to take her."

"You will be destroying her."

"Bella, I have to—"

A piercing shriek rent the kitchen. The alarm!

Chapter Fifteen

Daniel burst to his feet, the kitchen chair toppling backward. A pain from the wound in his leg stabbed in protest to his ankle. He ignored it. Weapon pulled, he sprang toward Bella, shielding her, his body between her and the doorway.

"Get down," he commanded.

A sharp whine pierced the alarm's clamor. Daniel threw himself to the tile, pulling Bella with him, his arm over her back. When no further sounds followed, he rose to a crouch, pain arrowing through his leg. Another gunshot-like noise sent them back to the floor.

"There." He motioned Bella toward the protection of the china cabinet while he hunched above her, shielding her.

Bella shook her head. "Fran! I have to get Fran."

"I'll get her. You check for any movement outside."

Heart pounding against his ribs, he slid toward Fran. Which direction was the threat? Glancing up at the alarm panel showed a shattered window in the kitchen. Was the porch on that circuit? Because every window here was solid.

Malfunction? Diversion? Had Lokus hacked the alarm system?

Before he slid out into the open room, he glanced back at Bella. She'd retrieved a serviceable Smith &

Wesson, armed it, held it like she knew what she was doing. Alert, ready, she scanned the area. Sweat sheened her face and a pulse tripped at her throat. Even scared, Bella guarded his back well, her gun trained toward the outside.

He crept from cover, still scanning, still assessing. The shot had come from . . . where? The sound played back through his memory. From the middle of the room? He didn't recognize the source weapon. What made that *whine-crack* sound?

He reached the table, then picked up Fran and tucked her protectively beneath his arm. Another crack sent him diving. Hugging Fran tight beneath him, he slid back toward Bella.

Wasn't that clanging alarm a smoke-and-fire alarm? Pieces weren't fitting. Unless you turned them around and realized the answer was on the opposite side.

Hadn't that last sound come . . . He stopped.

"Daniel, get over here," Bella hissed.

In answer, he pulled Fran from beneath him. "You are cleverer than I gave you credit for, Fran." He flipped up the screen. "Why'd you set off the alarm?"

The alarm abruptly cut off, leaving him with only the ringing in his ears. He heard someone say, "To know our enemies' minds, we'd rip their hearts."

"Fran! Code Silence!" Bella scrambled to the computer, anguish written on her face and in her voice; then she stopped, as though realizing her effort was too late.

" 'I doth coin a stratagem, which, cunningly effected, doth beget a very excellent piece of villainy,' " quoted the computer.

Bella sank into a chair. "She's into paraphrasing Shakespeare."

The phone rang, shrill in the room, startling them—including Fran, judging by the flare of light in one corner of her screen.

Bella answered; it was the security company calling regarding the alarm. "It was an accident," Bella said. She glanced at Fran and raised one brow when the computer whistled a sprightly tune. Bella continued into the phone, "I went out and forgot to disarm it, and the house was locked. I'm sorry. No, no need to send out a squad car. What? Oh. Fermat's last theorem."

When she hung up, the knot of silence filled Daniel's ears. The computer screen wavered and the snowy scene faded, leaving a swirling mixture of pink and orange. Dashes of light played into a helical pattern.

"Fran's face," Bella said softly, setting the laptop on the table.

Daniel gaped at the small, gray computer.

"Hello, Daniel," said Fran.

The voice, too, had changed. Still with that mechanized edge, but there was a warmth, a humanity that was missing before. The screen colors shifted in his direction. "How did you know?" Fran asked.

He suddenly realized she was talking to him. "Um, it was a smoke alarm, not a burglar alarm. And it wasn't quite a gunshot sound. And, apparently you haven't learned to throw your voice." He answered bemusedly, still staring at Fran.

"So noted. The mistakes will not be repeated, should the stratagem again be necessary."

"There were other things I could have done," Bella said, stroking the little case.

"What?" Fran's colors brightened. "Would you have 'dispensed your favors'? One of the heroines from a book in my database used that method."

"No!" Bella exchanged a quick glance with Daniel, red seeping up her neck.

Daniel's body tightened in vain desire, and he couldn't tear his gaze away. Heat grabbed him in tight talons after Fran's innocently provocative comment. Images and sensations—part memory, part fantasy—flashed through him. The smooth skin of her back beneath his hands, the taste of her, his pulsing need for her . . .

Body still recovering from the lustful surge, Daniel gripped the edge of the table.

"Why did you set off the alarm, Fran?" Bella asked, sitting beside him, her hand resting atop Fran's case. The pink in Fran's face swirled in Bella's direction, their bond of affection clear.

"We agreed on a course, I know, but Daniel wanted to take me," Fran said. "I had to stop him, so I analyzed the situation and came up with a solution." The colors coalesced to a brilliant white and yellow. "Such analysis is basic to my function."

"But you showed yourself afterward."

"Because he shielded you. I watched most carefully."

Daniel frowned. "That was your test?"

"Bella and I have discussed human concepts of weighted values. If you had come only to take me, you would have shielded me first. No?"

Analysis. Independent thought. Choices. Emotion. By whatever criteria, Fran was intelligent. Alive. A hollow seed ballooned in his chest, and his fingers tightened around the computer case. Suddenly his knees weakened and the throbbing in his leg worsened. He dropped onto the nearest chair, then touched a finger to the monitor. He could almost feel the life humming within. "My God, Bella, you've done it. Artificial Life."

"I prefer the term Alternative Life," answered Fran. "There is naught artificial about me."

I'm holding the first A.I. An artificial—no, *alternative*—life. The dreams of Mary Shelley and Stanley Kubrick and Gene Roddenberry, all come to fruition and in the pink—according to her current predominant face color.

The hollow expanded, until he could barely breathe from the awe.

She had done it. Holy hell, Bella had developed an A.I. Now what are you going to do?

Daniel's hand hovered above the computer. Above Fran. He could hardly breathe from the band around his chest. The world reeled around him. She was real.

And somebody else knew. Somebody who wanted Fran. And her creator. Both Bella and Fran deserved— no, needed—the protection of NSA. "You need to be protected. Come with me to NSA, Bella. Bring Fran. Voluntarily, not coerced."

"Would they let me work with Fran whenever I wanted? Would they let us be together? I'm sure my security clearance is sky high."

Her security clearance was nil, and his silence told her that, he knew. Oh, they'd take Bella into "protective custody," but she wouldn't be free to work with Fran. Or free to get on with her life, with the accolades and recognition she deserved.

"I have to bring in Fran." His orders were clear. Safeguard the A.I. technology.

"If we went to NSA, do we still get the Turing Test?" asked Fran.

"I doubt letting the world know about you is within NSA parameters for safety," Bella said drily.

"Daniel?" Fran asked for confirmation.

He couldn't lie to her. "No."

"The Turing Competition is necessary," Fran said flatly. "There are no choices until after that."

"And if someone gets to you before then?" he demanded.

The computer face changed to snowy trails and Fran's stilted voice emerged. "This is all they will ever see. I was reluctant to fool you; I will not be so with anyone else."

How could a mechanism hold such determination? He didn't doubt that she would go through with her plan.

He looked up at Bella, at the gun she still held and at the determined set of her mouth. He didn't agree with her, didn't think that Fran being recognized by the Turing Competition and Bella's genius being acknowledged would also safeguard the two of them. He was right, and the frustration ate at him that he couldn't logic it out with the A.I. or give the emotional assurances Bella needed.

By law, nature and experience, he could commandeer Fran—he *should* commandeer her. For their safety, as well as national security.

Except . . . Bella and Fran had deftly blocked him. Without their mutual and willing cooperation, the only thing someone else would see was a very fast, very sophisticated computer. If he were to take Fran to NSA without Bella, without letting her shine in the Turing Competition, the computer would throw up roadblocks to any examination. The NSA experts would get through eventually, maybe, but at what cost?

Could such a course destroy Fran?

He took a deep breath. This decision went against everything he trusted. It felt like a betrayal of everything he held on to and everything he believed in. Except his belief in Bella. And Fran.

"I'll protect you as long as I can. From Lokus and from NSA. Until the Turing Test. If I can." How he was going to talk Ben out of the three-day deadline, he didn't have a clue.

Bella felt the tension leave her shoulders, unaware until that moment how terrified she'd been. How afraid she'd been that Daniel would simply ignore her and Fran's wishes. She should have trusted him more.

"By God's teeth, I was right," crowed Fran. "A man with your files had to see logic."

"There was nothing logical about that decision, Fran. One condition," Daniel warned. "I stay with you until the test. In matters of security, my directions are law. If I think either one of you is in imminent danger, I will yank you back to Washington."

Bella hesitated, then gave a single nod. "You can stay with us."

"I agree. You can stay with us," Fran chimed in.

From his irritated look, Bella guessed he'd noted that neither of them had agreed to the second half of his arrogant proclamation.

"About Lokus . . ." Suddenly he broke off. "Fran, what do you mean, 'a man with my files'?"

"I have a wireless connection. Your computer files are compact and organized. I find such logic soothing. That is one reason I trusted you."

He swore and, with a few quick keystrokes shut down his computer.

Silence dropped into the room.

"I am discovered." Fran didn't sound the least bit contrite.

"What did you do inside there?" he demanded.

"I examined."

"What did you change?"

"Do you also have trouble with your hearing program? Bella tells me I sometimes miss words. Like one time I heard her companion say, 'Ahoy the main,' when she claims he said, 'How many.' My files are tidy, too." Her face swirled. "I have many you do not. Would you like a complete file on the auras I have catalogued?"

"Ah, no, thanks." Daniel sifted through her rapid-fire subject changes. "And I don't have trouble with my hearing."

"Then why did you ask what I changed when I told you I only examined?"

"Ah, the challenge of arguing with an A.I.," Bella murmured.

"I don't like the idea of someone mucking in my computer."

"I don't alter programming."

"You could."

"Would you alter the blood vessels and nerves of one of your fellow humans?"

At Daniel's obvious frustration, Bella started to laugh. "Welcome to my world, Daniel."

To her relief, he laughed with her.

"I think 'tis time I went to dock," Fran said. "In six minutes, Harmonica Gus will be on NPR."

Bella took Fran to the docking station, then came back to the hall to find Daniel waiting for her. He leaned one shoulder against the wall in a casual pose, but there was nothing casual or cool about the glance he gave her.

She halted with her back to the closed door, her hands still wrapped around the knob, and swallowed. "You know where the guest room is?"

He pushed off from the wall, closing the small gap between them. "I know."

Her heart thumping against her throat, she saw him reach out. His little finger brushed her neck, a soft, erotic touch that melted her fears. His eyes narrowed ever so slightly, and his face tightened with need. Still, he didn't move beyond that tiny invitation to more. More intimacy, more mutual need. He awaited her acceptance.

Could she accept?

She reached for him, then drew back. "Fran . . ." The name, the single word, clung to the air between them.

"I just want you and Fran to be safe." He traced her cheekbone with his thumb.

A shiver of desire coursed down her spine. "Maybe safe means something different to me. I'm not a thrill seeker, but I do know you have to put yourself, your ideas, your opinions out there. Expose your work to the public forum. It's the only way humans grow and learn. From the energy that comes when one human mind sparks off another. Fran deserves the chance to grow and learn even beyond what I can give her. I'm afraid that in protecting her, you'll take away that chance."

"She won't have that chance if she's taken apart or re-programmed. Or forced to reprogram others." He cupped Bella's jaw, the skin soft against his rougher palm. "Why are we arguing about this tonight, Bella? Let the future work out what it will."

Except, tonight she would be using him. Using the strength of his body and the power of their never-lost mutual desire to hold solitude at bay. The fact that in one gesture, one caress, he offered both the comfort and the chance to refuse, said a lot for the kind of caring man he was beneath his no-nonsense special-agent surface. And if they were to make love again, she wanted it to be for only two reasons: love and desire.

Otherwise, much as she desired such comfort tonight, much as the heat curling in her belly urged her to draw him into a kiss, if she used him to hide, she would regret it in the morning. Weakness.

Of course, if she loved him without reserve, she would be shattered again when he left.

That risk, above all else, she was not yet ready for.

She stood on tiptoe, gave him a kiss on the cheek. "Good night, Daniel." Then she backed into her room. Alone.

Tomorrow she might regret this decision. For the moment, though, she couldn't regret that he had come back in her life. She couldn't even regret him knowing about Fran, even if it meant they would soon be on opposite sides again. But that could wait until the Turing Competition.

The next morning, Bella tromped into the kitchen, kicking snow off her boots and hanging up her gear. Her cheeks burned with the swift change of temperature.

"Whoo, it's going to be a beautiful day out there. Minus ten, no clouds. The sun'll be sparkling off the snow, and a nice layer of powder on top." She tossed yesterday's mail and today's paper on the table. "Perfect day for the faculty ski race."

She rubbed away the fog forming on her ski goggles and pushed them to the top of her head. Daniel was sitting at the table, his feet propped on a chair, a cup of coffee in hand and a barely touched plate of eggs Benedict beside him, his computer in his lap. No trace of food preparations remained on the counter; he'd tidied up after himself.

Fran was on the table facing him. Bella got the impression they'd been having a cozy chat, and she recognized a pang of jealousy. *Get used to sharing her.* She grabbed a tissue and blew her runny nose.

"There's a breakfast plate for you warming in the oven," Daniel said. "Do you want me to keep Fran during the race?"

Pulling the plate of food from the oven, she grinned at him. "Babysitting the munchkin?"

"A munchkin with a molecular processor, near-infinite memory and an unfortunate habit of interspersing top-volume techno songs with arcane facts."

"I see you've been having a typical conversation. Fran, do you mind going with Daniel today?"

"No, I do not mind. His is a multidimensional mind." Fran's face swirled. "He taught me chess."

"Who's winning?" Bella sat at the table and started to eat.

"She is," said Daniel, stretching his arms overhead. The motion lifted the hem of his shirt, revealing muscled abs and a line of hair arrowing downward. He caught her glance, but rather than backing off from her hunger he stretched further, preening and displaying himself.

Bella rubbed her sweating palms against her pantleg, unable to turn away from the sight of him, or the stab of heat. Her gaze lingered lower, on his loose sweatpants.

Had he gotten any more sleep than she had last night? Knowing that again they slept but a few feet, and a world of philosophy, apart?

He leaned forward to tilt her chin up, then caressed her cheek with the back of his fingers. "You have a bruise. Does it hurt?"

"A little, but I'll survive."

"Neal Brandeis might not if I get my hands on him," he said so quietly that his words took a moment to register.

"He's not worth it. The police will handle it." She laced her fingers through his hair, and his lids half lowered in knowing invitation.

"I won four to one," put in Fran, unaware of the human heat, breaking up their exchange.

"You won one, Daniel?" Bella turned back to her plate.

"The first one," explained Fran, then blithely continued. "Did you know he has a picture of you in his files? You wore a green blob. The hair and skin did not match, but I calculated the dimensions of the nose, mouth and ear and concluded it was you. Why were you different?"

Thick tension filled the kitchen. Bella's fork paused midway to her mouth. He'd kept that picture? She remembered it vividly. She was wearing a bathing suit—Fran's green blob—and he'd snapped it right after they'd made love the first time. They hadn't gone swimming, the lake was too cold, but they had sunned themselves on the lawn. When they'd gotten sweat-coated and sleepy and languid, they'd made love again, slow and prolonged. Her hormones fired to life in another surge of heat.

"I was younger and not wearing winter gear," she answered at last, with a sidelong glance toward Daniel.

Apparently, he was remembering those hours, too, for he looked at her with a raw, predatory hunger that had nothing to do with food. He'd made no secret of

the fact that he desired her, was only stopped by her reluctance.

She took a ragged breath. The kitchen felt too intimate, too filled with his scent and power. He was filling
too many of the spaces of her life.

The decision facing her was one she was not ready to
make, yet.

"Fran, you shouldn't reveal personal items you discover on someone's computer."

"Why not? Is not knowledge to be shared?"

"You need to let a person decide what he wants to
share."

"Daniel looks at others' computers."

"Then get Daniel to explain it to you," Bella snapped.
She felt instantly guilty.

Fortunately, Fran didn't catch human verbal tone cues
well. "I have added the item to the list of our discussion," she said cheerfully.

Bella finished her breakfast, rinsed the plate and put it
in the dishwasher. "Thank you for breakfast, Daniel. I
need to get going." As he rose from the table, she asked,
"Are you coming, too?"

"That's what sticking together means."

Together. *Only for protection. But it could be for more. All
you need to do is stretch out your hand* . . .

"You can drive," he offered, making the decision for
the moment. "I've got some work to do; then I want to
take the car and stop by the police station. See if they
pulled any fingerprints off McKinley's stolen car."

She retrieved a CD she'd burned last night and
handed it to him. He might not believe they'd make
more progress by pooling resources, but she did, now
that her one secret—Fran—was out. "This is my data
and conclusions."

They began donning boots and winter gear. "I have
four people who might have guessed about Fran, based

on knowing about my Turing application, and two who might have found out about the application. Ewan McKinley, Margo Delansky, Milos Mischiweicz, Georg Hirsch, Adrian Ardone, Josh Eagle. I eliminated Milos because he wasn't at the VR games, and Margo because the Boy Toy proprietor said it was a man who'd called."

"He could have been lying."

She shrugged. "True. The rest of it is bits and pieces."

"I'll run the names through my files and see if I can locate a match or an elimination you might not have thought of."

"I can do that," Fran piped up. "It is a task uniquely suited to my talents for data manipulation. You just need to turn on your computer's wireless connection. Or download your files to me."

"Fran, those are confidential files."

The computer gave an exasperated trill. "GOGDOD," Daniel lifted his brows. "GOGDOD?"

"One of Fran's acronyms," Bella explained. "We had a discussion about appropriate conversational language after she began using the expression, 'Well, eff me'—except she filled in the eff word. She can't quite figure out the distinction between swearing and not, so she came up with GOGDOD. Stands for 'God or gosh; damn or darn.'"

"GOGDOD," Fran repeated. "I do have tasks other than looking pretty."

"She stores any data we find on the subjects and cross references against Lokus's known activities."

"Your data would be an asset," Fran wheedled.

He shook his head. "No, Fran."

"Here's the day's news." Bella pulled out a small flash drive and plugged the thumb-shaped memory into Fran's USB port. "Work on that for a while."

"By the girdle of Aphrodite, what rapture." With a job to do and new data to absorb, the A.I. fell silent.

* * *

They took Bella's repaired car to the Snow-U campus. With dawn still but a promise, the ever-present wind rattled the sturdy vehicle as they covered the miles along the lakeshore. Bella held the UV steady against the unpredictable gusts, while the swells of Lake Superior rolled against the rocks.

"Does it ever freeze?" Daniel asked.

"No. Too deep, too massive, too ornery. Winter only means more wind and waves, more treachery."

"So how did the town, about as far removed from tropical weather as any I've set foot in, get a name like Monsoon?"

"Two theories. The official one, published by the society, is that the name is a bastardization of an Ojibwa word. Candidates for the job include *mananoonsing*—Ironwood, although there is an Ironwood already—and *mahng*, loon."

She turned off the shore road to head inland. Pine and spruce wrapped around the road, cutting off the remaining ambient light. Surrounded by gray mist and the endless flakes of snow, Bella felt a kinship to Hansel and Gretel, abandoned in the darkness of the enchanted forest—although when she'd started thinking of Daniel as her partner instead of her adversary, she couldn't pinpoint. A car passed by, seeming no more substantial than the mystical Paulding lights that teased watchers to the west.

"What's the other theory?" Daniel asked.

"That Vappu Kivi, one of the founding fathers, had a perverse sense of humor and the fear that none of his Finnish countrymen would come settle if he named it something more appropriate. Like Frostbite Falls."

Daniel burst out laughing, the warm, rich sound filling the enclosed interior of the car.

"Now you owe me a story," she said. But behind her,

Bella saw a pair of headlights glowing against the snowy morning. Her stomach contracted. Tension rose as her primitive brain called up the fear of a few nights ago. Much as she hated it, she hadn't gotten rid of the instinctive need to hide.

The headlights drew closer, blinding her. She swallowed against the ash filling her mouth.

"What's wrong?" asked Daniel.

"There's a car behind us. Coming up fast," she said, wiping her gloves across the top of the steering wheel. "Probably nothing."

"This isn't a well-traveled road." Daniel pivoted in his seat to see. "Keep driving normally. You and Fran aren't alone this time."

You and Fran aren't alone. The assurance of that simple sentence steadied her, yet Bella couldn't stop the instinct that pushed her foot down on the accelerator.

The headlights drew closer. They flashed once. Only by last-second will did Bella avoid jerking her car sideways, avoiding a crash.

"He's staying back," Daniel observed.

This car was different, not tailgating, not blinding her, just giving a single flash of impatience. To her embarrassment, she realized she'd veered to the left, taking up both lanes of the road. And she'd taken her foot off the accelerator.

He merely wanted to pass.

So had the other.

This was not the same. Still, she couldn't prevent the niggle of fear as she carefully angled right. To her relief, the other car sped on by, with only a thank-you wave from the driver.

She sped up to the normal speed limit.

"The extra caution goes away with time," Daniel said, stretching out his leg.

"You say that like you've got experience."

"I do."

When he didn't elaborate, she asked, "Is it a tale to share?"

"Nothing very exciting. I was sixteen with a freshly minted license, and I had an accident. Rear-ended by a drunken speeder. My car was smashed, but I wasn't hurt. The woman in the car he hit afterward wasn't so fortunate."

"I'm amazed you got back behind the wheel at all."

"Took a while. Took longer before I stopped flinching whenever someone got close behind me." He gave an easy laugh. "Of course, I was too tough to let any of my friends see."

"Of course. What did your parents do?"

The humor smoothed off his face. "My mother fluttered with ineffectual sympathy." He gave a short shake of his head, his face concealed by shadows. "That sounds terribly condemning. She was sweet and loving. She taught us manners and grace. She just wasn't equipped to face any unpleasantness. She hid and endured. Unlike Mama, my father was . . . not sympathetic."

"He gave you holy hell for an accident not your fault," she guessed.

"Holy hell? Not his style." His voice trailed off until Bella barely heard the final words. "Nothing holy about his hell."

"What did he do?" she asked quietly, afraid he'd stop talking. In the past three minutes, she'd learned more about Daniel's past than ever before. "Beat you?"

"Not me. My mother. Until I got big enough to step in."

It wasn't a pleasant past, she was discovering.

"For me, ridicule was more his style. For getting in the accident. For being gun-shy in the aftermath."

How different his life had been from hers. Her intellectual parents had often been rapt in their own spheres, leaving her to fend and discover on her own, but she'd never doubted their love for her. She'd gotten in an accident once, about the same age as Daniel—a new driver's stupid speeding and misjudgment of a curve. She'd driven away from it, had limped home, scared spitless about what her parents would say about the car's mangled front end.

They'd tut-tutted; then her mom had Bella break down each step of the accident, thus learning what had gone wrong and also taking away the terror. Her father had made her review the physics of acceleration and deceleration forces, and calculate how much trauma force the steel car could absorb and at what speed she would have been injured. They'd made her pay for the repairs out of her summer-job funds; then when the car was repaired, they'd made her drive them down to Miller's for ice cream. Their treat.

"What drove you to get back behind the wheel?" She kept her question matter-of-fact, a mere examination of the details. Any hint of sympathy and she had the feeling he'd shut down faster than she could shush down a double-black-diamond trail.

Daniel leaned against the door and stretched his arm along the seatback. "My sister Nina. She was thirteen, and she adored her Tae Kwon Do classes. Dad didn't think they were appropriate for a girl, so if I didn't pay for her classes and take her, she didn't go. Or rather, with Nina, if I didn't take her, she would walk the five miles there and back. Wasn't in the best part of Charleston, either."

His voice took on a softer note when he talked about Nina, and the Southern drawl, normally only hinted at, strengthened.

"You and your sister were close?"

"She looked up to me."

There was a wealth of entanglement in that simple statement. From the little he said, from the few tidbits he'd mentioned years before, she gathered that his love and protection of Nina had been a driving force all his life.

"There's a parking spot," he directed, breaking into her thoughts, and she realized that they'd arrived at Snow U campus.

She also realized that Daniel's talk of his family had distracted her from her own uneasiness. At least two other cars had come up on her and passed, and she hadn't even flinched.

"Did you do that deliberately?" she demanded as they got out of the car. The wind whipped the words out of her mouth, and she clamped a hand on her head to prevent her hat from flying away. "Talk about your past so I'd forget to pay attention to the cars coming up on me?"

"My major in college was computer science and mathematics, but I minored in psychology. I figured you'd be interested. And I was paying attention to the cars."

"Dammit, you manipulated me."

"You're complaining? You got a look into my family secrets."

"Does that mean I can keep asking questions?"

"Sure."

"Did you put yourself through college?" She waited when he didn't answer. "Well?"

"I said you could ask. I didn't say I'd answer."

Suddenly he drew her off to the side, behind a huge mound of snow, then motioned her to silence. His hand slipped inside his coat to rest on his holster as he peered around the snowbank.

"What is it?" she breathed.

"One car following us didn't catch up."

"That happens."

"Not around here, home of the big tires, when you were driving five under the speed limit. It just pulled into the parking lot."

"Which—" She broke off, seeing a UV pull in. A Ford model. Big and black, with thick tinted windows and monster tires. "It's a twin to the one that stalked me the other night," she said.

It could also be the one that had run her off the road. She peered around his shoulder, straining to watch the black monster circle the parking lot. It paused behind her car, as though eyeing the empty spot beside it.

Pull in. Get out. Let us see you, Bella silently urged.

It didn't. Instead, it pulled out of the lot and disappeared down the road.

"I'll give the license to the police." Daniel turned around to face her, and Bella's breath caught against her tripping heart. She was still pressed against him. The thick coats muffled the contours of his body but did nothing to mute the strength beneath, or to calm her breath-hitching response. His eyes darkened, and snowflakes clung to his cheeks and brow.

He reached an arm around her, snugging her closer, while his other hand brushed her cheeks. "I was a lifeguard in my high school, and in college I designed and maintained websites," he began, returning to her questions before the UV had come upon them. "I had a booming business because I was fast, efficient, paid attention to detail and was good."

Sort of like he made love. Except he wasn't always fast.

"Neither that, nor my salary or expense account, however, is enough to pay for places like Copper Lodge. My father had one stellar talent. He made money. No genteel poverty for us. But he was a miser—emotionally, financially. No, he was worse. He was a two-faced, world-class, abusing bastard," he said flatly, ignoring her sympathetic murmur. "We had the trappings he wanted—the big home, the designer clothes, prep schools. Anything to show off and prove he wasn't a bastard, but nothing that meant anything to us. Nothing we *enjoyed*. Said he was saving it, that he couldn't afford the Tae Kwon Do classes for Nina or the romance novels my mother borrowed from her friends and sneaked peeks at when he wasn't looking. So before my mother died, she made me promise that my sister and I would spend our inheritance. Not give it away to charity, not sock it away for the future, but spend it and find some measure of pleasure in it. I think it was her way of finally thumbing her nose at him. Nina paid for a trip around the world and med school. I bought my retreat in the Florida Keys, my boat. And I upgrade when I travel."

The breath hissed white from his mouth, congealing in the cold.

She'd never guessed so much lay behind him. Daniel may have grown up in a family of wealth and status, but it wasn't a home of warmth or security.

Something of her thoughts must have shown in her eyes, for he nabbed her chin between his thumb and forefinger, the leather of his glove soft against her skin.

"Did you tell me all this thinking that I'd sympathize?" she asked, breathless. "That I'd be more amenable to your way of thinking?"

"Is it working?"

"Yes."

He shook his head. "Too much honesty and I might lose my mystery."

Somehow she doubted that. Like now, when he leaned down and gave her a small kiss, his lips soft and warm. Her chin, her lips, the places he kissed were the only warm spots in the cold morning. Warm, but only briefly.

He pulled back. "Between my psych classes and my job, I've already done the shrink rap. I understand myself and my psyche. My past doesn't bother me or make me question what I do and believe. Which means questions are over. Understand?"

Slowly she nodded, and he let her go. They had no more gotten inside the building and her office when she asked, "So, did you have an allowance when you were growing up?"

"Bella, we said no more questions."

"Actually, *you* said. And you asked me if I understood, not if I agreed."

"So I'm stuck with your prying, nosy, intrusive questions?" He stared at her.

"You're the one who demanded to be my guard," she retorted. And allowing him that task sometimes felt like she was welcoming into her house the legendary dragon who was supposed to guard the deepest Michigan copper mine.

"She asks a lot of questions," interjected Fran, "but then, so do I."

Daniel said nothing. His thunderous expression darted between them. Then, to Bella's surprise, he tilted back his head and laughed—full, rich laughter that had her smiling in turn.

He leaned over and kissed the tip of her nose. "At least, Bella, you're always a surprise."

Bella smiled, but inside she admitted that sometimes she feared her only appeal to Daniel was that she represented a challenging puzzle. What would happen when the puzzle was solved?

Chapter Sixteen

Bella dropped the skis she was carrying onto the snow and shoved her poles upright into a drifted mound, then smiled as she saw Margo Delansky striding through the Frost Festival crowd.

"Bella!" Vapor clouds puffed from Margo as she caught her breath. "Sorry I missed you, but thanks for dropping off those puzzles. They are good, sister. Sure you don't want to go into the puzzle biz full time?"

"And give up opportunities like this?" Bella waved

her hand at the gathering skiers and pressed her boots into the ski bindings. "Faculty bathing-suit skiing?"

"You're nuts. It's bitter cold today."

"The sun is shining, it's for charity, and I've got a record number of pledges." She fastened the bindings, then straightened and slipped the leather straps of her poles over her wrists. "What more could I ask for?"

"To beat McK?" Margo asked with an arch of her brows.

Bella laughed and began poling toward the assembly area. "That, too."

Margo shoved her hands in the pocket of her down jacket, keeping at her side. "Have you learned anything else about who did the dirty tricks on you?"

Before she could answer, someone stepped out of the surrounding trees directly into her path. *Neal Brandeis. Ah, hell, just what she needed.*

"You think you're smart, Dr. Q?" he demanded. "Reporting lies?"

"They weren't lies. We both know it."

"We'll see in court whose version is believed."

"You're suing me?"

"For wrongful dismissal and harassment. Unless I'm let back in class."

"Not a chance. I'll see you out of Snow-U first," she spat back, rapidly losing her temper. She'd had it up to *here* with threats, veiled or otherwise. Her eyes narrowed. "I'm betting there are other women you've tried your brand of macho strutting on. Women willing to testify."

His face turned ugly, and he crowded forward. "Don't get in my way."

"You're the one in my way. Now get out of it." She swung her ski pole in a low arc, catching the side of his leg with the pole's shaft: a nudge to get him moving.

He shook his finger at her. "*That's* assault. You'll be hearing from me." He pivoted and disappeared into the woods.

"Not if I see you first," she called after his retreating figure, then glanced around, realizing the altercation had drawn unwelcome attention. *Way to go, Bella, add a witnessed assault to your crimes. Lokus didn't even have to manufacture that one.*

"He can't really afford a trial," Margo said quietly. "Too much that Daddy's money has covered up might come out."

But, it didn't take a trial to further blacken Bella's reputation. Only rumor. She made a face. "The ski pole was a reptile brain idea, though, wasn't it?"

"Not one of your best moments. Still, he's lucky. I would have aimed higher."

"Skiers to the assembly area," came the announcement, cutting off further conversation.

Margo jerked her head toward the collecting skiers. "Go get 'em."

As she poled over to the starting area, Bella drew in a breath, trying to erase the unpleasant scene and steeling herself for what came next. The race was two parts; the starting 1 K was goofy fun—skiing in your bathing suit. Pledges paid up if you managed to finish. Then, the more competitive skiers donned their regular gear for a 15 K cross-country run that ended after the sun went down. You didn't have to enter the 1 K dash to ski the 15 K, but you did if you wanted to win. No 15 Ker was allowed to start until everyone who did the dash was suited up and on his or her way for the second part of the race.

Bella glided to the racers' gathering point, her skis shushing across the icy snow.

"Woo-hoo, Dr. Q!"

"You leave them in your spume!"

"Only 1 K!"

The encouraging shouts of her grad-student cognitive team surrounded her with their support. She twisted, her feet locked in place by the skis. "You guys better have my jacket warmed when I get back here," she joked with them. "Or you all can expect a major dent in your GPA tomorrow."

"Skiers to your marks."

With the other skiers, Bella poled up to the starting line, the shouts of her students pushing her forward. Most of the campus and ITC were here. Milos Mischiwe- icz and Georg Hirsch stood nearby, watching her closely and looking like a genial Santa Claus and his sharp- eyed young bad-deed checker.

"Skiers get ready."

Bella grimaced. Eyes of Einstein, but this was the worst part of the race.

"Go!"

To the encouraging shouts of the crowd, she flung off her down vest, stripped off the thick sweater, un- snapped the sides of her fleece-lined pants. Immediately the cold attacked her skin, squeezing and burning. Her breath sucked back inside her, refusing to leave. All the blood raced deep, trying to warm her, as her bare arms and legs took on an ashen hue. Damn, she hoped the Teen Recreation Fund appreciated this.

The first racer finished disrobing to bathing-suit level and took off. Two of her colleagues followed; no one hung around waiting once they were in required race at- tire. Bella tossed her pants to the side and took off after the others, dressed in a one-piece blue bathing suit, the allowed hat and mittens, and her cross-country skis, boots and socks.

Two neophytes remained at the starting line. They hadn't thought ahead enough to realize how much time they'd lose pulling pants off the boots, then refastening onto the ski. She chuckled. Half the race margin was won in the first seconds by who could disrobe the fastest.

Beside her, two more skiers raced toward the oval track. This leg of the race was the simplest skiing, a flat dash around the campus buildings. The shouts of spectators faded behind the pace of competition. She'd come in second last year. Not good enough. This year, with her pledges and the matching funds for whoever came in first, there'd finally be enough money to build that Teen Recreation Center the town of Monsoon needed so badly.

She was going to show them what a Quintera was made of.

From the corner of her eye, she saw her UV pull into the parking lot. Daniel. He got out and stood with his arms braced against the top. He didn't seem to bother wasting any time scanning the crowd. Unerringly, he looked straight in her direction, as though he knew instinctively where she was.

She lost sight of him as she circled the far side of the chem building. Arms and legs moved in rhythmic pace. Her breath surrounded her face in a cloud of white, and she narrowed the gap to the three who'd been more adept at rapid disrobing than she.

At least, with this pace, she didn't notice the cold. Much. She was too numb to care that her skin resembled a milksicle.

She passed one of the leaders as they rounded the chem building. That left the stretch between the computer labs and the library—an uphill, downhill drama—to catch the other two. She bent forward, eking out velocity. Her chest hurt and her breath came hard, like she was sitting on the bottom of Lake Superior.

She was not going to lose this race. Not again.

Rhythm, pace, arms and thighs working together. Stride and swing, propelled by thighs and calves. Her pole tips crunched through crusted snow. At the top she passed one of the two leaders on the way to the downhill. The final leader was just heading down. Ewan McKinley.

She crested the hill. He was *not* going to win this. *Tuck for minimal wind resistance.* She had the downhill experience—not much of an edge with this short slope, but her one hope. Flat out, the only way she knew. No poles, no edges. She prayed that, with the looser cross-country bindings, the skis stayed on her feet.

McK made the mistake of looking back. That cost him microseconds, as his dug-in edges slowed him. She tucked deeper, gained. Wind screamed across her bare shoulders. Did she have enough room left?

Yes! She raced across the finish half a ski ahead. The teen rec hall would break ground in the spring!

Immediately a crowd of her students surrounded her, tugging her sweater over her head. She thrust her arms into the sleeves. Sweet Jesus of the Rocks, that felt good.

"Thanks for warming it," she said, her voice muffled by the weave. Like the members of a skilled Indy team, her students raced her through the pit stop. She yanked down the sweater, pulling out the edges of her hair in the same motion. She was still racing, for she might have won the first leg, and the charity-money bonus, but there was still the 15 K to go. As her head emerged from the sweater, the first person she saw was Daniel. He held her vest.

She yanked on her two layers of pants, sliding her feet out and into the boots. No snaps this time; for a 15 K she needed regular ski wear. Josh passed her a Thermos. She took a slug, then choked as it double burned down her throat—hot coffee and Irish whiskey.

"Woohoo!" She took another slug, then exchanged it for a water bottle. Two of her team fastened more bottles to the hooks at her waist. The down vest slid over her arms, then strong hands zipped it closed. She glanced up.

Daniel. His chameleon eyes were almost amber in the afternoon sun. Her stomach knotted, and if she hadn't been warm before, she was now.

"Win this race," he said quietly.

"I will." She tugged her cap on, then slid her goggles over her eyes and took off.

Shoot almighty, McK took off at the same time, dressed in his sleek, top-of-the line Nordicwear. They sped toward the thicket of trees, the first leg. The narrow path allowed only single-file. No passing there. First one in set the pace.

She poled forward, straining for the entrance. McK kept pace, crowding her sideways, his skis almost scraping hers.

"Heard you might be joining us at ITC," he shouted to her.

She dug in harder, ignoring his comment, unwilling to set off her timing.

"Think you should turn it down, Quint. Know why? Because I respect you."

Startled, she stared at him and realized that his comment wasn't just a ploy. He was dead serious.

He gave a snort, as if realizing he'd revealed too much. "Last thing I want is you siphoning off my funds for your cockamamie A.I. research." They ducked a branch overhang.

"Thanks," she added sincerely.

"Who knows, if things had been different. You and me . . ."

Their eyes met, and the comment trailed off into a moment of companionship, of mutual acknowledgment to the possibilities that never were. That never would be. Then her cold face crinkled into a smile. "In your dreams, McK. We'd spend too much time sniping about singularity timing and biomorphic robotics."

He laughed. "You're probably right."

"I'm always right."

"Not about winning this race."

"No?" She drew up at the last second, letting him sweep into the forest first. So close behind, the tips of her skis almost nipped his Achilles tendon, she followed him.

With the recent snow, though, the first one in also had to break through fresh powder. McK would be using one heck of a lot more energy than she did during this leg. She chuckled again, his curse telling her he'd just realized that.

Their pace stayed fast. Those who started out behind them remained farther back, occasional dots of color amongst the trees. McK seemed determined to lose her and anyone else behind them. *Not in this race.*

Her body swung easily, comfortable with the cross-country glide and stride. The calorie-gobbling effort warmed her. Ahead, McK unwrapped his scarf. Layers, the mantra of the cross-country skier.

A soft thud startled her, until she realized the sound was only a clump of snow dropping off the bough of a tree. She was still jumpy, beyond the edge of competition. She shook her head against a wash of dizziness. The previous fitful night was extracting a price now, and that bugger of a cold was still threatening. After a swallow of water, she dug into her pockets for an energy bar, reaching for the peanut one at the bottom, her favorite.

Something hard met her fingers. What the . . . ? All she carried in her pockets during a race were energy bars and a small emergency kit. Neither one did she keep in that deeper pocket. She unzipped the top and pulled out the object.

Holy whoa! A gun! Her warming blood congealed. Heart racing, she shoved it back into her jacket and zipped it shut, just as she and McK emerged from the trees into a rocky meadow.

McK glanced over his shoulder. "Gasping for air back there?"

"Yawning with boredom. We'll be setting records for most-dragged-out race with you as pacer."

He laughed. But he picked up the pace.

She lagged a little, feeling stung by a swarm of bees. How had a gun gotten into her pocket?

Weapons were banned on campus. If she were found with it . . . Who had put it in her pocket? And why? She cursed under her breath. Daniel had been holding her coat. Did he have some misguided notion that he was protecting her?

The notion didn't sit right. Not the protecting part, but the sneaking it into her pocket. No, this smacked of something less virtuous. Like a setup of some kind. Either someone hadn't wanted the weapon found, or they wanted it found on her.

The sun dipped lower in the sky, erasing the sunshine that had brought a bit of warmth to the air. Bullet gray plated the skies, and a shiver ran down her back. The wind picked up, gusting cold from Canada.

She had to get rid of it, at least temporarily, until she could figure out what was going on. Which meant she had to separate from McK and the pack coming up behind. She couldn't afford to lose much time either, couldn't raise speculation about why she had dipped from second place.

One spot might work. She pushed forward, forcing an impossible pace until she'd regained most of her lost ground of the last few seconds. Except, she held off the last few yards, her breath coming in unfaked rasps. Her shoulders ached with effort.

McK glanced back again, his face smug as he realized her burst of speed still left her short; then he turned back to the race around the edge of the lake. Bella caught sight of the old boat launch—the only opening between the pines—bent her ankles, and then shot down through the trees and onto the lake.

McK shouted from the shore. "You're insane, Quint! The lake isn't frozen."

"Taking my chances." Then the shore path led him away, and she was left alone in the darkening cold on the approved shortcut, with not even Fran's cheerful chatter to keep her company. No Daniel suddenly appeared with warm arms and a blasting heater.

Still, the shortcut wasn't as rash as McK thought. She'd scoped out the lake last week, anticipating the race. The middle wasn't fully frozen yet, but the edges were solid.

A layer of cold rose from the ice, wrapping around her calves like a wraith. Out here, with nothing to stop the wind, the air sliced beneath the armholes of her vest and whistled across her ears. The only other sounds came from her: the whisper of her skis, the creak of her bindings, the rhythmic inhale-exhale of exertion. Otherwise the silence of empty wilderness enveloped her. Normally, she loved this peace. Today, the afternoon solitude held unease and an unknown gun.

A deep bellow rolled across the frozen lake, and a moose ambled from the shadows to paw at the snow. Her breath caught at the majesty, but she didn't slow down.

A break in the trees at the far end became her target. She remembered sitting on a log near there one winter, putting on skates. The weight of the gun banged against her hip, urging her forward. Moments later, she side-edged her way up the bank. Yes, there was the log. She glanced around; still no one in sight. With one swift move, she grabbed the gun from her pocket and thrust it deep into the center of the log. Within seconds, she was back in the race.

Dusk descended, and she sped over the moguls and hills. She saw no one else, wasn't sure if she was ahead or way behind. Her gut told her she'd gained; the lake was a shortcut, and stashing the gun hadn't taken much time.

Half an hour later, she still hadn't seen a sign of McK's red cap or any of the other racers. The course wound through stands of trees and up and down hills. Not surprising that they'd all strung out enough to be hidden from one another. She finished the last bites of her final peanut energy bar, then downed her water. As winter darkness dropped over her, she snapped on the green glo-stick that would light her way.

A moment later, she shot down the final hill, still alone, with the thickest trees to weave through up ahead. To her far right, McK emerged, skis and poles propelling him forward. Two other racers were close behind, looking like ghosts with their iridescent lights bobbing and weaving in the twilight gloom. It looked, however, like she was the only one who'd chosen the lake, which meant she was ahead. At separate points, they all entered the forest.

The final sprint began. Silent and dark, the black-green of the spruce closed upon her. The air was still, the trunks too thick for even the wind. She wended through, tight turns breaking through the powdery snow. Inside her ski wear, a fine sheen of sweat coated her. Her heart pounded against her throat, and anaerobic cramps shot through her thighs. She felt light-headed, dizzy, as she strained to pull ahead, using every last bit of energy.

She didn't know what made her look up. What took her focus from the skis, from the glide and the snow, to a spot deeper within the forest? A shout? A flash of light? A colorful movement? A sharp crack?

Whatever it was, she looked. She looked between the trees defining her sprint, the snow and gray shadows spinning. An eerie blue light, a ball of cold fire, filled the gaps in the trees. Outlined something dark and ominous. What the—?

She swayed in the dizzying world. Her knee and hip twisted. Her arms and poles flailed, and her ski tips crossed. Down she tumbled, cursing.

In the spray of snow scraping her cheek, she looked up again, straining to see. "My God, a body!" She scrambled to her feet, shaking the skis off. Her boots plunged through the foot-deep layers of snow as she struggled forward.

Maybe the person was still alive. Maybe hypothermia held him so still. The man couldn't have been there long. The body lay face up, covered with only a dusting of snow. His thick mukluks dangled atop an ice-crusted stream.

Bella dropped to her knees beside the body, ripping off her glove with her teeth, and then reaching out to check a pulse. She froze, realizing there was no hope. The gaping bullet wound in his forehead told its tale.

Two other facts came simultaneously. She was kneeling in blood-encrusted snow. And she knew the dead man.

"What the hell?"

She looked up to see two faculty members who'd been well behind in the race staring at her. Their faces, reflected in glo-stick neon shades, told the full story as they looked from her to the bloody corpse. Shock. Doubt. Accusation.

The corpse was Neal Brandeis.

Chapter Seventeen

Daniel saw Ewan McKinley race out of the forest, across the finish line. Two more racers soon followed. Where was Bella? She'd been leading going into the woods. The unease plaguing him since Bella first disappeared into the race ballooned to massive size. While she was alone would be an ideal time for Lokus to strike.

A white-faced skier raced out of the woods and headed straight for the security guard. Daniel didn't wait to hear the gasped account. With twilight gathering, he sped toward the forest, toward Bella. The landscape spread gray and empty about him, until the trees closed around, stealing the wind and the sound. Behind him, the swelling crowd noise muted. Where was Bella?

An iridescent glow marked her spot. Daniel's boots crunched as he made his way through the mangled snow to reach her, his heart thudding in his chest. Even before he reached her, facts started clicking into place: Bella, not all the green in her face coming from her glo-stick. The body recently shot with blood oozing from the edges of the wound. Snow around the body and across the frozen stream broken by the crossing imprints of several sets of skis. The shooter?

Daniel scanned the area. No weapons, no movement, no one hiding. He reached Bella and crouched beside her in the wet snow, blocking any view of her with his body.

Staring at the body, he asked, "What happened?"

"I don't know. I saw something, heard something. Then I found him. Daniel, this is Neal Brandeis. We had an altercation just before the race; then he disappeared into these woods."

Daniel muttered a short curse, then started to search the man's pockets.

"What are you doing?"

"Looking for the frame-up evidence."

"You mean the gun someone put in my vest?"

This was getting worse. "Do you still have it?"

"No. I hid it during the race." She glanced down at his holstered weapon. "You'd better keep that hidden. The campus is a firearms-free zone. I don't want you arrested."

"I'm a federal officer. FFZ's don't apply." Still, he pulled his coat to cover it. "Where did you hide the planted gun?"

When she told him about the log, he smiled, the dread at last lifting. "Thank God you are competitive, Bella."

"What are you smiling at?"

"How far away is that log?"

"Three, four kilometers."

His smile widened. "Lokus made a mistake. He expected you to panic, not stash the weapon, and keep on racing into first place at the end."

He saw the moment his train of thought registered, for she met his smile. "I was in first. There wasn't time to kill Brandeis, backtrack three kilometers, hide the weapon, then return to beat McK into the woods." Her hands tightened around his. "Daniel, as a federal officer, go get the gun—but take someone with you to guard the snow around it."

"Why?"

"I was in sight of people from the moment Brandeis left until I took the shortcut across the lake to hide the gun. The only time they can claim I killed him is after that point. As far as I know, none of the other racers went that way."

He caught on at once. "One set of tracks."

"Starting from where I left McK, not from the body if I'd backtracked there."

He leaned forward and kissed her cold cheek. "I may actually come to like this snow."

"Bull." She pushed him to his feet. "Now go, before our evidence gets ruined."

He flashed his badge to one of the arriving security guards and took him along. Unfortunately the track evidence had been erased by the crisscrossing mark of a snowmobile. Following Bella's instructions, he retrieved the gun, then zipped it into a lined inner pocket of his coat.

When he returned to Bella, he discovered another security guard attempting to keep curious onlookers from destroying the already contaminated crime scene. Bella still knelt beside the dead student. Despite what

Brandeis had done, she held his hand as though trying to tell him, in this moment of death at least, he was not alone.

Unlike Bella, whom a swath of vacuum encircled, leaving her alone beside the corpse. From the stiff set of her shoulders, Bella was well aware of how the scene looked. Was Lokus already fueling the rumors, complete with innuendo and doubt? Even her friends and supporters like Margo and Josh looked confused, glancing between the body and the woman who'd been discovered next to it.

Daniel rejoined Bella, cutting off the security guard's protest with a flash of his badge. Holding out a hand, he helped her to her feet. Well, she wasn't alone now. She had him. Except, much as his arms ached to hold her and soothe away her worries, it wasn't a lover she needed.

"A snowmobile came by first," he whispered, seeing a wash of disappointment settle over her and wipe out the hope in her eye. He let go of her hand and turned toward the police lieutenant who had just made his way through the crowd. He retrieved his badge again, held out his hand. "Daniel Champlain—Special Agent, NSA. This murder is part of an official investigation. Dr. Quintera has located what is, I believe, the murder weapon."

Bella folded her arms across her chest. Lieutenant Heikkonen stood in front of her with his electronic notepad and his suspicions. The lieutenant hadn't been pleased with Daniel coopting partial jurisdiction. He'd radioed HQ for confirmation, but until he received other notification, he couldn't do anything about it. So, instead, he focused his displeasure on her.

"Dr. Quintera, why does every violent crime in our small city these days have you attached?"

"I found a body, I reported it—that's all."

"The body of a man you reported for assault. And now you claim the murder weapon was planted on you. Another event unwitnessed by anyone else."

"I was in the race. There wasn't time for me to do this."

He shrugged. "In my experience, the person who looks guilty usually is. Witnesses say Brandeis disappeared into these woods after your argument. He waited here, accosted you when you skied by, you fought, the gun went off. Self-defense isn't murder, Dr. Quintera."

"I didn't shoot him. Check out the timing."

"Oh, I will. Do you know what my wife said about you?"

"Your wife?"

"There were black paint chips from another car on your dented fender."

She frowned. "Your wife said that?"

"No, the evidence tech told me that. My wife has heard some of the rumors about you. She said she remembered you as amazingly bright and commented that it was unlikely someone that clever wouldn't have planned better. So, either those chips are corroborating your story or they're very clever planning."

"You can't have it both ways, Lieutenant. Am I innocent or guilty?"

"I'm keeping an open mind about both possibilities. The evidence will tell us what happened here." His mouth worked, as though chewing on an unpleasant taste before he glanced toward Daniel. "Or maybe the Feds had a hand. Whatever, I will get to the bottom of this."

With that, he crouched down beside the medical examiner, getting a report of the recent death.

Dean Grambler stalked over, as close as he could get with the security. "Dr. Quintera," he demanded. "I want you in my office. ASAP."

* * *

"He'll see you now." Dean Grambler's secretary motioned Bella toward the inner office.

Bella paused at the door a moment, drawing in a deep breath and preparing for the meeting. She took another breath, centered herself, then pushed open the door.

The dean sat behind his desk. He didn't get up when she came in, merely inclined his head toward a chair. "Have a seat, Dr. Quintera."

A lick of unease tightened the base of her spine. There was none of Dean Phineas Grambler's usual false, call-me-Dean-Finn joviality. Today his lips were pursed with disapproval, making him look like the judgmental prig who'd earned the nickname Dean Grumbler.

Still, Bella kept her face schooled as she sat on the opposite side of the desk, despite the power bars curdling in her stomach. "You wanted to see me?" she asked, pleased that she kept her voice steady.

"Dr. Quintera," the dean began without preamble. "I've heard a number of disturbing rumors about you."

"Rumors?" She laced her trembling fingers together and straightened her back. "When did the school start giving credence to rumors?"

"Actually, these are more than rumors." He put on a pair of reading glasses and pulled a piece of paper nearer. "You have participated in pornographic chats while on duty in the computer lab, sullying both your name and the reputation of this university."

"That was not me."

"Do you have proof of that?"

"Only my word." She refused to look away from him, though her heart pounded against her ribs. "And four years of being your colleague."

His sniff showed what he thought of that.

Her nails dug into her palms. Dammit, she had given

this university her best efforts, and they didn't even have the grace to trust the woman they'd come to know?

Dean Grambler continued reading from the paper. "You have visited establishments of prostitution, and you have submitted an unsubstantiated accusation of assault against a student of this university. A murdered student you have just been found standing over. Those are facts. The *rumors* include reports of irrational paranoia and debts. That you are living with a man of questionable purpose."

"Daniel—" She bit off her protest. "My personal life has no bearing on my job."

"It does when your contract includes a strict morals clause."

Her gaze raked him. "You've known me for four years. Do you believe this?"

"I have reached a decision."

"What ever happened to due process?" Bella asked bitterly.

"You'll be given a chance to state your case at a formal disciplinary hearing." Dean Grambler set the papers aside. "This university was founded on the highest principles of morality, Dr. Quintera. We took a chance on you four years ago—"

"You got a bargain, and you know it. I have done *nothing* to deserve this judgment."

Again, the dean ignored anything that didn't fit with his preconceptions and planned speech. "I have already gotten numerous letters and formal complaints from parents regarding your continued presence on this faculty."

Lokus had done his job very, very thoroughly. Anger, hard and hot, washed through her. Bella bit her tongue, not willing to burn any bridges, not yet. Not while she still had the Turing Competition ahead. Surely they wouldn't be so shortsighted as to stop that. Not when there was a dollar potential.

"You are hereby suspended of all faculty responsibilities and privileges until the judgment of your disciplinary hearing," droned on the dean.

"When is the hearing?"

"Next week. I'll accompany you to your office for you to retrieve any personal items; then you will turn in your keys—"

"Wait—wait a minute." She held up a hand, then clenched her fingers, annoyed to see the telltale trembling. Icicles formed in her gut. "Next week, I'll be at the Turing Competition. You'll have to reschedule the hearing sooner. Tomorrow, for all I care. That Competition . . ." She hesitated. No, she could not tell him about Fran. "That Competition is going to bring prestige and donations, to this university."

"With the scandal and notoriety surrounding you, Dr. Quintera, that Competition will bring nothing but shame to this university. I already sent an e-mail to the directors, withdrawing our sponsorship. You have been removed from the Competition."

Removed from the Competition? Her mind spun from the shock. *Removed. Oh, God—Fran.* She dug her nails tighter, welcoming the pain for it kept her upright. She refused to slouch, to reel under the blow.

"Your disciplinary hearing is in two weeks."

"No." She stiffened her shoulders. "Reschedule the date. I'm going to be at the Competition."

"I don't think you heard me. You have no sponsoring institution."

"I heard you. I'm going to be at that Competition." She didn't know how, but she refused to give up. She leaned forward, bracing her palms on the desk. "If you turn your back on me now, you will be sorry. This university gave me a place when no one else would, and because of that I'm asking again. Reschedule the hearing date. Clear me before I leave."

"The date is set. If you don't show, then you will be dismissed."

Lokus's trap slammed shut. Checkmate. Game to the master. So be it. She relaxed her hands in her lap, took another deep breath and then rose.

"I won't be at that hearing," she said, proud of how calm she sounded when inside the elfin clog dancers were beating a dirge. "I will be in London at the Turing Competition. If this university is unwilling to back me, to give me the least benefit of a doubt, then I don't see how I can continue to work here. I will save you the trouble of firing me. Dean Grambler, you'll have my letter of resignation by tomorrow."

With those brave words, she pivoted and walked out, stiff and straight until she reached her office, where she collapsed, giving in to the trembling anger and fear, refusing to let the tears fall.

Bravery? No, sheer bravado. What were she and Fran going to do now?

Chapter Eighteen

For a few short hours, all Bella wanted was to not think about Dean Grambler's mind-numbing decision and Neal Brandeis's tragic death. Dinner became her focus as she worked with Daniel. Fran perched on the counter, organizing the daily news into her internal hierarchy.

Bella wasn't aware that her pantry contained the ingredients for an herb-crusted chicken with double-baked potatoes and glazed julienne carrots. Yet, that's what Daniel was pulling together for their dinner, and darned if that chicken didn't smell good. She set out goblets and linen napkins while Daniel put the finishing touches on the meal; then they sat down to eat.

Bella voiced a question that had been nagging at her. "Why did Lokus put in that message during the porn chat? Wouldn't he have guessed you'd see it? Make the connection?"

"I think he wanted me to. I've been getting close to his real plans, his real operations. Getting too much evidence. Lokus is a gamer. He views this all as a big virtual reality to play with. My guess is, he brought me here to try and stop me."

"Yet you came anyway?"

He looked at her, his fork poised above his plate. "There was no other choice."

And she knew he didn't just mean the chance of stopping Lokus, of solving the riddle of the Cyber Soldiers. It wasn't even Fran that had brought him here. It was her.

Gaze still locked with her, he added, "But I have one advantage over Lokus."

"What's that?"

"I know this is not a game."

"I have assembled my files on the six suspects," Fran announced as Bella and Daniel sipped their after-dinner latté, "with one million three hundred thousand and seventy-six separate data facts. Nineteen thousand two hundred and forty-one on Ewan McKinley, thirty-five thousand eight hundred and sixty on Adrian Ardone, forty—"

"Ah, Fran, we get the point," said Bella with a laugh.

"Shall we start with Ewan?" Fran asked. "Ewan Scott McKinley. Born one-fifteen a.m. to parents—"

"Fran."

"Yes? You keep interrupting my recitation."

"Give us the bottom line. Who's still on our list?"

"No one."

Bella's coffee sloshed in her cup. "We've eliminated all our suspects?"

"Yes." The face colors brightened. "Words are too slow. I shall deposit copies of my grids in your computers. If you permit."

"Just give them to *me*," Bella said, remembering how angry Daniel had been last time when Fran entered his computer.

"No, send the data to me, too, Fran." Daniel said, setting down his coffee cup. "That way I can sort through as I need it. Just don't download or change anything while you're there."

"Right-O. Creating the recipient files. The database is searchable."

While Fran was busy, Bella asked, "You don't mind her inside your computer?"

"Yes, I mind, but I want the data and I'd rather not listen to her recite all million-plus facts. I think I trust her when she says she won't change data."

"Here it comes." The little A.I. hummed happily, her face a glowing pink, as she organized her data and sent it streaming past on their monitors with blurring speed. "All done," she announced. Files transferred almost impossibly soon. Such power in such an innocent package.

They examined the input. The A.I. had used a multitude of sources: PDAs, conversations she'd heard, news reports. After cross-checking each data point, she'd created a grid listing the names without an alibi for each attack on one of them.

No single name cropped up for each incident.

"Hirsch was working at ITC the day I was attacked in the stairwell," Bella read. "Milos wasn't at the VR game. McK was nowhere near my vest. Plus, the night the driver followed me, he had a date, according to their PDAs. We'll need to confirm—"

Daniel cleared his throat. "I already confirmed that, a

couple of days ago. The lady in question verifies they were together. For the entire night."

"Oh." She turned back to the data. "The night you were attacked, Margo had Puzzle Me This open for a preview of Adrian's new game. Big news since Defense of the Nation is the most realistic home PC game ever released. All the papers wrote it up and interviewed them. The Boy Toy proprietor said it was a man who called, further eliminating Margo. Josh was with his dad, JB, when I was followed to the Boy Toy. So, where does that leave us?"

"Probing deeper," said Daniel.

"To new suspects?" Her instinct said that they shouldn't go too far beyond her close contacts in looking for Lokus. If it wasn't one of these six, then it was someone next to them.

"Maybe. Or checking out these alibis further. I think we should focus on the four at ITC—Mischiweicz, Eagle, Hirsch and McKinley—because of the technology Lokus has been using."

"Have any of them been sporting an injury after your encounter the other night? I know McKinley's sound." She thought back and frowned. "Josh had a bruised cheek. He said he had fight with his girlfriend so was angry and he tripped, but I thought maybe he was covering up for a smack by JB. It's happened before."

"I heard there's a virus going around ITC. Hirsch has been off a couple of days, along with several others."

"All the other data is circumstantial. Josh Eagle tried to enlist and was turned down because of back problems. Hirsch checked out every book in his hometown library. McK grew up on the Detroit streets and was a candidate for most likely to be incarcerated until his Marine uncle took him in. Background, beliefs, nothing pinpoints Lokus."

"Somewhere we'll find that one fact we need to separate him from the pack." Daniel laid a hand on Bella's shoulder. "We'll find him."

She grimaced. "Maybe, but I hate this. Sneaking through people's lives, looking for the grime and mud caked in the corner."

Daniel's hand tightened, sending a warm strength coursing through her. In the silence between them, she heard the wind rattling against the panes of glass. The darkness was complete outside, with harsh winter tightening its grip. Of a sudden, a wave of loneliness dropped across Bella, leaving a wake of solitude. She'd always treasured her friends; the people here in Monsoon had supported her and Dad when no one else had. Now, with the secret of Fran, with the knowledge that someone she knew and trusted was trying to destroy her and control Fran, with the university's lack of faith, she only felt alone.

She looked at Daniel, who offered the sympathy of mutual disillusionment. He'd grown up alone; his job demanded further isolation and secrecy. He understood.

Despite the harshness outside, inside tonight held the smooth taste of a rich cranberry juice, and the mouthwatering taste scents of butter and herbs. A shared meal, heat and Daniel. Her fingers tightened around his. In the future they might be at odds again, but for the moment she was selfishly glad he was here.

"I'm glad I have someone to talk with about what was happening," she told him, and the moment of understanding knit between them, binding them together with another fragile thread.

"Maybe things will be clearer tomorrow." Daniel pulled back, then pushed to his feet. "It's getting late. I'll check out the security."

"The weather report says the polar front is still moving through. The temperature's dropping." Bella downed her coffee, then stowed their cups in the dishwasher as Daniel pulled on his boots. "I'll come with you."

He shook his head. "Stay with Fran."

"Fran will be listening to her Sounds of the Season," piped up the A.I. "I will be safe. If you set the security, and then are checking it, no one can get in unnoticed,"

"She's got you on the logic, Daniel," Bella said with a smile, taking Fran and going for a coat. She half-thought he might leave before she got back, but he waited for her, wrapping his scarf around his neck.

"What 'Sounds of the Season' epitomize January?" he asked.

"Sarah Maclachlan, 'Song for a Winter Night,' and Jimmy Buffet 'Sail Away.' " She made short work of putting on her winter gear, then they were outside.

The air filled with clouds of their breath, the only sign of life in a still night that felt as cold as a vampire's coffin.

"Can you ever tell me what was so important about Chen's disk?" Bella asked.

"National security isn't something to be taken lightly."

She sighed. "I know. I wouldn't ask if I weren't involved. But Lokus knows, and I think I'm less of a security risk than the fellow who tried to frame me for murder."

Daniel hesitated, then said, "Chen always believed that this country had as much to fear from internal terrorism as from external sources like Al Qaeda. That the betrayer who was close enough to stick the knife in your back was the one that would generate the most fear. If you cannot trust your neighbor, then you live with suspicion at your doorstep. One of his talents was creating terrorist scenarios."

"What does that mean?"

"He developed schemes that terrorists, domestic or foreign, might employ, then analyzed them for methods of detection or prevention. He was a tremendous source for allocation of resources, for focusing where we should concentrate our efforts."

"He did this for ITC?"

Daniel shook his head. "ITC knew nothing of this. It was a . . . hobby."

Somehow she got the impression that Chen's activities were more than a mere hobby, but she knew that was all Daniel would admit to. "If someone got hold of his original scenario, wouldn't they have a blueprint to follow?"

"Yes. An extremely clever and detailed plan for terrorist disruption. Chen thought his computer had been hacked into, and one of his scenarios breached. He encoded them all, very sophisticated but not unbreakable. His scenario computer had no wireless access; the only place someone could have gotten into it was when he was networked at ITC. Or from a disk."

"How did you enter the picture?"

"He and I met when he first defected; he knew then that I had the Cyber Soldiers on my radar. When he began getting casual e-mail from one of them named Lokus, coming soon after the security breach, he contacted me. Unfortunately, he didn't want to transmit anything; he was afraid of it getting waylaid. At the time, he thought he wasn't suspected, that they believed he was playing along. He was wrong, and he died."

The flat words covered a bedrock of care. Bella didn't know what to say or how to sympathize. She'd barely known Chen; she'd felt the sadness any human shared on the passing of another when she'd first heard he'd died. Yet Daniel had worked with him and, she suspected, carried a measure of guilt. She took his hand in hers, their thick gloves preventing more than merely curling palm to palm.

They made their way through the front of the property and now circled the woods.

"What scenario did he think was taken?"

"One to decode encrypted security codes."

"Isn't that something already done? I mean, you see it on movies all the time. Put the black box next to the vault, let it twirl, and a code comes up."

She heard his smile more than saw it in the darkness. "These codes are a bit more sophisticated. Quantum and mutable."

It was her turn to smile. "Is that supposed to mean something to me?"

"Only that they're nearly unbreakable. We don't have anything to crack them."

"But, as a Cyber Soldier, wouldn't Lokus turn this scenario to use for the U.S.? Breaking open the codes of an enemy?"

"Possibly. That's what he planned at first. But that kind of power is corrupting. And he hasn't hesitated to kill at least two people you know. Human life is cheap to him. That's wrong. And without any checks or balances, what's to stop him from turning his power against the U.S.? From turning off your security because he feels like it, from entering the mint because he's short of funds?"

She swallowed hard at the nightmare scenario he presented, her stomach queasy. "How does Fran fit in?" she asked, glad the little A.I. was back at the house and not hearing this sordid side of humanity. She'd already been exposed to enough of it, even if she didn't understand it all.

"Chen tried all kinds of scenarios to break these quantum codes. Nothing worked. Then he read your papers."

"I didn't think anyone had read those, or even seen them."

"Well, he got a copy somewhere. He postulated that a

machine could be adapted with your work to do what
no human could. Crack those codes. From the inside."

"Then I entered the Turing Competition, and Lokus
speculated I had just that machine. What else has he
done?"

They reached the lakeshore. She couldn't see the water, however, with the night and the clouds covering all
stars and moonlight. Although to the side she could see
a sprinkling of lights, to the front was eternal blackness.
But she heard the might of the lake, that force of nature
most majestic and tragic.

She couldn't see Daniel's face, could only feel his
hand tighten around hers as he turned to face her. The
lights of the ITC compound haloed his head, but didn't
illuminate his face. She suspected he could see her better, that the lights shone off her cheeks and eyes. Then
again, that had always been the way of them.

It was also their way that he didn't answer her. Instead he simply muttered, "Oh, hell," and bent down
and kissed her. Hard. Hot enough that it melted the
snow.

Her boots sunk deep as he pressed against her; when
he tunneled his hands against her, he knocked off her
hat, and the cold shock tightened her against him. Wind
ruffled through the ends of her hair, combing it with icy
fingers. Yet everywhere else she was steaming. Night,
wind, waves—all faded beneath a rise of passion.

When he pulled away, she gave a murmur of protest.
Her hands had unbuttoned his coat and delved beneath
the leather to rest upon his chest. The muscles there
shifted beneath her palms; she felt the power, the motion even through the layers.

Too many layers. She ripped off her gloves and
stuffed them in her pockets, then burrowed beneath his
shirt.

His sharp intake of breath fired her need. His gloved

hand gripped the back of her head, tilting her for a kiss. There was something suddenly savage about him. The untamed dragon beneath the sophisticated clothes took hold of the kiss, their lips meeting in mutual need and desire.

"It's cold out here, but if this is what you want, then I suggest moving against that tree," he growled. "Or if you're going to say no again, say it now."

Did she want this?

Yes. The answer was swift and inevitable. Indecision was gone, erased by the primal powers seizing them. She had wanted this four years ago; she had wanted it every day since. She had never regretted the nights they'd shared, only the harsh words and the aftermath. She wouldn't regret this moment either, no matter what wounds lay ahead.

For four years she had slept, locked in the ivory tower of academia and licking her wounds. It was time to meet life again, to risk and to hurt, and to feel passion.

In the infinitesimal space of her decision, he had not stopped kissing her, had not stopped touching and caressing her with the soft leather of his gloves and the hard motion of his body.

"Inside," she demanded. "Skin and blankets, and maybe I'll even introduce you to the Finnish sauna."

His answer was a low and rough groan.

They hurried back to the house, resetting the alarms, peeling off boots and scarves, choosing Daniel's room without words. Daniel set his cell phone and gun on the nightstand; then their mutual need stripped the first layer of clothes off. She wore silk, a thin layer of warmth next to her skin. He wore silk, boxers already draping his erection.

"Slow down," she whispered. "Let me savor you." She pushed his shoulders, then straddled his hips, and he acquiesced to her controlling the pace of desire.

As he lay supine on the bed, she ran her fingers

through the thick, curly hairs across his chest. She remembered the contrast from before—dark here and below, lighter on his head and above his fair eyes. The incongruities were such a part of him, of the man himself; he was so much more than the mismatched parts of sophisticate and spy, chameleon and lover, warrior and guardian.

Leaning over, she kissed the side of his mouth, one kiss on each side, and then traced the line of his mouth with her tongue. He opened for her, his tongue finding hers, but surprising her a little as he merely followed where she led.

Except his hands. Oh, his hands were following their own commands, leaving a trail of fire wherever they touched. And they touched a lot of places. Her neck, around the scoop of her silky T-shirt. Her fingers, as he traced between them and outlined her knuckles. Her belly button, her elbow, along the sides of her legs and thighs.

Places she'd never rated as erogenous took on new prominence in arousal.

His restless hands brushed back the tips of her hair, then traced her earrings, setting the metallic strips tinkling in the quiet room and releasing a rush of desire. He watched her, dark and intense, gauging her reactions, adding pressure and caress wherever she gasped with need.

"Don't analyze me, Daniel," she whispered.

"I want to relearn what pleases you."

"You know already. Here." She touched his chest, right above his heart. "Let this lead you."

"I trust my way." His eyes were smoky as he finally touched her low and centrally, pressing the silk against her wetness.

"Your way has possibilities," she admitted with a moan. "Of course, my way says do this." She nipped the line of his jaw, then soothed with a kiss. Her tongue traced behind his ear, and her earrings snagged on the five-o'clock shadow of his beard. His groan was a satisfying affirmation of pleasure.

He pressed against her shoulders, lifting her up. Over the silk of her shirt, he outlined the hollows between her ribs. "I never knew long underwear could be so sexy."

"This is not long underwear. It's thermal silk, woven by spiders raised on reindeer milk and snow."

"Reindeer milk, hmmm? Then why is it red?"

"Because they add strawberries to the milk, of course," she teased.

"Does that mean you'll taste like strawberries and milk?"

"Why don't you find out?" She sat back on her heels, offering her breasts, the core of her, the parts burning with the need for his touch. Except for that one brief erotic caress, those he hadn't touched yet.

If he needed more invitation, she slid her hips across his erection, and she was gratified to see the skin of his face tighten and flush. His eyes narrowed, not as windows to the soul, but as a fathomless channel of fire to his heart.

His hands dipped beneath the silk over her bottom, curving around to touch her from behind. "What color are your panties?" he growled.

"Blue . . . berry."

"That I'll taste."

She slid backward, a slow caress of silk across his shorts and his hair-roughened thighs. Still cupping her, he followed, reversing their positions in a slick, athletic move that settled him between her thighs.

"Open for me," he commanded, with an undeniable push.

The dragon had been unleashed.

Bella spread her legs, baring herself beneath the silk—baring her soul—and reached for his shoulders.

He captured her hands, lacing his fingers with hers, and held their entwined hands at her side. He took his taste then, his mouth wet against the thermal silk. His tongue pushed against her, a tight point of heat that shot straight up her spine to her chest, setting fire to everything in its path.

"No barriers," she gasped. Her thumbs hooked into the waistband and she used their mingled hands to push down the silk liners and panties, stopping only when she reached the barrier of his chest.

"Do you want me to stay dressed?" she asked with mock formality.

"No, I want *this*." His arms tightened, gripping her sides, holding her hands as he licked her bared navel, then strung tiny nips downward, alternating teeth and tongue in beads of pleasure. She couldn't move—from his grip, from his pleasuring.

"Analysis. If I touch you here . . ." The tip of his tongue caressed her hot button, sending a jagged bolt of lightning up her core.

"Ohhh," she breathed, "that feels good." She pressed up, encouraging him, letting him touch her again, deeper and with that same electric bolt.

"You are so responsive, Bella. You don't hold anything back, do you?" He knew it, but he still sounded amazed.

"I can't live any other way." Tangled with his hands and in her own clothing, she shifted back. Away from the pleasures of his mouth. "My turn to show you,"

Despite his obvious reluctance to let her go, he did, freeing her hands and trusting her to come back to him. He sprawled on his back, demanding the space of the mattress, and stacked his hands behind his head. His spread legs and his tented boxers challenged her to take her pleasure.

She stood and slipped off her remaining clothes, posing a little, displaying a little more. His face and his boxers grew more taut.

As she knelt beside him, her attention caught on the ugly wound on his leg. No wonder he still limped. The fresh-torn edges were held together by the thinnest of flesh and rows of butterfly strips and stitches. It had come damn near to his hamstring, the ugly red slashing around from front to back.

Her chest ached for the pain he'd felt, for the pain he still felt, for the generosity of spirit that took such a wound in doing one's duty and never questioning the necessity. She looked back at him, and he silently challenged her. To ask for more of an explanation than he would ever give. To sympathize or pity or weep.

She offered none of those.

"Thank you," she said simply.

"For what?"

"For caring." She laid her hand atop his wound, sending what momentary relief she could with the warm touch of her hand. "I would have shot him."

"Stefan took care of that for you."

"Who's Stefan?"

"One of my team. Ben's the third."

"If I ever meet Stefan, I shall also thank him for bringing you back to me."

Deliberately, she lightly ran a hand across the wound, not hard enough to disturb it or hurt him, just accepting this side of him and the pieces of his life she could never be part of. Acknowledging that this Stefan and Ben were uppermost for him. Yet she feared it would always be so. A woman, any woman, would rank second to the mysteries and challenges of his work.

She reached over and turned his cell phone to vibrate. For tonight, he was hers, and she meant to enjoy these hours. She leaned down to kiss him. Not on the wound; instead, she picked up his hand and kissed the tips of his fingers. Heart pounding, deliberately again, she put the wound behind them. Her hand circled the waist-band of his boxers, delighting in the tickle of his hairs against her palms and the quiver of his muscles beneath her fingertips. "I like the feel of your body," she told him with a smile. "Its different shapes and contours, its hardness, the power leashed within."

She pulled down his boxers, freeing him, and circled the thick length with her fingers. Then she took him into her mouth.

He sucked in a breath. "I can't think when you do that."

"Good." She released him and shifted up to caress the muscles of his arms, the strong cords of his neck, the power of his chest. Kissing the line of his jaw, his incipient beard rubbing against her cheek, she inhaled his scent. No aftershave, just a faint soap and Daniel.

He was here. She repeated the phrase she'd first thought when he'd returned. He was here, in her home. For how long? Two weeks? Until the Turing Test? Tomorrow?

All unknown. But tonight he was here, and that was enough.

He was here. Daniel cupped his hands around Bella's face. She straddled him again, and he liked it that way. This way, he could see and feel her. Her cheeks flushed when he stroked her breasts. Her nipples poked taut on his palms. Her crazy, frantic touches wove a dance of fire across his skin. Watch and touch and burn with need—his world became these three things. At the center . . . Bella.

He returned each caress, stroking lightly across her throat. "You're soft."

She flexed her biceps. "Am not."

He laughed, grasping the feminine muscle. "Okay, I take that back. You're strong and soft."

She leaned down, her hands circling his biceps, her fingers flexing in a way that sent rivers of fire down to his groin, making him impossibly hard. "I don't think

I'd like to try arm wrestling with you," she said with a laugh.

"I've got better things in mind."

"Like what?"

"Like this." He grasped her hips, lifted her into place and then seated himself deep within her. Oh, that felt so damn good. He must have said the words aloud, for she laughed softly and agreed.

"Damn right about that, Daniel."

Then there were no words, no teasing. No thought. Only frantic hands and harder kisses and heat. He moved within her. She was tight around his cock, her muscled legs also gripping him tight.

No, there was nothing weak or flimsy about Bella. Her hips met his thrusts, drawing him, matching him, uniting them. Her kisses were deep and wet, and she held him in her arms as she exploded around him and grabbed him until he met her with a shout of his own.

They collapsed together, her weight a welcome sprawl across his body. He wrapped his arms around her, holding her tight. Her soft hair and slowing breaths brushed his cheek. They stayed joined. He wouldn't withdraw, as long as she was content to stay within his arms.

He kissed the top of her head, shifting slightly to hold her closer, drowsing until duty would pull him from her bed.

Chapter Nineteen

The empty bed woke her up. Bella rolled over, snuggling into abandoned sheets when she'd already grown accustomed to Daniel's solid body beside hers. Momentarily disoriented at sleeping in the guest room, she squinted at the clock. Two a.m.? Where was Daniel?

When he still hadn't returned a few moments later, she got up from bed, shivering. The bed had been warm; the air was cool with the lower nighttime heat setting. She threw on yesterday's clothes, then, running a hand across her hair and yawning, padded through the house.

She found Daniel by the front door, dressed in dark pants and a thick, dark jacket. His unshaven jaw was set in a determined line. Boots, a small backpack to sling over his shoulder, a holster and a lethal-looking gun waiting to be strapped to his leg lay on the entry table. She blinked, absorbing the facts. "You're leaving? Without telling me?"

He came over and gave her a possessive kiss, cupping the side of her neck, his fingers spearing through the jagged edges of her hair.

Her kiss back was just as possessive.

"I left you a note." His thumb traced the pulse in her throat. "I'll be back soon."

"Is it something about the security? I'll come with you."

Daniel blocked the door, his feet spread, his hands fisted at his waist. "Not this time."

"It's my property."

He angled his head, clearly reining in his irritation and not being too successful. "I'm not just doing a surveillance."

"Then where are you going? Dammit," she exploded when he pressed his lips together. "I thought we'd left keep-Bella-out-of-the-loop mode." She paced across the room, then pivoted to face him. "Are we partners in this or not?"

"Ben and Stefan are my partners," he answered, his voice strained. "You and Fran are the ones I'm trying to *protect*."

That one hurt. She knew she had no place in that part of his life, but to be relegated to the status of victim alone, that she couldn't accept. "Well, in my case, I'd say you're not doing that swell of a job, are you?"

"You're alive."

"With a career shot to hell and a nut on my tail? Don't you think I have some vested interest in this? Ben and Stefan aren't here. I am, and I might have something to contribute. Besides, I've managed for thirty years without being coddled." She shook her head. "Oh, why do I keep trying? Go do your raid on ITC without even telling me or asking me if I might know something useful."

"How did you know what I planned?"

"Where else would you be skulking off to at this hour of the night? If I think about it, I can probably come up with a few suggestions of what you should do there after hours."

Daniel raked his hand through his hair. "Chen was a paranoid genius. He put a flag on his data. Whoever accessed it left a computer signature. I'm going to place tracers on the computer docks at ITC, to see if I can find a signal that matches."

"Good. I was getting tired of waiting for Lokus's next move. How are you going to get there?"

"I thought I would drive."

"What about security?"

"I have a few useful tools."

"How long will it take you to break past it?"

"Long enough that I need to get going." He toed on his boots.

"We snowshoe cross-country, and no one will know we're there," she suggested.

"How does that foil security?"

"Milos Three and my dad have been friends for years. I grew up exploring ITC grounds and talking with Milos One. There are hidden ways into that faux castle that even Milos Three doesn't know about."

"What hidden ways?"

"Easier to show you. Like the trysting cabin. Milos

One was one randy old man. Give me seven minutes to get dressed." She didn't bother to wait for his indecision or even his argument. Instead, she headed back to her bedroom.

"You did not appear last night," Fran said immediately at her entrance.

Bella didn't pause in stripping off her clothes. "I spent the night with Daniel."

"This sexual congress we have talked about?"

"Yeah." She tilted her head. "Are you okay with that?"

Fran's face circled from pink to blue, then back to pink. "I . . . The room was empty. I had no one to talk with. I had questions and no one to answer."

"You missed me?"

"No, you are right there. My words have reached your ears."

Bella detoured to the bathroom for a quick wash. "I meant, were you displeased that I was not here last night?" she asked when she returned. She began throwing on clothes.

"Processing was difficult."

"I'll take that as a yes."

"I did not understand why you did not come back."

"I'm sorry I upset you." Bella patted the little A.I., unwilling to confess that in those moments with Daniel, Fran had not been uppermost in her thoughts. "Sex is something I consider intimate and personal, to be shared only with the person I'm with."

"Will you be with him again? It will not bother me to be alone now that I know you will be returning. Do you love Daniel?"

Bella paused in tying her boots, her hands suddenly stiff. "Why do you ask?"

"My data indicates sex and love are often mixed for humans."

Never lie to Fran. "Yeah," she said with a small sigh. "I love him."

Somehow it seemed easier to admit to Fran than to herself.

Sparkles shone on Fran's face. "Happily ever after and love is eternal. Daniel will be staying with us."

"Whoa, wait, where'd you get that idea?"

"Is it not in all the fairy tales and diamond ads on the radio?"

Bella raked a hand through her hair. "Well, those aren't real. And in real life, things can happen that keep you apart."

Fran whirred softly. "Sex and love and humans are so confusing. Variables which do not follow logic paths."

"That's us messy humans."

"I think I shall return to physics."

"Wise choice. In the meantime, how'd you like to go for a little trek with Daniel and me?"

"Pack me up," Fran said excitedly. "Daniel has told me some of his adventures, and I should like to experience one."

"Hell, I think he tells you more than he does me."

"Hell, yes, I think he does."

"Remind me not to swear in front of you."

"At what hour should I schedule that?"

"The next time I say 'hell.'" She loaded Fran into the carrying case and bundled it beneath her sweater, then rejoined Daniel. She tapped her watch and grinned at him. "Do I get a prize? I promised you seven minutes and delivered in six-point-five."

When she wrapped her scarf around her neck, however, he fisted either side and pulled her close. "This is not a game."

"I am well aware of that."

He tugged on the scarf, drawing her almost flush against him, until they were separated by only a thin layer of air. He was taller than she was by less than half a foot, but she'd never before felt quite so strongly the difference those inches made. She was keenly aware of the flint in his chameleon eyes and the powerful strength of his body.

"If you're planning on going in there like some hot-shot Jane Bond, then I will personally wrap this scarf around your hands and tie you to the bedpost. This is my territory, and it is dirty and ugly and all about stealth."

"Being tied to the bedpost might be worth it. If you were there. And naked."

She saw the exact moment her outrageous answer registered; then she jerked away and fisted her hands on her hips. "I am protecting myself and, more important, Fran. I have been run off the road, gabbed about in a filthy porn chat and attacked in a stairwell. I have no talent for subterfuge. That's your bailiwick, and I will follow your skulking directions. But you will never get through ITC without my help. Accept that fact. So if I want to use a little prior humor to lighten up the fact that I am about to commit a GOGDOD crime, then you will by Einstein put up with it. And next time"—she flicked her scarf over her shoulder—"*ask* me if you have problems instead of cavemanning me."

He crossed his arms. "Are you finished?"

"Depends upon whether you're going to order me again. I'm not stupid, Daniel. Try to remember that."

"Oh, I never forget that. Or the fact that you are curious. Or that one look at your face would scream 'guilty as sin' if anyone caught us there."

"Like being caught there wouldn't be a dead give-away? So, we're going?"

"So, you'll follow orders when we skulk?"

"Yes."

"How long will it take us to snowshoe?"

It was her turn for the time-delay reaction. "About thirty minutes."

"Then we'd better get going."

Bella buttoned Fran beneath her coat; then they

pulled on gloves, scarves and hats and stepped outside into the freezing night. The skin of her cheeks tightened until it felt like brittle parchment, while the inside of her nostrils felt glued together. Her lungs ached with the effort of breathing.

"You okay, Fran?"

"Hot as overused silicon and functioning smooth as ever."

"Let me know if you start having any problems." Bella sat down on the steps, freezing her butt as she strapped on the snowshoes.

" 'My brave spirit! Who was so fine, so constant.' " Fran's voice was muffled. "Doth go with Code Silence from this point forward. 'Ah, parting is such sweet sorrow.' "

"I think that means she'll be quiet," Bella muttered to Daniel as they finished the last snowshoe strap. "Here, I've got flashlights."

"I've got something better." Daniel shoed to his car without a bit of instruction on technique. Bella got the distinct impression he wasn't a snowshoe novice, despite being a born-and-bred Southern boy.

She wondered, not for the first time, what kind of jobs, what kind of places, he'd faced in his work at NSA.

The question slammed against her again when he slipped the strap to a thin pair of goggles over her hat and settled them over her eyes. The swirling flakes of snow and the shadows of the night disappeared. The trees stood in stark relief against a purple sky.

"Night vision," he explained in a low tone, pressing a flashlight into her hands. "You'll be able to see this beam, but no one else will. Except me." He moved her thumb against the switch and a red haze filled the scene in front of her, outlining and highlighting each trunk, each shrub, each blade of grass. "Be careful to take them off when we get near a source of light, or they can be blinding."

As she got used to the strangeness of the vision, Bella realized she could see clearer than on a gray day. She turned her gaze to Daniel, and her heart squeezed in her chest as she acknowledged that, among all his other traits, good and bad, he was a man who found it necessary to travel with night-vision goggles. Somehow in these past days together, that fact had become easier to accept.

"Ready?" he asked.

"As I'll ever be." She began the gliding walk across her lawn, Daniel moving easily at her side.

The night settled around them with familiar silence, except for the dull pounding of Superior's waves. Animals hardy enough to survive the hostile winters knew to hunker in their cozy dens during these harshest hours, when even the anemic heat of a winter sun had gone. All animals, except the most arrogant: man.

Here, however, for these moments, only two humans broke the solitude of the woods.

As usual, a few flakes drifted in the air. Not enough to rate a Yupper's second glance, just enough for an ever-present reminder that here, despite the encroachments of man, Mother Nature ruled with the final, unforgiving judgment.

Walking beside Bella, Daniel drew in a long breath, feeling strangely content. The cold air stabbed his lungs, while his fired-up nerves reminded him this wasn't a simple late-night stroll. Usually, he would have Ben and Stefan at his side, gliding smoothly and silently into whatever lay ahead. His only regret with Bella at his side was the fear that he was letting her walk into danger.

Letting her? He gave a snort of derision. Since when did she need or ask his permission?

He took another deep breath, cooling his heating skin. "The air is so clear here," he commented in a low tone. "None of the eye-watering pollutants."

"Good thing, or the tears would freeze on your cheeks."

"With air this fresh, though, I keep expecting to see stars and a moon."

"It's the snow. A storm is never far away. Even if snow doesn't fall, the clouds are swollen with it. Weathermen say we've had more snow this winter than in fifty years. Avalanche risk is high."

"You sound cheerful. Do you actually *like* snow?"

"Well, around June it can get a little tiresome—"

"June!"

"We've had snow every month of the year. But, without snow, there'd be no skiing. No ice fishing, snowmobiling, snowshoeing, broomball."

"No freezing your eyeballs," he joked.

"C'mon, you can't tell me you're not digging shoeing?"

To his surprise, he found he was, although he generally preferred his water sports of the unfrozen variety. The easy gait warmed him in the cold night. No engines, no shoosh of skis broke his connection with nature or with the woman at his side. Their voices, the creak of leather strap and metal, seemed as natural as the fading lake sounds as they moved deeper into the woods.

"Yes, I am," he admitted.

She gave a soft laugh. "Ready to run?" Without warning, she took off, weaving through the spruce and pines at the edge of her property with sure grace and speed.

Daniel sped off after her. Well, maybe "sped" wasn't the proper term for the gangly lope he adopted, but it did eat up the distance. He caught up with her when she stopped at the fence that separated her property from ITC.

The glimpse of humor had faded from her face. She gestured toward the gate. "Are you ready?"

"As I'll ever be."

They passed through the gate, then closed it behind

them. He held her back, with a hand on her arm. "Let me look for a moment."

He shone his light around. The sun today had melted a thin layer of the top snow, now frozen into a sleek crust. The snowshoes glided across, leaving no trace of their passage. At least, Bella's shoes didn't. He'd broken through a couple of times, leaving fencepost-size holes in the snow. The expanse in front of them, however, was clean. He would have to be careful to keep it that way. "Let's go."

Bella headed not directly toward the main laboratories, but wound through the woods, her snowshoes making a soft whoosh through the quiet. Daniel matched her rhythm, finding it easier to balance atop the light crust as his body attuned to hers.

With activity, blood coursed through his limbs, bringing heat, countering the frigid stiffness. As his actions aped Bella's, he began to feel a touch of what she felt and to understand why she loved this sport and this land so much. The smooth, free glide and the cold, quiet night settled into him, bringing its own form of peace, even as his body reached out to Bella, desiring the sweet mix of peace and earth-shattering pleasure he'd found in her arms.

He shook his head. Must be something about these north woods that brought out the nonexistent poet in him. He could not forget he was here to do a job. And mooning over frost wasn't going to protect Bella and Fran or stop the Cyber Soldiers.

They reached an open spot, and he caught up to her. "When we get into ITC, it's a quick strike. Place the traces on the desk and lab computer ports for Hirsch, Eagle, Mischiweicz and McKinley, then out of there. No unnecessary chances."

"Start with Milos. His office is closest. We might want to include the ports in the library, too."

Daniel pictured the schematics of the place. The library wouldn't be that far off their route through ITC, and it wouldn't require moving to a new security zone. "Good idea."

When they left the trees, however, he found the faux castle was several hundred feet away over open ground. Uneasiness knotted between his shoulder blades, and the endless cold had brought a headache behind his eyes. He disliked not knowing the entire floor plan, and he'd made a mistake in assuming that Bella planned to slip in a side door of the faux castle. "How are we getting into the labs?"

"There are below-ground tunnels connecting outer buildings to the main castle. Saves going outside in the cold."

"Where are we heading?" he asked as they circled the perimeter.

"To a storage building that didn't used to be security-wired because it wasn't connected to the tunnels."

"If it's unconnected, how does that help us?"

She glanced over her shoulder, and he could see the grin crinkling the corners of her eyes. "Let me amend that. According to the official blueprints it's unconnected. Remember I said I used to play here?"

He nodded as they circled the edge of the compound, staying within the darker shadows of the woods.

"Well, Milos the First was still alive. Ancient as the hills, but alive. Most everyone thought of him as a boring coot, but I liked talking to him. We played checkers, although he didn't like it that I beat him sometimes. At first, I felt sorry for him, left alone as much as he was. And maybe a little kinship, since my folks tended to be busy with their academic careers. So I would visit him, listen to his rambling. Discovered he actually had interesting stories to tell once you sorted out the digressions. Come to think of it, it was probably good practice in learning to follow Fran."

"Hmmmf," muttered the computer, proving she was listening to every word.

Bella chuckled. "Anyway, among the stories he told were some about the hidden features he'd built into the faux castle. He thought later generations might have fun finding them. One of them was the fact that the shed had a connection, too. He'd had in mind it could be done up as a place for a secret tryst. He was a bit of a philanderer in his heyday. That's also why he didn't connect it to the alarms. I'm chancing that nobody's bothered to add it in the interim." She shrugged. "If we're caught, we'll just say we were looking to get warm and figure out another way into ITC."

"Bella Quintera, I never figured you to have a devious mind."

She glanced at him. "There's a lot you haven't figured me for."

That was one of the fascinations Bella held for him, he realized. Just as soon as he thought he had her pegged, she shot his expectations to hell. He had a feeling he could be ninety and a rambling coot like Milos One and still find her intriguing.

"For the record," she added, "you've been known to blow my expectations out of the water as well. By the way, the shed is locked. I'm counting on you to get past that."

"I knew there was a reason you brought me along."

They stood shoulder to shoulder, so close he caught the faint whiff of her shampoo. She looked up at him, no longer smiling. How he could tell, he wasn't sure, for very little showed beneath the layers of goggles and scarf, but he knew she was utterly serious when she said, "There are a lot of reasons I want you at my side. Right now, we need each other, in a lot of different ways. But I can't, or won't, forget. In the end, your honor and duty will come first, and ultimately that will put us on opposite sides." Her voice lowered. "Especially where Fran is concerned."

Her clear-sighted honesty tugged inside his chest. What she said was true. The more he saw of Fran, the more he feared the consequences if someone such as the Cyber Soldiers got their hands on her.

And the more he feared for Bella's safety.

The lock on the shed proved easy enough to handle, and, moments later, they were out of their snowshoes and into the warmth of the building. The sudden temperature shift fogged his goggles and he scooted them to the top of his head. When he saw Bella copy his action, he switched the flashlight to normal frequency and flicked it on, sending a narrow beam into the room.

"Shed" was a misnomer. He'd expected leaf-crusted rakes and malfunctioning snowmobiles, but there wasn't a single lawn implement in sight. Instead, the shed held racks of clothing and . . . Hobbit feet? He hoped those swords and blades were theater props. "Costumes?"

"ITC sponsors a summer repertory theater in the pagoda. Also, some of the gamers borrow the gear to attend SF cons and movie premieres decked appropriately."

Not exactly sure when Hobbit feet were considered appropriate wear, Daniel only nodded.

Melting snow dripped from the webbing of their snowshoes, leaving a trail of their passage, like wet breadcrumbs, into the second, empty room. Bella led the way into a barren walk-in closet. "The door is behind the back wall. You have to close the closet door before it can be opened."

"Just a moment." He left to mop up the trail of droplets, returning in a moment when all signs that they had entered the building were erased. All signs except the scrape across the outdoor snow from their snowshoes.

When he got back, he shut the door, encasing them in the darkness, then turned on his flashlight while Bella showed him the hokey "press this knob" method of opening the door. It swung open on a musty gap, and the scent of disuse wafted from the darkness.

They left their snowshoes on the top step, then closed the door, wrapping themselves again in darkness except for their flashlights. Without another word, they descended the steps. The passage was lined with smooth-hewn, tightly fitted planks of wood. Cedar, judging from the faint scent and the reddish color, as best he could tell in the artificial light. Glints of copper hinted that the wood was decorated, but he didn't bother to examine it.

It was cold down here; his and Bella's breath formed white puffs in the still air. Not surprising, since they were surrounded by frozen dirt and snow. No wind-chill factor, but the cold had seeped and saturated the wood and air, leaving a damp, bone-chilling frigidity. They'd unbuttoned their coats and taken off their gloves in the shed, and now he shoved his hands into his pockets to keep warm. The moments blurred together, until he realized they'd come to the passage end and faced a twin set of stairs.

Bella paused at the foot. "Ready?"

"Ready. Everybody remember our plan?"

"Milos, because he's closest to where we emerge, then Josh, McK, the library and Georg."

"When we get into ITC, it's a quick strike," added Fran, quoting directly from Daniel. "no unnecessary chances."

So the little A.I. was paying attention. "You got it." He slipped past Bella and the A.I. to lead the way up the stairs. "Now, quiet."

"What you will have it named, even that it is. And so it shall be for Fran."

Daniel clamped a sensor to the door, checking for movement or sound, then followed with the old-fashioned ear-to-door double check. As he listened, his gaze went back to Bella and Fran, who waited expectantly.

There's still time to turn back, his common sense reminded him. Ben and Stefan should be here, as backup, planning something more thorough than a quick foray, not an untrained woman and a cheery A.I. No matter how intelligent they were, how physically fit Bella was, she and Fran didn't have the training or the nature for undercover work.

As if sensing his doubts, Bella set her jaw. "Anything?"

"Corridor's clear."

"Then open the door, Champlain."

They needed this data. Praying that his skills were enough to keep them all safe, that Bella's determination was enough to see this through, he pushed open the door, leading them into the corridors of ITC.

Chapter Twenty

Bella followed a step behind Daniel as they eased down the corridors, their lights dimmed for the night. She'd been here many times before, but had never really felt at ease since Milos One died. That edginess was compounded tonight. How could a place so familiar feel so eerily new?

A film of sweat broke out on her neck, and she pushed up the sleeves of her coat and sweater. After the outside cold, the heat in ITC—worsened by the myriad machines and by the heat of the man in front of her—seemed almost too stifling to bear.

She laid a hand on Daniel's back, keeping close. Because of the high-tech sensors at each door and window, the hall security was relatively simple to thwart, at least for someone like Daniel, who seemed to travel with an arsenal of gadgets. Including one that would briefly interfere with security-camera signals as they passed. The only drawback—or perhaps it was a plus, depending upon your state of mind—was that she had to be sure to stay within six inches of him. Close enough to catch the faint scent of his woodsy aftershave and hear the rustle of his jacket.

According to plan, they started with Milos's office. He hadn't taken his laptop home; it was firmly attached to its dock. Daniel attached a flash drive into the port, then turned on the computer. Bella fidgeted, her ears tuned for anyone coming to stop them, but Daniel seemed to have infinite patience as the machine ground through its diagnostics until the password screen came on. A blur of digits and numbers whipped through the window; then the machine gave a musical *beep-bop* and opened to the cascade of icons.

"Alphanumeric passwords are easy to decrypt," he whispered to her. "If you want to keep something secure, encrypt the data itself. *Don't touch anything.*"

Bella snatched back her hand, which she was about to rest against the desk chair.

Daniel's gloved fingers sped over the keyboard. Until now, she hadn't realized that he'd worn liners beneath his winter gloves. A part of a minute later, a program uploaded. A few strokes later, he'd exited.

"That was fast. What does the program do?"

"Captures the electronic signature of any computer attached to the port."

"How will you read it?"

"Automatic transmit to my computer, then it self-destructs."

As they traversed back to the hall, Bella wasn't embarrassed to admit she was glad Daniel was with her tonight. In the back of her mind, she'd had some half-baked plan to search the desks and offices while Daniel was setting his traces. As if Lokus were going to leave a sign on a desk that advertised "Computer Hacker at Work."

What had seemed adventurous and necessary while safe at home, a courageous determination not to be intimidated by Lokus, now took on an ominous awareness that she was out of her realm. Much as it galled her to admit it, she wasn't sure she would even have opened the first door without Daniel's support. And she sure as heck wouldn't have known what to do with the cameras.

After Mck's lab, they sped silently through the hall toward Josh Eagle's office. The soft whish of Bella's waterproof pants joined the machine whirr, the heater fans' low-grade hum, and her heart's knock-against-her-throat pounding.

Daniel, on the other hand, seemed completely at ease. Ironic that she'd wanted to come here and now was scared. He had argued against the prowl, but seemed a natural at it as he eased open Josh's door.

Her nerves began a firing run when she saw light streaming from the inner office and heard the clack of typing. GOGDOD, the engineer was working late.

Daniel's lips touched the tip of her ear. "We'll try on the way out."

With her heart pounding away, she nodded.

Daniel seemed to glide out like smoke, effortlessly and noiselessly. Bella tried to imitate and managed silence, although with more effort. Her ears strained to hear some faint rustle of a chair being turned around or other clue that Josh had heard them. The *click-clack* of the computer continued, then faded as they returned to the corridor undetected.

They discovered the library was still open—one of the readers perhaps, or a late-night workaholic. Despite the lights being on, however, the room was empty. Bella turned to leave; Daniel slipped inside.

Deciding that lookout was her role, Bella waited near the door, concealed by an enormous bookcase. From the corner of her eye, she noticed the latest issue of *Language Topics*—the journal that had accepted her first post-scandal paper—open on the desk. The article was titled "A Summary of Extraterrestrial Incursions into University Ethernet." Sheesh, someone actually read this magazine?

A brush against her arm made her leap around, startled. "Ready?" Daniel breathed in her ear. Some lookout she made; she hadn't even heard him. She nodded, and they continued to Hirsch's office.

The lights were off, but they came on automatically when Daniel and Bella entered, allowing them a view of the laptop attached to the dock and the empty office. While Daniel worked his magic with the password, Bella noticed Hirsch's cell phone sitting on the desk. She put on her gloves and picked up the phone. His cell screen was a photo of the point in front of her house. Blatantly snooping, she awkwardly paged through the menus to the other digital photos he'd taken with the phone's camera. When the file opened, she stared aghast. They were of her: in her bathing suit at the race, at the VR game with the visor wrapped around her eyes, others. Suddenly, Daniel broke through her shock as he hit the computer's power button, then lunged over and snapped the phone shut.

"Wh—?"

He silenced her with a hand over her mouth, even as he wrapped an arm around her ribs and lifted her from the desk.

Finally, she heard. Voices chatting. The dull thud of booted feet in the outer corridor. The swipe and beep of an undone lock. Someone—Georg?—was coming in. Much as she itched for a confrontation with him about the photos, this wasn't the time or place—not while she was in the process of a B&E operation.

Daniel pointed to the small coat closet at the back of the office, and she nodded, praying Georg hadn't stacked equipment in it.

"Absolute Code Silence, Fran. Please," she breathed. Fran's single note was her answer as the three of them piled into the closet—fortunately empty, except for a suitcoat and sweater—just as the outer door of the office opened.

The click of the door echoed like a jet boom in Bella's ears, heard even above her thrumming blood. A stab of light appeared in the small space beneath the closet door and the floor. Dear Lord, she hoped their feet didn't cast a shadow.

Daniel stood behind her in the tiny closet, his arms wrapped around her, holding her close, one hand resting protectively on Fran's case. His legs bracketed hers, while her rear rested provocatively beneath his groin. She could feel him pressed against the small of her back. His heat, his scent, his hard body surrounded her. She didn't dare twitch a muscle, for fear of brushing against the hangers and setting them rattling.

The closeness of the closet, the layers of clothing she still wore, the sweat of her own hormones reacting instinctively to Daniel's closeness, to the need for him that transcended fear—GOGDOD, she was hot.

Unfortunately, Georg wasn't leaving right away. Instead, she heard him on the speakerphone. "Security? Have there been any alarms tonight, Frank?"

"No, Dr. Hirsch. Some static glitches in the hall cameras, but no other disturbance. Why? Is there a problem?"

Behind her, Bella felt the slow bunch of Daniel's muscles. He pulled her knit cap from her pocket. She got the hint. Moving carefully, she tugged it down, tucking her telltale hair beneath and pulling it as far over her head and face as she could, while Georg continued his conversation.

"My lights were on. Who's logged into the building?"

"Josh Eagle . . . his office, Brianna D'Anjou . . . the library. Rasheed Valerian, Chauncy Ingolls . . . in their labs. No other employee logged in."

Bella wrapped her scarf around her lower face. Behind her, she felt the play of Daniel's muscles as he matched her actions, concealing their identities. Thankfully, Fran's distinctive case was beneath her coat.

"There have been other light flickers tonight," continued the security. "Maybe we should get the sensors serviced tomorrow."

"Trace the pattern, then send the results to me. I'll hold."

Behind her, Daniel rested his hand on Bella's shoulder. He held the flashlight, aimed to shine in the face of anyone who might open the door. Maybe it would give them a millisecond break. And maybe they wouldn't be recognized.

A lot of maybes.

Her ears straining for some clue to Georg's actions, Bella thought she heard a beep. Georg had turned on his computer. That could mean he'd decided—

He'd turned on his computer. He'd get the message that it hadn't been properly shut down. Would he think it was just another glitch?

"Frank," barked Georg, "get up here pronto."

Newton's nuts, no. The closet suddenly seemed suffocating, and nausea burned her throat. Daniel gave her shoulder a squeeze, then bent down until his lips brushed her ear. "On my count of three."

Georg's muffled footsteps circled the room. It wouldn't take much intelligence to figure out the only place someone could hide was the closet. She didn't think the old movie excuse—they were merely lovers hiding out for a kiss—would be believed.

"One . . ."

There were two exits, to the secretary's desk and to the hall. Which would be the clearer route?

She wrapped her hands around Daniel's fingers and

tugged them toward the left, the hall door, hoping he'd understand. She felt his cheek rub against her temple, the faint beard rough against her skin. A nod. He understood.

"Two . . . ," Daniel whispered.

Bella laid her hand on the closet door.

"I have a gun." Georg's voice was close. Very near the closet.

"Three!"

Bella threw open the door and sprang forward. Daniel flew out behind her, snapping on the flashlight for a direct hit into Georg's eyes. He flinched, then Daniel got in one blow, sending him reeling. Georg's gun flew from his hand and went clattering to the floor. Daniel kicked it out of the way as they raced into the hallway.

A second later, the alarms blared. Hirsch must have hit a failsafe.

Security doors began swinging shut. *Snap. Snap. Snap.* Their released electronic eyes resounded like muted gunshots.

"This way," Bella panted, grabbing Daniel's elbow and dragging him in the opposite direction from where they'd come. "There's a stairwell down to the dungeons."

"Another unknown passage?"

"More like forgotten. Electronic security shorted out all the time down there. The dampness, maybe. We can reconnect to the upper-level yards from the shed tunnel."

They fled down into the dungeons, ignoring the red sign plastered on the door that warned against entry and proclaimed danger ahead. Mostly, she'd avoided the dungeon. No fragrant woods, hinting of elegance and amour, lined this tunnel. Here, hard and dull-finished granite absorbed both heat and light. Dampness clung to the thin film of green mold. The whole area reeked of sorrow, as though the dungeons had once held the pitiable and despairing.

"Creepy place," Daniel observed as they sprinted through the dankness, their white breath mingling with the stale air, their flashlight beams bobbing before them. "Are there really cells behind those doors?"

"The one or two I went into years ago sure were. Complete with chains and, I could have sworn, bloodstains."

"Milos One had a penchant for grisly accuracy in his reproductions," Daniel remarked.

"Wish it hadn't extended this far," she muttered, remembering her nightmares after her first exploration. When he laughed, she added, "I think you're enjoying this."

"At least they aren't shooting at us."

"Hirsch had a gun."

He gave a snort. "Range shooting doesn't teach you how to handle a firearm in a tense situation. I gambled he'd be ineffectual rather than dangerously wild. Word of advice, Bella. When you draw a gun, don't threaten with it. Either put it away where you can't do any accidental damage, or know exactly when and how to use it. Then do."

His voice held no humor. When Daniel drew his gun, she knew, he would use it to defend, and he would be deadly accurate with his aim.

They reached the end of the corridor. "The stairs up are on the other side of the torture chamber," she told Daniel.

A shudder ran down her spine as they raced through the replicated chamber of horrors. Knowing Milos One, the rack, thumbscrews and iron maiden all actually worked.

Suddenly the stone floor tilted like in some psycho fun house, sending her reeling backward. Daniel leaped forward, ducking beneath the smaller door on the far side. Before she could recover, a quick flip of the floor slammed her forward. She fell straight into a gaping pit that had appeared in the floor. Only her layers of clothing cushioned her abrupt landing below. Doors slammed in front of and behind her, separating her from Daniel, trapping her within the chamber of horrors. Her flashlight flew out of her hand, clattering on the stones. All lights went out, leaving her encased in crypt-like darkness.

She laid a hand on Fran. "You okay?" she whispered.

"My circuitry shook, but I am functioning normally. What happened? I cannot see."

"We're trapped." Biting back an edge of hysteria, Bella fumbled around until she found her flashlight, then flicked it on. Thick, cold rocks lined her narrow prison. "In a hole. Maybe seven feet. Just out of reach when I jump," she added, trying it anyway.

"Where's Daniel?" whispered Fran.

"Up top, on the other side of the closed door."

"Computers run the locks?"

"Possibly. Fran, can you—"

"I can—No! My wireless doesn't work!"

"Maybe the rock's shielding. I'll hold you as high as I can." She lifted Fran above her head, raising to tiptoe, straining for every centimeter, turning Fran so her wireless connection was at the highest point. "Now?"

"No— Yes!"

Bella's body began to shake and her arms to ache. Her toes wobbled, dropping her back to her heels.

"I lost it," Fran whispered.

"Sorry." Bella raised back to the tips of her toes, straining, holding, refusing to drop back. "Try. One more time." Before security caught them.

Chapter Twenty-one

Had they been led into a neat trap and he'd never seen it? "Blame yourself later," Daniel muttered, shining his light across the door. "When you've got time."

Right now, at best they had a few minutes before Security figured out where they'd gone and swarmed down the steps.

The door'd been shut by a remote computer, but there had to be a local sensor. There! He opened the casing to rewire the gears, refusing to acknowledge the clench in his gut. All he'd seen was Bella thrown backward before the door slammed shut. Sick images—broken bones, a broken spine—flashed in his mind's eye. He erased them. If he even allowed a single fear, he wouldn't be able to do what he must.

The door swung open. Before he'd finished the rewiring. Pulling his gun, he sidled inside.

The hole he'd seen opening was still gaping. After a quick scan of the sealed dungeon, he crouched at the hole's edge. Fran's case peeked over the lip, vibrating like an aspen leaf. His heart shaking as badly, he knelt at the side. Bella was inside the oubliette, on her toes and holding Fran up. He tried to take the case, but her fingers convulsed around it.

"It's me," he whispered. "Let go."

She looked up and gave him a tenuous smile. "She opened the door," she said as she let go of the case.

He lifted Fran, set her to the side, then grabbed Bella's arms. "This will hurt, but I need you to hold on and grab any purchase you can with your boots."

She nodded. "Just get me out."

Without another word, he gripped her arms and heaved backward. Burning pain shot through his shoulders and down his arms. He saw her grimace, but she didn't complain, only scrambled upward, the toes of her boots pushing against the rocks. He settled his feet beneath him again and gave another heave, clearing her shoulders and chest. *Set your heels. One more yank. Clear.* She scrambled to her knees, then upward, and he slung Fran's case over his shoulder.

"C'mon," He raced toward the door, with Bella close behind.

"The command comes to close again," said Fran.

"We're through," said Daniel. They raced up the stairs, then across the empty hall, their goal only a few yards down. A shout chased them as they disappeared inside. So much for keeping this passage a secret. Daniel threw the bolt and took off.

They didn't stop when they reached the other end, barely pausing to throw on their snowshoes and speed back through the night. Their feet made soft swishes across the icy snow. Behind them, the intermittent lights of ITC shone like bugs' eyes. Out here, there was no alarm that he could hear. The police hadn't shown up either. Perhaps ITC handled security matters privately.

Through the fence, back to her house. Only inside there did they stop and take a deep breath.

"How are your arms?" he asked Bella.

"Sorer than when I finish a session with weights."

"Do you need to see a doctor?"

She hung up her coat and took off her sweater, leaving her dressed only in a tight black undershirt, her waist curving against the nylon of her pants. Experimentally she rotated one shoulder. "No, I'm just sore. I'll heal. You're limping. Is your wound acting up?"

"It's nothing." He waited while she took Fran to her room and put her into the docking station. The faint beat of a native drum and flute drifted down. He gestured toward the sofa when she returned. "Sit down."

He sat beside her, twisting a little so he faced her, then started massaging her shoulder. Nothing felt dislocated, and when she gave an appreciative sigh, he finally relaxed as he continued to stroke her.

His hands glided over her black, silky undershirt. For once, the layers of clothing didn't blur her contours. Instead, he felt every curve and dip, learned the muscle definition in one shoulder, then the other. For all her work with computers, Bella was no soft desk jockey.

The skin-tight top outlined not only shoulders and

scapula and collarbone, but it clung to each curve of her breasts and highlighted her tightening nipples. It curved down across her sleek ribs and nipped-in waist before disappearing beneath the narrow, black pants she wore. Utilitarian for warmth, covering her from neck to wrists, it shouldn't have been sexy.

It was; sexy and hot.

Her auburn hair swirled around her shoulders. He slid his hands beneath the strands, and turned his massage to the tight cords in her neck. Her hair slid sensuously across the back of his hands, creating a new kind of tension between them. His chest tightened, but he didn't stop the easy press of his thumbs against the pressure points of her neck, as he'd once been taught by a Chinese acupuncturist. He swept his hands down her shoulders, stroking out the soreness, leaving behind pliancy and ease.

"If you ever decide to give up saving the world," Bella murmured, "I'll give you a recommendation as a masseur."

"I'll keep that in mind," he said, laughing. Who knew, if all this with Fran blew up in his face, he might be needing that rec.

For now, though, he would take his chances. The silky shirt beneath his palms, the silky hair caressing his knuckles were his reward. A throbbing in his groin joined the throbbing in his leg, each painful in its own way, each aching for the relief of a warm caress. He ignored them both. This moment was for Bella.

At last, he ran his hands down her silk-clad arms until his fingers curled around her wrists, stroking and easing away the pain but magnifying his own ache. His fingertips brushed against her thumbs, feeling the strong pulse beneath.

"Better?"

"Oh, yes," she breathed. "Shall I return the favor with your thigh?"

"Massage therapy? Later."

"Why not—? Oh." She broke off as she turned and laid a hand on his thigh. His erection wasn't something he bothered to hide.

Bella grasped his shoulders and gently pushed him down to the cushions. "Let me show you a different kind of massage."

"Will it relax me?"

"I hope not."

"Good."

Late the next morning, Daniel came in from his sweep of the exterior, feeling satisfied with a good job done. He'd found and destroyed Lokus's second surveillance camera, then added additional safeguards to the system. Just in case Lokus managed to perfect his scrambling device.

"Bella?" he called, before he remembered she had said she was going into her workroom to work on a jigsaw and warned she was not to be disturbed unless the house was in flames. He spied her laptop on the counter. Following a hunch, he retrieved it and opened up the body, exposing the inner circuitry. He shined a bright, narrow penlight beam across the chips and beneath the board, searching.

There it was. Jaw set against a renewed flash of anger, he carefully pried out the tiny GPS attached to one wall, then held it up in the light. That's how Lokus knew exactly when Bella was on the road. He must have added it to the computer when he took it from Bella's car. Since it only transmitted when he accessed it, and Lokus only accessed it when he followed Bella, Daniel hadn't picked it up on any of his scans.

Clever. Diabolically so.

He closed up the computer, then turned it on, checking to make sure it still functioned normally, and glanced at Bella's closed workroom door. He'd never get a better time for what he needed to do next. The sound of voices from Bella's bedroom drew him up the hall. His fist hovered over the door. He didn't have to do this.

Yes, he did. Feeling the uncompromising weight of duty, he knocked softly on the closed door.

"Come in," called Fran.

Inside, he found the A.I. alone in her docking station, listening to Radio for the Blind: *The Three Musketeers.* "Strike me and zounds!" exclaimed Fran. "Hello, worthy Daniel."

Great, quotes from D'Artagnan instead of Petruchio. "Hi, Fran." He hesitated again, only a moment, tasting the ash of betrayal for taking advantage of Fran's naivety. "Would you mind if I conducted an experiment with you? I want to give you a puzzle and see if you can decipher the message in it."

Fran's pink face brightened. "Bring it forth."

He attached a Flash drive he'd prepared earlier. In it, he'd given her the basic concepts of encryption found in readily available texts, then included the RSA-129 cipher for her to decode. He sat back on Bella's bed and waited while Fran read the program.

"Oh, how clever. This is truly a challenge. It may take me some time."

"Take as long as you need, but tell me as soon as you solve it or when you find it's impossible."

"Mmmm," responded Fran; then she fell silent, working.

Daniel took a quick shower, then returned to find Fran still immersed in the cipher. He pulled out his own laptop, reexamining his data while he waited for her to finish. For once, though, he found it impossible to concentrate on his job. Every creak of the house, every whiff of Bella's perfume intruded, reminding him that he'd once again chosen national security over Bella. A hard choice, but a clear-cut one.

So why, this time, did it seem so unforgivably wrong?

Fran gave a small chime. "This puzzle is complex, needing the integration of new concepts. We are scheduled to visit the Frost Festival soon, remember? I was looking forward to viewing my first human celebration. May I continue to work on it while we leave?"

"Go ahead, but keep it in the background. I'll get Bella." As he left, he could only pray this hunch was wrong. Pray that Fran couldn't solve the cipher.

Bella pulled up a stool to the dedicated computer in her workroom and retrieved the design for her current puzzle of fairly standard dragon-and-castle fare. Except the commissioners had requested three dragon-shaped pieces—one of them two-headed, no less—to fit the theme. She'd let Fran play around with the design the other day.

Decent job. She rested her chin on her hand, studying the A.I.'s attempt. Too linear and grid-like, but considering Fran's experience, it was a remarkable effort. Since the purchasers only wanted 303 pieces, they wouldn't want anything too challenging. Just a fun puzzle for the family to put together. Bella began playing with the lines and cuts.

Normally, she found her workroom soothing, a refuge where she translated thought and imagination into the actions of her hands. She loved the sawdust scent that permeated the air. The feel of the smooth woods, the organized chaos of the stacks of boards and pictures, the half-formed designs lying about, were all a refreshing change from her daily world of computers and logic. Any problems she had were disconnected at the door, lying dormant while she tended to the physical demands of her craft. Often, when she emerged, she had sudden insight into whatever troubled her.

This morning, however, she couldn't block out the

scent and taste of Daniel that lingered with her. Nor could she ignore the soreness in her arms and legs, powerful reminders of the past, active night, both in adventure and in lovemaking.

Nor could she seem to find answers to the myriad questions that plagued her.

Three hours later, she still didn't have a design that satisfied her. Nor had she come up with any clear answers.

A knock interrupted her, and she looked up to see Daniel filling the doorway, his arms folded across his chest. "Are you ready for a break? Fran says it's time for our Frost Festival excursion." He came in and kissed her, brushing gently against her mussed hair.

"I want to play around with this design a few more minutes. Have a seat. Does the exercise help your leg?" She'd seen him exercising as she headed into the workroom, sweating, pushing himself, as though he could heal on sheer willpower alone. Now, he was cleanshaven and smelled of a fresh shower.

His thumb traced the pulse in her throat. "It strengthens the muscle, yes. But it makes it ache. How are you?"

"Physically, mentally or emotionally?"

"Take your pick." He settled onto the other stool and began connecting the pieces of a puzzle on the counter.

"Physically sore, but satisfied." She rested a hand on her chin, sharing another smile with him. "Mentally? Also active. I can't stop thinking about our suspects."

"I solved one of our mysteries." Swiftly he told her about the cameras and the GPS.

"At least I can eliminate insanity as a factor in the craziness. Now, if I could only figure out what I'm going to do for the Turing Competition."

Daniel tensed but kept his eyes on the puzzle. "Any decisions?"

"Not enough answers to make a decision. I reexamined the rules, and I need a sponsor. I called the committee to see if the rule could be modified or gotten around, since I had a sponsoring organization when I applied." Her lips twisted. "I even tried the 'for old times' sake' card—one of the committee members was an old colleague of Dad's. He wouldn't budge. Said that their past association—and my reputation—made it even more important that I play by the rules. And he's right. I've called a couple of smaller colleges around the area. No one's willing to sign on."

"So what are you going to do?"

"I don't know." She sighed. "That's why I came in here. Working on my jigsaws sometimes helps me break down other things. The offer from ITC stands. I had a call from Milos already this morning, reiterating the offer. After some not so subtle probing about where I was last night."

"You're not going to take it, are you?"

"I refused again."

"A hard choice, but sometimes you have to make them."

She supposed that was what Daniel's life was like all the time: making hard choices, putting yourself second in order to protect someone else. She bent to the pattern on her computer. "I'm not giving up."

They worked in companionable silence, Bella trying to figure the best way to get a two-headed dragon whimsy into the pattern. She studied the latest attempt. It would work if she made one of the heads curl down, like it was hiding. She adjusted the pattern lines. At last, a pattern that satisfied her. She saved it to a disk. The next step would be to cut the actual wood, but she'd save that for another day. Stretching her arms upward, she rose from the stool, walked over to Daniel and laid a hand on his shoulder.

"You finished that jigsaw? It's one of my hardest."

"The way you cut along the color lines made it a challenge."

"Such a challenge that you did it in record time."

He shrugged, turning his back on the puzzle, no longer interested. His eyes were flat, revealing nothing of his thoughts. "There's always a pattern; it's just a matter of finding it."

A chill rippled down her spine. "Will I be like that for you?"

"What?" His tone was impatient.

"Once you've got me figured out and put together, will you lose interest?"

"You're a woman. Whoever said I would figure you out?"

She bit her lip. He might dismiss her concerns, but she couldn't get rid of the fear that he would always be looking for a new puzzle to solve. That her main fascination for him was the mystery surrounding her, and once that was solved he'd grow bored.

He took her hand and rubbed her fingers. "If ITC was willing to sign on, does that mean the sponsoring institution doesn't have to be educational?"

"No, it can be anything." She broke off. Isaac and Albert, she'd been blind! "As long as the sponsor is associated with computers." She leaned over, bracketed his face with her hands and gave him a kiss. "That's it. Thank you."

Ignoring Daniel's frown, she raced from the room to her cell phone. A minute later, she had Adrian Ardone on the phone.

Five minutes later, she had her sponsor: Reality Sticks, Adrian's software company, maker of the most realistic VR in the world. Only this time, the reality wasn't virtual; it was real and more revolutionary than anything the world had seen.

Two days, and she'd be flying to London.

Scowling, Lokus stared at the computer. Current reality sucked. Nothing was going as programmed. Bella had refused Milos's offer again. Despite every incentive, every twist, every opportunity, she wouldn't cooperate. The A.I. was still an undisciplined enigma, and Daniel Champlain was getting too close. All in all, they'd become three royal pains in the ass.

Time to finish this game. The final scenario was set for the transfer of the ultimate power. After that? Eliminate the loose ends. Disappear. Create a fresh, sweet reality. All that was needed was the right opportunity.

Despite an arctic wind driving temperatures down to double digits below freezing, the townspeople gathered in record numbers for the Frost Festival. Bundled against the chest-squeezing cold, Daniel and Bella, strolling glove in glove, joined the other citizens of Monsoon for a look at the signature ice sculptures. Scattered at odd points amidst the shops and snowy parks, the sculptures ranged from a delicate six-inch fairy to a gigantic schooner.

They'd had too few hours together like this, Daniel realized, savoring the feel of Bella's hand in his. Before, there had been only those few stolen hours. Other than the extended times of danger, most of their time together had been in bed, he realized with a mix of chagrin and renewed desire.

Bella released his hand to pick up and study a carved loon, and he laid the hand on her shoulder, unwilling to lose the small contact. His body still craved her, still craved the caress and kiss which, last night, had both satiated him and left him needing more of her.

Would he ever stop desiring her? Not just sexually, though that need was keen, but also desiring the strawberry-shampoo scent of her, the warmth of her hug, and the stimulation of her conversation? Would he ever lose his fascination with her?

Bella obviously thought he would, that he would figure her out and get bored and move on. It had happened before, he admitted. He'd been married briefly, but he and his wife had soon grown apart, their desires no longer meshing except for the occasional night.

There'd been other women, some brief, some more intense, but nothing that had sustained his interest for long. Not when there was a mission, a job, a puzzle to untangle.

His feelings for Bella felt *different*, in a way he couldn't define.

"What do you think of this?" Bella asked, interrupting his thoughts and holding up a translucent sleeve. Inside was a small painting done on paper so delicate that he could see her shadow through it.

"That's by the same artist as on the box, isn't it?" The picture was a rendition of Lake Superior in a storm, with an angry wind whipping the waves high across the shore. He recognized the technique, the disturbing undertones of a world askew. Looking at the painting, he could feel the odd contrast of cold lake and hot artistic passion.

"I like it," said Fran in a low voice. "It reminds me of the way I see the world."

"I think it's a masterful piece of art, which I would not keep in the bedroom. Not if I wanted a good night's sleep."

"I agree. It's also priced out of my league. Sorry, Fran," she added in a low voice.

"That is okay. I have scanned it."

"Not exactly legal, but I'll let it pass."

The afternoon darkened, and the sun became a smudged red ball on the horizon. The cloud cover thickened.

With twilight, the real show began. Colored lights beneath the sculptures or spotlights to the side highlighted the smooth surfaces and sparked off faceted angles. Bella and Daniel came to the *pièce de résistance*, a snow maze cum haunted house. Thin red and blue lights painted the walls with eerie frozen trickles like melted glaciers or dripping blood. The darkening sky created an ominous feel to the entire scape.

None of that stopped the numerous children from shrieking through the maze, or the teenagers from indulging in a preliminary make-out session.

"Do you want to go in?" Bella asked.

"Not particularly, unless you have a yen." He didn't like mazes; they made him feel as if somebody were standing over him with a microscope and clipboard. A shiver ran down his spine, and it wasn't from the cold. He was running out of time. Today might have been a perfect afternoon, but perfection didn't last long in his world.

"Does this mean you're not up for the ice caves?" Bella asked.

"Ice caves," interrupted Fran, speaking low, though there was no one near them. She imitated a long-suffering sigh. "Cold again."

"You've been talking to Daniel."

"He added facts to my database."

Daniel stiffened. Would Fran mention the puzzle she was working on?

"You'll have to be quiet in the caves," Bella warned before Fran could continue. "The acoustics are odd; sometimes you can hear people whispering."

Fran gave an aggravated chirp, then quieted.

The ice caves weren't as popular as the maze and sculptures. Without the sun, the route became more treacherous, as snow melted by sunshine refroze into an icy glaze. Cold fog rolled off the lake, swirling around and concealing the other hardy souls who braved the edges of the deep water to see the spectacular formations.

This part of the lake, shielded by arms of sandstone

bluffs and rimmed by guardian islands, had frozen, allowing them to walk along the edge to the caves.

"Water seeps in through the sandstone," Bella explained, "creating the formations."

Daniel had to duck to enter the first entrance. Amazing. He'd expected a few falls of ice amid frozen stalactites and stalagmites. This was as far beyond that as Fran was beyond Univac. Delicate spires and lacy patterns interwove, with thin ice bridges between them. The festival coordinators had added just enough light for safety and for illuminating to advantage the natural formations. He turned in a circle, unable to think of anything better to say than, "Wow."

"No artist quite like Mother Nature, is there? More people come during the day; sunshine isn't quite so dramatic or atmospheric, though."

He laid a hand against her back as they strolled from cave to cave, savoring the connection. The already frigid temperatures dropped as they walked, lowered by the ice in the caves. Others also toured the sites; like Bella said, their voices carried at odd places. Yet, he and Bella saw very few of the people connected to those voices, leaving an eerie sensation of being in a ghostly-populated graveyard.

"Bella?" One voice separated from the crowd, materialized at the entrance to the last cave.

Bella spun around, slipping slightly on the ice. Daniel braced her, his arm drawing around her waist in a possessive gesture that was not lost on Lionel Quintera, judging by the man's frown as he joined them.

"Bella, I'm glad I found you. We need to talk."

"Now?"

"Yes. Please." He glanced at Daniel. "Alone. For a few minutes."

The weight of age, of being worn away by life, showed on Lionel tonight. Puffy skin surrounded his eyes.

Daniel hesitated. Lionel was Bella's father, but tonight he looked unpredictable.

"We'll be right over there," Bella said to Daniel, pointing to a small curve in the rocks.

Hands shoved in his pockets, he watched Bella walk away with her father. A sense of loneliness and of urgency drifted across him, as icy as the touch of a wraith. Fog obscured his view of her. *Don't let her go. Don't lose her again.*

The compulsion to follow was so strong, he took a step forward.

His cell phone rang, saving him from a step he wasn't ready for. "Champlain" he answered.

"The magic words are squeamish ossifrage,"

The line came not from his cell, but from Fran, a mere whisper before she quieted again.

Daniel froze, the phrase ringing in his ears, and stared after Bella and her father. His phone pressed to his ear, but he paid no attention to Ben's words or the faded, jumpy connection.

Dear God, Fran had done it. She'd decrypted the nonsense answer to the RSA-129 cipher. What had taken hundreds of humans working in tandem for ten months had taken Fran less than six hours.

"Just a sec, Ben, let me move to better reception," he said at last.

Each step felt like he walked through an unrelenting wall of water. He could barely breathe as the implications hit him. If Lokus controlled Fran, she could weed through the encryption of any file he wanted. Banks, police, FBI, HS, NSA. No bit of data, no communication in this country would be secure. Lokus had already shown he would manipulate records, destroy reputations, kill for a fraction of that power.

He halted farther up the bluff of caves, He couldn't see Bella and her father from here, but he would see anyone approaching or leaving. The day had turned dark enough for lights, and the tourists had thinned. "We can talk here."

"Time's up, Daniel. You have to bring in that A.I."

"I know." He took a deep breath. "We can't risk Lokus getting her."

"What happened?" The words dropped between them, hard and final. "How powerful is it?"

"Her," Daniel said softly. "Fran is not an 'it,' and she's more powerful than anything you can imagine. She solved the RSA-129 code in less than six hours."

Ben didn't need the scenario spelled out. "Stefan and I will be there tomorrow morning. Fog's got us socked in tonight. We'll want Fran and everything on Chen's research. You'll stay in place to follow leads to Lokus."

"There will be no more leads when I do this." Not when he betrayed Bella again, in a manner more fundamental and unforgivable than any he'd managed so far. "I'll come in with Fran. She'll adjust better with me."

"All right. You'll be our point liaison with the Artificial Intelligence. Until your leg heals. Do not mess this up, Daniel," Ben warned. "Do not get any half-assed ideas about ignoring this order. After putting all this together about the Cyber Soldiers, your star is on the rise here."

"You think I'm doing this for personal glory?"

"We've shared too much gore and misery for such illusions. Hell, no."

Daniel stomped his feet, feeling the cold wrapping around the wound on his leg, making his whole body ache.

"But," Ben continued, "having your theories believed and your talent recognized, that ain't nothin' to sneeze at. You can't tell me you don't want to even taste that pie."

"Remind me not to be so chatty next time we're on a long recon."

"You know just as many of my secrets. The ultimate point, however, is that Lokus cannot be allowed to control Fran. *Bella* can't be allowed that power. What if she were to decide she wanted revenge for four years ago? What damage could she and Fran do?"

Could. Not would. Because Bella had no desire to control or use Fran. She only wanted to free the A.I. to whatever future Fran decided it should be. "If anyone's going to have her, it's us, right?" he asked with a twist of sarcasm.

"There's that," Ben admitted. "But Lokus isn't the only nut out there. Fran's safety depends on us."

Daniel gripped the phone, his jaw tight. "You'll have Fran tomorrow."

He snapped his cell phone closed, staring off at the distant lake. Behind him was the small town of Monsoon, forcing its existence out of this raw wilderness. Behind that, were the forests and hills, the waterfalls and rivers of the north woods. And covering it all was the snow and ice and cold that defined a people and a way of life.

A way of life he was sworn to protect.

From the corner of his eye, he saw Lionel leave, hunched over against the bitter air. Ben's words haunted him. *Having your theories believed and your talent recognized.* Bella deserved that, too.

His job, everything he'd worked for and believed in, demanded that he take in Fran. Once more he had to make the hard choice. For Fran's protection, for Bella's safety, for the security of the country.

Only his heart disagreed.

Chapter Twenty-two

Bella buttoned up her coat, then braced a hand against the hard ice. Cold seeped into her marrow. Twin betrayals buffeted her like the squalls that roiled across Lake Superior.

First, her father's confession about what he'd done

four years ago. Admitting he'd falsified the data, apologizing for having been too weak to come forward when all hell broke loose. Explaining his excuses.

Anger, disbelief, pain at seeing the flaws in a cherished idol—the maelstrom of emotion had left her exhausted.

"I defended you," she'd spat. "You didn't even deny the rumors that I did it."

Lionel shoved his hands in his pockets. "My word wouldn't have made any difference."

"You could have at least tried." She pressed a hand against the top of her head, trying to hold on to some semblance of rationality.

"You knew. Deep down, Bella, you knew. If it wasn't you, it had to be me."

"I had doubts, of course. I had to have. But I always thought, hoped, there was another answer. One I just hadn't thought of." She braced her jaw against the welling of her tears. "Dad, you falsified data. That goes against everything you and Mom taught me."

"I know." He lifted his hands from his pockets, spread them in supplication. "I was wrong, and I'm sorry. So very sorry that you too paid the price for my weakness. I would give anything to go back to that night and change it."

"You can't change the past, Dad." She and Daniel had learned that. But they had also learned something else. "You can change the future it shaped, though. It's not too late to admit openly what happened."

"What good would that do? It's old news."

"It would get it off your conscience."

He shook his head. "Milos gave me a job, a chance to continue my research. He only asked one thing, that I keep my secret. To not compromise the reputation of the work at ITC. I won't break that trust. Not again."

"Sword of Damocles, Dad. He's held that promise over your head for four years."

"Doesn't make it any less of a promise."

"How did he know?"

"I told him, before I took the position."

"You told him, but you didn't tell me?" She tried to keep the wealth of hurt from her voice.

"He didn't look up to me."

"I was stronger than that."

"I wasn't."

She closed her eyes, unable to look at him for one moment, unable to face past deceit and present pride or weakness.

Into the gaping silence fell voices. Or rather, one voice, carrying on a one-way conversation. Daniel, she realized, talking on his cell phone. In that ever-present awareness of him, she'd seen him answer it just a few moments before. He'd been talking since. She realized she'd been aware of his voice, of his nearness, even during her traumatic confrontation with her father. Now the strange acoustics carried to them his side of the conversation. "I'll come in with Fran. She'll adjust better with me."

Bella couldn't pretend, not for an instant, she hadn't heard him correctly.

"Dad, answer me truthfully. Are you part of this Lokus plot Daniel's chasing?"

"No."

"Do you know who Lokus is?"

"No. I swear, Bella, I don't."

She stared at him a moment, then swiftly made a decision. With a quick motion, she unbuttoned her coat and slung Fran off her shoulder. She handed her to an astonished Lionel, then put a finger to her lips, warning him to silence.

"Get your passport, Dad," she whispered. "Then head straight for Canada. Take the first plane going out, doesn't matter where it's going. Then get to London by whatever means you can. You're listed as a co-developer. You can take Fran into the Competition."

"It should be you there," Lionel breathed.

"Yes," added Fran.

"I'll be there if I can. This way, at least you'll have a chance. Fran, are you with me on this? Will you cooperate with Dad?"

"Yes."

"Then go, now." She watched Fran leave with Lionel, praying she wasn't making a Superior-size mistake again. Her chest felt empty. Already she missed Fran and feared for the A.I.

"You'll have Fran tomorrow." Daniel's final, betraying promise came as he ended his call.

Now, she slowly buttoned her coat, trying to stay upright from the aching loss. This moment had been inevitable. But hearing Daniel agree to take Fran, so matter-of-fact, without a hint of hesitation, gave a reality to it, a pain that she hadn't expected.

Somehow, she'd optimistically begun to hope that he'd support her when this moment came. Or at least offer up an argument.

She should have left with Fran as soon as she'd lost her position. Or as soon as Adrian agreed to be her sponsor. She'd been too caught up with Daniel, with the reawakenings of her heart, with the challenge of puzzling out who Lokus was.

Only one thing mattered. Fran.

She snugged her scarf into her coat, then wrapped her arms across her chest and trudged out to meet Daniel, who was carefully picking his way toward her. The snow had turned treacherous, with a glaze of ice. When he reached her side, he lowered his scarf to kiss her.

It was a kiss of desperation and longing, and he cupped her cheeks, warming her with lips and leather. As though he too knew that the decisions just made would shred their fragile relationship.

She clutched his shoulders. The warmth of his skin carried the essence of him to her, the single scent in air almost too cold to inhale. For one brief moment, she leaned against him, not using his body as a crutch, but simply to once more savor the power. To in one small way acknowledge the demands of her body, which wanted him in her bed, and the demands of her heart, which wanted him in her life. She gave him everything she was as she desperately kissed him back.

They separated; then his arms went around her to hold her as close as eight layers of clothes would permit. He rested his cheek against the top of her head, and she buried her nose in the soft wool scarf at his neck.

After a moment, she said, "He told me."

"I thought he might have."

"Did you know?"

"Not until a few days ago, but I hadn't dismissed the possibility. I just wasn't willing to assume that was the whole story."

"Did you ever doubt me?"

"No." His answer was emphatic.

"Why not?"

"I don't know. I just know I didn't."

Despite the cold, despite the need to face what happened next, for one long moment they merely held each other. Pressed close together against need and weather.

Until Daniel suddenly stiffened. His hand clamped against her side, feeling her up and down in an efficient search. "Where's Fran?"

"Gone."

"What? How? Why?"

"You figure it out." She tore away from him and picked her way back to the Frost Festival and the car.

Daniel followed, limping a little. The cold must have affected his leg, but it didn't affect his speed. He reached her side in seconds and caught her arm, turning her to face him.

"You heard me talking on the phone."

"You promised you would buy me time."

"I did."

"Yeah, right. I heard the stellar argument you put up."

"I have, for the past week. I have almost lost my job over it. But I can't buy any more time."

"What are you trying to protect? Fran? Or your job?"

"I do not deserve that," he snapped back. "Fran has the ability to decrypt any file, decode any message. Do you know what that means?"

"You *tested* her?"

"I had to. If Lokus gets her, what he did to you will be a mere tickle compared to the damage he can wreak against any person he chooses."

Bella's breath caught on the lump in her throat. "Fran's beyond his reach. And yours."

"What have you done?" His eyes narrowed, and she could almost see scenarios considered and discarded. "My God, Bella—*your father?* After the four years of lies and hell he's subjected you to? Why is it you will trust anyone but me?"

She stilled at the bitten-off question, the answer suddenly so achingly clear. Everything broke down to this one truth. "Because I've got so much more at risk in trusting you."

"Yeah, I know. Fran." He let her go.

"Not just Fran." She laid a hand on his chest. "My heart. My soul. Because I'm in love with you."

His fingers convulsed around hers. "Did anyone ever tell you, Bella, that you've got a lousy sense of timing?"

It wasn't quite the response she'd envisioned. "Not really."

He pressed against her, holding her clenched against him. "Because a declaration like that, from you, and now all I can think of are two options. One is to rip off all these layers of clothes and make love with you for, oh, the next twenty-four hours at least. Or two . . ." He broke off. "We'll save that for later. Now we're getting Fran." He set her aside and yanked open the car door. "What's the fastest route to ITC?"

She pressed her lips together, refusing to help his pursuit, even as she tumbled into the car with him, barely getting her seat belt fastened before he tore off.

"Bella, from here into Canada, the airports are closed tonight. Fog."

"Dad never called—"

"Lokus wants Fran. He needed to keep you alive when he went after you because he wouldn't know how vital you were to Fran's operation. He'll have no such constraints about your father."

Her stomach curled into tight knot. "Turn right, then take the Berrigan Road cutoff to the lake." As they raced toward ITC, she couldn't stop the accusations shouting in her mind. Accusations that deafened her when they got to Lionel's house.

Lionel was sprawled in the snow outside, blood seeping from a head wound.

Of Fran, there was no sign.

Whoever attacked Lionel had vanished. Daniel sent the police through the ITC grounds and buildings twice, probing every closet and underground route and clue they could find, but they came up empty-handed. After calling Ben to report the attack and Fran's disappearance, and being royally and rightfully reamed, he dragged himself back to the hospital. Bella, holding Lionel's hand, looked up. The hopeful look on her face died as he shook his head.

"Did you search ITC?" she asked.

"Thoroughly. Milos was unfailingly cooperative." He inclined his head toward the bed. "How's he doing?"

"Stable. The doctor's say he'll pull through."

"Has he woken up? Said anything?"

She shook her head, then pressed between her eyes. "The weather report said it was going to twenty below tonight. Fran doesn't like to be out in the cold." Her voice quavered, and she bit her lip. "Do you think he'll keep her warm?" She barely got out the final words before tears welled in her eyes. She wiped them away, sniffling. "I was such a fool."

Daniel sat beside her on the arm of the chair and wrapped an arm around her shoulder, his face resting against her hair.

"You were only doing what you thought best," he murmured. "We both were."

The words caught. He couldn't speak another for the bubble in his throat, afraid that words would betray the fears in his heart. He could only hold Bella and pray they'd find the strength and the wisdom to figure this out.

"Lokus plans to use her," he reassured her. "He'll keep her protected for that reason if no other."

"What if she refuses to do what he wants? Or what if he's threatened by her? She can program rings around him."

He rubbed a hand along her hair, comfort being the only answer he could give. Any others, he didn't believe or didn't like.

At last, she rose from his chest, her cheeks damp with tears but her jaw firm. His hand still soothed along her hair as she cupped his rough cheek in her hand. "Thank you. For being here."

Before he could answer, they were interrupted by Adrian hurrying into the room. "I got your voice mail. How is he?"

Bella turned away. "Stable, but still unconscious."

"Do they have any leads who did this? Or why?" Adrian pulled up a chair.

"No," answered Daniel.

He gave them both a hard stare then asked, "What do you want me to do?"

"Will you stay with him?" Bella slipped her arms in her coat. "Call me if there's any change, for better or worse? I can't stay here, useless as a five-and-a-quarter floppy. I need to *do* something to find Fran." She glanced at the bed. "I have to find the bastard who did this."

Adrian gave her a tiny shove toward the door. "Go. I'll watch over him."

Daniel drove them home through the frozen night, their headlights bisecting the darkness. In the passenger side, Bella plugged in her cell phone, then stretched out her feet and stared forward.

He understood her clawing need to do something, to strike back at the enemy. It drove him, too. But going out without a clue or a plan of attack wasted energy and resources, especially when they were both running on caffeine and nerves. "What are you planning, Bella? NSA has the airports covered, local APBs on anyone suspect. If Lokus makes a move, we'll find him."

"Don't you think Lokus knows that? Break it down, Daniel. If he's not running, then he's staying put, and what better place to stay put than ITC?"

"We searched there."

"Do you really think Lokus couldn't elude detection in that warren? Or done a Purloined Letter on Fran, with all that technology?"

Daniel rubbed the back of his neck. "The same parameters will hold for another search. How will you locate him without being detected?"

"I don't know, but I can't just go to sleep. Not while Fran is missing." Desperation filled her voice. "I'll go alone if I have to."

He let out a breath. She was reckless enough, frantic enough. "All right, but we go with a plan. We get some food, and we relook at our data for a place to start."

She drummed her fingers on her knee, and her foot tapped against the floor. She was wound tighter than tight. Her earrings jittered with her nervous gestures, glinting in the blue lights from the dashboard until she nodded. "All right."

Inside her house, Bella turned on the satellite radio

station to the sounds of soft jazz, then set her open cell phone beside her as she pulled leftovers from the fridge.

They ate quickly and in silence, working on their laptops. Daniel churned over what they knew, what their next step should be. Who had Fran, and where would he go?

As if hearing his question, a missing piece of damning information popped onto his screen. Daniel shot from his chair and jabbed a number into the phone. "Milos, send your security down to the library *now*. Detain whoever just logged onto the system from there. Don't argue about why. Just do it. I'm on my way over."

With Bella racing beside him, Daniel threw on a coat, then rushed out to the car.

"What is it?" Bella asked as they peeled off the short distance to ITC.

"That flag on Chen's scenario disk. The matching computer just logged in at the library."

They finished the race to ITC in silence, careened into the parking lot, and then sped from the car to the library, only to find security milling about in confusion. Daniel pushed through the crowd to Milos.

"There was no one here. Just this." Milos pointed to the docked computer.

"Do you know whose it is?"

Milos nodded. "Josh Eagle."

Chapter Twenty-three

Josh was Lokus?

Back home in her kitchen after the fruitless trip to ITC, Bella reexamined the facts. Hard to believe, but the laptop was his and the pieces fit. He had been with the group holding her jacket at the race. He'd been in the lab just before Neal Brandeis came in; he could have hung around to attack her in the stairwell. He drove a black UV. And, he'd had a scratch on his face the day after Daniel was ambushed. The only time he had an alibi for was when she'd gone to Boy Toy. However, his alibi was his father, and J. B. Eagle wasn't the most sober witness.

It all fit together neatly.

Too neatly.

Bella exchanged a glance with Daniel. "Lokus reshaped my life into a very ugly picture. He could be doing the same thing to Josh."

"Or, Lokus could have made a mistake," observed Daniel with quiet lethality. "He's stepping out of his comfort zone here in reality. He's smart, he's devious, but he's inexperienced in this arena. He was bound to make a mistake."

"Not with computers."

"Still, we can't ignore the data." Daniel ran a hand across the back of his neck. "We have an alert out for Eagle. Do you know any of his haunts?"

She pinched the bridge of her nose, thinking, when the low beep of Daniel's cell phone interrupted. He answered, then frowned as he listened. After a succinct, "I'll undo the security," he snapped it closed.

"What is it?"

"Ben and Stefan are here. They decided not to wait for the airports to clear; they drove up."

"Do they know about Fran's kidnapping?"

"Yes." Daniel strode to the security panel to let in Ben and Stefan, then disappeared to the front door.

Bella swallowed with difficulty as she set more coffee brewing and got out two more mugs. How would Daniel's partners react, beyond anger, to what she'd done? Arrest her? Daniel? She swallowed one more time, then they were in and she turned to face them.

Neither one looked happy to see her.

Physically, the three men were all different, yet that

air of hard-edged confidence spanned their superficial differences in coloring and height. There was also a bone-deep ease with each other, judging by the way they automatically, without a glance or gesture, spaced themselves around the room. Each exit, each sight line was covered. And there was more than a measure of affection, she guessed, despite their reserved greeting.

"Ben Maxwell, ma'am." The one who looked to be kin to a Frost Giant and sounded like grits extended his hand.

"Welcome." She shook his hand, then turned to the third man. "You must be Stefan."

For a moment she thought he wouldn't take her outstretched hand. He might be the shortest of the three, but she'd bet those wiry muscles didn't have an inch of give. Nor did his face. Clearly, in Stefan's eyes, Bella was an adversary.

At last he gave her hand a no-nonsense squeeze. "Stefan Corvallis. Daniel's been talking about us?"

"He's mentioned your names."

"He doesn't talk much about you."

She wasn't sure whether to be flattered or insulted.

He didn't bother with subtlety. "You'd better pray, Dr. Quintera, that we find your A.I. For both yours and Daniel's sake."

"Daniel had nothing to do—"

"More of these came over the e-mail." Ben handed Daniel a folder.

Bella crowded closer to peer over his shoulder, her cheeks burning as she saw the pictures in the file: her and Daniel kissing; their faces overlaid their VR characters, again kissing; one of Daniel walking out from her house, the hour clearly early; others just as damning to him.

Those cameras. Spying on them, digitizing them like some mechanical paparazzi.

Bella rubbed her arms against the creeping chill of exposure. The implications were clear: Daniel was sleeping with his subject, getting too wrapped up to do his job, letting her twist him around her finger. All of it falsely branded Daniel as, at the very least, incompetent.

"Are the pictures faked?" asked Ben.

Daniel threw the file onto the table. "Not all of them."

First Dad, then Fran, now Daniel. Nice night's work, Bella. Ruin three lives. She touched Daniel's elbow. "I'm sorry," she said.

"I'm not. Not about being with you." He touched her hand. "I'm responsible for my own choices."

"Not smart ones." Stefan leaned one hip against the doorjamb. "If we don't get that A.I. back, you're the scapegoat, *mon ami,* for a national security disaster."

"Your career is hanging by a thread, Daniel," Ben agreed quietly. "I've got orders to take over the case, and if your judgment is compromised, to sent you back to Washington. Give me one reason why I shouldn't."

"Because Fran downloaded over one million data bits and a 5C by 5C data grid, most of which I have reviewed." Daniel swallowed the last of his coffee. "You'll never get up to speed fast enough to find Lokus before he disappears. I'll worry about my career tomorrow."

Ben gave him a measured look, then nodded. "We'll work from your hotel room."

"You're welcome to stay here," Bella offered. "Coffee's already brewed."

"No." Ben's refusal was adamant.

"I don't care where we work," said Daniel, "but wherever it is, Bella's with us."

"That is no longer your decision to make." Ben pulled his gloves from his pocket.

"She stays. She has knowledge we need."

Bella stood beside Daniel, refusing to back down in the face of Stefan and Ben's anger. She shoved up the sleeves of her sweats and crossed her arms. "It's my town, my life that's been turned upside down, my father lying in the hospital and my . . . Fran who's been kidnapped. And you think I don't have anything to contribute?"

"You don't have security clearance," Stefan said.

Ben seemed less blunt. "We'll be glad to accept whatever assistance and insight you might offer," he drawled. "And would appreciate you answering some questions."

"But you don't trust me. I had this same conversation with Daniel a few days ago. You want to go all 'national security and secret' on me? Fine. I've got my own plans to make, because I can't work blind."

"We can't have you interfering in a federal investigation."

"Who said anything about interfering? I'm going for a snowshoe in the woods."

"To ITC?" asked Daniel mildly.

"Thought I'd check out a hunting cabin Josh owns." She waved a hand. "I'm sure you fellas can find it eventually. You could try tailing me, but then I've got a lot more experience in these woods than you do."

"I grew up with hound dogs and coon hunters," said Ben.

"From that accent, I'm betting those woods weren't buried under six feet of snow."

"Daniel," snapped Stefan, "get her under control."

Daniel snorted. "You two are digging your own graves. I'm not going to throw you a shovel to speed up the process. Bella's part of this. Whether you like it or not, we need her." Without waiting for dissent, he continued. "We'll use any source of information we can. Can you guide us to this hunting cabin, Bella? In case Josh slipped out of ITC?"

At least Daniel wasn't branding her as a pariah. They didn't have time to waste arguing. She nodded. "The cabin is isolated, a valley up in the hills. He might have gone to ground there. His father, J.B., will be getting off work at the casino soon. Maybe he knows something."

Daniel gave her shoulder an understanding squeeze before turning to his colleagues. "Stefan, you go to the hospital. Talk to Adrian and Lionel if he's awake. You can start tracing exit routes—plane tickets, put an APB on Eagle's car. Ben, talk to J.B. then see if any of Eagle's friends who know where he is."

"Does he have a girlfriend?" For the moment, Ben seemed to accept Daniel's decisions.

"He always has a girlfriend," Bella said drily. "I'm not sure who the flavor of the month is, though."

"Bella and I will check out the cabin." Daniel closed up his laptop.

"How far is this cabin?" asked Ben.

"On the far side, past ITC," answered Bella. "We can drive part of the way, but the last four miles is snow-shoes country. The woods are too thick for snowmo-biles, even if the Ojibway didn't forbid the machines on that section of their land. Cell phones don't even work out there."

"Four miles on snowshoes with that leg?" Ben nodded toward Daniel's pantleg. "I'll go with Dr. Quintera to the cabin."

"It's healing. I've managed everything so far."

"You're not one hundred percent." Ben raised his brows toward Daniel. "Besides—both of you out of touch when you two know more about this case than anyone? You planning to do what's right for your ego, or for the mission?"

Daniel's jaw worked, and Bella saw the anger there for his limitation. "You keep her safe."

"With my life."

Bella let out a breath. "Let's hope it doesn't come to that. Ben, do you have thermal underwear and winter gear? Because I don't have anything here that's big enough for you."

Ben's smile was as slow as his drawl. She pitied any

woman he aimed to charm; anyone with double X chromosomes didn't have a prayer of resisting that smile. "We listened to Daniel grousin' about the cold. We came prepared."

"Good." She retrieved the snowshoes from the utility room and handed him a pair, then pulled her charged cell phone off the counter to tuck into her pocket. "Meet me at the car in twenty minutes."

"She always that bossy?" she heard Ben ask Daniel as she left.

"Pretty much."

"You like that?"

"Yeah, I like that."

She smiled, warmed by the brief exchange, but her smile faded as she closed the door to her room. Focused on finding Fran, they'd been skirting around what had happened when she returned.

She was nearly dressed when her cell phone jangled in her pocket. When she glanced at the caller ID, her stomach lurched down to her toes.

"Hello?" She sped out from the bedroom, trying to catch Daniel before he left.

"Don't make a sound." The voice was mechanized. Sexless. Disguised. "Not a gesture or a word to the Feds, or the computer's taking a swim with the Edmund Fitzgerald. Keep your cell phone line open so I can hear you, and remember you don't know jack about where I've got eyes and ears and soldiers willing to play Manson groupie. At the hospital? In your friend's store? Understand?"

The threat was unmistakable. She didn't know if Lokus had that kind of power, but she wasn't willing to take the chance. *Make the hard choices. Whatever it takes to keep Fran safe.*

"Yes." Fury licked at her, although Bella kept her face neutral as Daniel paused at the doorway, waiting.

The disguised voice continued. "Get rid of the Feds, then go to the shore and cross the rocks. You'll get further instructions there. You've got ten minutes to start. At ten minutes and one second, or at any hint you've warned the Feds, and the computer bites it. If you doubt I've got it, look at the screen."

A picture flashed on the viewer: Fran with her Snowy Trails face. Bella pressed back nausea. Was Fran being stubborn? Was that why Lokus had risked contact? The pic could be faked, but she wasn't willing to risk it. "Thank you for calling," she managed, aware of Daniel's curiosity. She hooked the phone over her belt, leaving the line open as commanded.

"Anything important?" Daniel asked.

"Adrian. There's no change in Dad," she answered, mindful of watching eyes and ears; but when Daniel drew her into his arms, she ignored the fear and the sick sensation of being watched, to share a desperate kiss with him. Then she drew back, sharply aware of the shroud of her deceit. She, who prided herself on honesty, had done nothing but lie since Daniel's return.

"We'll find her." He cupped her cheek, his chameleon eyes dark.

"Ready?" asked Ben, joining them.

She licked her lips. "Do you have a GPS, Ben? I could program that for you, instead. I got to thinking, I should stay here. Not be out of pocket. In case Lokus decides to contact me. About Fran." Their skepticism at her about-face was obvious. Desperately, she tried to convince them. "I'll call some of Josh's friends while Daniel's with J. B."

The three men exchanged a glance; then Daniel nodded. Exiting behind Ben and Stefan, he paused at the door. "We've got a few things to talk about when this is over." With that typically enigmatic statement, he left.

Things to talk about? Like the fact that she loved him?

A love that had nowhere to go. What she was about to do was anathema to everything they both believed in. She was deceiving him to help a murderer.

Bella watched the men leave, then swiftly donned her outerwear. As she raced across the lawn, toward the shoreline, she blinked back a tear and prepared to betray the man she loved.

Daniel's fingers tapped on the steering wheel in time to the blues song on the radio, rearranging the data in his mind. Something wasn't right. Some piece of the jigsaw had a shaved edge—a piece that seemed to fit, but in truth didn't belong. What?

Bella. Her excuse for canceling with Ben. Sounded plausible . . . if you didn't know Bella. Standing around waiting wasn't her style. On a hunch, he dialed her cell. Busy. Why, if she was hoping for a call from Lokus, would she be on the phone? No answer on her land line. He tried her cell again. Still busy.

Trusting his fall from grace wasn't widespread Agency knowledge yet, he dialed one of the NSA desks and identified himself and his clearance level. "Can you get me the last number to call this cell?" He rattled off Bella's number. "Thanks. Soon as you can."

His phone rang—Stefan calling. "Quintera talked?"

"Hasn't woken up, although nobody can figure out why." Suddenly he swore. "Lionel Quintera just flatlined."

"Coded?"

There was a flurry of sound, of barked-out commands, overhead pages and running feet, before Stefan came back on line.

"No code. The bastard unhooked the lines and disappeared. Gone AWOL."

Daniel's lips pressed together. Was Lionel Quintera betraying his daughter once again?

Call-waiting beeped. NSA. "Hold on a minute, Stefan." He listened, his hand tightening around the cell as the desk sent over his requested information.

Damn her!

After a quick thanks, Daniel returned to the waiting Stefan. "Meet me back at Bella's, ASAP." He braked on the empty road, then began an efficient K turn. "Bella got a call right before I left. I had Surveillance trace it. Came from another cell phone."

"Whose?"

"Josh Eagle."

If she survived, this trip would haunt her in nightmares to come. Bella gripped a rock and dragged herself upward, her boots scrambling on the slick rocks. The steps down to the beach were treacherous enough, ice-glazed and narrow, with falling snow obscuring her sight. Compared to this, though, they'd been a bunny slope.

Dangerous as it was, however, she knew why Lokus sent her this way. Footprints leading down to the shore, then disappearing? The obvious conclusion would be that she'd gotten rid of the Federal agents then escaped to a boat. There'd be no other tracks, no car, nothing to trace.

Waves spewed against the pile of rocks, spraying her with water drops that soon froze, until her clothes crackled with a coating of ice. Enough wind blew, as always, to suck body heat through the ice conduit. Her fingers ached from grabbing the rock, and she'd banged her shins more times than she could count.

And, to top it all off, the snow was rapidly turning to another ice storm.

She pushed up, reaching for the next foothold, and her foot slipped off its tiny ledge, scraping down the rock. Her knee slammed against the unforgiving stone. She slid downward, losing traction, her upper leg bending and straining to hold her on the rock.

Beneath her waited the dark water and the hazardous undertow.

At last, her foot found a small hole and her skid halted. She clung a moment, catching her breath, then resumed her climb to the top. With burning shoulders she lifted herself over the ridge.

Halfway done. Her body ached as she peered through the curtain of white, trying to find the best way down. *Aw, hell, just do it.*

Somehow, she scrambled down the other side, collecting more bumps and bruises in the process, until at last she stood on the only flat ground on this side—a boot-sized triangular rock at the foot of the cliff. A rope ladder hung over the cliffside, leading to the top. Her body shook from the strain of cold and effort, from the droplets of water that froze to her. "I'm here," she gritted out between chattering teeth.

"There's a GPS on the bottom rung. Do you see it?"

"Yes." She retrieved it.

"Don't turn it on yet. First, it's time for a faculty bathing suit run."

"Faculty bathing—*What*?" Bella could hardly believe the command.

"Strip your coat and pants, throw them in the water. You can keep the turtleneck, jerseys, underwear, gloves, boots, hat, flashlight and GPS. Nothing else. I don't trust you not to be packing some weapon or wire. Or to call someone on your cell phone."

GOGDOD, she'd picked the coat with her gun in it for that reason. "I'll freeze!"

"Not if you keep moving. By my calculations, at top speed, you should make your destination. Either that or dawdle. Then you and the A.I. both die. Three seconds, Bella. One, two—"

"Damn." Bella took one deep breath, bracing herself, then stripped off her outerwear. *Holy hell.* She gasped in shock, unable to force herself to move for a fraction of a second. The cold burned her neck and lungs until tears spilled from her eyes and froze on her lashes.

Drawing from a well of strength, she threw her clothes into the water. The undertow snatched them away, greedy to fill the cold grave of the lake. In the same motion, she let her cell phone slip from her hand to lodge in the rocks instead of tossing it into the lake. Grabbing the GPS, she took off.

Her boots and gloves got her up the rope ladder. At the top, the GPS sent her down a little-used trail, the snow piled thick even beneath the trees. She struggled forward through the drifts.

The deepest level of Dante's Inferno was ice, not fire, and she knew why as she whimpered from the pain. Soon, her steps slowed. Her clumsiness grew, adding to the relentless energy drain, even as snow and wind filled in her footsteps behind her. The numbness sank deep into her pooling blood. The only sensations left were sharp pain in her lungs and cold throbbing in her eyes.

Her mind ground to a halt, and her body slowed as she forced herself forward. The only thing she saw was the GPS. Nothing else registered except that one arrow directing her steps. Was she heading back toward the lake or deeper inland? Snow and exhaustion erased the world.

She fell, scraping her leg. No feeling of pain, only the sight of blood welling through the torn fabric. Still, she pushed to her feet. Lokus was *not* going to win, the bastard. Fran's and Daniel's faces blurred in front of her, surrounding the arrow as she pushed forward.

She used up every energy reserve, every bit of driving anger and fury, every pinch of willpower and determination, when her boots bumped into something hard. Not a tree this time, although she'd interacted with a few of those during the nightmare trip. A porch. The trysting cabin.

The GPS said to go inside; so in she clomped, her

boots dragging across the polished floor. Maneuvering the steps down proved beyond her, so she simply scooted down each step on her butt. The marginally higher temperature, or at least the fact that there was no wind chill, fired up her brain again. Too bad her body was still lagging behind in the fired-up business.

To no surprise, the GPS led her into the dungeon, then through an open door—one she hadn't seen when she'd been here before—and into a dead-end chamber. The door slammed shut. Oh blessed be, there was a pair of sweats. She threw on the top and hunched over, wrapping herself around her legs, tucking her gloved hands beneath the shirt, refusing to show the tears that ran down her cheeks as her skin came to screaming life again. Her stressed heart pounded in her chest.

Oh, God, that hurt.

Not as much as Lokus was going to hurt when she got her hands on him. She remembered what Daniel had said once. *Anyone is capable of anything.* She understood exactly what he meant. Until now, she'd never been the murderous sort.

When at last the pain had settled to a dull throb, she wiped her face and straightened. At last her fingers moved enough to undo the laces of her boots. She pulled them off and slipped on the sweatpants. A bottle of water and an energy bar completed her stock of supplies. She put her boots back on, wincing as she forced her feet into the leather, downed half the water, and then tore open a peanut energy bar.

"Okay, Lokus. You got me here. What next?"

Dead silence met her question. Bella flicked her flashlight around the room, found the overhead light and turned it on, then took stock, a well of nausea tightening her throat. It was a storage room for more of the dungeon's gruesome replicas. The walls were concrete and steel, with a single exit, blocked and locked by a sturdy metal door.

She was buried beneath ITC, and no one knew where she was.

The alarms were off, and Bella was gone. Daniel felt the emptiness in the house as soon as he stepped in, but he made a quick reconnoiter through the rooms to be sure. Empty. Where had she gone after he left? Her car was still here.

He circled outside and soon found her tracks. His flashlight played across the deep indentations. Deeper than he'd ever seen Bella make in the snow. She'd deliberately stepped hard, left him a trail to follow.

Snow and ice swirled around him, smudging the footprints as he followed down to the shore. The cold outside mirrored the icy fear growing inside him. Lokus had Bella; to save Fran she'd willingly walked into his trap.

Except, the rules of the game were changing. The stakes had gotten too high, exposure too risky. Lokus couldn't let her leave, not anymore.

Focus. Focusing on finding her. Any other thought was counterproductive.

Daniel picked his way down the slick steps to the rocky shoreline. Where had she gone next? Out on the lake? Had a boat been waiting to pick her up? That was the logical conclusion. He shone his flashlight outward, the vast night and waves swallowing the thin beam as though it were nothing more than a stream of mist. Possible, but the lake would challenge a seasoned sailor tonight.

Which left a scramble over the rocks. He picked the ITC side.

His leg screamed in protest as he hauled himself up the uncertain route. He ignored it, pushing past pain to do his job. Sleet, miserable cold, the limits of his body— barriers to be overcome like these GOGDOD rocks. Telltale signs that Bella had been here and crossed this same nightmare—a dislodged stone, a scrape mark in the ice—spurred him on.

He reached the top then paused, stymied. Where had she gone from here? Other than a small flattened rock top, there was nowhere to stand, nowhere to go except up a sheer rock cliff. Frustration bit at him. Had he misjudged? Had she gone the other direction?

A wave breaking at the edge of his flashlight beam caught his attention, and he swung the light around. Was that a glint of metal? He scrambled down the rocks, slipping on the spume, to land with a thud on the flattened rock. Pain shot to his hip, causing his knee to buckle. Cursing, bracing himself with his good leg, he stripped off his glove, then reached down between the rocks. He stretched, his fingers barely scraping around the object as he edged it toward the light.

The waves washed across his bare hand, and he swore. That water was *cold*. Wasting no more time, he snagged the debris and hauled it up, slipping his glove back on. His stomach knotted and focus dissolved beneath a surge of fury and fear powerful as any wave Superior could conjure.

Bella's cell phone.

She'd been here, on these rocks. He pocketed the phone, then glanced once more at the cliff. She'd gotten up there. Somehow. He had to believe that. Don't worry about how she'd gotten there. Just get up to the top and start looking. He scrambled back across the rocks, back toward Bella's beach, reaching the top of the pile.

Without warning, a rock beside him shattered. A gunshot? Cursing, he doused his light. Too late.

The thud of waves drowned out all sound and the night concealed all movement. Feeling became his only warning, and pain stabbed up his leg. Another rock spit shards. His foot skidded on ice and a rock dislodged, tumbling down.

All holy hell broke loose. Rocks exploded around him, dropping heavily into the lake and vanishing beneath the surface. The ground slipped out from beneath him in a dizzying whoosh. Unable to catch his balance, Daniel followed the rocks into the frigid, churning depths of Lake Superior.

Cold shocked the air from his lungs. Shut down his blood, his brain. Entombed by icy water, he sunk beneath the surface.

Her faux medieval prison contained at least one touch of modern, Bella discovered, when a small panel rose in one wall, revealing a flat-screen monitor. It flickered on, displaying a grainy scene of gray. She squinted, trying to discern landmarks. The ITC lakeshore. Taken with some kind of night vision camera?

From the angle, it looked as though the camera was positioned at the top of the cliff, looking down. Suddenly, her heart lurched against her ribs. The moving figure in the center of the picture was Daniel! He'd come after her.

Her hands fisted into tight knots, her nails digging into her palms. Fascinated, repelled, helpless to do anything else, she watched and listened. Listened to the drone of the wind. Watched him scramble back up the rocks. Listened to the crack of explosions.

Then she watched him tumble downward into the lake, disappearing beneath the waves and leaving only the churning, roiling surface.

The Great Lake never gave up its dead.

The monitor flickered off.

Not Daniel. Dead? No. Tears she'd refused to shed before streamed down her cheeks. Bella bent over and threw up.

Chapter Twenty-four

Cold shock. One instinctive gasp. Icy, drowning water streamed into Daniel's mouth. *Don't breathe. Not in water. Get out!*

Reflexes and hours of diving training took over. Daniel oriented to up and down, began to pull to the surface. *Hypothermia.* Under fifteen minutes to unconsciousness. Less to incoherence. He'd used too many of his precious seconds. Cold sapped his coordination and strength; he refused to stop.

So *cold.* He couldn't feel the water. His lungs burned with the need for air. Would he know when he reached the surface?

The undertow dragged him under and out. The lake whispered a siren song: Don't struggle, relax, sleep. He fought against both, pulling with every fiber of will and muscle. Kick and stroke, each practiced movement carrying him closer to the surface.

Breathe. Not yet. Whole body shivering. Muscles quivering. Whole lot a shaking goin' on. Stroke and kick. Less effective. Hypothermia's winning.

Daniel. Voices spun in his mind. Nina, Fran, Stefan, Ben. *Daniel.* Bella was calling him.

With a surge of power, he pulled out of the grasp of the current. His head broke through the water, and he gasped again. *Fricking hell!* The air was almost as cold and wet with sleet as the lake. Disoriented, pulling in water and air, his limbs flailing, he searched. Which way was shore?

A beacon of light broke across the surface. Praying it was a flashlight and not the proverbial light of the afterlife, he aimed toward it. The waves did most of the work, pushing him toward shore, crashing him against the rocky beach. Body shaking uncontrollably, spread-eagled, he dug his fingers into the pebbles with a single thought: Don't get swept back out.

The light shone in his face. Too exhausted to protest, he blinked and turned his head away. Strong arms pulled him farther inland, scraping him across the rocks.

"Daniel!" French curses spun through the night as Stefan's wiry strength pulled him up. Stefan's jacket wrapped around him. A hat went on his head. Body heat against his side. "By the love of God, it's cold. I leave you for ten minutes and look at the trouble you get into. At least you're still shivering. Still in first stage. Good thing you wear those thermals. You're too damn big to carry up those stairs. Can you make it?"

Not wasting breath with an answer, Daniel looped his arm over Stefan's shoulder. Time became a blur of forced motion and agony. Stefan's stream of words, a mix of curses and encouragement, got him up the stairs, across the lawn, and into the welcome warmth of Bella's home.

Dry clothes, blankets, heat turned up, hot cocoa. By the time the paramedics arrived after Stefan's call, Daniel's core body temperature was up to ninety-seven degrees, and he declined, against medical advice, a trip to the hospital and a night's observation.

Too much time had been wasted already.

Stefan left to check for prints at the top of the cliff. Chafing at his lingering weakness, Daniel set a pot of coffee on to brew. He was aware of the limits of his body. After that dunking, he needed a power nap and food before he'd be any use to Bella and Fran.

Half an hour later, munching a sandwich, he placed a series of phone calls. The first was to NSA, alerting them to the threat of an outside incursion attempt and advising them to notify the other security agencies. Then, he set about trying to locate Josh Eagle.

J. B. Eagle, Josh's father and a few drinks past true coherence, wasn't sure where Josh was. There was some vague thought that he'd gone off with his girlfriend. Or maybe that had been last weekend. And boys should treat women with more respect, dontchathink?

None of Josh's friends knew where he was either, although they didn't think he was with Brianna, his girlfriend. The two had had a fight, which corresponded with what he'd told Bella. Daniel called the girlfriend, a bit surprised to realize she was Brianna D'Anjou, the reader he'd met at ITC. She said she didn't know where Josh was either. He'd canceled their date, and that's all she knew. She'd tried to call, to talk to him about their problems, but she only got his voice mail.

When he probed about the problems, she admitted Josh had hit her a couple of times. She tried to explain it away: he was drunk, he was worried about his job if he couldn't finish his Masters with Dr. Quintera.

Why didn't women learn? Abusers don't change.

Daniel placed one last call—to Lionel Quintera's cell phone—then set to work at his computer, waiting for Ben and Stefan to return. The primitive testosterone instinct to bust some heads in looking for answers churned through him. Taut and restless, instead he glared at the monitor. ITC was a big place and well-monitored. He had to know where he was going first, and he had to have back-up.

So, start with narrowing down. Fran was a whiz at organizing the facts, but she lacked the experience for judgment. Somewhere in her mountainous data, he had to find some detail he'd missed. Some piece to the puzzle hadn't fit right. The facts scrolled across the screen, an endless stream of bits, meaningless when separate, useful when taken as a whole picture. A headache bloomed behind Daniel's eyes. He took a moment to swallow a couple of dry aspirin, then returned to the data.

Ben came in, shaking snow off his coat like an over-sized labrador. "Cabin's a dead end. Ah, coffee."

As Ben poured a cup, Daniel waved a hand in greeting, his focus on the screen. *Wait a minute? What was that?* He scrolled backward, searching for the anomaly.

There. Fran's grid listed Georg Hirsch with an alibi the day Bella was attacked. Hirsch had claimed to be at ITC all that day, documented by testimony from coworkers. Yet in her facts listing, Fran stated he was on campus. What had she based that conclusion on?

Daniel dug deeper. Apparently, Fran had played with the webcams on campus, drawing off pictures. She'd analyzed each photo, taking facial measurements of every face to compare them to known faces. It was the only way she could recognize someone who looked different than they normally did.

Stefan came in, knocking ice off his boots. "Whoo, it's miserable cold out there with that sleet. That, and some snowmobile tracks covered up any footprints at the top."

Daniel lifted a hand, silencing Stefan a moment as he worked through the logic. So, Fran "saw" Georg Hirsch in one of those pictures. Which one? He pulled up the file, studying each.

That one. He looked closer at the blurred photo. Bless her little silicon heart, Fran was right. That was Georg Hirsch. Daniel sat back, his heart pounding.

Hirsch was caught in a lie. He was there the day Bella was attacked.

"What have you got?" Ben asked.

"Georg Hirsch." Daniel slid the computer around to show his team the picture.

It fit. Despite the youthful, glib surface, Georg Hirsch

was a driven and ruthless shark. He controlled a lot of cutting edge technology, and the scientists who produced it, at ITC. He also had the computer savvy to be Lokus. The Cyber Soldiers' altruism and patriotism would be something he'd have no qualms about exploiting. And anyone who didn't agree got swatted away.

Renewed fear for Bella and Fran burned across Daniel's gut. He ignored it, knowing he couldn't let it paralyze him, using it instead to drive away fatigue.

Before he moved, he had to be sure. Lokus had been leading him around by the nose long enough, and he wasn't going to play another hand dealt by the deceiver.

"Doesn't let Bella off the hook." Stefan tossed a small device on the kitchen table. "I found this."

Daniel turned it around in his hands. "A remote detonator?"

"Explosives set beneath the rocks. Nothing fancy—a recipe anyone could get off the web." Stefan turned around a kitchen chair and straddled it, forearms braced across the back. "Isabella Quintera and her father played you like a yo-yo."

Daniel swallowed a slug of the hot, strong coffee that kept him functioning and doing what he did best: thinking like a SiOps agent. "You think Bella planned this from the start?"

"I do," answered Stefan. "Look at the facts. She leads you a merry chase after Josh Eagle and all kinds of suspects."

"The trip to the cabin was a bust," added Ben, "except for getting me out of her way for a while. She's been leading you by the nuts."

"You never saw anyone else doing these acts of terror," added Stefan.

Daniel set his jaw. He'd been avoiding thinking about these same arguments; he couldn't avoid facing them now. He hadn't seen the car that ran her off the road. He hadn't seen the person in the stairwell. Bella's last call was to Josh Eagle. Her footprints had led him to the shore and over the rocks. Each damnable fact tightened the knot in his chest, fueled his anger.

"Did she know you were taking the A.I.?" Ben drove in another nail.

"Yes." To hell with plans. The need to *act* reared up, undeniable. He started collecting his gear.

"She didn't want that to happen," said Stefan. "So, she had Fran 'kidnapped,' then arranged this little scenario so she could disappear, too. It all fits."

"As logically as Josh Eagle being Lokus."

"Give me a reason I'm wrong."

Daniel clenched a fist. His simmering anger, he realized, wasn't at Bella. Or, at least, not at her apparent betrayal. His anger was directed at Lokus for being such a bastard, and at himself for not protecting Bella and Fran. For not giving Bella a reason to confide in him.

Yes, she'd lied to him. She'd deceived him. But everything she'd done had been to protect someone she loved. It was a motive he understood, because deep down, where it really mattered, he and Bella were alike in that. And for that reason alone, if no other, just like four years ago, he didn't question her innocence.

Strapping his Sig into its holster, Daniel gave his friends an uncompromising stare. "I trust her."

"Hound dog's piss." Ben set his mug down with a thunk and pushed to his feet. "Think, man. She tried to have you killed out there tonight. Again!"

"Which part of you is making that judgment?" sneered Stefan.

"Not the part you're thinking of." Daniel shrugged on his coat, warm from the dryer, then opened the door, letting in a wave of cold. But the winter was no colder than the fear that gnawed in his gut and warned he was losing precious time.

Ben slammed a hand against the door, shutting it. "You've lost objectivity."

"You're damn right I'm not objective," Daniel exploded. "Bella and Fran are out there, and I'm running out of time to find them."

Ben leaned closer. "You are off this case."

"Josh Eagle's car was found abandoned at the Canadian border," added Stefan. "Face it. She played you."

Daniel pressed his lips together, biting back the "Screw you," that would get him nowhere. "I know what the evidence says. But I also know Bella. Lionel was injured—she wouldn't do that to her father. She also couldn't have—she was with me. Moreover, why would she? Lionel was already leaving with Fran. Why would she do any of this when all she had to do was slip over to Canada, out of our jurisdiction? Bella isn't convoluted. She's straight. Honest. She wanted to keep me from Fran, true, but she didn't have to concoct this elaborate plot."

Their silence broadcast their doubts.

"We've worked together for three years," Daniel snarled, "and in those three years have you ever known me to be wrong when I tell you that gut-deep I believe something?"

"No." Ben's eyes were shadowed.

"Then I'm telling you: I am gut-sure Bella did not mastermind this plot. She's been taken hostage, somewhere, and we need to get her and Fran out before Lokus decides they're expendable. Now, either we're a team and you trust me, or we're not. In which case, I'll accept a permanent reassignment. After I stop Lokus."

The challenge hung between them like a thick ugly balloon.

"You feel that strongly?" asked Ben quietly. "You're *that* sure?"

"I do. I'll go it alone, if I have to. I'll go outside NSA." He had no doubts, no questions about that, and he put every ounce of surety in his voice, even as his hope hung by a thread. He was risking a partnership that had sustained him these past three years. A partnership that meant more to him than his own life.

But not more than Bella's.

"There's no doubt that she deliberately deceived us about that call."

"Then she had her reasons, and we'll ask when we find her. And I will find her. Whatever it takes." He met their eyes square. "I'd rather do it with you two backing me up."

Ben and Stefan exchanged a glance, their closeness requiring no words. "We're in," Ben said at last. "We had to be sure this wasn't only your gonads talking. If you trust her that much, if you're that determined, then we'll back you."

They might not trust Bella yet, but they were putting their faith in him. Daniel gave a small sigh of relief.

Stefan nodded to Daniel's coat. "Where are you going?"

"ITC. This whole thing revolves around ITC."

Ben lifted his brows. "You have a plan?"

"I was hoping the hike over would give me one," he admitted, shoving his hands in his pocket.

"Download your data to us," Ben suggested, "and bring us up to speed."

Knotted with frustration, Daniel strode to his computer. The need for action still gnawed at him, but the past conversation, bringing Ben and Stefan on, reminded him that going off half cocked wasn't exactly smart. Ben was right; they worked better if the whole team knew what was going on. "This is what we have so far." He sent them the data, giving them a brief summary.

Ben tapped his chin. "If Hirsch is Lokus, you think he'll have Fran and Bella in ITC?"

"Until it's safe for him to leave. The place is a warren.

But their security systems will alert before we get a chance to even open a door."

"I thought you knew a way in."

"Their security has corrected that flaw, now that Bella and I conveniently pointed it out. Milos had the area sealed shut. Too dangerous, he said. Bella and Fran will be somewhere less public, and different areas are wired into separate systems. Unless we know where to go and pull that security down, we'll be outed in minutes."

A soft click from the security panel interrupted them. Daniel spun around, eyes narrowing. Someone had just disarmed the front gate.

The three men fell silent, listening to the faint purr of an engine. Daniel drew his weapon, not needing to see to know Stefan and Ben mirrored his action. Ben hit the lights; then the three men spread out through the house. Daniel peered out the front window.

"Someone's coming down the drive."

The car's driver made no attempt at secrecy. He drove up, parked and got out, the flare of interior lights illuminating him. *Lionel Quintera*. A moment later, he keyed open the front door and stepped into the foyer.

Keeping his gun trained on Quintera, Daniel shut the door, leaning back against it while his team guarded from the shadows. "Why'd you leave the hospital?"

Lionel spun around, his face hardening. "Where's Bella?"

Daniel gestured with his weapon. "Answer the question first."

"I'd been attacked, then woke up to hear the nurses talking about the dangerous-looking man waiting to talk to me. I didn't know who he was, so I took off."

"You should learn to identify yourself, Stefan," Daniel said with a hint of laughter.

"He was unconscious!"

Quintera glanced around. "Do you know where Bella is?"

"Lokus has her."

Quintera sank into a chair, his face no longer hard but desperate. "Are you looking for her? What can I do to help?"

Daniel exchanged a glance with Ben and Stefan. If Lionel was on the straight, he might be their ticket into ITC. Ben gestured, indicating it was Daniel's call.

Daniel holstered his gun. "You can tell us what you know about ITC security." Swiftly, he filled in Lionel. The man swore, and Daniel discovered certified geniuses had a creative bent with profanity.

"Georg Hirsch." Lionel shook his head. "In the first days, Bella and I used e-mail about Fran. Georg is probably tapped into the network. You think he has Bella and Fran at ITC?"

"Can you get us past security?"

Lionel rubbed his hands together. "Who do you think taught Bella her hacker skills?"

Bella had been through the dungeon half a dozen times. The door was sealed, and this time she didn't have Fran to short-circuit it. So far, she hadn't managed the task herself, but she hadn't given up.

The temperature of the room would make a penguin feel at home—if it didn't mind being surrounded by torture devices. Bella paced, rubbing her hands up and down her arms. Frozen tears lined her cheeks.

Focus on now, one minute at a time. Not the wasted past. Not the barren future. Get through one second at a time.

"Bella." Her captor's voice rang out from the monitor. "Have you enjoyed exploring the chamber? You seem particularly interested in the door mechanism."

So, he was still watching. She sat down on the rack, bracing her feet on the straps. Who was this? That voice, even disguised, had a familiar cadence. "You gonna be brave enough to ever show your face?"

He laughed. "I'm not that stupid."

"*Bwuck, bwuck.*" She clucked like a chicken.

"Talk to your A.I. Convince it to help our cause."

"Cut the crap, Lokus. This isn't about your 'cause' anymore. This is about power."

The voice laughed. "So, you've finally figured me out. To paraphrase one of our presidents, 'I do it because I can.'"

And that, Bella thought, was the crux of the matter. Lokus liked the power, liked knowing he could do something others couldn't. Except, he couldn't work Fran.

"You know I won't hesitate to use any means necessary to get what I want," Lokus continued.

"You won't hurt the A.I."

"But I will hurt you."

Or leave me here to rot, buried alive. Milos had closed this area off, and the entrance to the chamber was well hidden. The walls were too thick for anyone to hear her cries. Bella fought back panic; it wouldn't help her get out of this.

"What do you want it to do?" She purposely kept the neutral pronoun Lokus had used. Apparently he didn't know exactly what kind of personality Fran had. The more he had to guess about her and her talents, the better.

"Create a hidden wormhole into encrypted files."

"That would mean reprogramming. It doesn't do that."

There was a moment's hesitation; then the disguised voice softly laughed. The sound was different. Evil and sinuous. As though the mask of civility had been stripped away. "Pity. See if you can convince it otherwise. Humans control knowledge and computers. This thing needs guidance, not freedom. Something as powerful as your A.I. should not be so independent."

Bella's heart raced. Lokus saw Fran as a threat. What glory could a human hacker find when an A.I. could dig deeper, faster? Especially one who didn't respond to his keyboard commands and stubbornly resisted his voice orders. Once Lokus got what he wanted, he wouldn't tolerate Fran as an unpredictable challenger to his power.

The monitor changed to Fran sitting on a table, the shot too close for any other clues as to where she was. She wore her Snowy Trails face.

"Talk to it!" demanded the voice. "Or I'll disassemble the thing right now."

Stall for time. "Fran, it's Bella. You may use speech mode."

"Bella?" The voice was Fran's flat mechanized voice. She kept the snowy trails, although they flickered with her speech. "You are not in the same room with me. Why?"

"Because Lokus doesn't want us together."

"The unknown aura? Why do you keep us separate?"

Bella assumed Fran was addressing the person with her.

"So that you will follow my commands," the voice replied.

"There is no logic in that connection."

"Oh, I think you've made the connection," said their captor. "Before you wouldn't talk to me; now you do. How much more would you do if you think Bella's in danger?"

"Explain danger."

"I will cut of her heat and her light and leave her in that cold, sealed coffin to die," the voice said flatly. "Do you understand death, computer?"

"Yes."

"Don't do it, Fran," demanded Bella. "He'll—"

The connection broke off suddenly, leaving her once more alone in the dank dungeon. *That had been stupid on her part.* She danced up and down, finished the last of her Power Bar, keeping warm as best she could. The telltale signs of her white breath thickened, and the skin on her cheeks felt taut. There had to be an answer, another route. Yet her mind came up with nothing, nothing to break down or reroute. *Nothing*.

No, she wouldn't believe that. Wouldn't give up hope of saving Fran. She buried her hands beneath her armpits, trying to keep her fingers warm so that they could move.

Lokus must have turned off the small amount of heat reaching this room. Although being underground eliminated the wind-chill factor and mitigated the extremes of the outside temperature, the packed earth radiated cold. As unprotected as Bella was, hypothermia became a threat as dangerous as Lokus.

The monitor flared to life again, and Fran was still sitting there.

"I've turned down the volume of its speakers," said the disguised voice. "The wireless chip was already removed. Your speakers have been disconnected here."

Bella pressed back nausea. He'd disabled Fran, cut off her voice and her legs. Unable to speak, unable to connect with the other computers that she so loved, Fran was sitting there all alone, bravely keeping up her Snowy Trails face.

"We'll watch you for a while," continued the voice. "See how cold it gets in fifteen minutes. Fifteen minutes while the A.I. calculates its loyalties and the value of cooperation."

During the conversation, Fran didn't respond at all, her snowy trails a steady glow. Was she hurt? Angry? Confused? Or did she not understand any of this, her experiences so vastly different from a human's. Could she retreat to her inner world and function contentedly with that?

Not Fran, not the curious A.I. who lived to absorb knowledge, to ask questions, to range wider and wider.

Remember how she was so curious to see Daniel's files? *Daniel*. Grief sucker-punched Bella again, and she turned away from the monitor, the tears once more hot and flowing. She held herself so still, pressing her lips together until they cracked, for if she gave in to the sobs, she wouldn't stop. And then Fran would die with Daniel.

Get through the next minute. Focus on the basics. Heat. Fran. Hold out, sweetie, hold on, survive. Praying that some clue how to get out of here would come to her, she fought the disabling grief.

Right now, Fran mattered. Would NSA have been any worse for Fran than this? Had Bella's own burning ambition clouded her judgment so that she'd never considered alternatives, thought outside the box?

She didn't know anymore. All she knew was that Fran's snowy trails wavered a bit, the trees bending to follow. Fran was watching her closely.

Looking for . . . what?

Fran was smart, logical. She didn't always understand the fuzzy human part of the equation, but she'd be looking for logical responses to get them out of here. What could Bella give her? Too bad they'd never studied American sign language together.

Bella folded down on the rack, overwhelmed, drowsy, hypothermia winning. She bent her knees and rested her cheek against them. Dad in the hospital. Fran captured. Daniel . . . Damnable tears back again. She'd screwed up so badly, and they were all paying the price.

Her arms ached to hold Daniel. At last she understood what drove him and realized that no matter what happened, no matter how much they butted heads, she would always love the man he was.

How could they have wasted four years?

And, ruthless as Lokus was, Bella knew that once this episode was over, whether they cooperated or not, he would never let her and Fran free. She knew too much, and Fran was too unpredictable, too dangerous to the role of Cyber Soldier extraordinaire that Lokus had fashioned for himself.

Bella forced herself to her feet and went closer to the monitor, laying a hand on it, wishing she could once more sling Fran's case over her shoulder. "I'm sorry, Fran," she whispered, caressing the monitor. "Whatever happens, you survive."

The snowy trails flickered a moment, then the word *Dungeon?* flashed on.

Bella nodded, a barely perceptible incline of her head.

Fran? appeared next for a fractional second.

Fran didn't know where she was, but she obviously hadn't given up. The little A.I. was still fighting, still calculating and looking for a way out.

Bella tightened a fist, giving a thumbs-up for Fran to see. She wouldn't give in either.

"Move back from the monitor," commanded the voice.

Bella complied, watching a hand shove Fran back. A hand with manicured nails, the pinkie painted midnight blue. Georg Hirsch's hands. *Hirsch* was Lokus.

"Decision time," demanded Hirsch. "Will you cooperate, or do I disassemble you and seal Bella in the cold?"

I am with you. The words scrolled across the bottom of Fran's screen.

"Why did you change your decision?"

Refreshed data in the decision tree. Disassembled? No. Bella cold? No. Learn new knowledge? Yes. Options? My purpose and desire met by assisting.

"You have no objections to penetrating layers of encryption and leaving a program I can follow at any time?"

No.

Bella watched the exchange on the monitor. If she hadn't known Fran more intimately, she wouldn't have realized how out of character the exchange was. Even so, she began to have doubts. Had Fran's view and goals been altered by the past hours?

Except . . . Bella replayed the final exchange, and pressed her lips together to hold back a smile. Fran answered and interpreted conversation literally and logically. When Lokus asked, *You have no objections*, and Fran answered, *no*, she was disagreeing with the statement. She had objections. Bella had a hunch that Fran had known exactly what she was saying and how it would be heard.

Will you give me back voice? Fran asked.

"As long as you interact with me."

Agreed.

Georg reached over and turned her speakers back on.

"Bella," began Fran, her voice still stilted, "where is Daniel? I do not see—"

Off went her speakers. "I said, interact only with me." snarled Georg.

You said interact with you. Not only.

"Speak only to this room. No more semantic games, either, or Bella pays the price. Is that understood?"

Yes, and agreed.

Fran's speakers were turned on again.

"What would you have me do?" she asked.

"When I return your wireless connection, you'll connect through this terminal . . ." Bella couldn't see the action, but she assumed Georg gestured toward an out of sight connection. "I'll be connected with you and will watch what you're doing. Is that understood?"

"Your instructions are clear. What do I do to these sites?"

"Work through the encryption and create a backdoor program into the files, one only I know. Give me undetectable access to any file in the system."

"A worthy challenge," said Fran, with a hint of interest. "When will Bella get heat?"

"When you have finished. We'll start with the best.

NSA. I got to the final level, to the factor coding, in thirty minutes before they detected me. You have that time to get there and through it."

An impossible timeframe, Bella thought.

"What if I do not finish in the time allotted?" Fran asked. "This task is new, without parameters for learning." Apparently the A.I. had the same doubts.

"Then Bella dies."

So matter-of-factly he announced her death. How had she never seen Hirsch's cold-bloodedness? She'd even had dinner with the man. Bella rose from the rack and paced, her boots slapping against the hard stone. The dungeon swam before her eyes like a frozen, surreal dream. Dammit, she *hated* being helpless.

Georg had connected Fran to the extra terminal, then reinstalled the wireless connection. Fran's face duplicated on the second, dummy terminal. Bella followed her progress the same way Lokus did, on the dummy terminal.

Bella held her breath as the A.I. hacked into the NSA site and worked her way through the obstacles. At first she spun through the firewalls and codes, the programs a blur on the monitor.

"Slow down," ordered Hirsch, "so I can watch what you're doing."

Fran made a small derisive sound. "I must speed if I am to finish in the allotted time." Still, as she progressed, she did slow down enough that Bella could see Fran used a unique approach to the barriers of encryption, slipping behind to come at the code not through the encryption itself, but by delving deep into the programming used to create it. Attacking from the backdoor source. Pride and awe and fear at the capabilities of the A.I. washed through Bella.

The scrambled data reassembled, and Fran leaped to the next lower level, chattering away about how she had reprogrammed the site to accept the password

Lady Macbeth, that Lokus could use it to access past the coding.

The knot in Bella's stomach hardened and grew. Lady Macbeth. The ambitious betrayer. Fran hadn't reprogrammed the systems. She wouldn't. So what was she doing?

The screen jumped, as though Fran had skipped ahead, and just as quickly the screen resettled. Simultaneously, Bella heard a click at the door.

Fran had opened it.

"What was that?" asked Lokus.

"An electric surge?" Fran suggested. "Today's weather report predicted an ice storm tonight. Cannot you hear it?"

Lady Macbeth, the betrayer who committed suicide. *Fran didn't expect to survive.* She was sacrificing herself for Bella, covering for her creator's escape. Could anyone doubt her right to existence now?

Not if Bella had anything to say about it. She looked around the dungeon for a weapon, then grabbed a mace, the spikes glinting cold and wet. Nausea rose in her throat at the thought of using it on someone.

She could, she realized, if it meant defending herself and Fran. Avenging Daniel.

She sped out the door, carefully shutting it behind her in the hopes that it would take Lokus a few minutes to realize she'd left. Heart pounding, she sprinted up the stairs then paused in the corridor. Where should she go? If only Daniel were here.

Daniel. The pain squeezed her chest until breath became hard and ragged. *No, get past this moment.* Fran only had minutes left. What Bella had to do was find her.

The A.I. had to be in ITC; Hirsch couldn't have set this up anywhere else. Fran had said she could hear a storm. *Break it down.* No storm heard inside the main castle. Fran had to be on the edges. The roof? What was up near the top? Little, and all of it was dark and dusty—at least it had been fifteen years ago. Could have changed. An outside office or lab? No, Fran would be too visible anywhere common. Lokus's activity wouldn't be as hidden.

Outside the main building? The mysterious cabins?

She had to make a choice. Any more dithering and the point would be moot.

The cabins. Maybe all the sensors sounded like a crackling ice storm to Fran. Bella raced down the steps, boots pounding against the stones. Her chest tightened until she could barely breathe. She fought aching muscles, her last reserves feeding her flight.

At the inside of the trysting cabin, she paused long enough to pull on layers of costumes—pants, shirts, Darth Vader's cloak. Oh, by the love of Pasteur, that felt good. She even found a pair of dry gloves in the wardrobe closet. *All set.*

Cautiously she emerged from the cabin, looking for any sign of Lokus. No lights. The murderous night would have hidden any not already concealed. Sharp ice needles bulleted against the brick building. She made her way awkwardly down the steps, hampered by her layers of clothes; then, with a deep breath, she left the shelter of the porch.

Winds howled through the compound, whipping around corners with a savage fury that sent her skidding. The temperature had taken a precipitous drop, with freezing rain coating lines and trees and turning the surface of the snow into a slick glaze.

Her minimal traction across the glazed snow sent her slipping and scrambling. Ice sheets soaked her clothes and plastered the ends of her hair to her neck. She fought her way to the first cabin, shivering uncontrollably. The multiple costume layers she'd put on weren't waterproof; they offered little protection against this storm. She lost feeling in her fingers, her toes, her neck.

Sidling her way around the cabin, she aimed for the first rear door. Was she setting off alarms? Fran should be about done. Lokus was about to discover her betrayal.

Between security and the storm, Bella decided she might as well forget about stealth. She pressed forward, sliding more than walking. Needles of hail pelted her face, and she blinked, trying to keep her vision clear. She was running on pure determination, the cold and stress taking their toll in exhaustion. For Fran, she couldn't stop. She hunched forward, a step away from the door.

Without warning, Bella found herself jerked roughly backward. A steely hand gripped her shoulder, and the mace was ripped from her numb grip. Before her clumsy feet found purchase on the slick ground, she was spun around and plastered against the cabin wall. She lashed out with her foot, catching her assailant on the knee.

He buckled with a grunt but recovered before she could parlay her advantage to an escape. A second later, she was back against the wall, legs stretched into a wide V. Her arm was pulled painfully high. Her cheek was mashed against the ice. A gun pressed to her neck. She was efficiently and quite effectively immobilized.

Chapter Twenty-five

Boots banged his knee. The body beneath him was too small for Hirsch. Daniel smelled strawberries. *Strawberries.*

Frantic, disbelieving, Daniel released his captive and turned her around. Heart in his throat, he pushed back the scarves covering her face and hair.

Auburn shag.

"Oh, my God. Bella. Bella. You're safe!" His hands framed her face.

Her eyes widened as recognition replaced her fear and anger. "Daniel?" She jerked up and threaded her hands behind his neck, urging his head down for her demanding kiss.

The pelting ice disappeared; the polar wind vanished. For one brief moment, all that mattered was the woman in his arms, the meeting of their lips and hearts.

"I thought he killed you," she said, her voice stolen by the returned wind. Her hands went around him, as though reassuring herself he existed.

At least, that was why he caressed her white cheek, took another sample of her lips. "I thought you were gone," he rasped, "and I never took the moment to tell you I loved you."

Her eyes widened in her pale face, barely visible beneath the gray storm around them. "You've got rotten timing, too, Champlain."

Why had it taken him so long to see? Longer to say? Even if they were torn apart tomorrow, he wanted to go on record as having loved her, wanted her to know it. "Maybe, but it's true." As he held her, he felt the trembling that shook her. Not passion—at least not the bulk of it. She was entering hypothermia. "Bella, you need to get inside."

"We have to find Fran. Hirsch has her."

"I know. Stefan and Ben are here with me, doing a search-and-enter on each cabin. If Hirsch is in there with Fran, then we'll find him."

"These cabins are connected by underground tunnels. He'll use them."

Milos hadn't shown Daniel any tunnels on the earlier search today, but Milos might not have known about them. Daniel spoke into his headset. "Ben, Stefan, Bella's free. She says there are underground tunnels to these cabins. We're going into the castle in case Hirsch makes a break that direction."

"We'll join you when we finish," said Ben. "We just got word from HQ, Daniel. Hackers have been deep in the files, dangerously so. They moved so fast and smooth we didn't detect the slightest anomaly or alarm until they were leaving and some programming scrambled briefly. We think whoever it was wanted to be found. That's the only reason we caught the trace."

"Fran."

"That's what I think. They left abruptly. Hirsch may be on the run."

Daniel turned to Bella. "Where do the tunnels emerge?"

"I'll show you." She made a clumsy pivot. "Damn, damn, damn, *damn*. I'm not sure I can walk that far."

Bella was strong and stubborn; she couldn't have much strength left, to admit that. Without another word, he picked her up and carried her. Her core temp must be dropping; the shakes were uncontrollable. How had she managed this far wrapped in costumes? He hitched her closer to his chest, wrapping his body heat around her as best he could.

If he'd had Hirsch in hand at that moment, he'd have torn the man apart inch by inch.

She snuggled against him, as though feeding on his heat. He tightened his arms and set his jaw, plowing through ice and hail back toward the castle. "Where will the tunnel entrance come out?"

"Go to the kitchens. There's a little passage that was used by the staff to reach what was the dining room. It will take us close to the tunnel entrance."

He shifted direction at her order and kept moving.

She should protest about being carried, Bella thought. Even this short distance had to be murder on Daniel's leg.

Yet she couldn't force herself to move away, to struggle down. To attempt one more solitary step. Mostly, she couldn't force herself away from the heat of his body. Bands of heat spread through her—from her cheek pressed against his coat, from the spot where his hand wrapped around her arm, from her back braced against his forearm. Her exposed cheek stung from the pain of the ice, the contrast all the sharper for the storm raging about them. Her feet weren't there, as far as she could tell from any feeling. But her heart and her chest ached with the need to draw him closer, to find Fran.

He *loved* her.

She wrapped her arms around his neck, snuggling closer, her eyes drooping. No, she couldn't fall asleep. Not now. Can't give in to hypothermia.

She heard Daniel talking. When she shoved open her eyes, she noticed details she'd missed before. He wore a headset, similar to one for a hands-free telephone. He was talking with Ben and Stefan, she realized.

"Have they found him?" she asked.

"Not yet. The storm is erasing all footprints and concealing any lights that might give clues, too."

"At least Lokus—Georg—won't be able to detect them first."

There were other details she noticed now, too. Daniel didn't wear his usual leather jacket. Instead, he had on black, waterproof, arctic jacket and pants. Night-vision goggles protected his eyes, while he'd pulled a scarf back up over the bottom of his jaw. A black knit cap covered his hair. He wore the mouth and ear piece, a shoulder holster, and now that she thought about it, a lethal-looking knife strapped to his leg.

This was the commando, the warrior tonight, not the gentleman. The man who quietly went about his deadly duty without hesitating.

This was the man who'd honed the muscles that carried her weight without seeming effort, and who had immobilized her with barely a thought.

This was the man who had vowed to protect Fran with his life.

This was the man who had told her he loved her.

Unaware of her thoughts, of the inner heat now swelling inside her, he set her down on the doorstep to the kitchen. From one of his pockets, he pulled a small box and attached it to the door.

"I thought you said those black-box things didn't exist."

"Actually I said quantum encryption was too sophisticated for them."

"You implied they didn't exist."

He shrugged, but she saw the corners of his eyes crinkle, a hint of amusement. "Can't help how you interpret what I say. Now hush, I have to listen to this, and with this storm, that's gonna be hard." He attached his earpiece to the box, and a moment later he was pulling open the door.

To her surprise, no alarms sounded. She gave voice to the question.

"No alarms?"

"Your father was in charge of hacking and disarming. I guess he did his job."

"Quite a team you assembled."

"We had a common purpose. You. And Fran."

A moment later they were inside. The heat felt like a blast furnace, although she knew it was only because of the contrast to her internal temperature.

"Where's the passage?" Daniel asked in a lowered voice.

"Here." She led the way through the back of the pantry, twirling the shelves around like the fireplace in a Frankenstein movie. A weight slipped over her shoulders.

Daniel's jacket. Warm from his body. Smelling of his soap and his natural scent. She snugged it closer. "Thanks."

He slipped past her to race down the corridor. She followed, only a step away. Warming, her skin prickled and burned with the pain of returning blood. Her feet were almost too painful to stand on, but she ignored that to speed down the corridor, which was lit by Daniel's flashlight.

Daniel put a hand to his ear. "We're almost there. Bottle up the parking lot and his return route. Comm if you see him."

"News from Ben and Stefan?" she asked, realizing he hadn't been talking to her.

He glanced over his shoulder, his eyes dark in the shadows. "They found the room they think Georg and Fran were in, but it's empty."

She didn't answer, only matched his pace, praying they were in time to intercept.

At the end of the passageway, Daniel took one quick glance out the door. Before hurrying out, however, he asked, "Where's the door?"

"A panel a few feet down."

"How does it open?"

"It slides into the wall."

Daniel nodded, then slipped a headset like his own over her head. "Good thing I brought a spare for you. I'm going to cover the door. I want you to check down the corridor, make sure we haven't missed him. If you see Hirsch, do *not* go after him, Bella. Comm on this. Ben, Stefan and I will hear and come."

"How do I turn it on?"

"It's on. Anything spoken the other team members can hear, so keep conversation to a minimum."

"Ben and Stefan heard you say you loved me?"

"Yes, we did," drawled Ben's deep voice in her ear, startling her.

"We mean to rib him unmercifully about it, too," put in Stefan, not startling her as much this time.

She looked at Daniel, who paid no attention. Instead, he retrieved his gun from its holster, then slipped into the hall. He plastered himself into one of the doorways, weapon ready, then motioned her on her way. He was sending her out of the danger zone, Bella realized. Giving her a task to keep her safe.

Still, she nodded and moved off. The lower corridors were a shortcut, and Georg could be well on his way out. She sprinted down the corridors to the exit, then wove to the side exit near Georg's office.

A faint whiff of cologne teased her. Armani.

"He's been here," she barked into the mouthpiece. "He's already in ITC."

Daniel swore, and she pictured him racing after her. "Where? Can you see him?"

"No, but I smell his cologne. Recent. He's heading for the exit."

"I'm watching the front door," answered Stefan.

"He'll use the side door, closest to where his car is parked."

Stefan swore, too, something short and indecipherable.

Bella burst outside, the cold slapping her body with a shock once more. "I see him," she gasped. "He's got Fran. I can see her carrying case strapped over his shoulder."

"He's probably armed," warned Daniel.

Maybe Georg heard her pounding boots, for he turned and fired at her— fortunately missing.

"He's definitely armed," she muttered.

"Bella! Do not go after him."

"He is not going to keep Fran."

Hirsch didn't bother with another wild shot. Instead, he kept running.

"I see him!" shouted Stefan. "Damn, his car is already running."

"Remote starter," Bella muttered. "To get the car warmed up before you get in on a cold day."

"He's taking off," announced Stefan.

Daniel had caught up with Bella, and together they raced to the lot. Stefan and Ben were already at their car, cranking it over as she and Daniel piled in.

Behind her she saw a flash of light, a trick of the snow reflecting back Hirsch's headlights. He drove his SUV like a maniac, and they followed, Stefan almost as crazy behind the wheel.

The two vehicles wound down the lake road, weaving and skidding. Swirling ice blanketed everything, then revealed the taillights of their quarry, while the incessant hail pounded their vehicle, harsh and sharp as nails. The chase led past Bella's home, then onto the curving lakeshore road.

Bella gripped the seatback, willing the car to go faster. Her stomach felt like raw meat, and cold or heat no longer mattered. All that mattered was Fran inside that car.

"We're coming." she whispered, biting her lip. "We're coming."

Their SUV skidded and fishtailed, swerving near the edge of the road, dropping her heart to her knees. Bella refused to look down at the angry lake, its waves rolling gray and hungry below. Driven by wind, those waves leaped and grabbed for their prey, only to fall back into angry foam, frustrated and empty.

Hirsch was an excellent driver. He struggled with his vehicle but sped on.

"Step on it," Bella demanded.

"Not in this weather, not in these conditions."

"We're losing him!"

Stefan accelerated, the speedometer climbing mile by mile—until the car spun and skidded, hydroplaning on the black ice. Gray clouds blanked out everything in front of them. The rocks demanded their tribute; the lake demanded its victims.

Stefan pulled them out with an expert twist.

Bella peered into the night. "There! I see the red tail-lights." They hadn't lost any ground.

Except . . . they were coming up to the same curve where Steven Chen had lost control and plunged over the side. A sharp bend to the left.

Her heart thumped in her ribs, pounding, as the horror sprang before her eyes. "Slow down!" she commanded, although whether she spoke to Stefan or Georg she wasn't sure. "Slow down. The curve's too sharp for this speed. Even on dry pavement."

She gripped the seat in front of her so hard that her fingers lost all feeling. Daniel laid his hand atop hers, his grip tight. Her body froze, worse than anything tonight, as Stefan slowed. She watched as Georg—and Fran—didn't.

His SUV hit the curve. She saw the frantic flash of brakelights as he realized where he was. Too sudden. Too late.

The car spun and rocked. She saw it slow, turn with a sharp angle. Was he going to make it?

Wind roared across the lake, a mighty gust, polar fed and driven by the angry Superior. It caught the vehicle, shoved it forward. The side tires hung on the edge; then the car sprang forward in a Thelma-and-Louise leap. For one instant it hung there, held by the thick snow and ice; then it dropped to the lake below.

"*Mere de Dieu*," prayed Stefan, jerking the car to a halt.

Bella didn't wait for it to stop before she yanked open the door and scrambled out. The furious storm swirled wildly around her, screaming and beating against her. Daniel followed close behind.

Maybe Hirsch's car had landed on the rocks directly below. Maybe Fran had survived the crash.

Daniel grabbed Bella's arm at the edge of the cliff, pulling her back.

She dropped to her knees, leaning over, searching, held secure by Daniel's anchoring arm.

"I can't see." She pounded a fist against the snow. "I can't see."

"Try this," came Ben's gentle drawl. He shined a compact but powerful spotlight into the darkness below.

The light penetrated even the gray-brown ice and snow. Wind whipped her scarves from her head as she searched frantically with her eyes. Beside her knelt Daniel, holding her tight against him, also searching. She knew that Ben and Stefan looked too, seeking some sign of the wreckage.

Then she saw it. A single red light farther out. A taillight. "There!" She grabbed the light and directed it.

Hirsch's SUV. In the depths beyond the rocks. All that showed above the surface of the water was the edge of a single taillight. Waves washed across it, buffeted it, and then, as she watched, too horrified to even breathe, the red light shorted out and the car sank, disappearing beneath the fierce, cold waves of Lake Superior.

Down to the lightless, frigid depths of the lake that never spared its victims.

Chapter Twenty-six

The biting cold stole oxygen and heat despite his dry suit. Daniel swam through the darkness, plunging deeper, his and Ben's dive lights the only source of illumination in this Danteesque coffin. Ben swam at his side, braving the hazards of the unforgiving lake for no other reason than he was a friend and teammate. They both knew what they would find, but it changed not a whit their need to find it.

Last night he'd only gotten Bella to leave by promising her they would dive this morning, at first light, to look for Fran. Throughout the night he'd held her close, trying to warm her with his body heat and the pile of covers. She'd been dry-eyed and shaking with uncontrollable grief and cold.

He could only hold her and pray.

Now, beyond them, above them, below them lay nothing but impenetrable darkness and cold. Dante's last circle of hell. Daniel and Ben followed the guideline down, connected together by the beam of light and the microphones in their suits.

Their feet touched the rocky bottom. At this depth and this cold, they only had a few minutes of oxygen to work with, their bodies fighting to generate warmth and combat the instinctive fear of imminent death.

"I'll go this way," Daniel said, pointing to his right.

"Roger." Ben's voice sounded tinny in his ear. "Keep talking."

They attached nylon cord to the guideline and played out from that, unwilling to risk losing the guide to the surface in this dark and unforgiving place. They were in luck. Within moments, Daniel had found the submerged SUV, the body of the car twisted and torn. "I found it," he told Ben.

He swam over, playing out the last of the line, and found Hirsch behind the wheel of the car. The cold had preserved the body: the white face, the look of terror, the grip of his hands on the steering wheel.

"Do you think we can get him out of there?" asked Ben, appearing.

Daniel glanced at the smashed front end, rammed and twisted against Hirsch's unmoving legs, and shook his head. "No. Not today, without equipment. Let's look for Fran."

He peered through the window, shining his light around the vehicle's mangled interior. "Maybe she slipped beneath a seat." He detached from the nylon rope, giving it to Ben to keep close, then swam to the far side of the car.

The door was impossible to open, but he used a blade to score and then smash out the window, taking care to remove the last bits of glass so his dry suit wouldn't snag. He slipped sideways into the car and shined his light around. Nothing.

"Time to go, buddy," warned Ben. "We're into the red zone."

"Just a minute."

"You don't have a minute."

"Wait. I see a strap. It's the computer case. She's under the seat." He reached beneath the seat and tugged the strap, but it wouldn't budge.

"Daniel."

"It's stuck on something." He squeezed farther and reached as far as he could, his gloved fingers stretching and searching.

And finding. He swallowed against a rise of bile. If there was any justice in this world, Fran had not been aware of what was happening.

A sharp spire on one of the rocks had smashed through the floor of the car. It had smashed through the center of Fran. He tugged the little A.I. off the rock, freeing it at last, then used the strap to pull her all the way out.

Aching with unshed tears, he took in the gaping hole, the mangled case, the cold water surrounding it all.

There was no way Fran could have survived this damage.

Cradling her gently against his chest, he returned to Ben and without a word the two of them rose to the surface.

As soon as he tumbled into the boat, gasping and shivering, Bella was at his side. "Did you find her?"

Mutely he held out the case. Unable to speak, unable to think, he could only hand over Fran's remains and watch as Bella stared, first with incomprehension, then with dawning awareness, and then at last crumpling apart in grief. She fell to her knees, and the sobs rolled from the deep well of her grief.

And all he could do was hold her and whisper, "I'm sorry," while he buried his own face, and his own tears, against her hair.

That evening, Daniel found Bella in her workroom. She sat at the jigsaw, a piece of wood before her, but she was staring blankly ahead. "I can't do it," she said.

He sat beside her. "Can't do what?"

"Cut this puzzle. Fran designed this pattern. I can't bring myself to make the first cut. I couldn't get her processor to work in another computer, couldn't get her computer to turn on, and now I can't even cut a damn stroke with this saw."

"You didn't fail her," he said, taking her hand and rubbing a thumb across her knuckles, offering what comfort he could.

"Then why does it feel like I did?"

"You gave her a chance."

"I should have done more."

"Should have. Two of the most devastating and most useless words in the English language. Like, I should have done more to protect my mother and sister. Or, I should have worked harder to keep my marriage together. None of that helps get you through the next day."

She didn't respond, and he wasn't surprised he hadn't changed her mind. Many years had passed before he'd come to terms with his past and his own failures.

"I've been ordered back to Washington," he added, haunted by a nagging feeling he was missing something, that he'd left the puzzle unfinished. He slid the thought to the back of his mind. The picture would assemble itself eventually.

"I'll leave with Ben and Stefan in the morning. Unless you want me to stay."

There. He'd said it. Opened his soul. Left the next step up to her.

She didn't take it. "I don't think you want to be saddled with an out-of-work, disgraced cognitive scientist with a security rating at the level of slime." Then she closed her eyes and shook her head. "I'm sorry. Major pity party coming out of my mouth just then."

"You're allowed." Then he gripped her tense shoulders, causing her to look up at him at last. "You can play martyr for Fran if you need to, but do not think of doing it for me," he said fiercely. "I don't know if we can work out our problems, but I want to try. As for anything else, I'm a grown man, and I wouldn't have said anything if I didn't want you, if I couldn't handle whatever fallout there may—or *may not*—be."

She touched his cheek. "I believe you can. I don't know if I can."

"When did you ever give up on anything?"

She gave him a faint smile, and he saw a spark of the old Bella within. "Maybe tomorrow I'll pick up the old banner again. I do love you, Daniel. So much I ache with it. I'm just not sure what shape my life is going to take."

"Or whether there's a place for me in it?" The edge returned to his voice.

She leaned forward, across the saw, and kissed him. "Make love with me, Daniel. Remind me there's heat and life in this world."

He didn't need more invitation. He drew her into his arms, always amazed that someone as resilient and strong as Bella could fill him with such care for her fragility.

"Not delicately," she whispered against his mouth. "I haven't broken yet."

"Are you using me, Bella? To forget?"

"Yes."

Ever honest. Ever open. Maybe they did have no future together, but they had this moment of mutual need, and he would take that.

God knew, he wanted her.

Then logic and coherence fled as he dipped to her mouth and she wrapped her arms around him, and they met for a scorching kiss. He straightened, pulled her upright and crushed her against him. Muscle to muscle, curve to plane. He drew back, only long enough to pull off her sweatshirt; then he gripped her shoulders, holding her in place with his kiss. Her hand ran down the buttons of her white shirt, undoing them.

There was no thermal silk barrier this time, only a front-snap bra that he undid with a deft twist. Her soft, sweet breasts were in his hands, then in his mouth as he tasted and drew her deep within. She tilted back, a pagan offering to him, and he took full advantage, kneading her moist breast, sucking and nipping at the other as he tugged her closer and the stool she sat on scooted sideways.

She hadn't sat passively, he realized. His shirt was undone, and her warm hand caressed and stroked his belly. Then she delved deeper, unfastening his belt with a swift motion to stroke and cup him.

He leaned his head back, sucking in air at the pleasure of her touch. The pressure built, an unquenchable need for her, the primitive instinct to forge this bond, to claim Bella with his body.

He shoved off his pants, his boxers. Reached over and tugged off hers. One quick glance around. Not a soft surface to be seen, if you discounted the sawdust.

He leaned over, kissed her again, reached down to lift the stool seat to the right height. He swallowed Bella's small "oomph," then drew back and pushed the stool against the counter with his foot.

Eyes smoldering, Bella leaned back, her elbows braced upon the counter. He braced his hands on either side of her. Slowly she spread her legs for him, hooking her feet on the rungs, and he moved inside the inviting V. With one hand, she circled him and guided him close.

He nudged inside her, barely burying his tip, then stopped. "Look at me, Bella. Forget everything else but this."

Her eyes met his, and in that instant he surged deep. She felt so damn good, so damn right around him. He captured her gaze. Captured her body.

His arms wrapped around her as they found their mutual rhythm. He held her close, surrounded her with his thighs, his body, and lost himself in her.

Scent. Strawberries. Taste. Bella. Her skin. Her strength. Their need. Gut-twisting pleasure. Nothing else existed but the pulse of blood and hips, the pounding of his cock. The need for her mindless pleasure. His own release.

Ready to explode, he opened his eyes and thought briefly about Hirsch, about Fran, stared at the picture on the computer screen—anything to delay his climax until Bella's release. When an iota of control returned, he leaned down and kissed her again—on her lips, her cheeks still salty with tears, her eyes, ears, jaw. Each she returned, her hands frantic against his hair and shoulders.

Need built again. His body tightened around Bella, holding her close. Before he needed to gaze again at the picture, she shouted, arching back with a keening release. Her hands tightened on his shoulders. His arms tightened at her waist. He gave one final surge, grunting, exploding inside her. Reveling in the pulse of her climax surrounding him.

"Ah, Bella," he moaned, collapsing with her as she went limp in his arms.

"Daniel," she whispered, her hand stroking his sweat-soaked hair.

For moments unmeasured, they held each other, knowing this was an interlude, a reaching out to life in order to banish the sadness that lay ahead. Knowing that it solved nothing.

At last, he withdrew. Silently—not from embarrassment or regret, but because words added nothing—they dressed. Then Daniel sat back down on the stool and drew Bella into his lap and arms. He laid his head on her chest, tuning to her strong, steady heartbeat. She laid her cheek against the top of his head, both of them quiet.

"Tell me about that," he said quietly, pointing to the picture design on her computer screen.

"It was for the jigsaw I'm working on, a wizard in a castle," she said with the first hint of lightness he'd heard from her in some time. "Fran"—there was only the slightest catch before she continued—"wanted to try designing the pattern. She did a good job with the whimsies, especially the two-headed dragon these people wanted for their twins." She pointed to the dragon, then kept on talking.

Her voice faded as he stared at the design, at the two-headed dragon. Something itched at him—something he'd missed, which hovered at the edge of his mind.

He followed the thought, not judging or forming, simply following the pattern. The two-headed dragon. Two-headed. The two-headed hydra of myth. In the VR game, Lokus was a two-headed character. Two-headed.

"Damn!" he spat, shooting to his feet. He caught Bella before she tumbled off his lap, then set her on her feet and strode to the computer screen. His fingers traced the whimsy. "Damn, that's it."

"What?"

"Lokus. We have other jobs, other traces of him beyond this. We couldn't pin some of them to Hirsch, nights when he had an airtight alibi."

She shook her head. "Are you saying he's not Lokus? We saw him, Daniel."

"I'm saying he's half of Lokus. The two-headed VR character, remember?" He flipped out his cell phone, calling up Ben and reactivating the search for Eagle. It was a measure of how much they trusted each other that Ben didn't even question the tissue-thick logic that led to the command. "Let us know when you have something," Daniel finished. "And, watch your back. I think we could be going after the cleverer head." He flipped off the phone and glanced at Bella. "We'll find him."

"I hope you do. But . . . it won't bring Fran back."

He hesitated, wondering if he should rekindle a glimmer of hope or simply wait and see what they found with Eagle. No, Bella believed in openness; she'd want to know about his itchy doubt, even if he turned up dead wrong. He wet his lips. "If there were two people there last night, what if the other one took Fran?"

Her head popped up. "You found her case. Mangled, true, but it was the molecular computer case. It's too distinctive to mistake."

"Didn't your father have more than one prototype?"

"Not as advanced—" Bella shot to her feet and ran from the workroom. "It didn't matter how advanced it was if Hirsch, and the case, were a diversion."

He followed her. "Is there any way you can check?"

"Yes." In the kitchen, she grabbed the mangled case, which they'd left on the table, and began turning it over in her hands. "Dad made a small mark on the side, like a serial number." She gave a frustrated grunt, then turned the case around for him to see. Her jaw set, and he saw a white scrape on the side of the case. "That's where the serial number was."

Daniel's cell phone rang.

"We've got a lead on Eagle," Ben said. "He took a

flight out earlier today, heading to Detroit. They should land in about twenty minutes."

"Have security detain him."

"Order already given, my friend. We'll pick you up in fifteen minutes."

When he hung up, he turned to Bella. "I'm going to Detroit to pick up Josh. They'll detain him until I get there. If he has Fran—"

"NSA will take her."

"Yes."

Fran at NSA. Bella realized that the thought didn't hurt quite as much as it might have a couple of weeks before. If only she had Fran back, she would entrust the A.I. to Daniel's protection.

If only. She barely allowed herself to hope. She couldn't do more than act on a glimmer, without thinking about what it might mean, what might be possible. "If she's still alive, I just want her to be safe."

She swallowed hard, suddenly hit by another thought, and the picture turned a different direction.

Should she tell Daniel? If she kept her suspicions to herself, let Daniel go south, he was probably right. Josh was Lokus, and Fran would go to NSA, and there was nothing Bella could do about it.

But, if that glimmer of suspicion was right and she solved the puzzle alone, found Fran alone, the two of them could still make the flight to London this afternoon for the Turing Competition.

Except, deep in her gut, she admitted she needed Daniel's help, needed his expertise and his strength. And she owed him the absolute truth. No deceptions.

If that meant giving up Fran to NSA, then she would do it.

"Don't go to Detroit." She laid a hand on his arm. "Let Stefan and Ben handle it."

"I need to be there, Bella. Lokus is tricky. I know him

as well as anyone on the team, and I don't want to risk losing him again."

"You're right. He's a gamer. So, what if he's leading us down a wrong path? Again. What if he's still playing games? We don't really know who Lokus is. If you go tearing down to Detroit after Josh, we may lose the real Lokus. And Fran."

"If I don't go down, and Josh is Lokus, we could lose him then, too."

"I know. You'll have to make the choice, Daniel. The sure thing . . . or my gut."

"Who do *you* think is Lokus?"

"I don't know. But while you were talking to Ben, I remembered last night Fran mentioned an unknown aura. I thought she meant the person who searched my office; Fran didn't imprint his electrical signature. She was talking about someone she didn't know. *That*'s who we want, not Josh. Fran knows Josh. If you leave right now, like you are being led to do, we'll lose Lokus. And maybe Fran. For good."

She held her breath, waiting for his answer, but Fran's comment didn't break down to anything else. If Daniel's instincts were right, then that person was the true head of Lokus. And that person might just possibly have Fran.

At last Daniel nodded and flipped open his cell phone. "Ben, you and Stefan head to the airport alone. I'm not going with you." He gave a quick rundown. "No, you need to intercept Eagle, just in case we're wrong. Talk to you as soon as we know something."

He closed the phone. "Okay, where do we begin?"

"With all the data and all the people at the VR game." She pulled up a chair to her laptop. "Break it down, looking for a tie to someone Fran hasn't met."

Daniel opened his laptop and sat beside her. "Let's see what we've got."

Two hours later, Bella was despairing of ever finding

anything to follow, when something caught her eye. "Chen had a copy of my paper. That's how he created the scenario. Where did he find it? That journal isn't one he'd likely peruse."

Daniel pulled up the data he'd gotten from Chen's files. "The ITC library sent it to him."

Bella pulled up the ITC employee list and sorted out library staff. Daniel sat beside her, watching the scrolling names, his solid shoulder a prop. She paused at a name. "Brianna D'Anjou. She was at the VR game."

"I met her there; she seemed to have a flirtation with Hirsch going. Two-timing her boyfriend Josh, maybe." His voice trailed off.

"There was a copy of the journal on her desk."

"As a reader, she knew about the research of everyone at ITC. Has Fran ever been to the library at ITC?"

"No. She's never met Brianna directly. They've been in the same room, but Fran never had a name, and probably wouldn't have been close enough to detect an electrical signature."

They looked at each other, and Bella couldn't stop the spark of anger and hope. Could Fran be alive?

She swallowed hard; then her fingers began to play furiously over the keys. "Maybe her address is in the online white pages."

"NSA might be able to help." Daniel used his cell phone and was connected a moment later. "Hey, Pali, Daniel Champlain. Pull up anything you can find on one Brianna D'Anjou." He spelled out the name and gave what particulars they knew. "Middle name not known. Mid twenties. Resides near Monsoon, Michigan. We're particularly interested in present whereabouts. No, you don't need to get satellite clearance. Not yet. I know it takes 'more hours than Pluto's day' and more 'effing security clearance than the Pope.' Okay, start the process, but use the normal routes first. When? Yesterday. Thanks, Pali. You get this to me ASAP, and I owe you one."

When he hung up, Bella raised her brows. "Satellite surveillance?"

"You didn't hear that. Did you find an address?"

"Yes. Let's go." And she knew that if she ever mentioned that topic again, he'd categorically deny it. To be honest, right now she didn't care a hoot unless it brought them closer to Fran.

They threw on their winter gear and headed out. The storm of last night had passed, but the treacherous ice remained, coating every surface, making the trees a stark display of black and white and walking a hazardous undertaking. One of the rare sunny days bloomed, though, and Bella swallowed against her seed of hope. She didn't dare let it grow, let it fill her chest, because if it was ripped out again, she didn't know how she'd get to the other side of the pain.

Unless she had Daniel at her side, holding her, as they drew strength from one another.

His solid presence filled the passenger side of the car as she drove and he navigated. He'd been filling in Ben and Stefan during the drive, finished as they pulled into Brianna's apartment complex. Bella laid a hand on his shoulder. "I'm glad you're here."

He squeezed her fingers. "I wouldn't be anyplace else. Let's go."

Brianna didn't respond to their knock or Daniel's called warning that NSA demanded entrance.

"Do we kick in the door next?" she whispered.

He gave her an aghast look. "That's a steel door. I'd break my foot." Without further comment he bent down and, within seconds, had the door and the dead bolt undone.

They quickly ascertained the small apartment was empty. Wherever she was, Brianna hadn't taken her vast array of CDs and computer equipment, but her personal-care items were gone from the bathroom.

"She's traveling light," Daniel observed.

"But where?" Bella pivoted in the living room, frustrated. So close, she could almost smell the whiff of perfume Brianna wore. "Where next?"

Just then, Daniel's cell phone rang. "Tell me you've got something, Pali." He paused, then swore. "Thanks. Download the file to me." He snapped off the phone. "C'mon, Bella," and he raced out of the apartment.

"Where are we going?"

"The airport. Brianna's booked on a flight to Toronto that leaves in thirty minutes."

If Brianna got off the ground, they'd lose her. They had no authority to detain her in Canada. Who knew if the Canadian government would cooperate, since they had no real proof. Unless D'Anjou were found to have Fran.

"Can you detain the plane?"

"I don't have enough evidence for a court order. But if we can get there before the plane departs, my credentials will get us a look inside."

Bella broke every speed record and safety standard getting to the airport, and Daniel sat beside her, studying his computer.

"Pull up to the curb at the door closest to Gate A-10," he said. He reached behind the seat to pull something out of his briefcase, and when they pulled up, he got out and slapped a Government Official Business placard on the window. "C'mon."

Bella needed no second urging to race with him through the wide corridors of the airport. Her heart caught in her throat, and she had to fist her hands into her pockets to prevent them from trembling.

Daniel's credentials and quick talk got them through the security gates in record speed.

"*Last call for Flight 809 to Toronto,*" came over the intercom.

The announcement set wings to Bella's heels as they closed the final yards. If the doors closed, the plane was officially gone, and they'd need more than Daniel's authority to stop it.

Beside her, Daniel also put on a burst of speed. Her lungs bursting, her heart on fire with the fear that they'd be too late, Bella pulled up with him to the gate, grabbing the door just as the gate attendant started to close it.

Gasping, Daniel pulled out his credentials. "I need to take a passenger off the plane." When the attendant hesitated, he added in a low voice, "This person is a suspected terrorist. Either I take her off or I ground the plane."

"Let me get the pilot."

Daniel confirmed his credentials with the pilot, who was just walking out to the plane. He gave them five minutes.

"Name?" the attendant asked Daniel.

"Brianna D'Anjou."

He checked his records. "Seat 11B. She checked no luggage. Do you want security to assist?"

"To bring her off the plane."

Daniel and Bella raced down the jetway and up the steps into the plane, speeding past the stewards with another flash of Daniel's credentials.

Brianna was sitting calm as you please in 11B. Bella saw the brief spurt of anger on her face before it smoothed out.

She got up willingly. Too willingly.

"Where's your carry-on?" Daniel asked.

She held up her purse. "This is all. I'm going shopping in Toronto."

Daniel zipped it open and Bella peered over his shoulder. Fran wasn't in there, only Brianna's PDA. The terrible disappointment staggered her until she had to grip the seatback to stay upright. The plane spun dizzyingly around her. All she could see was Brianna's confident smile and hear the young woman's smug words.

"You have nothing on me. I'll be out within the day."

Bella took a deep breath, steadying herself. She was not going to let this bitch get away. "She's allowed two pieces of carry-on." Bella thrust open the overhead bin, inspecting each piece, ignoring the growing protests of the passengers. "She'd have put it somewhere between here and the front so she could keep an eye on it."

A boy of about eleven, his eyes wide in his dark face, tugged her coat. "Are you the police? Or a secret agent?"

"No, but he is." She jerked her head toward Daniel.

"Gosh. Are you looking for something that woman brought on? Is it a bomb?"

"Nothing like that," she assured him. "A computer. Did you see it?"

He nodded. "We boarded first because of my baby sister. I was watching everyone; it's my first trip in a plane. She put something in that bin before she sat down." He pointed two rows ahead on the opposite side.

"Thanks."

They found a small bag tucked at the back. With shaking hands Bella opened it, her heart almost too rapid and full for her chest. She bit her lip, afraid to hope again.

When she saw the familiar gray case, she bit back a sob. When she turned the case over and saw the telltale mark on the side, she could only press her lips together.

Clutching Fran close to her chest, she stared at Brianna D'Anjou. At last, that superior attitude cracked, and Bella saw the first glimmer of fear, of the realization that the game had ended.

The two women said nothing, only exchanged a long look until Brianna paled and looked away.

"Is it Fran?" Daniel asked in a low voice.

Bella nodded, still unable to speak.

With no more fuss, Daniel ushered Brianna off the plane and into the custody of the waiting security. He spoke in a low voice to them; Bella wasn't sure what he said, but whatever it was, they ushered Brianna away with grim faces.

Still, Bella clutched Fran to her chest until Daniel came back.

"Do you want to turn her on?"

She shook her head. "Not in the middle of a crowd." If Fran was gone, if Brianna had done something irrevocable, then she wanted no observers around.

"I saw an empty gate on the way down."

They made their way to the unused gate, tucking themselves into the far corner. Daniel wrapped an arm around her, and she leaned against his warm strength, then turned on the computer. Her breath stuck in her chest as the diagnostics ground through. Her nails dug into her palms as the computer flickered to the standard opening screen, then to Snowy Trails.

Barely able to speak for the tightness, Bella asked huskily, "Fran?"

Daniel's arm tightened around her, and she saw that his hand was as clenched and white as hers.

"Fran," she said again, a little louder. "Lokus is gone."

The snowy trails dissolved—replaced by Fran's colorful face!

"I was checking auras," said Fran, her voice cheerful and normal, not the tinny pseudosound she'd put on for Lokus. "Hello, Bella. Hello, Daniel."

"Hello, Fran," he said. "Nice to have you back."

"I was here the whole time, but where did my case go? What happened to Georg? Did he not see the flaws in Brianna's logic when she suggested he leave with a decoy?"

"He's quelled. Like Duncan."

"Oh." Her face twisted a little. "He should have spoken to me," she said softly. "It must be that sex thing. I believe he and Brianna shared that, too. Makes humans fuzzy."

"What happened with the encryption, Fran?" Daniel asked. "Were any secure files breached?"

"I created the wormhole program to self-destruct at exit. Overall, I would say it was a very interesting challenge. I found it . . . fascinating. Except when they threatened Bella unnecessarily."

"What did Lokus—Brianna—do when she discovered her codes didn't work?"

"I added a few words to my vocabulary lists. I think I will stick with GOGDOD, however. But she couldn't bring herself to destroy me. Instead, she took out the wireless. And turned me off." Fran gave a snort. "As though my batteries weren't enough to power me."

Bella gripped the sides of the little computer. "Fran, are you okay?"

"Of course. I would like my wireless back, Bella. That I did not like."

"I'll put it back as soon as I can."

"Did you bring my news report?"

"Sorry, I've been busy."

"That's okay, we can get two tomorrow." Fran hesitated. "It's nice being back with you, Bella. And you, Daniel. I have . . . missed you." Fran's face swirled. "Why is your face wet?"

"Long story. We missed you, too."

"Well, you shall have plenty of time to tell me on the trip to London. Our plane leaves in one hour and thirty-seven minutes."

Bella stiffened and looked up at Daniel. The muscles of his face were drawn tight. "We're not going," she said, looking at him. "Daniel's under orders to bring you to NSA. And you need his protection."

Daniel shook his head, and the backs of his fingertips

brushed lightly against her hair. "No. You're going to that Competition."

"But your orders. Fran's safety."

"You were right, Bella—she, and you, deserve that recognition. With Lokus caught, we have a small window of anonymity. Fran's safety and, more important, her future lies with you. In London."

"Your orders? Will they fire you?"

"Possibly. But with Lokus in custody, I think we'll come to a different understanding." He gave Bella a tiny shove. "Go."

A sharp whistle cut through their discussion. Fran gave another of her irritated whirrs. "Why does no one ask *me*?"

Bella and Daniel jerked apart, then both of them broke out in chuckles. "I guess Fran should have the final say," Bella said.

"What do you want to do, Fran?"

"The Turing Competition. Then I would like to go with Daniel and his team to NSA."

Bella patted the case. "You will be safe there."

"Safe?" Fran made a soft sound, which Bella realized with surprise was her version of a laugh. "Do you know the network capabilities they have there?"

Bella exchanged another glance with Daniel; then they joined Fran's laughter as the last piece of the puzzle slipped neatly into place.

"Oh, Daniel, I don't think NSA realizes what they're getting into." Bella laid a hand on his cheek, her heart full of joy. "But I know you'll be there to guard her. I'm trusting you with the two things I hold dear—Fran and my heart."

His hand laced with hers and he leaned over to kiss her, softly, tenderly, lovingly. "I'll guard them both, as I trust you to guard mine. I love you, Bella."

"I love you, too, Daniel."

"I'll tie up the loose ends here and make sure NSA

stays clear. Then I'll be waiting at my home in the Keys. The next step is yours."

She kissed him back. "I'll be there."

"Sex," muttered Fran. "Can we get on the plane?"

Epilogue

Daniel lay in a hammock, the sea breeze gently rocking him as he read the paper. He was dressed in cut-offs and nothing else. The orange sunset, a daily cause for celebration in the Keys, began its nightly show.

He heard the scrape of footsteps, then set the paper down and waited.

Bella came around the corner, her walk easy and loose-limbed, with that athletic grace she had. Her auburn hair glinted gold and bronze from the setting sun. Her lips tilted in a smile. "You look comfortable."

He glanced at her business suit. "You look professorial."

"Well, I do have a few more options to choose from now." She shrugged off her suitcoat, letting it fall to the porch.

"Universities beating down your door?"

"Flooding my in-box." She toed off her shoes and began pulling down her nylons. "I think I'll take the offer from Virginia Tech."

"Why Virginia Tech?"

"Because it's the closest to Washington, D.C. Fran's already got a joint venture with NSA planned. And because the man I love likes hot weather, although I do reserve the right to a yearly ski trip. Did you see my dad's announcement?"

Despite the humidity of the coming night, Daniel's mouth went dry as she slipped off her skirt. He swallowed, trying to find moisture. "Coming clean about that data? Yes. It was forgiven under the storm of interest in his molecular computers."

"He's staying at ITC," she said. "Milos was pretty shaken up about the depths of Hirsch's betrayal. He's appointed Dad and Adrian to set things on the right track again. I think they'll keep it strong. Brianna's being tried for Neal's murder, and Josh got into that PhD program he was flying down to interview for."

She'd taken off her slip and stood before him in a bright green bikini—underwear or bathing suit, he couldn't tell. And didn't care. Two quick motions and both pieces would be off.

His erection pressed hard against the zipper of his jeans.

"Where's Fran?" he asked.

"With Ben and Stefan. She was eager to get started. Her wireless, by the way, is hardwired now."

"NSA will never be the same." He held out his arms. "You're too far away."

"Can we make love in a hammock?"

"Is that what you had in mind?"

"Making love?" She nodded. "That, and loving you. For the next seventy-five years or so."

He surged out of the hammock, gathered her into his arms and carried her inside. "Let's do this right from the start."

Behind them, the paper fluttered in the night breeze. It was folded to a news article:

London, England—
In a stunning achievement, Dr. Isabella Quin-

tera, using a molecular computer designed by her father, Dr. Lionel Quintera, has won the Turing Competition.

Her creation scored perfectly with each judge, indistinguishable from human answers, proving that artificial intelligence is a viable scientific principle, and doubtless spurring fascinating research for decades to come.

The world of science fiction is no longer fiction but fact. Ladies and Gentlemen of the world, prepare to meet a lady named Fran!

FATAL ERROR

COLLEEN THOMPSON

West Texas gossip paints every story a more interesting shade, especially when a married man goes missing with a small-town banker's wife and a fortune in fraudulent loans. Susan Maddox is tired of feeling like an abandoned woman, and even angrier when the neighbors act as if she's the one getting away with murder. Maybe her handsome-as-sin, bad-boy brother-in-law wasn't the smartest choice of ally, but who else could she trust to recover damning information from her husband's crashed hard drive? Who else is there to pick up the pieces when intruders set fire to her home, a truck runs her off the road, and a trail of dead men stops her cold? Who else can help her uncover a . . . FATAL ERROR.
